BIRDY

ALFRED · A · KNOPF · NEW YORK · 1979

BIRDY

by WILLIAM WHARTON

This is a Borzoi Book
Published by Alfred A. Knopf, Inc.

Copyright © 1978 by William Wharton
All rights reserved under International
and Pan-American Copyright Conventions.
Published in the United States
by Alfred A. Knopf, Inc., New York,
and simultaneously in Canada
by Random House of Canada Limited, Toronto.
Distributed by Random House, Inc., New York.

The art on the title page is based
on a photograph by © Harold E. Edgerton from the
National Audubon Society Collection / Photo Researchers.

Library of Congress Cataloging in Publication Data
Wharton, William. Birdy.
I. Title.
PZ4.W5377BI   1978   [PS3573.H32]   813'.5'4   77-28023
ISBN 0-394-42569-3
Manufactured in the United States of America
Published January 9, 1979

There are bird tracks
And nothing in the sky;
Something lived, left,
And left something.

BIRDY

Aw, come on, Birdy! This is Al here, all the way from Dix. Stop it, huh!

I lean back and poke my head out into the corridor. The queer looking guard-orderly type in the white coat's still at the other end.

I peer through the cage door. Birdy's squatting in the middle of the floor, not even looking at me. He's squatting the same way he used to squat in the loft when he was sewing feathers on that creepy pigeon suit of his. If this doctor-major-psychiatrist here ever finds out about that pigeon suit, he'll sure as hell chain Birdy right to the floor.

Sometimes it'd scare the crap out of me. I'd climb up to the loft expecting only pigeons and Birdy'd be hunched in the back, in the dark, sewing feathers on those long johns. Birdy could come up with the weirdest ideas.

And now, here he is again, hunkering in the middle of this white room, ignoring me. I sneak another look along the corridor.

—Come on, Birdy. Cut it out! I know you're not really a bird! This section eight crap doesn't make sense. The stupid war's over for Christ's sake! Hitler, Mussolini, Tojo, the whole shitload; kaput!

Nothing. Maybe he is a loon. I wonder if this psychiatrist knows we call him Birdy? Birdy's old lady wouldn't tell; probably doesn't even know.

Birdy turns his back on me. He just spins in his squat. He keeps his hands against his sides and twists around. He's staring up at the sky through a small, high window on the other side of the room.

The doctor-major told me I'm supposed to talk about things Birdy and I did together. They shipped me out of the hospital at Dix to come down here. My face is still wrapped in bandages. I'm between operations. It hurts to eat or talk and I've been talking like crazy since nine o'clock in the morning. I can't think of any more things to say.

—Hey Birdy! How about when we built the pigeon loft up in the tree down in the woods?

Maybe talking about that'll get him. Birdy's old lady made us rip down the first loft, the one in his yard. Birdy's house is part of the Cosgrove estate; used to be the gate house. The Cosgrove house and barn burned down years ago. Birdy's house is just over the left-center field fence of the baseball field. The baseball field is built on the old Cosgrove pasture; last open place left around there.

—Hey Birdy! What in hell did your old lady do with all those baseballs?

Birdy's old lady'd keep any baseballs that went over the fence into their yard. Ball players didn't even try anymore. Semi-pros, everybody, gave up. Hit a homer over that fence, into Birdy's yard; good-bye, ball. Nothing to do but throw in a new one. It got to be expensive playing in that ball park if you were a long-ball-hitting right-hander.

What the hell could she've done with all those baseballs? Birdy and I used to look for those baseballs everywhere around his place. Maybe she buried them, or she could've sold them; big black market source for used baseballs.

—Hey Birdy! Remember those Greenwood bastards? They never did find our loft up in that tree. Shit, there sure were some creeps in our neighborhood!

Those Greenwood kids'd bust up anything they could get their hands on. They'd steal bikes, pigeons, everything not nailed down.

This loft was a great place for pigeons to home on and nobody'd have any idea it was up there. We kept a rope ladder in a hole under some bushes. We had a hook on it and used to throw it over a branch to climb up.

—Remember that rope ladder we used to climb up, Birdy? Jesus, we were screwballs when you think about it!

I keep talking, watching Birdy, trying to tell if he's listening. He's still staring out that high window on the back wall.

He's certainly pitiful-looking squatting on the middle of the floor in thin, white hospital pajamas. He's squatting flat on his feet with his knees together, his head thrust forward, his arms against his sides, his fingers hooked behind him. The way he squats, you'd think maybe he just might spring up, flap his arms a few times and fly out that window he's got his eye on.

It was a terrific loft we built down there in the woods. It was smaller than our first place, the one in his yard. Our first flock in Birdy's yard was big. There were ten pairs, and two extra cocks. We had all good stock, no junk birds, no cornys, all purebred. I figure if you're going to spend money on feed, you might's well have good birds. Birdy's always trying to bring in some kind of shitty bird just because he likes it. We used to have big arguments about this.

We had three pairs of blue bars, four pairs of blue checks, a pair of red checks and two pairs of white kings. No fancy birds, no tumblers, no fantails; none of that crap.

Now I think. I know.
Know. Think. Nothing.

When we sold the old flock, Birdy's mother made us scrape the pigeon shit from the front porch where the birds used to roost. She had the whole porch repainted with our pigeon money.

Birdy's mother's a first-class bitch.

Anyway, so we have no money to buy birds for the new loft in the tree. Birdy isn't supposed to have pigeons at all, anywhere.

We get our first two birds down at Sixty-third Street under the el. There's a big flock of street pigeons there, mostly pure junk. We'd go watch them after school. We'd take the free bus from the railroad terminal to Sears. We're about thirteen, fourteen then.

We'd watch the pigeons strutting around, eating, fucking, the way pigeons do all day, not paying much attention to anything else. The el'd go by and they'd soar up in big arcs as if it hadn't been happening every five minutes for about fifty years. Birdy shows me how they usually go back to the same place and do the same things they were doing. We'd watch and try to figure who the flock leaders are and where the nests are up in the girders of the el. We try to work out the pairs. Pigeons are like people; fuck practically all year long and mostly stay in the same pairs.

Usually we'd bring along a bag of feed. Birdy can get almost any pigeon to come sit on his hand in about two minutes. He'd tell me to pick one out of a flock and he'd concentrate on that one pigeon and start making pigeon noises. Sure as hell, that exact pigeon'd begin twisting over and hop right up into his hand. He tells me once he just calls them over. How'n hell can you call a particular pigeon out of a flock? Birdy's a terrific liar.

—Ah, come on, Birdy. Get off it, huh? This is Al here. Let's cut this shit!

Nothing. Anyhow, this one pair of blue bars adopts Birdy. They're beautiful birds but not banded. Birdy gets them so they'll sit on his head or shoulders and they'll let him hold them around the wings. He'd stretch out one wing after the other and ruffle their flight feathers. These pigeons act as if this is the most natural thing in the world; seem to like it.

Birdy'd let them go, throw them up with the other

pigeons and they'd come right back. Usually pigeons will always fly to the flock. One day Birdy and I walk home instead of taking the bus, and that pair stays right with Birdy all the way to our tree loft. Those crazy birds are homed on Birdy.

Must not listen.
To hear something, must not listen.
To see something, must not look.
To know something, must not think.
To tell something, must not listen.

We had to lock the loft to keep those blue bars from following Birdy home. His old lady'd poison them if she ever caught on.

—Hey, Birdy; remember the blue bar pair you had homed on you? Jesus, that was weird!

He's still not paying any attention. I don't care if he is a loon, he shouldn't just ignore me.

—Birdy, can you hear me? If you hear me and don't say anything, you really are a loon; nothing but a fucking loon.

Christ, I'm wasting my time. He acts like he's deaf or something. Major-doctor says he can hear, hears every word I say. Those bastards don't know everything either. Maybe Birdy's just scared and doesn't want to listen. What the hell could've happened to him?

When we had the old flock at his house, one thing Birdy and I liked to do was take a bird or two out for a ride on our bicycles. We built a special box to carry them. These were birds already homed to the loft. Birdy'd rigged a string on the pigeon gate with an old alarm clock so we'd know exactly when they got back. We'd go out to Springfield or someplace and let them fly home with a message to ourselves.

One time when I go to the shore with my family, I take two birds with me. I wade out in the surf and let them loose; less than two hours later they're back at the loft. That's over ninety miles. In the message I wrote the time and told Birdy I'm letting the birds fly loose over the Atlantic Ocean.

Birdy'd sit by the hour in our loft watching those pigeons. Christ, I like pigeons myself, but not all the holy day sitting in the dark watching. Then, there's that pigeon suit he used to wear. He started making it while we still had the loft in his back yard. It began with an old pair of long johns he dyed dark blue. He gathered pigeon feathers from everywhere and kept them in a cigar box. He'd squat, like I said, in the back of our loft, sewing feathers onto those long johns. He began at the top and worked down, round and round, one feather overlapping the other, the way a bird is.

When he got it finished and put it on, he looked like some kind of scraggly giant blue check. He'd wear this crazy suit every time he went into the loft. It's one thing that definitely bugged his mother.

When we built the tree loft, it got worse. He started wearing gloves covered with feathers and slipped reddish-yellow long socks over his shoes and up to his knees. This was all finished off by a hood with more feathers and a yellow cardboard beak. In the back of the loft, in dark shadows, squatting, sometimes he'd look like a real pigeon, only about the size of a big dog. Somebody accidentally looking up into that tree and seeing him walking around would probably go completely nuts.

—That's what you need here, Birdy, need the old pigeon costume. Really freak out your fatass doctor.

Birdy didn't have any feeling for quality birds. I never could figure just what it was he looked for in a pigeon. Take this next pigeon we get for the tree loft; it's one of the ugliest things you can imagine. She's so corny, I wouldn't think even a corny'd have anything to do with her. Birdy thinks she's beautiful.

It's about a month after we got the blue bars, Birdy comes to the loft with this pigeon one rainy day and says he found her down in the dump fighting a rat. Now, who'd believe a thing like that? Birdy's lies are so way out nobody'd believe them. Another thing about Birdy is he'll believe other people's lies. Birdy'll believe almost anything.

The earth turns and we are caught. The weight invades and we struggle in a cage of shifting tons.

This corny's absolutely black, not shiny black but a dull smoky black. Except for her beak and the way she walks like a pigeon, you'd swear she's a pint-size crow. She's so small I think she's a squab, this is after I'm convinced she's a pigeon. I don't want her in the loft. An extra hen in a loft is bad news, but Birdy insists. He keeps raving about how beautiful she is and how she can fly.

First thing she does is steal that blue bar cock away from the hen. He doesn't know what hit him. He's wearing himself out strutting around, chasing, fucking her; not even eating. Poor blue bar hen is moping on the nest.

I'm pissed; I want to throw the goddamned corny out. Pigeon witch's what she is. Birdy says OK but he's not happy. We throw her up and out the next day. I figure she's a wanderer and we'll never see her again.

When I get to the loft that afternoon, Birdy's already there; so's the witch. She's with a great red check cock. They're strutting all around the loft and the red check's giving it to her while the blue bar's trying to get his in but making zero. We watch all afternoon. Finally the blue bar goes back to his hen. I say, OK, the witch can stay now she has her own cock. She must've gotten homed to the loft in only two days.

No one knows more than they have to know. All of us locked in gravity graves.

Well, that witch is unbelievable. Next time she goes out, she comes back with a beautiful pair of purebred, banded ash. Birds like that cost a fortune, eight, nine dollars a pair. These are really show birds. We can't imagine where they come from. The ash cock goes for the witch and the hen follows them into the loft. They're so beautiful they light up the whole place. So now the ash is fucking the witch and the red check's out. It's not natural.

Things go on like that. The witch goes out and comes back with a cock or sometimes a pair. Most times it's quality birds. This witch has sex appeal for good pigeons. She always lets the cock she brings home have it till the next one comes along, then never lets him near her again. During the three months she's in our loft she shows no sign of nesting. Birdy says maybe she's a whore pigeon, but I'm sure she's a witch.

I break inside my aloneness to knowledge, the end of knowing; a billowing of an air current; a movement toward necessity.

Shit, before we know it, we have more pigeons than we can keep in the loft. Nobody even knows we have pigeons, so nobody suspects us. With our witch, we're the biggest pigeon-nappers west of Sixty-third Street.

We start taking extra pigeons out to Cheltenham or Media on the train and selling them. Not much chance of anybody recognizing them way out there. We're making three, four dollars each weekend that way. Working a whole paper route every day you can't make that.

And do we ever have great pigeons in the loft. Makes our old loft look like a pig sty. Birdy insists on keeping those first blue bars and, of course, we keep the ashes. Then, we have the sweetest pair of blue checks you ever saw. Checks as clear and unblurred as a checkerboard and they're big but still slim, with high heads. They have feet red as persimmons and clean. Banded birds, both of them, beautiful. I could watch them all day. I really go for quality pigeons. We have two pairs of red bars almost as good, so good anybody'd trade three pairs of purebreds for either pair.

The witch is in and out. Sometimes she's gone three, four days at a time. Even though she's making us all that money, I wish she won't come back some time. She gives me the willies. I don't like the way Birdy is with her, either. They're creepy together, especially when he's wearing that stupid pigeon costume.

I take another peek up and down the corridor. For a loony bin, it's awful quiet. Most rooms have double doors. The outside door only has a small glass window so you can look in at the crazies; the inside door has bars. I'm sitting in the space between the two doors.

It's a lot better looking hospital here than the one at Dix. I'm in plastic surgery there and everybody's in and out all the time. We have to wait two, three weeks, sometimes a month, between operations. We're not sick so they let us out while we're waiting. I'm heading home between operations; big hero in the hoagie shop. They tell me one more will do it; but I'll never be able to grow a beard on that part. Who the hell wants to grow a beard anyhow?

—Hey, Birdy boy!! Remember that old corny we had? She really had hot pants for you, buddy. How'd you like a little pigeon nookey, right now, huh?

I have a feeling for a minute there I got to him, just the way his fingers unfold and fold again. He really could be putting this whole thing on. What the hell, it's no sense bucking for section eight. They're letting everybody out anyway.

That corny used to parade back and forth in front of Birdy, cooing low and shimmying down her back the way a pigeon hen does when she wants a cock to jump her. She's flirting with him, the witch. When Birdy'd spread some feed on the floor, she doesn't go down and hustle with the others; oh no, she flies over on Birdy's hand and gets him to feed her. She makes all the same moves a hen makes when she gets fed by a cock. Birdy even puts some grains between his lips and she picks them out. Christ, sometimes I used to think Birdy actually thought he was a pigeon.

To bend the tree or fill the sail is nothing. Knowledge only, not knowing. A bird knows the air without knowledge.

I want to see if I can remind Birdy of when we went on the treasure hunt. This was after the gas tank and after they made us break up the loft. We'd already graduated from elementary school and Birdy was going to a Catholic school. I'm going to Upper Merion, the public school. My parents are Catholic too, but they're Italian Catholics and don't go to church much. Birdy's old man and old lady are big for mass and all that crap.

Anyway, I have to write a story for my English class and since I have practically no imagination, I decide to work this gag on Birdy and write it up just the way it happens. We're reading "The Gold Bug" in class and maybe it gave me the idea.

—Hey, Birdy!! How about when we went looking for old man Cosgrove's buried treasure? Jesus, what a riot.

I came over to Birdy's place with the map. I'd spent almost a week making it and getting everything else ready. I have it all browned with fire and burnt on the edges. Christ, it's a masterpiece. It's all in code and we figure it out in Birdy's room. We move a model for one of Birdy's crazy birds off his desk so we can spread out the map. It's raining that day.

Birdy's always making bird models. He makes them with balsa wood and paper the way you make a model airplane, only his are bird designs with rubber-band power to make the wings flap up and down. Some of them are complicated, with wings that rotate so they twist vertically on the up stroke and horizontally on the down. He's actually gotten some of them to fly. Trouble is, none of them fly as far as a regular model airplane; it takes too much rubber-band time to flap the wings for any kind of long flight.

—Boy, you really fell like a ton of bricks for that crappy map, Birdy.

The message part has all kinds of complicated directions, like from this tree to that rock, all that treasure map talk. It leads us to a wall where we're supposed to find another message. Birdy eats it up; Christ, he'll believe anything. He's talking about how he's going to build a giant aviary with his money. I almost give away the whole thing; I don't want to hurt Birdy, I'm just having a joke and getting my English homework done.

We go down that night. It's raining like hell. I try getting Birdy to postpone but nothing can stop him. He believes things so hard he's getting me to believe; I almost expect to actually find some treasure myself.

We tromp around in the dark, sopping wet, no flashlights. Birdy's leading me to a treasure I didn't put there. We do find the old tobacco can where I hid the second message; it's shoved between stones of the Cosgrove ruin, beside where the fireplace used to be. Birdy slips it into his pocket and we hightail out of there and run all the way back to his house. We go in through the cellar so nobody'll see us. Birdy's a little runt but he runs like the wind.

We sneak back up to his room again and spread out the new map. I've used the same code and burnt off a part of the writing but left enough for us to figure out it's a treasure map. There's an X to mark the spot. Birdy wants to go straight out again. I talk him into going the next night. We need proper tools and stuff. I'm wishing I'd never started the whole damned thing. I'm sorry I don't have some kind of treasure to bury for Birdy to find.

The treasure is supposed to be buried at the northeast corner of the old barn ruin. This is all said in treasure talk again so we have to figure it out. I help Birdy over some hard parts but he gets most of it himself. He deserves a treasure all right.

We agree to get together after supper when it's dark. I have no trouble getting out, but Birdy has a fancy plan with a dummy in his bed and a way to lock his door from inside. He could probably just say he was coming over to my place but he's deep into the treasure business. The Tom Sawyer of Upper Merion.

We have a shovel and he has a compass and a string and I bring along my twenty-two just in case. Naturally, it's started raining again. Didn't rain all day but now it's pouring. It's a thick, dark night. We go across center field, down the hill behind the flagpole and along the path leading to the Cosgrove barn. It's late fall, past my birthday, so there isn't much grass or bushes. Summer, you can hardly get into this part; wouldn't even know the old walls are there.

I didn't come down here when I made the map. I just made up the spot, "northeast corner of barn." It turns out, with a compass, there *is* a northeast corner. Turns out, eerily, that there's a slight depression in the ground right where the X should be. I'm ready to dig for gold myself. Maybe I'm getting messages from the other world. Maybe old man Cosgrove's been getting through to me. Everybody always says Cosgrove buried his money. For years people used to dig around here hoping to find some of it.

We start digging, taking turns every five minutes. I'm torn between laughing my balls off and shitting my pants. Birdy's dead serious, checking my watch to see I don't get more'n my share of digging. He's digging when he hits something. "That's it!" he says. I'm turning green. What if there is a treasure; it's too spooky. He digs like mad, clears a corner of something made out of metal. I start digging on my turn and turn it up finally. It's an old can of motor oil. I laugh; I figure now's the time to tell him. I'm mud up to my ass and wet. We're getting into clay and it's slippery. Digging in the dark when you can't even see the rocks you clink against is no fun.

"There isn't any treasure, Birdy, I made the whole thing up."

He takes the shovel and starts digging again.

"Christ, no sense digging anymore, Birdy, there isn't any treasure here! I made up the map and everything. I did it as a school project."

Birdy keeps on digging.

"Aw, come on, Birdy. Let's go home and get dry."

Birdy stops, looks over at me. Then he says he knows the treasure is here and we shouldn't give up. It's got to be here and I only think I made up the map. That's too much. I tell him he's crazy and I'm leaving. He keeps digging. I stand around another five minutes, then take off. He's still digging madly, not saying anything.

I don't see Birdy for another two or three days. I decide not to write about the treasure hunt for school. I go down to where we'd been digging and there's a hole at least six feet deep, deep as a grave. I don't know how the hell Birdy got out of the hole when he was finished.

When I finally do see Birdy again, we don't talk about the treasure hunt at first. A few days later, Birdy says he figures somebody got to it before us; that's why the ground was sunk in like that. He still won't believe I made it all up; even when I tell him how I did it. He only gives me one of his crazy eye-wiggling looks.

I want to think to make real this that I know and can't hold. I'm pulled down. The earth in me is strong; the drifting dust is in my bones.

We get such a good business going, selling pigeons, we decide to go out and get some birds ourselves. That's what we were doing up on the gas tank that night. It's a big storage tank at Marshall Road and Long Lane. This is a place where several different flocks of pigeons roost and nest.

—How about us up on top of the gas tank, Birdy. That was wild. That night you almost convinced me you might just be part bird.

Damn; he's not paying any attention to me at all.

—Listen here, birdbrain! I'm tired talking to the back of your head; you can't be that crazy! Maybe if I come in and give you a coupla hard ones you'll hear better!

Crazy ass thing to say; anybody hear me, they'd lock me up too. Anyway, Birdy's not afraid of things people are supposed to be afraid of. No way you can make him do something he doesn't want. No way to hurt him; like he just doesn't feel anything he doesn't want to. Typical of what I mean is the way I met Birdy.

Mario, my kid brother, comes in and tells me this freak down at the Cosgrove place took his knife. I ask him where he got the knife; he tells me he found it. I figure he stole it but I'm always looking for fights anyway. I'm naturally strong and I've already started lifting weights; have my own miniature gym down in the cellar. I'm walking around squeezing spring things to increase my grip; reading *Strength and Health*; York, Pennsylvania, is a kind of Mecca for me. I start all this crap when I'm only about eleven—probably because the old man used to beat me up so much. Anyway, I've got all this strength and I want to try it out with fights.

I'm just starting these crazy ideas when Mario tells me about Birdy taking his knife. I'm thirteen. Birdy must be all of twelve. I see us in my mind as older, not as little punks like that.

I go down and walk across the ball field. I'm wearing my new brown leather jacket and Mario's tagging along behind me. He shows me the place. I lean over the gate in the wall and Birdy's sitting on the steps of his back porch cleaning off the knife. I tell him to come over. He comes with a look on his face as if he's glad to meet me.

Living things grow upward but are not free. The highest branches trap air and light but only feed endless grindings of earth. Growth itself is without meaning.

I tell him to give me the knife. He says it's his; says he bought it from a kid named Zigenfus. He tells me I can check with this Zigenfus if I want. I ask him to let me see the knife. He gives it to me. We're talking over the wooden gate in the wall to his house. It's the wall of the baseball field.

I see right away this is a really good knife, a switchblade. I try to work it. Tricky kind of catch and spring; seems to be broken. Birdy reaches over to show me how it works. I pull the knife away and tell him to keep his crummy hands off *my* knife. He looks at me with his wiggly eyes as if I'm nuts. I turn and start walking away with Mario. He opens the gate and comes after us. We keep walking. He gets in front of us, walking backwards, and asks for his knife. I stop. I hold it up. "This knife?" I say, "Try and take it." He reaches for the knife. I'm holding it up in my left hand so I can give him a good one with the right. Somehow I miss, and he gets hold of the knife. I snatch the knife out of his hand. I hold it up and he reaches again. I swing and miss again. His head is right there, but by the time my fist gets to that place, he's gone. I swear he moves after I start the punch. I put the knife in my pocket so I can use both hands; I figure I'm really going to massacre this fool. He keeps reaching for the pocket. He's always there and I keep swinging but can't hit him. I start trying to set him up. Nothing doing; it's like I'm doing everything in slow motion and he's at full speed. He's not doing anything like bobbing and weaving; he just moves away from the place I hit at, the way you'd step from in front of a car.

I decide to grab him. If I have to, I'll put him on the ground where he can't move, then clobber him. Mario's not saying anything. Next time Birdy reaches in for the knife, I step forward and get a good headlock on him. I bend to throw him over my leg and he's gone. The feeling is exactly the way it feels when a snake slips out of your hand. He squirmed or vibrated.

I try everything. I try tackling him. I try getting him in a bear hug. I try another headlock. Nothing holds him.

Later, when Birdy switches to old U. M. High, I want him to go out for wrestling but he won't do it. The only exception is one time when we have an intramural competition and there's nobody to wrestle against Vogel at a hundred thirty-five. Vogel is district champ; Birdy says he'll suit up to fill in.

The whole school is out to see the match; intramural sports are a big thing at U. M. At the opening of the first period, Vogel misses the takedown a couple times, then he dives at Birdy. Birdy steps aside and falls on Vogel for a takedown. Birdy can't weigh more than one twenty-five soaking wet. Vogel's getting mad. He tries to roll. Birdy slips loose and lets Vogel roll alone onto his back. All Birdy has to do is flop on him, hold him down and he has a pin, or at least a near pin. Birdy stands up and smiles down at Vogel. Vogel scrambles for an escape. Birdy has two points for the take-down and Vogel one for the escape.

Same thing happens again and Birdie has another two points for takedown. Vogel escapes again just at the end of the period. Score: Birdy four, Vogel two. The crowd's beginning to laugh; everybody's rooting for Birdy. Birdy's walking around looking goofy as ever, the wrestling suit hanging all loose on him.

The second period starts in referee position with Vogel on top. He really hunkers in on Birdy. Birdy's not even looking at anything, just smiling to himself. I figure this is where Birdy gets pinned. Vogel's a strong kraut bastard; he's all red in the face he's so mad.

The ref slaps his hand on the mat and calls "wrestle." Vogel pulls Birdy's arm for a breakdown and somehow, I don't know what he did, some kind of forward roll, but Birdy's standing and Vogel's there all alone on the mat. Jesus, the crowd breaks up. Vogel's on his hands and knees like an old bear, and Birdy is standing, looking down at him.

Vogel charges across the mat at Birdy. He fakes going into a wrestle position, then goes down for a leg drop. Birdy twists around and winds up sitting on Vogel's head. It's too much. I get so excited I bump my knee into the back of the guy in front of me. He has a sharp pencil in his hip pocket. The point jams into my knee and sticks there. I still have the mark; souvenir of the day Birdy beat the district champion hundred thirty-five pounder. Beat him twelve to six on points, didn't even work up a sweat. Vogel's so pissed he spends all season trying to make up for it. He just misses being state champion by two points; gets beaten in the final at Harrisburg.

When brought to meaning, all importance becomes small, as in death, all life seems nothing. Knowing is destroyed by thinking, not destroyed but sterilized; distilled into knowledge. Thinking, the processing of knowing to knowledge.

Finally, I'm puffing so from trying to catch Birdy, I straighten up and look at him. He smiles at me. He's still playing games. He wants his knife all right but he's not mad at me. I'm just the long arm of fate. I take out the knife. I open it slowly to scare him. I go into a crouch like I'm going to kill him. He stands there watching me. I begin to suspect there's no way I can get him with that knife, even if I want to. Throw it and he's liable to reach into the air and catch it. I begin to see how funny the whole thing is. Mario's still standing there. I throw the knife into the ground at Birdy's feet. Birdy picks it up. He cleans it, closes it, then walks over and gives it to Mario. He says if it's really his knife, he can have it. Says, maybe Zigenfus found it, or stole it, and maybe it's Mario's all the time. I tell Mario not to touch the fucking knife. I take it from Birdy, then give it back to him. I feel like General Lee surrendering his sword. That's when Birdy asks me if I like pigeons and invites me into his yard to look at the loft he's building. Mario goes along home and Birdy and I get to be friends.

—Birdy, you know you could've been state champion if you wanted to. You could've wrestled all those shrimps at a hundred twenty-five without even trying. Could've broken all kinds of track records too.

We'd sit across the street on Saturdays watching pigeons on the gas tank. Birdy has great binoculars he got at a pawn shop. They're perfect for watching pigeons. We'd watch all day, taking turns and eating hoagie sandwiches we bought on Long Lane.

Birdy makes drawings of the pigeons. Birdy's always drawing pigeons or any kind of bird, the way other guys draw hot rods, or motorcycles, or girls. He draws details of feathers or feet and he makes drawings of birds like blueprints, with arrows and top views and side views. When he sets himself to draw a pigeon like a pigeon, he can do that too. One of the things Birdy is, is an artist.

One day some cops sneak up on us. They say we're peeping into people's windows with the binoculars and they've had complaints. People are nuts. By luck, Birdy has a lot of his bird drawings and we say we're making a report for school. This is something even a cop can understand. He's going to have a hard time explaining to some lady why we'd rather look at pigeons than peep through her window and watch her pee.

There are a few good strays in those flocks at the gas tank and we want to get some. Birdy, most likely, could've talked them into his pocket, but we're both sold on the idea of climbing that tank. It has to be done at night when the pigeons are roosting. There's a fence and a night watchman but we've been checking and know where to go over.

It's hard for me to do this. I must kill each bird, defeather it, disembowel it, for one bite. I must. I am hungry; I starve for knowledge. My brain spins in knowing. We trade all for knowledge.

We use our rope ladder with the hook to throw up and pull down the bottom section of the ladder on the back side of the tank. I go first; we both have gunny sacks to put birds in. We have flashlights, too, so we can see the birds and choose the ones we want.

We get to the top OK. There's a fantastic view up there; we pick out the Tower Theater and lights going all the way into Philadelphia. We sit up there and promise ourselves we'll come up again sometime just to watch the stars. That's something we never get to do.

Scary as shit catching birds. We have to reach over the edge into the slits on the tank where the pigeons roost. I try it first with Birdy holding my legs, but I can't make it. The top of the tank slants to the edge and you have to lean out so your shoulders're clear over. I can't get myself to do it. No matter how strong you think you are, there're some things you can't make yourself do.

Birdy doesn't mind at all. He reaches under and hands them to me. If they're junk, I hand them back; good ones I shove in the bag. We go all around the tank, stopping and checking whenever we hear pigeons. First time around, we get about ten reasonable birds that way.

Birdy says there're more good ones in the next slit down. He shimmies out till he's practically hanging from his waist over the edge. I put the bag of birds down and sit on his feet to keep him from flipping over. I'm ready to quit. It scares me just sitting on his feet that close to the edge. He's leaning out so far now he can't hand the birds back, so he takes another bag to put them in directly. I figure we're liable to get all kinds of crap with Birdy choosing, but we can always let them go later.

That's when there's a clatter, and some pigeons flap in the dark behind me. I look around and see two birds getting out of the bag. Without thinking, I lean back to shut the bag. Birdy's legs swing up in front of me and over the edge!

There's a rush and pigeons fly out and up into the dark. I'm scared shitless; I wait, afraid to move. I have a feeling the whole tank is rocking. Nothing happens. I slide on my stomach toward the edge. Birdy's clinging to the slits. He still has the gunny sack over his arm. He looks up and gives me one of his loose smiles. He holds out a hand.

"Gimme a hand up, Al."

I reach out but can't make myself lean far enough out to grab him. I close my eyes but then I get dizzy and I'm about to fall off. He takes his hand back and shifts his grip. He tries to leg up over the edge of the tank but can't make it. I'm beginning to shake.

"I'll go get somebody, Birdy!"

"I can't hold on that long. It's all right, I can do it."

He pulls his feet up to the next rung and tries to reach with one hand to the top edge of the tank. I try to reach for him but I'm absolutely paralyzed. I can't make myself go near that edge. Birdy hangs there with his ass leaning out into the dark. I get down on my stomach and try to reach as far as I can. I get my hand to where he can reach it if he lets go with one of his hands. Birdy says, "When I say three, I'll let go and grab your hand."

Birdy counts, lets go and I catch him. Now we're really shit up a crick. I can't pull without slipping down off the tank. We're just balanced there; every time he moves, I slip a little further toward the edge. That's when I pee my pants. Jesus, I'm scared. Birdy looks back down.

"I'll try making it to the coal pile."

I don't know what he means; maybe I don't want to know.

With his free hand, Birdy arranges the burlap bag in front of him, then lets go of me. He hovers for a second, turning himself around against the side of the tank, then leans forward into the air and shoves off. I can see him all the way down. He stays flat out and kicks his feet like somebody swimming. He keeps that burlap sack stretched across in front of him with his arms spread out.

The first time I flew, it was being alive. Nothing was pressing under me. I was living in the fullness of air; air all around me, no holding place to break the air spaces. It's worth everything to be alone in the air, alive.

Birdy does get over to the coal pile and, just before he lands, closes up into a ball, twists, and lands on his back. He doesn't get up. I can barely see him, a white spot in the black coal. It's a long way down.

I don't expect him to be dead. This is stupid because it has to be over a hundred feet from the top of that tank. I even remember to bring the pigeons with me. I climb down the tank ladder, not thinking too much, just scared. I run around to the coal pile. The night watchman must've been asleep.

Birdy's sitting up. He looks dead white against the coal; blood's dripping out his nose and into the corners of his mouth. I sit down on the pile beside him. We sit there; I don't know what to do; I can't really believe it's happened.

The tank looks even higher from down here than it did from on top.

Birdy tries to talk a couple times but his wind's knocked out of him. When he does talk his voice is rattly.

"I did it. I flew. It was beautiful."

It's for sure he didn't fall off that tank. If he'd fallen, he'd've been smashed.

"Yeah, you flew all right; want me to go get somebody?"

"No, I'm fine."

Birdy tries to stand up. His face goes whiter; then he starts to vomit and there's a lot of blood. He sits back on the coal pile and passes out.

I'm rat scared now! I run around to the night watchman's shack! He won't believe me! I have to drag him out to Birdy. He calls an ambulance. They come and take Birdy off to the hospital.

I stand there with the birds in the bag. Nobody pays much attention to me. Even the ambulance men don't believe he fell off the tank; think I'm lying. I stop on my way home and put our birds in the loft. I hang around there for a while; I hate to go home. Something like that happens and all the things you think are important don't seem like much.

Birdy shuffles over to the john in the corner to take a crap. No seat on the toilet or anything. No privacy. God, what a hell of a place for someone like Birdy.

I turn around. I'm looking up and down the corridor when the orderly or guard or whatever he is sees me. It must be some crummy job walking up and down a corridor checking on crazies.

"How's he doing?"

"He's taking a crap."

This character looks in. Maybe he likes to see guys take a crap. Maybe he's a part-time nut. I ask if he's a civilian. You can't tell anything when they all wear those white coats. He could even be a piss-ass officer or something. Never know in a hospital. He tells me he's a CO. I think at first he's trying to put on he's the commanding officer. Turns out CO means conscientious objector. He's been working in this hospital most of the war.

"You want to knock off for lunch now? I have to feed him anyway."

"Whaddaya mean, 'feed him'; can't he feed himself?"

"Nope. He won't eat anything; wants to be fed. I have to spoon-feed him. No trouble or anything, not like some of them. I just shovel it in. He squats on the floor and I put it in."

"Holy Christ! He really is a loon! Won't even eat?"

"He's nothing. Guy across the hall there won't wear any clothes. Squats in the middle of his cell like your friend here; but if anybody tries to go in, he shits in his hand and throws it. Boy, he's fun to feed. More like a zoo than a hospital on this ward."

He looks in the cell. I look too. Birdy's finished. He's squatting on the floor, in about the same spot, like the pigeons after the el goes by. The orderly comes with a tray of food. He takes the key, opens the door and goes in. He tells me to stay out. He squats down beside Birdy and starts feeding him. I can't believe it! Birdy actually flaps his arms like a baby bird being fed! The orderly looks around at me and shrugs his shoulders.

"I forgot to tell you, Doctor Weiss wants to see you after lunch."

"Thanks."

Weiss is the doctor-major. I look in once more at Birdy and go down the corridor. I know where the cafeteria is because I had breakfast there. It's really a cafeteria, too, not a mess hall; doctors and nurses eat there; good food. I eat and think about Birdy being fed like a baby pigeon. What the hell could've happened?

When I go to see Weiss, I ask what's the matter with Birdy, but he's sly and manages not to answer. Suddenly, he gets to be the major talking to the sergeant.

He's watching me with a shit-eating grin on his face as if I'm some kind of nut myself. He starts out asking about what they're doing to me at Dix. I tell him about how the jaw is smashed and how they put in the metal part.

When they first told me, I thought I'd have a steel jaw like Tony Zale. Doctor there tells me, actually I'll have to be very careful, a punch could undo the pins and shock me into the brain. So now I've got a glass jaw. That's about right.

I'm telling Weiss all this stuff and then I *see* him. He's smiling, *hmm*ing and *ahh*ing just to keep me going. He doesn't give a damn. I decide I don't want to tell too much about Birdy.

He asks how long Birdy and I were close friends. I tell him we've been friends since we were thirteen. He asks this in a way so you know he really wants to know if we were queer together; if we jacked each other off, or gave each other blow jobs. I'll say this, there's a lot of that crap in the infantry. A four-hour stint in a foxhole with the wrong guy can get awfully funky.

Actually, I can't remember Birdy being interested in sex at all. Take that whole scene with Doris Robinson. If he couldn't make it with her he's hopeless. Maybe all he had it for was birds. This quack'd sure flip if I told him that.

The doctor-major keeps trying to pump me about Birdy. I'm completely turned off. If he could just *look* sincere. He knows I'm holding back. He's no dummy. I have to be careful. Under that white coat he's solid brass. He's liable to lower the boom on this buck-ass sergeant any minute. So far, he's been talking like a doctor but I'm waiting for the old military manner to strike again. All doctors in the army ought to be privates.

Just as I'm thinking this, he comes out with it: "OK, Sergeant, you go back there this afternoon and see if you can make some contact. It's probably the best chance we've got. I'll make an appointment to see you again here, tomorrow morning at nine." He stands up to dismiss me. I fuck him with the salute and hold it till he returns it. Son-of-a-bitch.

On the way back to Birdy, I have a little talk with the CO orderly. Nice guy; probably not queer. I get him to talk about being a CO. He says he spent some time being starved for experiments on how little food a person really needs and then he was up in a forest planting trees and he's been here at the hospital the last eighteen months. He tells me all this as if it's what's supposed to be. He's a bit like Birdy; hard to hurt. Real losers never lose.

He asks me about my face and I tell him. He's truly sympathetic, not like Weiss. You can see it in his face and how he reaches up and touches his own chin to see if it's there. He opens Birdy's door for me and I get my chair from the corridor.

Birdy's still squatting in the middle of the floor and staring up at the window when I come in.

—Hey Birdy! Just had a long talk with Weiss. He's sure one sweet pain in the ass. If I were crazy, I'd pretend I wasn't, just to get out of his fat hands. How about that?

Birdy actually turns his head. He doesn't turn all the way around and look at me. He turns halfway, the way a bird does when it wants to look at something directly with one eye. Of course, Birdy isn't looking at me, he's looking at the blank wall across the room.

—Birdy! How about the time we took off and went to Wildwood. I'll never forget the way you jumped around in the waves.

I have the feeling Birdy's listening. His shoulders are lowered as if he's roosting and not getting ready to take off. It could be just my imagination, but I don't feel alone. I keep talking.

After the gas tank, Birdy was in the hospital more than a month. It was all in the newspapers about how he'd fallen from the tank and hadn't been killed. There was a picture with a dotted line showing where he'd jumped from, and an X where he landed. Reporters asked me what'd happened and I never should've said anything about flying.

Naturally, the whole business with the pigeons comes out.

Birdy's father tears down the loft and burns the wood. The pigeons fly around there for a week looking for the loft. It's the place they're homed to. Those first blue bars fly up to Birdy's house and hang around there till his mother poisons them. I don't know what happens to the pigeon witch.

The kids at school ask me the same questions about Birdy flying. Even before he gets out of the hospital, they're calling him Birdy, the bird boy. Sister Agnes has us all write letters to Birdy and we collect money to send flowers. I don't say anything much in my letter; I don't tell him what's happened to the loft and the blue bars.

When Birdy comes out of the hospital, he looks even runtier than usual and his hair's long. He's pale as a girl. I tell him about the loft but not about the blue bars being poisoned. He doesn't ask. We're in the eighth grade; Birdy catches up and graduates with us.

After the gas tank, I knew I had to fly. Without thought, a bird denies all in a moment, with an effortless flick of wings. It would be worth everything to learn this.

If I could get close to birds and enjoy their pleasure it would be almost enough. If I could watch birds like watching a movie and become inside them, I'd know something of it. If I could get close to a bird as a friend and be there when it flies and feel what it's thinking, then, in a certain way, I would fly. I wanted to know all about birds. I wanted to be like a bird and I still wanted to fly; really fly.

That summer, Birdy and I take off. We don't plan it. We're always bicycling down to Philadelphia and the Parkway. We'd go down there, play around the art museum, the aquarium, and the Franklin Institute. There's a place on Cherry Street where they have a room full of bird pictures. We used to go look at them. Birdy's pictures are better. Birdy says artists don't know much about live birds. He says a dead bird isn't a bird anymore; it's like trying to draw a fire by looking at ashes.

We'd go down to South and Front streets where there are

hock shops and stores full of live chickens and pigeons for eating. One day we buy a pair of meat pigeons. We spend all day shopping for them. We take them over to city hall where there're some tremendous flocks. We pull a feather out of each wing, put the feathers in our shirt pockets, and throw the birds up with the others. We watch all afternoon while they find a place in the flock.

I show Birdy how if you get at a certain angle, the big statue of Billy Penn on top of city hall looks as if he has a gigantic hard-on. We have great fun there in the square with the pigeons; every time some ladies pass by, we start pointing up to Billy Penn and they look up to see old Billy with his dong sticking up.

One day we decide to bicycle across the bridge and into New Jersey. We get across and hang around Camden. We're going to go right back that afternoon, but then we see a sign pointing to Atlantic City.

We have our whole bankroll with us, money we made selling pigeons: twenty-three dollars. Usually we kept it in the hole where we used to keep the rope ladder, but we have it with us this time.

We start down back roads leading toward Atlantic City. Now we know what we're doing, we start watching for cops. We want to sack out before it gets dark.

That night, we sleep in a tomato field. It's summer but it's cold. We each eat about ten tomatoes, with some bread and coke we bought at a store in Camden. In the morning, when we wake up we're frozen. I begin to think of going back. Birdy wants to go on to the ocean; he's never seen it. His folks are poorer than mine and they don't have a car. Already I'm going to get the shit beat out of me for staying out all night so what the hell. What can they do anyway? Old Vittorio can just beat me up again; he can't kill me.

That afternoon we get to Atlantic City. Birdy goes berserk when he sees the ocean. He likes everything about it. He likes the sound and he likes the smell; he likes the sea gulls. He runs up and down the beach at the edge of the water flapping his arms. Lucky it's late afternoon; not many people to see him.

Then, Birdy takes off, running, flying, jumping into the water. He still has his clothes on. He gets knocked on his ass by the first wave. He's dragged out by the undertow. I think he's going to drown, but then he stands up soaking wet, laughing madly, and falls backwards into it just as another wave crashes over him. Any ordinary person would've been killed. He rolls around in the water thrashing and throwing himself into the waves. Some girls start to watch and laugh. Birdy doesn't care.

When he comes out, he flops in the sand and rolls. He rolls and rolls till he rolls limp under the water and under the waves deep into the water again. He rolls back and forth in the surf like a log or a dead person. Finally, I have to drag him out. For Christ's sake, it's getting late, and now his clothes are all wet.

Birdy doesn't care. We wheel our bikes along the board-walk to Steel Pier. We have a great time buying as many hot dogs as we want and riding all the rides. We buy a two-pound box of saltwater taffy for dinner; and move on back up the beach to where it's deserted. We find a good place with warm sand and bury ourselves in it.

I tell Birdy about his mother poisoning the blue bars. We decide not to go home and not to write where we are, either. Hell, my old lady's always complaining about how much I eat; it'll save her having to feed me. I'm sick of having the old man jump on me, too. Birdy says that, except for falling off the gas tank, swimming in the ocean is probably the closest thing to flying. Says he's going to learn to swim.

Nobody ever learned to swim the way Birdy does. He doesn't want to swim on top of the water like everybody else. He goes out under the waves and does what he calls "flying in water." He holds his breath till you think he's drowned and then comes up someplace where you aren't expecting him at all like a porpoise or something. That's when he starts all the crappy business with breath holding, too.

In the water I was free. By a small movement, I could go up and move in all directions without effort. But it was slower, thicker, darker. I could not stay. Every effort would not let me stay more than five minutes.

We have left the water. Air is man's natural place. Even if we are forced to walk in the depths of it, we live in the air. We cannot go back. It is the age of mammals and birds.

One hundred billion birds, fifty for every man alive and nobody seems to notice. We live in the slime of an immensity and no one objects. What must our enslavement seem to the birds in the magnitude of their environment?

We decide to take off down the coast to Wildwood. That's the place my family usually goes every summer. Atlantic City is bigger but Wildwood is more open, more natural.

We roll down on the bikes. We're still looking out for cops. It's terrific, free feeling, no house you have to go back to, nobody waiting for you to come in and eat; nothing to do but roll along and look at the scenery. I never knew before how much I was locked in by everything.

On the way down, we decide we'll sleep on the beaches at night, spend the days there in the sunshine. We'll lift whatever we need from the stores. There're also lots of garbage cans behind the restaurants where we can find all the food we need. We'll buy a couple old blankets at the Salvation Army and a pot to cook in under the boardwalk.

It works out exactly like that. Things hardly ever do. All we spend any money on after we get the blankets and the cooking pot is the rides at night and saltwater taffy. We get to be dedicated saltwater taffy addicts. We both like the kind with red or black stripes and a strong taste.

We don't have any trouble with cops. There're all kinds of people down on vacation, and so a couple strange kids are hardly noticed. At nights we've fixed a hidden nest down where the boardwalk is only about three feet higher than the sand. We tuck ourselves in there and hide our cooking pot in the sand during the day.

Birdy is going crazy with his swimming. All day long he practices holding his breath, even when he isn't swimming. I'd be sitting there talking to him and I'd see his eyes are bulging and then he'd blow out his breath and say, "Two minutes, forty-five seconds." He asks me to count for him sometimes. The way he wants me to count is Mississippi-one, Mississippi-two, and so on; really nuts. All day he's in the water "flying," coming up once in a great while and taking a deep breath. He's found the local public library and is reading about whales and porpoises and dolphins. He's a maniac. When Birdy gets started on something like that, there's nothing you can do.

The worst thing of all is the sideshow freak called "Zimmy, the Human Fish." Birdy spends a fortune watching this guy. This is a truly creepy set-up. Zimmy has both his legs chopped off just at the top, so he looks like an egg with a head and arms. He's fat with gigantic lungs. He has a big sort of swimming pool with a glass front, like a goldfish bowl, and people look through the glass to watch him do his tricks. This guy is Birdy's hero. You see, Zimmy can stay underwater without breathing, doing tricks down there, like smoking cigarettes, for as much as six minutes at a time.

I get tired of watching so I spend my time at the act just next to Zimmy. Two madmen drive motorcycles around the inside of a wooden bowl. They race each other. It's wild. Then, there's a woman who climbs into a motorcycle with a sidecar and they put a big hairy lion beside her. She revs up the motorcycle and spins around the inside of the bowl, hanging out sideways with that lion roaring all the way around. Christ, it's amazing what people will do. There's one young guy in the act who does acrobatics on his motorcycle— standing up with his hands on the handlebars while he's hanging out sideways on that wooden wall. He has tremendous deltoids and forearms with tattoos all over them. He looks like he'd be one hell of a tough nut to pin.

Nights, Birdy and I ride the rides. Birdy chooses all the rides that throw you against the sky. There's one where they start you spinning so you go faster and faster till you're upside down, with nothing to hold you in your seat. Everybody screams except Birdy. He sits there with a big grin on his face. I do that once, that's enough.

Another time I'm trying my strength on one of those things where you swing a sledgehammer and try to ring the bell. I ring it three times in a row and win a little Teddy bear. There are a couple cute girls watching us and I give it to one of them. We get to talking. They're from Lansdowne. Birdy stands around but he's bored. I talk them into going on the roller coaster with us. One has red hair and nice beginning tits pushing out her sweater. The other is quieter, more the type for Birdy, if there is any type of girl for Birdy.

On the roller coaster, I hold her hand in her lap, tucked sort of between her legs. I can feel the slippery flesh under her dress. I put my arm over her shoulder and she leans her head against me. While the car is clickety-clicking up for the downhill run, I look back at Birdy and his girl. He's leaning over the edge looking down and she's looking straight ahead, holding her own hand in her lap. She smiles at me; Birdy doesn't notice. He could even be thinking of climbing out of the car and jumping. I wouldn't put it past him.

After that, I talk them into going for a walk along the beach, and we walk over to where we have our nest. We get out the blankets and spread them. The girls are getting nervous. They're here with their parents and have to be home by ten o'clock. I ask Birdy what time it is; he looks up and says it's about nine-fifteen. I've never known Birdy to be wrong about the time. Birdy's girl is more nervous than mine. She wants to take off right away. My girl, whose name is Shirley, says maybe Birdy and Claire, that's the other girl, ought to take a walk down to the clock at the parking lot to see what time it really is. She looks at me. Now, I'm getting nervous myself. I've got a hard-on, and here it is coming right at me.

As soon as they're gone, we get down on the blanket and start kissing. She opens her mouth and sticks her tongue between my lips. I begin feeling her up and then, bango, I come off. I try not to let on but she must know. We keep kissing, but it's not the same. She lifts her sweater and puts my hand under. I touch her bra and can feel her little nipple, hard, under it. She looks around, reaches back, and undoes the bra. I put my hand over her whole tit. Jesus, my hard is coming on again. Just then, we hear Birdy and Claire. Shirley pushes away and hooks herself up. She brushes back her hair and stands up. I get up, too.

"It's almost nine-thirty, Shirley. We'd better get home."

Claire stays out from under the boardwalk. Birdy stretches himself on the blanket where Shirley and I just were.

"OK, party pooper. Good-bye Al. See you, Birdy. Maybe tomorrow night about eight, near the merry-go-round, OK?"

I say OK and they leave. I'm still shaking, and the inside of my jockey shorts are slimy with jit. I go down toward the ocean as if I'm going to take a piss. I wipe myself off. I never knew any girl like that before.

We meet a couple more times before they leave. Birdy's bored with the whole thing and Claire's bored with Birdy, but Shirley and I are going hot and heavy. One night, we're down on the blanket and I get my finger under her panties. I can feel her little hole and I slip my finger in. That's getting close. But she pushes me away, and that's it.

When the girls leave I'm ready to go, too, but Birdy's still wrapped up with his swimming. I swim some myself, but Birdy's in all day long. He keeps going without stopping till he's pooped, and blue with cold. Then he'll come out and lie face down in the sand till he gets his wind back, then out he'll go again. It doesn't look to me as if he's having any fun, but he has a big ear-to-ear grin on his face all the time. He's only swimming, but he's talking about "flying." That's typical Birdy.

Well, after a few weeks, we run out of money and decide to sell the bikes. This is our big mistake. We go into a bike shop, and while we're trying to sell them I notice the lady go into the back and phone but I don't think much of it. The guy keeps us in front dickering over price, and we're about ready to walk out when two cops come in the door.

They take us down to the station house, leaving the bikes at the bike store. First, they accuse us of stealing the bikes, want us to show some papers to prove we own them. Who the hell has bike-ownership papers? Then they find us on the runaway list. Birdy's old lady's turned us in. We'd both written saying we were all right and we'd be back in time for school. What a bitch.

Well it all comes out that they ship us home on a train first-class with a stupid bald-headed cop. He goes all the way, eating in the dining car and everything. They stick our parents for a ninety-two dollar bill and we never see the bikes again.

My old man beats the living bejesus out of me. He chases me around the cellar with his big leather belt, hitting me with it or punching, kicking, whatever he can get me with. The old lady's standing at the top of the cellar steps yelling, "Vittorio, VITTORIO! BASTA VITTORIO!" Nothing's going to be enough for old Vittorio except to kill me. Finally, there's nothing for it but to roll up in a bundle on the floor and pretend I'm dead. I just about am. I swear, there on the floor nobody's ever going to get me so they can beat me up like that again. Somehow, I'll get so I can beat the crap out of Vittorio, too. I'll do it before he's too old to appreciate it, if it kills me. I'm curled up on the floor with my hands over my eyes and ears, and he's swinging away at me and that's what I'm thinking. What a lot of shit!!

I'm in bed for a week. I look like I've fallen off three gas tanks. I'm black-and-blue, sore all over. Mostly I'm sore inside. The old lady won't let me out of the house till the worst swelling is down on my face. Old Vittorio's a strong son-of-a-bitch. You wipe big joints and cut six-inch steel pipe all day and you get strong. I pin the bastard on my sixteenth birthday.

She is so beautiful; she's everything I've imagined, everything I want to be. It's impossible she's mine, not really mine, just with me. If she doesn't care to stay, I'll let her go. I want her to love me. I want us to be close, as close as living things can be to each other. How close can we come?

When Al and I finally paid back the money, my father said I could have a bird in my room as long as I do my schoolwork and help around the house with chores. I can't keep a pigeon indoors, so I decide on a canary.

First, I read everything I can about canaries. I find out that the original canaries came from Africa and were shipwrecked on the Canary Islands. They were dark green. The canary is valued because it can sing. However, only the male canary sings. The female looks exactly like the male but cannot sing. She is kept in cages for breeding purposes only. It seems unfair to the females.

I like canaries because of the way they fly. The canary has an undulating flight. It flies up into an almost stall, then loops down, then up to a stall and down. It's like Tarzan swinging through the trees but without vines. It's the way I'd like to fly. A few finches hang around down by the Cosgrove barn. I've watched them with my binoculars; they fly that way.

I could never keep a wild bird in a cage. If a bird already knows how to fly against the sky, I could never cage it. I know

I have to buy a bird born in a cage, a bird whose parents, grand-parents, ancestors had lived only in cages.

There are many types of canaries. Some are called chop-pers and sing a loud song; their beaks open, ending each note by closing the beak. Others are called rollers. They sing with beaks closed and deep in the throat. There are different kinds of rollers and choppers and there are contests for singing. There are also various shapes and sizes of canaries; some are so peculiarly shaped they can scarcely fly.

I decide to buy a young female because they're less expen-sive. I'm interested in flying, not singing. I buy a bird maga-zine that comes out every month; it gives addresses of people who sell birds. I start looking at all the canary aviaries I can find, and get to, on my bicycle. It's two months before I find her.

She's in a large aviary in the back yard of a lady called Mrs. Prevost. Mrs. Prevost is fat and has little feet. She has aviaries in her back yard and breeding cages on the sun porch. She doesn't care much about song or color or how her birds fly. I don't think she particularly raises them for money either. She just likes canaries.

She goes into the aviary and all the birds come flying down to her and land on her arms or on her head. She's trained the birds and has some who'll hop up and down little ladders or ring bells to get food. She has some she can take out of the cage on a perch. They won't fly off the perch even when she waves it around.

Mrs. Prevost looks carefully for cats and hawks before she takes out a bird. She's terrific; she should be in a circus.

Mrs. Prevost lets me sit in the aviary and watch her birds as much as I want. It's in her aviary I decide I like canaries more than pigeons. It's mostly in the sound of wings. Pigeon wings whistle and have a crackly stiff feather sound. Canary wings make practically no sound at all, only the kind of sound

you make with a fan if you flip it quickly, a pressure against
the air.

I sit out there in the aviary with the females every Saturday
for over a month. I never see Mr. Prevost. Mrs. Prevost brings
me cups of tea in a thermos when it's cold. Sometimes she puts
on a coat and sits there with me. She points out different birds
and tells me who the parents are and how many were in the
nest and which ones got caught in the wire or were sick so she
had to save them. She tells me which ones she's thinking of
breeding and why she's choosing them. She's going to breed
thirty females that next year. She chooses them to breed just
because these females are good mothers or come from good
mothers. She isn't trying to breed for anything special except
more canaries. Mrs. Prevost would sure make a good mother
but she doesn't have any children. I didn't ask her; she told me.

She shows me one of her females who's six years old and
has given over sixty birds. This female comes and sits on Mrs.
Prevost's finger. Mrs. Prevost transfers her to my finger one
afternoon. She perches there a few minutes while Mrs. Prevost leans down and talks to her. Mrs. Prevost talks to her
birds. She doesn't peep or whistle; she just talks in a low voice
the way you'd talk to a baby.

Mrs. Prevost hates cats and hawks. She has a continual
war with them. There're always stray cats coming in hoping for
an easy meal. She's tried fencing, but you can't fence out a cat.
She says she can't get herself to poison them. A couple times
there're cats sitting outside the aviary, turning their heads back
and forth watching the birds fly. Mrs. Prevost'd dash out on
her tiny feet and chase them. I tell her she ought to get a dog.

Once, when I'm sitting in the aviary, one of the cats comes
and doesn't see me. It must scare hell out of a bird having a cat
with those little slit green eyes watching—twisting its tail back
and forth. After a while, this one can't wait and throws itself
against the wire. It hangs there with its mouth open, pointed

teeth against a thin ridged pink top of mouth. The sharp claws are wrapped into the wire. It almost makes me glad I'm not a bird.

I saw Birdie the first day I sat in the aviary. I actually keep going back just to watch her but I don't tell Mrs. Prevost this. The aviary is taller than it is wide either way. Birdie is the only bird who flies around the inside of the upper part of the aviary. The others fly from perch to perch or down to the floor to eat but Birdie flies around and around in banked circles. It's the kind of thing I'd do myself if I were a bird and lived in that aviary.

Birdie is very curious. There's a piece of string hanging from the top of the aviary. It's not more than two inches long. Birdie has to turn herself upside down to pull it and she hangs there minutes at a time, pulling and tugging, doing her best to hang on and backing off with her wings, trying to pull it loose.

There's another thing I like better about canaries than pigeons. Pigeons do a lot of walking. They swing their short bodies back and forth like a duck and walk around on short legs, or sometimes when they're courting, they pull themselves up and take short soldier-like marching steps. Canaries never walk. If they move on the ground, they hop. Most times a hop means a little flit with the wings. It makes them look so independent. They hop in place, then hop to another place. I've noticed robins both running and hopping but canaries never walk.

Sometimes, Birdie'd just hop all over the cage. She'd pick up a tiny stone here and move it over there. She'd dig in the sand with her beak. She won't bring anything out, just digging. It's like she's doing some kind of bird housekeeping.

Then, sometimes, she'll hunch back and take a flying leap for the highest perch. This takes a careful aim because perches are spread all over the place. Mrs. Prevost puts in lots of perches; she doesn't think much about birds having long free places to fly. Birdie flies between the perches as if they aren't there. She's beautiful.

I go downtown and hunt around junk shops till I find a cage. It costs twenty-five cents. I take it home to fix up. First, I scrape all the paint and rust from the bars. There are two broken places; I repair them. I straighten and clean the tray in the bottom. I boil and wash out the food and water dishes. It isn't a big cage, fifteen inches deep, thirty long and twenty high. I hate to think of taking poor Birdie away from the big cage and her friends to put her into this small cage, alone. I know I'll make it up somehow.

After it's all clean, I paint the cage white. I give it two coats till it looks practically new. I put some newspaper in the bottom, and bird gravel. I buy roller mix seed and put it in one cup and fresh water in the other. I'm ready to bring Birdie home.

I carry her on my bike in a shoe box with holes punched in the sides. I can hear her scrambling around inside, sliding on the slippery bottom of the box. I wonder what a bird thinks when her whole life is suddenly changed like this. She isn't one year old and she's lived her whole life either in the nest or the breeding cage, or in the aviary with other birds. Now she's in a dark box with no perches, she can't see and can't fly. I speed home as fast as I can.

I go in the back door and up the back stairs to my room. I don't want to show her to anyone.

I cut a hole carefully in the end of the box and put the hole next to the cage door. In only a few seconds she hops into the cage. She lands on the floor and stands straddle-legged. She looks around. She seems even more beautiful than she did in the aviary. I don't want to scare her, so I back up to the other side of the room where I have my binoculars. I turn the chair around and rest the binoculars on the back of the chair so I can watch her without my arms getting tired.

After a few little hops, rattling sand on the paper, she hops up onto the middle perch and peeps. It's a single note going from low to high and watery. It's the first time I hear her voice. In the aviary, there's so much sound you can't hear any particular bird.

She cocks her head and looks from side to side. She knows I'm there across the room and she looks at me first with one eye, then the other. Canaries don't look at any particular thing with both eyes at once. Most birds don't. They only see with both eyes when they're not really looking at anything. When they want to see something particular, they look with one eye and blind out the other. They don't close it, just blind it.

Birdie moves lightly and quickly, heavy air means nothing. She hops up to the top perch and wipes her beak, sharpening it, checking, the way dogs sniff trees.

She's yellow, the yellow of a lemon. Her tail feathers and wing tips are lighter, almost white. The feathers on her upper legs are lighter too. Her legs are orange-pink, lighter than pigeon legs, delicately thin. She has three toes forward and one .back like all tree birds, and her nails are long and thin, translucent, with a fine vein down the center. She's medium-sized for a canary and has a rounded, very feminine head; her eyes are bright black, her beak exactly the color of her legs. Small pink nostril holes are tucked under the feathers of her head at the top of her beak.

She peeps again and turns around on the perch to face the other way. She does this without seeming to use her wings. She springs lightly up, twists her body, and is facing the other way. It's the same move an ice skater makes when she jump turns, only with much less effort. Birdie does this while still eyeing me left and right, shaking her head back and forth, a bird "no."

Her eyes lose focus and she goes into total vision. She isn't looking at me anymore. She jumps down to the bottom perch and sees the water cup. She tips her head in, dips her beak into the water, and tilts her head back. She does this three times. Like pigeons, she can't swallow up. She lets the water flow down into her throat. It looks as if she closes her beak over a certain small quantity of water, not more than a drop, then holds it till she tilts up so it rolls down her throat.

After drinking, she hops to the floor of the cage. A bird needs sharp gravel to grind food in its crop. She hops around, making sand rattle on the paper again, takes a few grains, then jumps up on the bottom perch again for some birdseed.

The seed I've bought contains rape, a tiny black round seed; canary seed, a thin tan-colored shiny seed with a white fruit; rolled oats; and linseed. She dips into the food dish and spreads seeds around till she finds one of the rolled oats. She picks it up, peels off the shell and eats the fruit. It's done quickly. While she's eating, she looks over at me twice. Birds are very suspicious while they're eating. She eats about five seeds; the rolled oat, two rape seeds, and at least one canary seed. She uses a different technique to peel each type. She doesn't eat any linseeds. Linseeds are to keep the feathers in condition.

It's amazing how well birds can work seeds out of the shell using only their beaks; no arms, no hands.

Later, I try eating birdseed to see what it's like. I spend hours cracking seed with my teeth. One mouthful takes a full hour. You can't eat the shells because they're bitter.

After Birdie's eaten, she leaps with one slight flick of her wings, a hardly noticeable flick, from the bottom perch, turns around in midair and lands on the top perch, at least four times her height. It's as if I jumped off the porch right up onto the roof. She peeps at me from there. I try to peep back.

She checks the bars of the cage with her beak and nibbles

some cuttlebone. Cuttlebone is from a fish; it has calcium and other minerals for birds. She constantly tries to talk to me, or maybe she's trying to discover any other birds around. There's a sad sound in the peep, interrogative, going up at the end, peeEEP? She opens her beak halfway when she says it and often says it just as she leaves one perch for another. Perhaps it's a signal to let other birds know she's changing position. I don't really know enough about canaries.

When it gets dark, I cover her cage with a cloth to protect her from drafts.

The next day is Sunday. I see her trying to bathe in the water cup so I put a saucer of water in the cage. She goes down immediately with a peep that's different from the others, shorter, more like PEep? She stands on the edge of the dish, dips her beak in, tests, then lowers her chest into the water and wiggles. She jumps out and up onto the edge of the dish, shakes her feathers impossibly fast, stretches out her wings to show feathers individually, then throws herself into the water with another short PEep? She goes in and out, splashing, wiggling. There's a concentration, a total involvement; nothing passive. I've watched hundreds of pigeons take baths in water or in dust but it was slow motion compared to Birdie.

After she's splashed all the water from the saucer and made a soggy mess out of the newspapers on the floor of the cage, she flies wildly around, almost crashing into the bars. Her flight feathers are so wet, they hang bedraggled, resting on the perch. The feathers around her face clump in little bunches. She dashes back and forth, from perch to perch, shaking, vibrating her whole body. Drops of water fly across the room even onto the lenses of the binoculars. They're like comets charging into my miniature world.

Finally, most of the water shaken off, Birdie begins to preen herself. She takes each feather in her beak and combs it out to the tip. She leans back frequently to the oil sack at the tip of her tail and spreads a thin film of oil over the newly washed feathers, one at a time. The bath, from beginning till end, finishing with a satisfied flurry of fluffiness, takes almost two hours.

I'm really in love with Birdie now. She's so dainty, so quick, so skilled, and she flies so gracefully. I want to have her fly in my room free but I'm afraid I'll hurt or frighten her putting her back into the cage. It's very hard to wait.

That afternoon, I give Birdie a first taste of treat food. I try peeping when I give it to her, the question peeps, peeEEP? I give treat food in a special cup shaped to fit between the bars of the cage and rest on the edge of the middle perch. I keep my hand as near to it as I can when she comes to eat.

The feed has a smell of anise and is sweet. I only put a few grains of seed in the dish. Birdie looks at me where I am with my hand near the food. She cocks her head and tries to see me from different angles. She comes close, then flies away. She pretends she isn't interested at all and goes down to eat the regular seed. I know she's curious. At last she comes up and quickly steals one seed out of the dish. She goes to the other end of the perch to eat it. She queeEEP?s at me and I try to queeEEP? back. She comes again and takes another seed. She eats it looking me in the eyes. I don't move.

She puts one foot onto the little dish to hold it and eats the rest of the seeds. Her foot's within an inch of my fingers. I can see the tiny pink scales and light veins running down her legs next to my own massive whorled fingerprints. I can smell her, the smell of eggs when they're still in the shell, probably the smell of feathers. I don't remember just that smell from pigeons. Pigeon smell is musky with something of old dust; this is a thin perfume.

When she's finished, she lets go of the dish and wipes her bill on the perch but doesn't go away.

I queeEEP? at her but she only looks at me. I queeEEP?

again. She sees me; she's questioning what I really am. It lasts maybe ten seconds, a long time for a bird. Then she goes down to the floor of the cage and eats a few grains of sand. I'm very happy.

Next day, I think about Birdie all day at school. I don't even want to look at people. People can be so gross, especially grown-ups. They grunt and groan, make swallowing and breathing noises all the time. They smell like putrid meat. They crawl around with heavy movements and stand as if they're nailed to the ground.

At lunch, walking around the track, I practice jumping and turning around. It's hard to do. It's much easier if you do it when you're running. Standing still and jumping up is almost impossible. You've got to twist hard enough to get around in the little time you have from the jump and yet not so fast you're still twisting when you hit the ground. You have to twist back against yourself with your shoulders in the air. I almost do it once by getting down in a crouch and taking an easy jump up and a slow twist. For a second, it feels right, a little bit free, but then I hit the ground wrong and fall. I get too loose up there. I have to speed up my body thinking somehow.

When I come into my room after school, Birdie queeps at me. We keep queeping back and forth while I change from school clothes. I have to go down again and sweep off the back porch. If my mother ever gets an idea I'm spending too much time with a bird, it'll be like the pigeons all over again.

After the gas tank, I hid my pigeon suit up in the rafters of the garage. I know she's still looking for it, says she's going to burn it—going to burn it for my own good, she says.

I can't figure what she thinks is unhealthy about birds. Does she want me to spend all my time chasing after girls at school or making myself the strongest man in the world, like Al; or maybe hopping up cars and tearing them apart. What's so healthy about that?

I don't want any trouble, that's all. I do a good job on the porch and water the flowers on the window sill. I pick up some papers and a couple of old rusty cans from the back yard. Kids are always throwing tin cans over the fence. If my mother'd stop running out and shaking her mop or broom at them, they'd quit. I still haven't figured out where she keeps those baseballs. They must be worth a fortune.

Back in my room, I get out some treat food and walk quietly over to the cage. Birdie's queeping with me. I'm listening to hear if she has anything else to say; I can't hear anything different. Canary is still a foreign language to me. I got so I could understand most of the things pigeons have to say. They don't really talk, they only signal each other.

I slide the dish between the wires of the cage onto the perch. She comes up to the perch and stands on the other end. Now, there's definitely a change in her voice. It's still queep but much louder, like somebody saying, "really?" It's qurEEPP?, from deeper in her throat. I can hear it but I can't do it; I give her a regular queeEEp? back. After a half dozen of these loud qurEEPP?s, she hops left and right along the perch over to me. With each hop she completely turns her body direction to the perch, at the same time keeping her head toward me. Each hop lines the other eye up with mine. She's shifting her vision from eye to eye as she advances. Incredible, almost impossible to describe, but she does it without seeming to notice.

When Birdie gets to the dish, she puts her feet on it the same as last time and takes her first seed, shelling it without going back along the perch. She has her wing and leg muscles flexed to jump back if I make a move. I'm yearning to shift my finger through the bars of the cage and touch her foot. I feel caged out of her cage.

When she's finished with the treat food, I stay there with my hand on the cup and bring my face up till my eyes are looking through the bars not more than a foot from where she's standing. Birdie stands there and looks at me, cocking her head one way, then the other. She gives a qurEEPP?, then jumps down to the perch below. I watch her eat some seed, then some gravel. Being really close like this is even better than watching through binoculars.

When Birdie shits, it's a semi-hardened mass much smaller than pigeon shit. She tosses it off with a slight thumping of her ass. Most times it's a single flip, but sometimes it takes two or three. She shits once every five minutes or so. The shit itself has three parts I can see. There's the outside part which is clear as water, just wetness, then there's the white part, more solid, something like cream, and then the center which is brownish-black, blacker than human shit and somewhat shaped to come out the ass, like human shit. There's practically no smell.

Every day that week, when I come home from school, after I've done chores, I go upstairs to my room and watch Birdie. First, I change the feed and water; then, if she tries to take a bath in the new water, and she usually does, I give her some water in a saucer. After that, after I've watched her bathe and talked to her, I give her some treat food on the end of the perch. She isn't afraid of me at all now. That is, not for a bird.

The only thing a bird has going for it is that it can fly away. If Birdie knows that living in a cage makes her so vulnerable, it must be terrible. Still, she always keeps herself ready to escape even though there's no place to go. I try to think what it would be like to have some gigantic bird come and stick his claws into the window of my room with some potato chips or a hoagie. What would I do? Would I go over and get some, even if I had enough regular food in a dish somewhere else?

After the first few days, when I come into the room, Birdie is down on the floor of the cage, running back and forth, looking out over the barrier that holds in the gravel. I think she's glad to see me, not just because I give her treat food, but because she's lonely. I'm her one friend now, the only living being she gets to see.

By the end of the week, I rubber-band the treat food dish onto the end of an extra perch and put it into the cage through the door. I lock the door open with a paper clip. At first, Birdie's shy, but then she jumps onto the perch I'm holding and side-hops over to the treat dish. It's terrific to see her without the bars between us. She sits eating the treat food at the opening to the door and looking at me. How does she know to look into my eyes and not at the huge finger next to her?

After she's finished eating, she retreats to the middle of the perch. I lift it gently to give her a ride and a feeling the perch is part of me and not the cage. She shifts her body and flips her wings to keep balance, then looks at me and makes a new sound, like peeEP; very sharp. She jumps off the perch to the bottom of the cage. I take out the perch and try to talk to her but she ignores me. She drinks some water. She doesn't look at me again till she's wiped off her beak and stretched both wings, one at a time. She uses her feet to help stretch the wings. Then, she gives a small queeEEP?.

Generally, Birdie looks at me more with her right eye than her left. It doesn't matter which side of the cage I stand. She turns so she can see me with her right eye. Also, when she reaches with her foot to hold the treat dish, or even her regular food dish, she does it with her right foot. She'd be right-handed if she had hands; she's right-footed or right-sided. She approaches and does most things from the right side. Even when she's stretching her wings, she always stretches her right wing first. The only exception is she sleeps on her left foot. I think when a bird sleeps you get a good idea of what birds think of the ground. A bird will usually search out the highest place it can find to sleep and then separate itself as best it can from the ground by standing on one foot; in Birdie's case, her lesser foot. A bird, balled up in puffed-out feathers, standing on one foot, looks nothing like flying. A lizard looks more capable of flying than a sleeping bird.

Because of the way Birdie sleeps, I want to build my bed up against the ceiling of my room. My mother gets all hot and bothered, but my father says it'll be all right if I pay for the wood myself and don't knock holes in the walls or floor. We only rent the house.

I pinch wood from the lumberyard at night. I do it the same way Al and I got the wood for the pigeon coop. I sneak in at night and push it out under the fence in back, then go around and get it. I buy bolts and use my father's tools. Because I can't attach to walls or ceiling, it has to be self-supporting. The job takes me two weeks. When it's finished, I fit the mattress and springs into the frame up high. I put the old bedstead out in the garage. I check my pigeon suit and look around for the baseballs.

I build a ladder up to the bed by drilling holes and pegging in steps. It's like a ship's ladder when I finish. I even run electricity up there and hang curtain rods from the ceiling. I snitch some material from Sears and make curtains. It's a great little nest, even better than the loft in the tree. I can crawl up there, pull the curtains and turn on the light. A private place.

By now, Birdie jumps right on the stick when I put it in her cage; even without treat food. She'll eat the treat food off my finger, too. I wet my finger, push it into the feed bag and some sticks on. I hold my finger at the same place on the perch where I usually put the treat dish and she comes over to pick it off. Her little beak moves fast and is sure and gentle. She cleans it all, down to the little bits caught in my fingernails.

Next day, when Birdie jumps on my perch, I pull it slowly out of the cage. I've practiced a lot with moving the perch up and down or back and forth inside the cage so she knows how to stay on and not be scared. As I pull her out through the door, she looks up at the top of the door passing over her head and hops backward to stay in the cage. When she comes to the end of the perch, she hops off into the cage. I begin all over, but it's the same. After three or four times, I get the idea to put some treat food on my finger so she'll be eating as I pull her through the door.

This works and when Birdie looks up she's out of the cage. She gives me a strong qurEEPP? when she sees where she is. I hold the perch as steadily as I can and she stands there looking at me. Then she unfocuses and lets the room come to her. It must feel to her like going on a rocket ship and getting out of the earth's atmosphere.

I hold her there a minute, then slowly lower the perch back to the cage. As I push it through the door, she jumps off the perch and down to the floor. She goes over and eats one seed, then hops to the other side and takes a drink. It looks as if she's checking to see if her world's the same as when she left it. She queeps back and forth with me for about half an hour after that. She's as excited as I am. It's wonderful to have her free right there in front of me, to know she can flip her wings and fly out into the room. It makes everything different, it makes my room seem as big as the sky.

I'm getting better at queeping. You have to do it with your throat, tight, deep, and use your lips. It can't be done by whistling.

The next day I take Birdie out of the cage again. This time she only ducks under the crosspiece at the door. I put some treat food on my finger and she hops over to eat it. She touches me for the first time when she puts her foot onto my finger while she eats. I keep her out on the perch for almost five minutes and give her some rides by slowly moving the perch up and down or back and forth. She queeps at me each time and watches my eyes.

I take her over to the cage and instead of putting her in the door, I lean the perch on top of the cage and she hops off. Then, I put the perch just into the opening of the door. After a few queeps and some peEEPs, she jumps onto the perch and into the cage. It's really a shame to close the door after that.

She knows she's been smart and brave. She goes over to the perch where I feed her treat food and gives a couple good loud QREEP?s. She actually is saying something new like QREEP-A-REEP?. I put some grains onto my finger and she eats them.

In a few weeks, I have Birdie so she'll fly out of the cage when I open the door and then she'll land on the perch when I hold it up to her. She'll fly off the perch to the other parts of the room, up on my bed, or on the window sill or on the dresser. Then she'll fly back to my perch. She flies so beautifully with her head out and her feet tucked back. Her wings in the room make a whispering sound. If I want her, all I do is hold out the perch and call her with a PeepQuEEP. This is a sound she knows. Probably it's more her name than Birdie. "Birdie" doesn't mean anything to her when I say it. I keep thinking of her to myself as Birdie but PeepQuEEP is the name I call her with.

At first, I give her a little grain or two of treat food when she comes to me, but after a while I don't. I know and she knows we're playing together.

Sometimes she teases by flying back toward the perch and then, at the last minute, swerving away and landing somewhere else. One time she lands on my head this way. I can watch her fly all day, and I even like to watch her hopping around. She searches all over the floor and finds little things I can't even see. I watch her carefully to get any droppings. If my mother finds any bird shit on anything, the whole game is finished.

It's a long time before Birdie lets me stroke her head or her breast. Birds are that way; they don't even stroke each other. Birdie learns to like it though. She'll come to my hand and puff up when I run my finger over the top of her head or down her wings. Her toenails need cutting, but every time I try to wrap my hands around her to pick her up, she panics.

Usually when I let Birdie out, I pull the window shade, but one day I forget. She flies out of the cage door when I open it and straight at the window. She hits the pane of glass in full flight and falls fluttering to the floor!

I dash over and pick her up carefully. She's unconscious, limp in my hand. There's nothing deader than a dead bird. Movement is most of what a bird is. When they're dead, they're only feathers and air.

One of her wings seems dislocated. I carefully fold it back and hold her in my two hands to warm her. She's still breathing very lightly and quickly. Her heart's beating against my hand. I look for something broken or bleeding. Her neck is hanging loosely over the end of my fingers and I'm sure she has a broken neck. The way she flies, with her head so far ahead of her body, confident with her flight, this is what would happen.

Her eyes are closed by a pale, bluish, almost transparent lid. There's nothing I can think to do. I pet her head softly. I PeepQuEEP at her and try to breathe warm air over her. I'm sure she's dying.

The first sign she shows is to move her head and lift it from hanging over my finger. She opens her eyes and looks at me. She doesn't struggle. She blinks her eyes slowly and closes them. I PeepQuEEP at her some more. I stroke her head. Then, she opens her eyes and straightens her head. She couldn't do that if her neck were broken. I begin to hope. I pull her legs out between my fingers and straighten the toes so she's standing with them on my thigh while I hold her. She closes her eyes again but she keeps her head up. She doesn't grab with her feet on my thigh. The toes are limp and fold in on themselves.

I hold her quietly some more, petting her head and queeping at her. Then she queeps back; tired, a faint queeEEp?. I queep and she queeps again. I loosen my grip and she manages to stand on my thigh. She's all puffed out in a ball and her feathers are ruffled from the sweat of my hands. I cup her on both sides with my hands so she can't fall. I hold her again and try to smooth her feathers. I feather out her wings one after the other. They seem all right. I let go of her and she stands alone on my thigh. She bristles and fluffs out her ruffled feathers. She leans back and runs each flight feather in turn through her beak. She shits. Then, she straightens herself and hops along my knee and queeps, quite like her old self. I queep back and put my finger out to her. She hops on it and turns. She wipes her beak on my finger. She'd never done that before. It's wonderful to see her moving again. I didn't know I was crying but my face is wet. I carry her over to the cage and she hops off my finger and into the cage. She's glad to be back in her safe place. She eats and drinks.

I watch her for about an hour after that but she's fine. I can't believe my luck. It would have been awful without her. From this time on, I can always pick her up and hold her. A few days later I cut her toenails.

I begin wanting to tell somebody about Birdie and all the things she can do. I try talking to Al about it but he isn't interested much in birds anymore.

She's such fun. I leave her out at night sometimes and train her to sleep on top of the cage so her droppings fall onto the cage floor instead of all over the room. I put her cage on the shelf behind my bed so she feels comfortable. It's the highest place in the room. In the morning, she hops down onto my head and picks at my nose or the corners of my mouth till I wake up. She never picks at my eyes.

I learn a lot of canary words and can tell her to stay and to come and I learn a sound for eat and hello and good-bye. I'm beginning to hear the differences in the things she says.

That night they put me up in quarters with the orderlies. The CO guy on Birdy's ward shows me around. I pump him about Birdy. He tells me Birdy's been here almost three months. He says, for a long time they didn't even know who Birdy was; had to go through all the records for somebody missing in Waiheke, the place where Birdy was hit. That's an island off in New Guinea, he says. He tells me Birdy has bad malaria on top of everything else.

That night I have one of my screaming dreams. I wake up hollering out loud. At Dix, on the plastic surgery ward, nights, it's more like a damned loony bin than this place; everybody trying to work it out. The CO comes over but I tell him I'm OK. I'm having the sweats again, whole bed soaking wet. I move over to another empty bed. I wonder if the CO will tell anybody; Christ, they're liable to lock me up, too.

Next morning I go see Weiss. He's not in yet but there's a fat T-4 with a typewriter; Underwood, stand-up job. He says he just wants some information for the doctor. I try to explain I'm not one of the crazies but he's got out a blue form and turns it into the machine. He sits there grinning at me. He's got me pegged as a loon for sure.

Great questions he asks, like, How many people in my family have done themselves in? or, Do I get pleasure when I take a shit? What creepy questions! But that's not the really weird part. First, he asks me my name. He types it out, four finger hunt and peck, then he looks at it and spits! Spits right at my name on the paper! Jesus! I figure maybe something got caught on his lip; try to ignore it. Then he asks me my serial number and outfit. He types this out, stares at it, and spits again! Maybe he's a loon, slipped in here while the doctor's out. Maybe it isn't happening at all and I'm nuts myself. I try to get a look at the T-4 without his noticing. He grins back at me, a bit of spit still hanging on his fat lip. Maybe it's some kind of a new psychological test, the spit test. Who knows?

He starts asking more questions. Same thing every time. Not big goobers or anything gross, just a fine spray kind of spit. The whole typewriter must be rusty inside. He asks another question, types it out, looks and spits. I check the door and distances. This light blue form he's typing on is turning dark blue. He's almost finished when the doctor-major passes through to his office. He gives me his psychiatrist smile; holding out on the military this morning.

We finish. The T-4 gently pulls the form out of his typewriter. He knows what he's doing; he's pulled wet forms out of that machine before. He holds it by the corner and carries it into the doctor's office. Then he comes out, thin grins at me, rubs his hands together, probably wiping off the spit; and tells me to go in. The doctor-major is staring at the wet paper and reading it. He motions me to sit down. The paper is flat on his desk; he's not touching it.

I'm waiting for him to comment on the spit. Maybe congratulate me for passing the spit test or blaming me, or something. Nothing! He's used to spitty papers. He might just be the nut himself, won't read anything that doesn't have spit on it; hires this T-4 especially to spit on his papers. Could be anything. He looks up; very serious, very dignified for a fat man. His eyes are glinting behind his glasses; very much the working psychiatrist this morning.

"You say here you were court-martialed?"

"That's right, sir."

Give him the old "sir" bit; get no doctor-ing from me. Got to get out of here with my skin. Should've lied about the fucking court-martial.

"What type of court-martial was it, Sergeant?"

There it is; Sergeant; now we know.

"Summary, sir."

"And what was the offense?"

"Attacking non-commissioned officer, sir."

He gives the old *hmmmm* and two *ahhhaas*. Then he looks to see if the door to the office is closed. It is. Almost expect him to get up and open it. Here he is locked in with the mad officer killer. I give him my killer stare from under one eyebrow; Sicilian, Mafia, contract-killer look; all rolled in one. I used to practice it in front of the mirror; have to get some advantage out of being Italian.

I'm not giving an inch. I'm thinking of getting up from the chair slowly and moving in for a pin. He clears his throat and folds his hands just behind the spit pile.

"Do you get these violent impulses often, Alfonso?"

The psychiatrist is back in the office. He's got the Santa Claus grin on and all. Hell, I'd be a better psychiatrist than this moron. He doesn't quite know what to do. I don't know which way to play it myself. I'm wishing this had happened in the middle of the war instead of after it's all over. Maybe I could've gotten myself a big pension as a homicidal maniac. That's right; they turned this little neighborhood boy into a raving maniac by horrible war experiences. I'd live the rest of my life in gravy, just growl every now and then or beat up some old man.

He's still grinning at me; not a single flinch in that grin; he's got the psychiatrist grin down to the nickel. He's trying to shake me up. I'm tempted to tell him how much I enjoyed pushing that hunky's face in with the shovel. Niggers in the coal truck sure were scared shitless, too.

"No, sir. Not often, sir."

"Would you mind telling me how it happened?"

Sure I would, but I know a direct order when I hear one.

"Only in the army four days, sir. Corporal at Fort Cumberland grabbed me by the arm and I reacted instinctively, sir."

"Oh, I see."

He doesn't see and he knows he doesn't see. I smile back at him. Big smiling game. Great being Italian; all the movies make everybody afraid of you. When people think of a bad guy, they think of an Italian. I give him my dangerous look again. He's going over the wet form; doing the *hmmm, ahhhaa* thing some more; we're not getting anywhere.

"Sir, should I go back to the ward this morning?"

"That's right, Sergeant. I think it's the best chance we've got."

I wait. I can't really get up and leave till he does something. When you're in the army, you're tied down all around. I can't figure why he isn't asking me if I've ever clobbered Birdy. That's the first question I'd ask.

He stands up at last and I stand, too; give him the salute. I have a feeling he's pissed at me and pissed at himself for being pissed. I scare him; this makes me feel good. I keep hoping I'm finished with that crap but when somebody starts leaning, it all comes back.

"OK, Sergeant, I'll see you tomorrow about this time."

"Yes, sir."

Bastard's going to write to Dix for my records. Please Lord, just let me out of the goddamned army!

I get back to Birdy and even though he's still squatting on the floor, I know it's different. I know he's knowing I'm there. I know it's Birdy and not some fake, freaky bird.

—Had another session with your doctor, Birdy. You're going to have a great time with him when you decide to talk. Whatever you do, don't tell him about the pigeons and the canaries and all that bird shit. He'll have you pinned into a case as a specimen.

I know he heard me that time. I want to hang in there, keep it going.

—Hey Birdy, remember when we were selling the mags? Christ, that was a scene!

After we get back from Wildwood and I finally recover from old Vittorio's revenge, we have to figure some way to pay back the money. We owe our parents ninety-two dollars in train fare. We get the idea to sell magazines door-to-door in apartment houses.

We work out a smooth deal. The building superintendents try to keep us out but we push all the call buttons and somebody is always lazy enough just to push the door buzzer without calling back. Once we're inside, one of us keeps the elevator busy while the other goes from one apartment to the other selling the mags. We're selling *Liberty*, *Saturday Evening Post*, *Collier's* and *Cosmopolitan*. The best time for selling is from right after school till about five-thirty, when the men start coming home. A lot of the ladies are alone because their men are off fighting the war. We get a regular route of ladies who buy from us. I'm the one who usually does the selling; Birdy does the elevator business and keeps the superintendent chasing after him. Fat chance that super has of ever catching Birdy.

Most of those ladies are bored out of their minds and I'm always getting invited in for a cup of tea or coffee. If I were older and knew what to do, I could probably really make out.

Birdy's already started with all his crappy breath-holding. He's getting to be more and more of a freak. He shows me once how he can hold his breath for five minutes. He sticks his head in a pan of water in my cellar. He tells me he turns his mind off breathing. That's nuts!

Then he's always talking about flying. He tells me once, "People can't fly because they don't believe they can. If nobody ever showed people they could swim, everybody'd drown if they were dropped into the water," is what he says. Really weird ideas. He's going to a Catholic high school, now, down at Forty-ninth Street in Philadelphia. The things he tells me about that school, I begin to understand why he's turning so crazy. It's a regular prison.

He's also beginning with his canary thing. He talks about that canary all the time and he starts different goofy exercises. I try getting him to work out with weights to build himself up, but he only does his arm flapping and jumping up and down. Sometimes he talks about his canary and I think he's talking about a real person. I think maybe he's finally noticed there are girls in the world but it's just the canary. He calls her Birdy, named after himself I guess.

The school he goes to is too cheap to have buses so he rides in on his bike. I cut one day and ride in with him. What a miserable place. Freshmen and sophomores use outside staircases like fire escapes and everybody is always robbing everybody else's locker. They have Christian brothers teaching there. They wear long black skirts like priests except they have little stiff bibs sticking out from under their chins; real bunch of creeps; guys who want to be priests but are too dumb or don't have the guts.

The whole school smells funky, like a gigantic jack-off party going on all the time. Big places like that without any girls are always funky. On wet days, Birdy says it smells so bad you have to wear a gas mask.

The way you eat lunch in this school is to walk round and round the track. Brothers are standing in the middle like lion tamers. If you want to take a piss or something you have to ask for one of these wooden passes. They've got five passes for more than three hundred people. Everybody walking around, holding a lunch bag, eating and holding back from peeing.

Birdy starts faking library passes to get to the library during lunch. He has the inside of a book cut out and he's eating sandwiches out of it. He gets away with it for almost three months but they catch him just before Easter vacation. Some brother bears down on Birdy in the library and bops him on the back of his head. Birdy throws books, sandwiches, the whole works at him and scoots down one of those fire escapes and away. They toss him out. He comes over to old U.M. to finish the year with the human beings. I figure it might turn him on with all the girls and everything but he only gets worse. People at U.M. start calling him Birdy, too. Jesus, he's actually beginning to look like a bird.

He's getting even skinnier and his chest's beginning to stick out in front like his ribs are broken. His head juts forward from his shoulders and his eyes are always darting around loose in the sockets so he never seems to be paying much attention to any one thing. I know he's seeing everything. Birdy sees everything but he doesn't, what you could really call, "look" at anything. Like the weather; somehow Birdy always knows about the weather. If the paper says it's going to rain and Birdy says no; Birdy's right.

The next summer, Birdy and I take the job as dogcatchers; Birdy's deep into his creepy canaries. We're standing on back of the truck with those huge nets and Birdy's talking about how many eggs are in this nest or which bird is already cracking seed. He's out of sight.

Then the next year, Birdy and I don't see too much of each other. I go out for track, throw the discus; make varsity running guard, and wrestle. Birdy has no interest in sports. He's back there with the birds.

In my junior year, soon's I'm seventeen, I join the State Guard, I want to learn how to shoot rifles, pistols, all that shit. I go down to the Armory on Thursday nights to drill. Birdy comes along with me sometimes. He sits up in the balcony bleachers in the dark and watches us. I get issued an old Springfield o6 and learn how to dismantle it. I'm a gung-ho soldier bastard. Going to get me a few Japs before the whole thing is over.

I start going with Lucy then, too. She's one of the cheerleaders at school and totally dumb; a commercial major. One afternoon, I'm sitting out in the parking lot at school in Higg's car, making out with Lucy, when Birdy comes rolling up on his bicycle. We're both juniors and he's still tooling around on this wreck of a bicycle. Same crummy bike he got after we lost ours in Wildwood, trying to sell them. It won't go more than about three miles an hour without wobbling. Birdy's the only one who can ride it; he doesn't even lock it in the bike rack. He just stands it there. Nobody's going to steal it. It's the only bike in the rack anyway; they built those racks back in the twenties when people rode bikes to school. Birdy's tooling that bike to school every day, rain or shine; won't take the school bus. Jesus, what can you do with somebody like that?

Birdy comes over and we talk about exams we're having.

Birdy and I are in a lot of the same classes; both academic, both half-assed B students. Lucy's looking at Birdy. I don't think she ever knew we were friends. To her, I'm big killer Al, wrestler and football player, something to cheer about.

Birdy starts talking about his canaries. Everybody at school knows he has about a thousand canaries by now. He brought some of them in to Chemistry class once to study their blood and he built a flying model in Physics that actually worked, his crazy ornithopter. He even writes about them in English. Birdy, the bird freak. I'm still half interested in pigeons but Birdy's too much. I've visited his aviaries and it's about the same as his coming down to the Armory with me. We're more a habit with each other than anything.

Birdy's telling about some bird he's gotten to fly with weights tied around its legs. This bird can carry almost three times a normal bird weight and still fly. The weight lifting champion of the bird world. He's been training this poor sap of a bird since the nest. Lucy says something about Birdy being cruel and Birdy gives her one of his quick shifting glances just to show he notices, a fast almost-smile. Lucy's mind's too slow for it; she doesn't see anything happening that fast.

Birdy's so thin you can almost see through him. It's late May and he's wearing a sleeveless shirt and his sharp chest bone sticks out against it. He gets more spooky looking all the time. He's the only guy in school with hair long enough so it drops in his eyes and he never pushes it back. He talks through that hair.

He's spinning his bike around in small circles as he's talking to us. Down inside the car, I've got my hand slipped up Lucy's crotch. She's flexing her muscle on and off against my fingers. Lucy's got great strong legs; she can jump straight up and come down in a full split. That's her specialty as a cheerleader. Break your heart to see her do it.

Finally, Birdy rolls off. After he goes, Lucy wants to know all about Birdy. I tell her we went to elementary school together. She opens up her legs a little so I can slip in my finger; she's juicy already. I'll take her down to the park in back of school. I know a great place under a bridge there. Whole bank is practically paved with condoms. Lucy gives me a good, stiff, strong tongue kiss and leans back.

"Is he queer or something?" she says. "He looks like some kind of homeysexual."

Honest to Christ; that's what she says, "homeysexual."

$\mathcal{I}$ got Birdie just before Christmas and by February she's already showing mating signs. She stands in one place and flaps her wings without flying, a kind of nervous flipping. She also starts carrying around bits of paper or thread. She's developed a new short Peip, and sometimes a trill of little peeps. When she eats from my finger, she Peips and goes into a mating squat with her wings quivering, wanting me to feed her. I put some on the end of my wet finger and Birdie opens her mouth and wants me to put it down her throat the way you do with a baby bird. A female bird gets to be a lot like a baby when she wants to mate.

About then, my mother finds out I've been letting Birdie fly out of the cage and there's a big scene. After all kinds of hysterics, my father says I can make an aviary under the place where I built the bed. My mother throws another fit but has to go along. My father understands things sometimes.

I want the aviary to be as invisible as possible, so I make it with thin steel wire. I put staples in the floor and into the joists under my bed. Then I stretch steel piano wires tight up and down between the staples. I put them the same distance apart as the bars on a canary cage. I make the door separate, just big enough for me to wiggle through. I hang it on the bed frame.

When it's finished, you can barely see the wires. Inside, I

cover the walls with light blue oilcloth and hang a light from under the bed. I put oilcloth on the floor, too, and white sand on top of it. I make different perches with dowelling and trim down a piece of twisted bush to make a natural little tree in the back corner. It looks great. I take Birdie out of her cage and carry her on my finger, through the door, and into her new house. She flies from my finger onto one of the perches and flies back and forth all over the cage. She tries the tree and eats from the new dishes on the floor. She takes a bath. While she's still wet, she comes over and sits on my knee, sprinkling me with water when she shakes. It's a terrific place for a bird.

I still have twenty dollars left from magazine selling. Paying off my share of the ninety-two dollars to my parents took the rest. I want to buy a male for Birdie and I want a first-class bird, a real flier.

On Saturdays, I start going to different bird places on my bike. I carry Birdie with me in a small traveling cage. I could take her on my shoulder, but you never know when you'll see a cat or a sparrow hawk.

Besides Mrs. Prevost, there're other people who sell birds and live near enough. The biggest is Mr. Tate. He has six or seven hundred birds. He's a short man who's almost deaf although he isn't very old. He wears a hearing aid and is married but I never see any children. It's strange that a man who can't hear should be raising singing canaries. It's like Beethoven.

Birds are Mr. Tate's business and all he knows or cares about is production and how much they cost. He has large flight cages filled with birds and tremendous batteries of breeding cages. He breeds two females on a male to cut down feed costs. He thinks I'm peculiar bringing Birdie with me but he doesn't mind.

I stand in front of the male cage and take out Birdie so

she can see. She flies against the side of the cage and some males come over to visit. A few sing to her or try to feed her. I watch but there aren't any I like especially.

I'm looking for a green male because the books say you should breed a yellow bird to a dark bird for good feather quality. Two yellow birds give young with thin, ragged, under-developed feathers and two darks give thick, short bunchy feathers. I feel I'll know the right bird when I see him and so will Birdie.

Another grower nearby is a lady who only has about fifty breeding birds. She's Mrs. Cox. Mr. Tate has his birds in his back yard, but Mrs. Cox has hers in a covered back porch. She likes her birds and knows each one. She's like Mrs. Prevost; she tells me which of her females are good mothers and which males are good fathers. She knows who all the mothers and fathers of all the birds are. Listening to her is like listening to somebody talk about people in a small town. Sometimes she even whispers when she tells me about some particular bird which did something she thinks is wrong. She has a name for every bird. She's glad I brought Birdie with me to help select a male; she says Birdie can fly free in the cage with the females.

The males are in one half of the flight cage and the females in the other. There's a wire partition between them. Mrs. Cox says she watches the birds and when two birds show they love each other, she puts them into a breeding cage. Listening to her is like reading Gone With the Wind or something. She points out all the flirtings going on and which bird is after which; when you listen for a while, you begin to believe it.

Mrs. Cox doesn't use any breeding system. Her only rule is she won't let brothers and sisters from the same nest mate; it's in the Bible, she tells me. In her breeding cages she uses one male to a female. She thinks Mr. Tate isn't very nice the way he does it. She talks half of one whole afternoon just about that.

Mrs. Cox and Mrs. Prevost are friends. Mrs. Cox recognized Birdie immediately as one of Mrs. Prevost's birds. Sometimes the two of them exchange birds to get new blood in the aviary. They're a lot alike, except Mrs. Cox is skinny.

Mrs. Cox says I can leave Birdie in the female cage and visit whenever I want. If Birdie takes a fancy to one of her young males, she'll sell him to me. It's very nice of her but I don't want to leave Birdie like that.

I come every Saturday and let Birdie fly around with the other females. A lot of the males come over next to the partition and sing to her, but there doesn't seem to be any particular male she prefers. There's one male I like myself; he has a green back and a yellow-green breast with white flight feathers on the outside. His head is flat and his legs are long. There's a definite turn under his throat but I never see him sing. He flies very gracefully with much dignity. Mrs. Cox says he's a chopper; he sings very strongly but has some bad notes; these notes run in the family. His great-grandfather had been a roller but the rest of the family are choppers.

Mrs. Cox tells me about another bird breeder named Mr. Lincoln. He's black and lives a square off Sixty-third Street on the other side of the park. She says he has all his birds in an upstairs bedroom in a row house. He's married and has five children. He doesn't do anything but raise birds and the whole family is on relief. Mrs. Cox tells me all this in the same voice she talks about the birds and what they've done or haven't done.

The first time I go to Mr. Lincoln's, he acts as if he doesn't have any birds. It's only after we've talked about birds a bit and he's seen Birdie that he shows me three or four birds he has in a cage downstairs. We talk about them for a while and then he winks and tells me to follow him upstairs.

He's fixed up a terrific aviary. The only trouble is it's all inside and smells strongly of birds. He keeps it clean but with a couple hundred birds and no air, it gets smelly. He says he can't screen and open the windows because of his neighbors. He's afraid they might tell the relief people he has birds.

The birds are all in one room. One side is breeding cages and the other is flight cages. The door of the room opens onto a hall. He makes all his breeding cages by hand and paints them different colors according to his breeding plan. Color is what Mr. Lincoln is interested in. He shows me the different projects he has. He experiments with breeding canaries to different kinds of birds to get new colors. He has some canaries he's bred to linnets; they're a nice buff red-orange with pale stripes. Other canaries he's breeding to a little North African siskin; these are dark with bright red-orange breasts. He's also breeding to something he calls an Australian fire finch. These come out with red heads and dark bodies.

Mr. Lincoln talks about first crosses and second crosses and shows me birds he calls mules. He has to explain to me that a mule's a bird who's sterile. I don't tell him I always thought a mule was a special kind of horse with long ears. He tells me most of his first crosses are mules. He says sometimes he has to breed ten times before he gets a fertile bird. The only way to check is by breeding.

Mr. Lincoln has tremendous books with diagrams and drawings of his breeding charts. He explains line breeding to me. He has different special foods he's developed to make birds want to mate. He says if a man ate any of that stuff he'd probably be able to breed with a bird himself. Mr. Lincoln never says "fuck" or "shit" or stuff like that. It's always "breed" or "mate" and "droppings." Maybe it's because I'm young or white but I don't think so. Mr. Lincoln doesn't seem to mind my color much.

The main thing he's trying to do is get an absolutely black

canary bird. He says he wants one so black it'll look purple. He says there's a lot of black hidden in green birds and he's trying to get it out. The way he does this is breed the greenest birds, the ones with the least yellow in them, to white birds. The first time they come out white or gray or spotty. He takes the darkest ones without spots and breeds them back to the dark green father or mother bird. He's been line breeding back like that for nine years and some of his birds are blacker than street sparrows. There isn't a yellow feather on them; the parts that are black are deep dull black and the lighter feathers are deep gray. Mr. Lincoln shows me a feather he keeps in his wallet. He says when he has a whole bird as black as that, he can die happy. This feather must be from a crow or a blackbird, it's that black.

The interesting thing is, his dark birds are such fine singers. Mr. Lincoln couldn't care less about this but most of the young males in the black cages are singing away, beautiful deep-throated rollers. Mr. Lincoln says it's " 'cause us niggers is always singin'." Mr. Lincoln doesn't really talk that way at all. He smiles and looks at me closely when he says it.

He lets me put Birdie in the female flight cage. I can tell he doesn't think much of Birdie as a bird; she's just a dumb blonde to him, but he's impressed with the way she lets me pick her up and handle her. He says he's never seen a bird so tame and I must be good with birds. He says I can sit up there in his aviary and watch the birds all I want. I go there a lot and I watch Mr. Lincoln cleaning and taking care of the cages as much as I watch the birds. His hands are sure and quick like birds themselves.

After a while, his wife starts inviting me to eat lunch with them. You can tell Mr. Lincoln's kids think he's wonderful. He probably is. While I'm spending all this time at Mr. Lincoln's, I tell my mother I'm with Al. Al says he'll cover for me. He wants to know if I've finally got a girlfriend but I tell him

I'm going to watch birds in Philadelphia. I tell him about Mr. Lincoln. Al says my mother will kill me if she catches on to where I'm going. He's right.

Mr. Lincoln says he won't sell me any of the birds he has marked in his breeding charts, but he'll sell me any of the others. There's one bird I really like. I could watch him fly around all day and he knows I'm watching him. It's the only canary bird I've met who comes over to the wire and tries to bite my finger.

This bird is constantly fighting with all the other males. That is, he's trying to pick a fight. He'll fly onto a perch and clear off everybody to the left and then everybody to the right. Then, he'll go to another perch and do the same thing. If he sees a bird at the food dish for more than a few seconds, he'll swoop down on it like a hawk. I point him out to Mr. Lincoln and he shakes his head. He says, "That's one of the bad-blood ones."

It turns out that in his breeding for black this one strain came through. It carries a lot of black in it, practically solid black but it's all mixed in with yellow so they're a deep green color. He says he's tried everything to get that black separated out but finally had to give up. This is the last one of that strain. All the rest he's sold off. He says the other thing is, the males in this bunch are meaner than bumblebees. They fight amongst themselves so much they practically kill each other off. They actually begin fighting before they get out of the nest. They fight the other birds until they either win or are half killed trying.

Mr. Lincoln says they all came originally from a Hartz Mountain roller female, the daughter of a singing champion. Mr. Lincoln bought her because she was so dark; he had to pay ten dollars for her five years ago. That's a lot of money for a female, especially since she was six years old, sick, almost bald, and molting all the time. Mr. Lincoln doctored her up,

fed her some of his sex food and got two nests out of her before she died. Mr. Lincoln's convinced the mean blood comes
from her. He says there's nothing more stubborn and mean
than a German.

That's when he tells me he's a racist. Mr. Lincoln thinks
different races and people are different in their blood and this
is the way it's meant to be. He says each people should try to
live its own natural life and people should leave each other
alone. I ask him how this fits in with breeding canaries to linnets and siskins. Mr. Lincoln gives me another one of his close
looks. He says he's a racist for people not for birds; then he
laughs. He tells me most people are unhappy trying to live
lives that aren't natural to them. He wishes he could take his
family back to Africa. I'd never thought about American black
people coming from Africa. Sometimes it surprises me to find
out the perfectly obvious things I don't know.

I call this bird Alfonso, because he's always looking for a
fight, just like Al. You get the feeling he thinks he can take
on anybody and win and if he can't win he'd rather die. I try to
get Birdie interested in him but she doesn't pay much attention.

One time she's forced to notice him. There are two or
three males after Birdie. She'd go over near the screen between the male and female cages and these males would come
over and start singing to her. Most times she flits back and
forth from perch to perch as if she's not listening but she always comes back to that perch and has her wings flitting up
and down. Well, this once, Alfonso decides to cut this mob
down. He comes over and pecks the nearest one till he breaks
off his song and flutters to the bottom perch. The next bird
turns and half jumps up with his wings spread and his mouth
open to fight, the way birds do, but old Alfonso gives him two
quick pecks near the eyes and he's had enough. The third bird
takes off while this is happening. Poor Birdie watches as her

cheering squad is wiped out. Alfonso gives her one look, then flies against the wires of the cage with his mouth open in the canary equivalent of a roar. Birdie almost falls off the perch.

Anyway, I decide that's the one I want. Birdie'll have to learn to love him. He's dark and has a flat head like a hawk, a long body with only a slight difference between the grass green of his breast and the moss green of his back feathers. There's not a white feather or even a yellow one to be seen anywhere on him. His legs are long and black and his feathered thighs show under his tight, slim belly. He's really a fearful-looking bird. His eyes seem to pin you down; bright black and close together for a bird. It's hard to believe he's only a seed-eating canary.

When I tell Mr. Lincoln that's the one I want he tries to talk me out of it. He says it's hard to breed this bunch because they beat the females up something awful and sometimes even turn on the babies when they come out of the nest. He says they're nothing but trouble. The females are good mothers, but the males can break your heart.

It doesn't do any good talking to me. I'm crazy in love with the way he flies. He flies as if the air isn't even there. When he flies up from the bottom of the cage, he's two feet in the air before he opens his wings. When he drops from the top perch, he closes his wings and only opens them once just before he hits the bottom of the cage. I have the feeling you could pull all the feathers out of his wings and he could still fly. He flies because he isn't afraid and not just because it's what birds are supposed to do. He flies as an act of personal creation, defiance.

Mr. Lincoln sells him to me for five dollars. He's worth fifteen at least. Mr. Lincoln says he wants me to try him and come back to tell what happens. If it doesn't work, I can bring him back and he'll give me another bird. Mr. Lincoln's a terrific person. I wish there were more people like him.

When I get home, I put Alfonso in the cage where I used

to keep Birdie before I built the aviary. Then I hang that cage in the aviary where Birdie lives. I'm afraid to put them together right away. Mr. Lincoln said he might kill her and I have to be careful.

Just catching him was really something. He'd flown like a mad thing and when Mr. Lincoln finally cornered him, he shrieked out and twisted his head trying to bite the hand that was holding him. He was completely helpless, held down, but when I put my finger out to pet him, he twisted his head and gave me a hard peck. Birdie was sitting on my shoulder watching all this. I wondered what she was thinking. She did give me some serious questioning queeEEPs when I put her in her traveling box. I put Alfonso in a cardboard box to carry him home; I was half afraid he'd chew his way out.

Well, it's fun to watch. Of course, Birdie is all excited. She flies to his cage and tries hanging onto the side looking in. He gives her a couple sharp pecks at her feet and breast as she hangs there. One time he snatches a few feathers out of her breast.

He seems happy enough in his new cage; eats, drinks and generally makes himself at home the first day he arrives. It's as if all he wants is to be left alone. I'm waiting to hear him sing. I'd never heard him sing at Mr. Lincoln's. Mr. Lincoln'd blown away his vent feathers to show me his little dong, as if there were any question about his being a male, but I don't know if he can sing. Mr. Lincoln said he didn't remember ever hearing him but he didn't listen for it. He couldn't care less if a canary sang. I don't think I care that much either, but I'm anxious to get him in the big cage so I can watch him fly.

That afternoon, I go visit with Birdy again. I'm beginning to think there's not much use. The trouble is I'm not sure I really want Birdy to come back. It's such a rat-shit world and the more I see, the worse it looks. Birdy probably knows what he's doing. He doesn't have to worry about anything, somebody's always going to take care of him, feed him. He can live his whole life out pretending he's a lousy canary. What's so terrible about that?

Christ, I'm wishing I could get onto something loony myself. Maybe I'll play gorilla like that guy across the hall; just shit in my hands every once in a while and throw it at somebody. They'd lock me up and I'd be taken care of the way I was in the hospital at Metz. I could do it. Maybe that means I'm crazy. I just know it's not so bad letting somebody else make the decisions.

God, it'd be great to be a running guard again; feel the mud sticking in my cleats, smell the mold in the shoulder pads around my ears, hear my own breathing inside a helmet. Everything simple, just knock down anybody with the wrong color shirt.

Who the hell knows who's really crazy? I think this Weiss is crazy along with his spitting T-4. They know Birdy's crazy and probably think I am too. I should talk to that CO. He's been around looneys long enough, probably knows more than most doctors. One thing I've learned; you want to know where an OP is, never ask an officer. He's liable to send you to a Post Office.

I'm even beginning to wonder if the way Birdy and I were so close all those years wasn't a bit suspicious. Nobody else I've ever known had such a close friend; it was as if we were married or something. We had a private club for two. From the time I was thirteen until I was seventeen I spent more time with Birdy than with everybody else put together. Sure, I chased girls and Birdy played with birds but he was actually the only person I was ever close to. People used to say we sounded alike, our voices I mean; we were always coming out with the same sentences at the same time too. I'm missing Birdy; I need him back to talk to.

I sit there for over an hour between the doors not saying anything. I'm not particularly watching Birdy either. It's like a long guard duty, I'm turned inside myself, only half there. I don't know how I get to thinking about the dogcatching; maybe I'm remembering how it was all such a shock to us, especially hanging around the squad room talking to the cops. That was a quick injection of life-shit all right.

—Hey, Birdy!

He tenses up; he's listening to me. What the hell. I don't feel like talking to him about it. What good would it do. It's not what I want to talk about anyway. Birdy hops up and turns around to look at me. He cocks his head both ways looking out of one eye, then the other, like a pigeon.

—Aw, come off it, Birdy; quit this bird shit!

It was the summer before our junior year when Birdy and I got the job as dogcatchers. Actually, we invented the job. There'd never been any dogcatchers in Upper Merion and so there were whole packs of dogs running around wild. This was especially true in the poor part of town, our neighborhood.

These packs would have ten or twenty dogs in them and they didn't belong to anybody. People'd buy their kids a puppy for Christmas or a birthday and then when they found out how much they ate, they'd throw them out and the dogs would find each other It was like a jungle. Mostly they were mangy-looking mongrels, with short legs and long tails or pointed faces and thick fur; all kinds of strange-looking animals.

They'd roam around in the early morning knocking over garbage cans and spreading crap around. Daytimes, they'd usually avoid people and mosey around independently or sleep. Sometimes they'd even go back to the people who owned them; but at night they were regular wolf packs.

Once in a while they'd gang up on a kid or some cat or the garbage men and there'd be a big fuss in the newspapers. This happened just as we were about ready to get out of school that summer. I got the idea of trying to pick them off with my twenty-two. By then, I'm already a real gun nut. I don't know if I would've ever done it but I told Birdy. He said we should go to the police and tell them we'll work over the summer as dogcatchers. He already has all those canaries and big feed bills.

Surprisingly, the police buy the idea; the commissioner signs procurement slips and in only two weeks it's all set up. They rip the back off one of the old patrol wagons, build a big cage on it, rig a wooden platform on the back bumper where we can stand with handles to hold on to.

They assign a sergeant named Joe Sagessa to drive the wagon and we're in business. Joe Sagessa had been on the desk and isn't too happy with the job but he's stuck. He has a pack of hunting dogs out in Secane so he's the likely one for the detail.

The deal is we'd be paid a dollar an hour plus a dollar a dog. That was a lot of money in those days. My old man was only pulling about thirty-five bucks a week as a plumber.

While the truck is being fixed up they send us down to Philadelphia for training. We're just on the straight dollar an hour but we don't have to do a damned thing but watch.

The township bought us gigantic nets especially made for catching dogs. They have short handles, only a foot or so long but the net part is almost four feet in diameter. They weigh over thirty pounds. There are racks built on the side of the wagon to hang the nets when we ride on the back.

Down in Philadelphia the dogcatchers are all black. They're genuine professionals and one of them has been catching dogs for seven years. These guys catch dogs the way the Globetrotters play basketball. They made a real joy out of it.

They have a regular dog wagon, designed for the job; they can clamber around the fender and get inside behind the driver whenever they want. Only one of them at a time would ride on the outside. He sings out whenever he sights a stray dog.

They give us lessons with the nets first. They'd worked out left-hand hook shots, right hooks and straight-on jump shots. This last, they say, is for when the dog jumps at your throat. They're having fun kidding around with us.

It's all worked out like big game hunting. They talk about different dogs they'd gotten and about the big "mothers" they'd had to wrestle into the truck, and they show us all the places where they've been bitten. They get a straight dollar and a half an hour no matter how many dogs they catch.

For a week we ride along on the back of the trucks with them. Now, down in Philadelphia, most of the houses are row houses, so they have a system for trapping dogs between the rows. When they spot a dog, one netman jumps off right there and the wagon goes down the street toward the dog. They drop another netman off beside the dog, and the truck goes on down to the other end of the street and swings around. The third guy, the one driving the wagon, gets out there. They all have their nets with them.

The one in the middle, beside the dog, sneaks up and tries a drop shot; just drops the net over the dog. This is rarely successful. Somehow, the dogs catch on and take off. Then it's up to the netman at either end. The one in the middle hot-foots it after the dog to keep him moving. As the dog charges past the guy on the end, he'll try to net him with a right or left hook shot. If the dog doubles back, he has to run past two nets. It's a lot like a good baseball play where they catch a player off third base and run him down. Finally, the dog takes the plunge one way or the other and most times winds up under the net.

Then there'd be a lot of laughing and pushing the dog into the wagon. People'd start crowding around and cursing and if it were somebody's dog, there'd be big arguments. They have a way of lifting the dog up in the net and dumping him into the cage. They told us one time a character came out and cut the net to get his dog. They laughed till they couldn't breathe telling us about it. As soon as they've locked a dog in the wagon, they'd hightail on out of the neighborhood.

There'd been dogcatchers a long time in Philadelphia so there aren't really any packs. What they need down there is a catcatcher. There're beat up cats wandering all over the streets. You just never see a bird in that part of town.

These dogcatchers have girlfriends all over. After they've gotten seven or eight dogs they take off one at a time for an hour or two to go visit the girls. The rest of us would drive around. Sometimes if a dog looks as if he wants to be picked up, we drop off and try to slip a net over him. Most of the girlfriends are married and these guys would come back laughing and giggling and bragging but scared, too. There are all kinds of jokes about who's the most tired. They're actually catching dogs about three hours a day. The rest of the time they are, without doubt, the oldest established floating stud service in Philadelphia.

They'd ride around flirting. Women are hanging out the windows, leaning on pillows and waiting for them. They'd yell and try to get us to stop. The guys have on-going arguments about who has how many kids with which women. Most of the talking isn't really words, more just smiles, looks, and deep throat noises. It sure looks like a hell of a lot better life than our fathers have.

At the end of the day, we'd go back to the dog pound. They have cages there and a setup for gassing unclaimed dogs. This means just about all the dogs they caught. Nobody is about to pay two dollars for a license and a five dollar fine to get out a dog.

They'd empty the wagon, then gather the overdue dogs into the gas chamber, close the door, a door like a safe with a twisting handle, turn on the gas, then go over and clean out the cages where the dogs had been.

Birdy and I are fascinated by the gassing. After half an hour, they turn on the fans to suck out the gas, open the doors and pull the dead dogs out by the tails. Neither of us has had much to do with anything dead. It's hard to watch them go in live, jumping, barking, trying to get attention, then come out dead with their eyes open. There's a special incinerator designed to burn the dogs. It has a long, movable grate they can pull in and out for dumping the dogs into the flames. They clean out the gassing chamber and the day is finished. They laugh and joke while they do all this but we can tell they don't like it either.

That first morning when we go out alone, with our own wagon, we chase about fifty dogs and don't catch one. The houses where we're hunting aren't row houses and the dogs run off between houses and into the next street. Joe Sagessa almost laughs himself sick watching us. We could probably have walked up to most of those dogs and picked them up. We both feel this would be cheating. We have to catch our dogs with the net to be dogcatchers.

That afternoon we go back to our own neighborhood because the houses there are in rows. We manage to catch four dogs, including the dog of Mr. Kohler, the paperhanger; he lives three houses away from us.

The township had made arrangements to keep the dogs for forty-eight hours in the kennels of a vet named Doc Owens. We take the dogs out there and then quit for the day.

When I get home, Mr. Kohler is in our living room. He's hollering at my mother. When I come in, he turns on me. He wants to know where his dog is. He says if it's dead, he's going to kill me. He calls me an Italian Fascist. I push him out the door, across the porch, and down the steps. I'm hoping he'll take a swing at me. I haven't knocked down a grown man yet. He stands on the lawn and tells me he's going to call the police. I tell him I'm working for the police. I tell him it'll cost five dollars to get his dog back because it didn't have a license, the dog is a criminal and so is he. If he doesn't get down there right away tomorrow I'll slit the damned dog's throat myself. He calls me a Fascist again. I call him a shithead kike. I'm about ready to start chasing him down the street; I'm wishing I had my net. My mother tells me to come inside. I go in and she tells me to quit the dogcatcher job. I tell her I won't; I'm just beginning to enjoy it.

The next day we get twelve dogs. We've worked out our own system. We catch the dogs cowboy style, by more or less rounding them up. When we come on a pack we don't drive up to them, we follow and maneuver them from street to street, till we get them at a dead end or a place where we can surround them.

We're watching to find out who the leader of the pack is. All those packs have one top dog. We watch for this when we're rounding up the pack. He's easy to spot because he runs at the head of the pack and the others look at him to see what to do. We concentrate on catching that pack leader, then the rest are easy. The way we do this is drop one of us, usually me, right in front of this dog. I stand there with the net down like a bullfighter's cloak and growl at him. Usually he has to defend his honor and the pack so he'll bristle up and growl back. Birdy, meanwhile, has dropped off behind him, perhaps twenty, thirty yards, and sneaks up through the pack. By the time the dog's discovered what's happened it's too late, and one or the other of us takes him. After that, the rest of the pack is easy. They stand still as we walk up to them or wag their tails trying to make friends. Most dogs are big cowards. We net them or pick them up. We figure we deserve the pack after catching the leader.

We catch this whole twelve dogs between eleven and eleven-thirty in the morning of that second day. Twelve dogs is all the wagon will carry. It's half an hour drive out to Doc Owens's, so Joe Sagessa suggests we get some hoagies and beer, then sack out up behind the golf course. We do that and lie around telling jokes till about three, then drive over to Doc

Owens's with the dogs. Mr. Kohler has already come and paid to get his mutt.

That night, the cage is a filthy mess. Luckily there's a hose for cleaning off the squad cars, so we use it to wash out all the dog shit, dog piss, vomit and dog hair. Joe gets us lockers in the squad room where we can keep our work clothes. We shower in the squad showers and keep an extra set of clothes there.

It's almost like we're in the police ourselves. It's terrific being able to handle those slick thirty-eights and forty-fives. Those cops keep them in perfect shape. Some of the belts and harnesses are beautiful to look at, with the ideal combination of sweat and oil, molded to fit the waist or the shoulder.

There're always card games going on. Joe introduces us around and they don't seem to mind our being there. I begin to think I wouldn't mind being a cop. A guy like Joe Sagessa is still young and ready to retire with a good pension. People might hate you but they holler when they need you and you get a lot of respect. There's another idea I can write off.

The next day we do the same thing. By ten o'clock in the morning, we have ten dogs including a huge German shepherd. This time we drive them out to Doc Owens's first, come back to get our hoagies and beer, then lie around for two hours. That way we don't have the dogs locked up all the time, barking, howling and crapping all over everything. In the afternoon we go out for a second load. We get eight more dogs. Joe's having as much fun catching dogs as we are. He's on regular salary, but that day Birdy and I split eighteen dollars in dog money plus the eight hours in salary. What a racket.

Doc Owens is beginning to back out on the deal. He's running out of places to put the dogs. His fancy clientele is up tight about having so many mangy mongrels hanging around. That first set of dogs is over the forty-eight hour mark, too, and nobody's come to claim any of them except for Mr. Kohler. Doc Owens makes us take them with us. Joe says he'll drop them off out where he likes. That's about twenty miles out Baltimore Pike and outside the township.

The next day we get eleven dogs in the morning. When we arrive at Doc Owens's he won't let us unload. Joe is smiling like crazy. They've got mutts tied to stakes all over the back yard. It looks like a very low-class dog show. Doc Owens wants us to take those twelve dogs we got the second day before we unload any more. So, we go out of there with the twelve dogs in the back. We go back to the police station in the municipal building and Joe explains the situation to Captain Lutz. Lutz phones down to Philadelphia and they agree to gas the dogs, but at a dollar a dog. There's nothing else to do, so we drive all the way into town, deliver the dogs, feeling like real bastards, and drive back. By then, it's too late to go out again so we wash and clean out the wagon. Birdy and I spend that night trying to think of another job.

The next morning, we catch ten dogs in less than half an hour. The catching is getting to be the easy part. We go out to Doc Owens and he comes over with a worried look on his face. He blows up when he looks into the wagon and sees this really motley bunch of dogs, including a mean-looking Spitz. Joe jumps out of the car with two wires in his hand and a smile on his face.

Joe's system is simple but awful. He says it's the best way and the dog doesn't suffer at all. He electrocutes the dogs. The way he does it is to stand the dog in a wet spot on the cement floor in Doc Owens's cellar. Then he shaves a spot of hair off the back of the dog's neck and another spot just above the tail joint. He snaps alligator clips on to these spots. The alligator clips are attached to wires which join in an outlet plug.

He hooks up one of the dogs this way, stands back, and pushes the plug into a 220-volt socket. The dog sort of jumps into the air, with its legs stiff and its eyes wide open, staring; then comes down on its feet, standing like a toy dog, its hair sticking out straight. After about a minute, Joe pulls the plug and the dog collapses into a heap.

It's a terrible thing to look at but can't be any worse than being gassed. The trouble is you have it happening in front of your eyes. I've seen some cats smashed by cars but that wasn't on purpose. This is awful.

We'd reach in, choose one of the dogs, hook it up, the dog having no idea of what's happening, and then ZAP, the end. Birdy and I hose the floor after each dog. We're hearing rumors about the Nazis' concentration camps; we're running a concentration camp for dogs.

We do all twelve dogs. After the first few, I've made up my mind to quit. Maybe somebody has to do it but I don't want to be the one. Birdy is pale green in that dark cellar and we're watching each other. I know we're both torn between taking off and bursting out laughing or crying. I know Doc Owens and Joe are watching us.

Doc Owens asks Joe what we're going to do with the dead dogs. Joe says he's made arrangements for that, too. Birdy and I carry the dead dogs out and put them in the back of the wagon. They seem one hell of a lot heavier dead than alive. We drag the heavy, bigger dogs out by the tails, then lift them together and push them through the door. It's amazing the difference between dead things and live things.

We jump on the back of the wagon and Joe drives us over to the next township. Birdy and I stand so we block the wire screen door. We don't want anyone looking in and seeing all those dead dogs when we're stopped at a red light.

We drive to the big incinerator in Haverford Township. It's one of those tall tower jobs that burns all the time. The smoke and smell are supposed to go straight up so nobody will smell it. We get the dogs out, two apiece, throw them over our shoulders and climb to the top on winding steps. The dogs are already getting cold and stiff. Up there is a manhole cover. Joe opens it and we can look straight down into the flames. We drop the dogs down that hole. It's enough to turn a person religious.

By the time we come up with the second set of dogs, it's already smelly. We drop them in, put the cover back and Joe says, "Let's get the hell out of here." It's about one-thirty in the afternoon now, so we get our hoagies and beer, and drive up behind the golf course again.

Birdy starts off by telling Joe he's not sure he can stick it out. The killing of the dogs is too much. Joe begins telling us stories about the things he's seen as a policeman. He says we should quit if we really feel like it but we might as well get our feet wet here as anywhere else. We're probably going to be cannon fodder for the war and we'd better get used to it now. He says this seeing dogs die and learning to live with it might actually save our lives later on. In twenty years on the force he's seen all kinds of shit and life is no bag of cherries.

Joe is medium height and thick, not fat, and he looks strong. He has a full head of graying hair cut short. He looks so much like a man that even the other policemen look like boys beside him. He has a deep voice and a deep laugh; he laughs a lot. We listen to his stories about all the rot going on in just our township and we know he isn't lying. It's the first time Birdy and I really begin to learn something of what a mean shitty world it is. What makes it all worse is Joe laughing at some of his worst stories and expecting us to laugh with him. We don't have the guts to quit either. I think we can't face up to having Joe laugh at us.

Well, it turns out that all the smell from the incinerator doesn't go up. A regular war starts between Upper Merion Township and Haverford Township. Joe is called before the commissioner and bawled out. The commissioner's getting mixed reviews about the whole dogcatching operation anyway. Gardeners, mothers of small children are sending nice letters, but dog lovers are up in arms. They're threatening to get the ASPCA after us. It looks like Birdy and I won't have to quit after all. The dogcatching operation is suspended for three days. Birdy's glad because he has a lot of work to do with his birds. He's catching dogs so he can build that dream aviary of his; the same reason he was digging for buried treasure in the rain.

I go over to his place and help him out some. He has more crazy canaries than you'd believe. Birdy gets all excited showing me some of the experiments he's carrying out with weights on the birds' legs and pulling flight feathers from the wings to see how little a bird needs to carry a heavy weight. He's also built some beautiful models. He wants me to help when he turns one of these into a working model big enough for him to fly. He wants me to help with the launching. I say I'll do it when we get some time off from dogcatching. I've got an idea for an underwater diving bell myself and I'm going to need help when I try it out. We agree to do both those things when the dogcatching thing folds.

The next Monday we're back on the wagon again. Joe tells us he's found another place to get rid of the dogs. Birdy wants us to take the afternoons off and ride out to the Main Line where all the millionaires live and dump the dogs there. If we could do it, that'd be fun. We'd start all kinds of new breeds mixed in with French poodles and Pekineses.

We catch a truckful by noon. The dogs are getting smarter; survival of the fittest is beginning to set in. We go out to Doc Owens's. He's ready to go through the roof after keeping all those dogs five days. He rants and raves at Joe. Joe smiles, shakes his head, and promises we'd take them all today. Joe's enjoying Doc Owens's being mad.

For all the noise the dog lovers are making, there's nothing being done about it. Just about all those dogs we caught are still there, ready to be killed. To tell the truth, most people are glad to get rid of their mutts.

That afternoon at Doc Owens's is like a combination of Sing Sing and a slaughterhouse. We're piling up dead dogs three high. The smell of burning flesh and hair is sickening. The poor dogs begin to catch on to what's happening and start trying to fight away from the alligator clips. One beast, half setter, part shepherd, part wolf, gets so mean we can't get the clips on him and Doc Owens gives him a shot of strychnine. He goes out about the same as the ones with the electricity.

Some dogs, though, still walk right up, smile at us and wag their tails, looking up at us expectantly, as if we're going to put them on a leash and take them for a walk. Some walk; a walk right into nowhere. Birdy and I have to keep going outside for breaths of air and to hold ourselves together.

When it's done, we carry all the dogs into the truck. We pack them in tight and even throw a few onto the floor in front beside Joe. It's three-thirty before we get them all in. Joe starts driving out into the country past Secane. Joe doesn't tell anybody anything until he's ready, so we don't ask questions. I'm thinking he's found another incinerator, or is going to pile them up in a dump.

Slowly, as we get further out from any houses, we begin to pick up the most horrendous smell I've ever smelled. Nothing can describe it. We go onto a small dirt road and pull up into an open place in front of a stable. There are spavined-looking horses tied around to the buildings. The whole place is swarming with big blue flies. Usually there are flies around horses, but not like this, and this smell is something else. It doesn't smell like horses.

But it's horses all right. It's horses being cut up. This is a slaughteryard for old plugs. I look over at Birdy and he's absolutely green. Joe jumps out of the truck and seems to know everybody. Joe knows everybody, everywhere. I guess that's part of being a cop; probably, too, he buys meat for his dogs out here.

We get off the wagon and are immediately covered by flies. It's a hot day and they're drinking our sweat, then they start on our blood. They're big flies with shiny blue-purple bodies and dark red heads. There's no way to get away from the bastards; they fly into our noses, eyes, ears. Joe comes back and tells us to get up in the wagon again. He drives us around in back of long sheds. Inside we can see men standing in blood, hacking away at huge chunks of horse flesh.

Behind the shed, there's something that looks like a gigantic meat-grinding machine; it's run by a gasoline motor. Joe jumps out, walks over and pulls a cord, the way you'd start a motorboat or a lawn mower, and it starts chugging, slow then fast, a one lunger. Blue smoke comes out in clouds. Joe switches it into gear and the grinder begins making a tremendous racket. Bits of ground flesh leak from small holes in the bottom.

There's a huge funnel-like hole at the top of the grinder, almost big enough to put a human body into it. Joe tells us to get the dogs out of the wagon. We drag them over and he starts dropping them into the funnel. Jesus, he's still smiling! He's holding the dogs away from himself, to keep the blood, shit, and slobber from getting on him, and dropping them in. He's in his uniform shirt with his badge and regulation pants. His belt and pistol are around his waist and he's not wearing his cap. He glistens in the sunlight, dropping the dogs into the machine. Thin lines of dog flesh, mixed in with hair, are coming out the bottom. Birdy and I are staggering back and forth with the dogs, trying to pretend we're men and trying not to vomit all over the place. The stink, the flies, and now grinding up the dogs; we're earning our dollar an hour. Joe motions us to help him put the dogs in; he steps back and rubs his hands together.

We grab hold of the dogs. The best way is to lower them in by the tail. The sound of the grinding is grisly. We get it done somehow. Birdy and I are glad to climb into the front seat of the wagon while Joe talks with some of the men standing around. We're never going to make it as men in this world. The seats are plastic and hot. Birdy says if we can get used to this we can get used to anything. That's after I tell him we'll get used to it.

We're just about getting our stomachs settled when Joe comes over and invites us into the shed to watch how it's all done. He sees our faces and starts laughing. He slides into the wagon; we climb out onto the back, and take off.

While we're cleaning the wagon that afternoon, I ask Joe what they do with all the meat they grind up in the grinder. Joe says they make dog food with it.

*T*he days pass; Birdie and I try everything. I sit for hours with treat food in the dish. So long as I stay near it, Alfonso hovers in the back of his cage raising the front edges of his wings and opening his beak in a threatening growl. As soon as I go away he comes over and eats. It's hard to believe he's the same species as Birdie. Birdie becomes more and more fascinated by him as he remains hostile to us. She lands on top of his cage to watch him and queeps, peeps, trills; everything she can come up with. The only answer is a sudden lunge when he thinks she's not paying attention.

I decide that maybe if I try starving him for a day, then offer him food, he'll be more cooperative. No; he just acts meaner than usual. I try two days without food. Nothing. You just can't keep food away from a canary for three days. I try giving him special tidbits like bits of apple or celery top or a dandelion leaf but it doesn't matter. He'll eat it only when I've removed myself to a distance. He'll eat it, keeping an eye on me every minute, as if he expects me to charge up and take it back. He most definitely is the mad bird.

St. Valentine's Day comes. It's the traditional day for beginning to breed birds if they're going to be kept inside, but Alfonso stays mean, and keeps apart from us. I give both Birdie and Alfonso a big leaf of dandelion that day. It's supposed to get them all hot for breeding. Mr. Lincoln told me that. He also told me it's French and means "lion's tooth." That's the kind of thing I like to know. He told me not to eat any dandelion leaves or flowers myself or I'd get all hot and bothered and maybe wet the bed. He said the French also call dandelion "pissenlit," which means "piss in the bed." Urinate is the way Mr. Lincoln said it. He must be the smartest man I've ever met.

I'm dying to get Alfonso out so I can watch him fly. One afternoon, I can't wait any longer. I open the door to his cage, then go back to my corner in the aviary. It doesn't take him long to figure out the door is open. In about five seconds he's on the door sill looking around. He's awfully suspicious and looks over to where I am. Just to be safe, I hold Birdie in my hand. Finally, he decides to take a chance, and shoots out like a dart for the highest perch across the aviary. He wipes his beak all over the perch; showing it's his and maybe smelling Birdie out. He looks down at me. The way he looks down, with his pointed head, thin body, and long legs he makes me tense up a bit. Then he pulls one of his wings-folded sky-dives down to the food dish and water cup. He stomps all around, looking for traps I guess, then eats and drinks. He's an incredibly messy slob; scattering seeds over the floor before he finds a seed he'll accept. After he's eaten, he starts hopping over in our direction, like he's preparing to charge. Birdie makes a few queeps and I make some myself. He cocks his head from side to side trying to get a good look at us. Up till now, he's usually looked at us straight on, more or less just to see if we were going to make any fast moves or try to get behind him. He doesn't care about us individually; we're just a vague danger he wants to be ready for. That's the way it is. If you only look out for yourself you're a lot safer. You're vulnerable when you let yourself go out.

So, for the first time, Alfonso gives us a real going over. He's trying to find out what the hell we actually are. After five minutes of this, he flies up on a near perch and scans us from a new angle. We don't move. Finally, he gives a rusty peep. It sounds like a voice hailing a ship after spending twenty years on a desert island. It's the most reluctant peep I've ever heard. You feel he wishes he could put it back into his beak almost as soon as he's made it. Birdie and I peep back enthusiastically. We peep back and forth a few times but he gets tired of that, too. He flies over onto the top of his cage, hops down onto the sill, then hops into the cage. We wait. I know he's testing me to see if I'll jump up to close the door while he's in there. I can't see into the cage from where I am but I'm sure he's in the back, waiting to spring out if I make a move toward the cage.

He comes out again. I think about letting go of Birdie but I'm afraid. Mr. Lincoln's probably right. I don't want to take any chances with Birdie. I wait until Alfonso's on a perch away from the cage, then I carefully get up and put Birdie into the little cage. She gives me every kind of nasty peep she can muster but I turn around and go out of the aviary. I want to watch what Alfonso does when he thinks I'm not there.

At first, all he does is enjoy the size of the aviary. He flies from one end to the other, twisting in mid-flight and catching himself at the end of each run. He flies straight up, trying to catch himself a high place under the bed springs. He does quite a few of his straight drops. He can really fly. He's like a test pilot checking to see if all the mechanisms are still in order after a plane's been grounded for a while.

He goes down and splashes more seed around and eats a few. He washes his face off in the water cup but he doesn't take a bath. He ruffles out his feathers and combs them down again; fast, nothing like the leisured preening of Birdie.

Birdie in the meanwhile is practically hanging out of her cage trying to see him. I think she's gotten the idea of my strategy. At least this way we can watch him do things.

After a few more gymnastics and some more exploration he lands on top of Birdie's cage. She queeps madly. He hops around and shits so he just misses her head. Then he jumps over the edge and slides down the bars on the front of the cage till he can look into the empty treat cup on her perch. Birdie hops near him and gives him a gracious peep; he gives her a half-hearted growl. She stands her ground and they stay like that, next to each other; Birdie queeping and he looking at her as if she's in a zoo. He scrambles around the side of the cage to the regular food dish and Birdie hops down to join him. Just to be sociable she dips her head into the dish for a seed. Alfonso flies into a regular rage. He lets go, makes a flurry of wings, and screeches. He attacks the side of the cage. Birdie jumps away. She recovers and cowers at the other end of the cage. Stupid Alfonso keeps attacking for about five minutes. He flies back to the floor of the aviary, then attacks again. He hangs onto the door as if he's trying to pull it open. I begin to think there, just for a minute, he might manage it. It's a snap-swing hinge and I'm getting to the point where I'll believe anything. I'm also beginning to think maybe I've made a mistake. He seems hopeless.

Things go on the same way for a week. Birdie trying to be nice and Alfonso being a bastard. To give Birdie some exercise, I take her out of the aviary at night while I'm doing my homework or working on my models, to let her fly around. She keeps flying to the wire of the aviary, trying to attract Alfonso's attention. I'm coming along fine with my flying model. This one flies, but in a long down glide. The rubber-band motor doesn't give enough flapping power for lift. I don't know how much weight it could carry, not much. I have to get some calculations on the weight and density of birds.

In the evenings, when I let her out to fly, I turn the light on in the aviary. Birdie keeps flying over and hanging onto the wire. She peeps and queeps until it's embarrassing but Alfonso just ignores her. You'd think he didn't like birds. He doesn't seem to know what it is to be lonely, or even care.

I've about decided to give up and take him back to Mr. Lincoln when something happens. It's a Friday night. I'm in bed reading. The light on my bed is the only light in the room.

At first I think I hear water running. I listen hard, then realize it's coming from under me. The sound increases in volume, then develops into the unmistakable sound of a long rolling note. Alfonso has finally decided to sing. He sings as if he's trying not to wake us, as if he doesn't want anyone to hear; as if he's a trombone with a mute, practicing some complex piece of music to himself before a performance.

After the long roll, continued unbroken, undulating in volume and pitch, for half a minute, he breaks into three almost sobbing, soft, drawn-out melodious notes. Those three notes are enough to break your heart. Then he quickly crescendos to the top of another roll and brings it down slowly, tortuously, to a sound that has a clicking rather than a whistling quality, the kind of sound that had first caught my attention.

He stops. I hold my breath. I wish I could see him; I try to calculate where he is from the direction of the sound, but I can't. He starts again, the same low clicks becoming melodious, increasing in volume, tone, pitch, simultaneously, moving over at least an octave but in a different register. This time there is a single drawn-out note at the top and then directly across with another very round sounding roll to a stop; three staccato, almost unmusical peeps and then the descent. He stops. I wait but nothing more happens. I turn out the light; somehow I've got to keep him. Listening to him sing in the dark like that was close to flying for me. I feel myself somehow unbound.

I sit there all afternoon till it's dark. Nobody bothers me. I watch Birdy. He doesn't do much except take a crap or pee once in a while. He does this by squatting over the toilet with his feet on the toilet seat. A bird doesn't even know when it craps, so Birdy isn't a real bird.

A few times he turns toward me and watches. He turns his head back and forth, shifting his whole body each time. There's a sink in the corner filled with water and once he goes over and drinks like a bird, lifting his head to let the water run down his throat. What the hell's he trying to prove?

When he moves anywhere, he hops. He lifts himself from the squatting position with each hop and then squats again; hopping, squatting, flipping his bent arms as wings, exactly like some awkward giant bird; like a hawk or an eagle, hopping on the ground, slow hops.

It's getting so it doesn't bother me as much. When he looks at me, I try smiling but he doesn't notice. He's curious but there's no kind of recognition. I can't help wondering what in hell could've happened to him. I don't want to ask Weiss again, he obviously doesn't want to tell me; probably doesn't know. Most likely, Birdy's the only one who knows.

I look up and down the corridor; nobody's around. The CO's already fed Birdy. This time I stayed on to watch. That's the creepiest part all right. I don't know if the CO or Weiss or anybody realizes that Birdy is imitating a baby bird being fed when he flips his bent arms like that. I'm sure as hell not going to tell.

What happens to somebody like Birdy? Will they keep him locked up like this all his life? Are there hospitals all over the country filled up with war nuts? Birdy isn't hurting anybody. Trouble is, if they let him out, he'll probably go jump off some high building or try to fly down a staircase or out a window or something. What the hell, if that's what he wants to do they should let him. Birdy never was dumb, most things he did made sense in a special kind of way. I'm still not sure about this crazy business either. What's crazy? Wars are crazy for sure.

Speaking of crazy, Birdy and I did some goofball things. An example is the spring of our sophomore year. I'd been working all winter on a diving helmet. My old man'd taught me how to cut, braze, and weld, so I made a diving helmet from a five-gallon oil can, some lead pipe, and brass fittings. I'd tested it for leaks and it was airtight. I pumped air into it by mounting two car pumps on a seesaw arrangement with an airhose going into the helmet. The pressure of the air would keep the water from coming in and the extra air came out in bubbles from the bottom.

I'd also made a spring-mounted underwater gun from some pipe. My idea was to hunt fish underwater at the Springfield reservoir. Nobody's allowed to fish there and it's crowded with fish. Mario said he'd help but I needed two for manning the pumps and the air line when I went under. Birdy said he'd pitch in. My half of the deal is that I'd help him with his crackpot flying machine.

Birdy'd taken one of his models that sort of worked and made a man-sized version of it. There were huge wings with harnesses you slipped your arms into. You had to flap the wings with your arms. These wings were each over eight feet long and there were vanes turning vertical on the upswing and horizontal on the downswing. The whole thing was designed so it rotated forward on a crankshaft arrangement when it was flapped. Birdy said you had to catch the air under the wings to get any lift.

Birdy'd made it with aluminum framing, thin aluminum

panels, and bicycle parts. He'd worked hundreds of hours on it in the machine shop at school. I don't know where he got the aluminum; that stuff was rationed to build airplanes for the goddamned war. Birdy also had a silk piece sewn between the legs of a pair of pants that he wore when he flew this thing. When he spread his legs he had a tail like a pigeon.

I tried the wings on and I could hardly flap the monsters. Birdy has a board over two sawhorses in his back yard. He'd lie out on this when he practiced flapping. That year of arm swinging and jumping up and down had really paid off. He could flap those wings and keep it up for more than five minutes. He'd also lie out on his back with five-pound weights hanging from the tips of these wings; then he'd flap them up. He'd calculated that five pounds on the ends was the equivalent to twenty pounds pressure under each wing at the middle. He said this gave him forty pounds of flapping power, whatever that meant. He calls this contraption an ornithopter. I thought he made up the word but I looked it up in a dictionary and it was there. It said an ornithopter was any aircraft designed to derive its chief support and propulsion from flapping wings. Who'd believe it? There's a word for everything.

I insist on doing my thing first. I'm thinking I might be getting into another one of those gas tank affairs where he's going to wind up in the hospital for a while. I even try to talk him out of his crackpot project, but Birdy's hard to talk out of anything. He says he'd thought of jumping from the gas tank but he needs to get up speed before he can lift off.

His plan is to have me pedal a bicycle, with him standing on a contraption he's rigged in front of the handlebars. Then, on a signal, I stop suddenly and he takes off. This is all going to happen down at the dump, the old part, where they don't dump anymore. The pile of crap has piled up about thirty or forty feet, right to the edge of the creek there. Birdy's planning to take off the edge of the pile and fly over the creek. I figure at least he'll have something to fall into. He says he can slip out of the wings by unbuckling two buckles. I know he can hold his breath underwater forever, so I should be able to get down and pull him out.

As I said, we're doing my thing first. One evening we pile the helmet, pumps, and pump rack onto our bikes and head out for the reservoir.

It's just getting dark when we short the electric fence with a jumper wire and start to climb over. I have on swimming trunks under my clothes and pipe nipples tied with ropes around my ankles to weigh me down. The top of the fence has barbed wire, so we throw burlap bags over it. Birdy goes up first, then I give Mario a boost and he drops on the other side. I hand the stuff up to Birdy and he drops it to Mario. We work our way down to the reservoir. There are some trees where we can set up the pump hidden from the guard house by the dam. I figure I'll just slide down the slanted sides of the reservoir into the water and nobody will see me.

We get the pump ready and the air line laid out. I strip and put on the helmet. I'm beginning to wish I hadn't made the damned thing. Mario and Birdy try out the pumps; I'm getting air fine. We have a rope tied around my waist so I can signal them to pull me up if I get in trouble. I also have a flashlight I waterproofed to see my way around down there.

I start into the water and it's ice cold. I pee into some of the cleanest drinking water in the Philadelphia area. The side of the reservoir is slippery with green moss and I've no idea how deep the goddamned thing is. I'm sliding down and feeling there isn't enough air coming into the helmet. I can't get my breath from the shock of the cold water. The glass face plate is already fogged so I can't see. I don't want to turn on the flashlight until I'm completely under. If the guard sees the light he'll be all over us.

The water starts coming up past the face plate of the helmet. I'm wondering if I'm going to be able to climb back up the slippery sides of the reservoir. I can feel panic grabbing me. Where the fuck did I get such a screwy idea anyway; who the hell needs to walk around underwater shooting fish. If it weren't for Mario and Birdy watching me, I'd scramble right on up out of there. I try a few slow deep breaths. At the least, I have to get the whole helmet underwater. I take a few more sliding steps down. My feet start sinking into soft cold mud over my ankles. I turn on the light but all I can see is a blur. There isn't going to be any shooting fish, that's for sure. I'm just managing to beat down surging panic. I take a few more steps and the mud is up to my knees.

Then, I don't know what brought it on; the helmet is working perfectly, the air bubbles are plopping out of the bottom, I have enough air, everything is perfect; but I need to get out of that helmet.

I rip it off and pull on the rope. I've ripped off the helmet before I realize I'm really underwater and I don't know how deep. Nobody is pulling on the rope either. I'm not sure which way is the way back. I don't even think of pulling myself back by the rope. I'm completely ape. I drop the flashlight and try to swim up to the surface. I can't make it because of the mud and the weights on my legs. I breathe in a full swallow of water; I'm choking, drowning, when Mario and Birdy start pulling me out. They pull me sidewise up the side of the reservoir like a gaffed fish.

The air feels wonderfully warm and thin. Mario and Birdy are bent over me. I'm stretched out, shaking, choking. Jesus, I'm glad to be alive. Birdy leans close.

"What happened, Al? Did it leak?"

I nod. I don't look at him. Now it's Mario.

"You all right, Al?"

I nod again. Mario starts pulling in the helmet. Birdy is undoing the rope from around my waist; the knot slipped when they pulled me up the side of that wall and I can hardly breathe. Mario leans over the water.

"The light's still burning down there. Look at that."

"Forget it. Let the damned thing burn itself out."

Birdy's taking apart the pumps.

"What happened, Al?"

I look over at him. He'll believe anything. He wants to believe.

"Water began coming in. It started rising up past my mouth, then past my nose. I ripped the thing off and tried to swim up but I couldn't move; these fuckers weighed me down and the mud on the bottom is thick as cow shit."

I'm sitting up now and trying to untie the weights from my legs; I'm starting to get cold. Birdy gives me a hand. Then I get dressed and we take all the stuff back with us. Later, I use the diving helmet as a project in Science, get an A for it. I write it up as if it really worked. Actually it did.

To try out Birdy's crazy wings we have to wait till the wind's blowing from the right direction. This wind has to blow on a Saturday or a Sunday when we don't have any school. Birdy has the whole thing planned out with written instructions so it'll only take the two of us to pull it off. He's already gone down and cleared a path about a hundred yards long for the bike to make its run. He's cleaned off all the tin cans and used a shovel to fill in any dips and knock down any bumps. I hope nobody saw him flattening out the top of the dump; they'll figure for sure he's crazy. I go down and look at it; it's like a short narrow runway for an airplane; in fact, Birdy's rigged a little wind sock with an old, starched silk stocking.

Birdy doesn't want anybody to see his machine, so we take it down at night and hide it up where we used to have the pigeon loft. We still have the rope ladder; Birdy's old man didn't find that. Everything's set.

Finally, after about three weeks, the wind is blowing perfectly on a Friday night. We make arrangements to meet at home plate at seven o'clock the next morning. When I get there, Birdy's already waiting with his crazy bicycle and the platform hooked to the front. We've been practicing riding around the block with him standing up there. This itself is a hot trick both for Birdy and for me. The kids in the neighborhood are laughing their asses off watching us. We don't care; they're just a bunch of morons anyway. I give Dan McClusky a clout on the side of the head, for the sheer hell of it. Nobody can hurt an Irishman by hitting him on the head.

When we get down to the dump, Birdy straps on those wings and runs around a little flapping them. He'd run fast into the wind, jump, and flap like mad. It does look as if he's getting some lift. He says he can feel it. He tells me he hasn't eaten any dinner or breakfast. He's been dieting for a month so he's thin as a rail. I try to talk him out of the idea again but no go. He's all fired up to fly out over that creek. He really thinks he's going to take off and fly into the blue. I'm glad nobody else is around; they'd lock us up.

Birdy's figured it all out. He has a special stand to hold the bike so he can climb up on the rack while I hand him the wings. Then I help hold the bike, steady it, while he straps them on. He looks super weird standing on the front of the bike with those wings on. He looks like a gigantic Rolls Royce radiator cap, that's what.

There's a mark he's made at the edge of the hill. I'm supposed to throw on the brakes there and he's going to spring off the bike. He goes over everything with me again. He should be nervous. Here he is about ready to jump off into the air at about thirty-five miles an hour over a forty-foot drop with all that hardware on his back. Not Birdy. All I can see is he's anxious to get started.

I start pedaling the bike like mad, trying to keep on the path. After I get moving, I'm going straight. I have powerful legs and I'm giving it all I have. It's one of those things you don't just half do. Birdy's crouched in front of me, wings outspread, ready to spring off. We're really moving when we reach the line and I hit the brakes.

Birdy springs off and over the edge. He's flapping those wings like a mechanical seagull. For a few seconds he goes straight out, his legs spread, soaring, a gigantic, silver winged bird. He actually begins to go up, but he's losing forward momentum and he goes into a stall. Out there, way off the hill, he begins to drop, feet first, with the wings spread and still flapping but flapping sideways. They're designed to flap down, when Birdy's flat out. Now he can't get his feet up again. He's dropping down into the creek, flapping his wings uselessly all the way.

I run after him. I'm sliding down the dump hill, getting ashes into my shoes and all over me. I scare the bejesus out of a rat. When I get there, Birdy's standing up in the middle of the creek unbuckling his wings.

"You OK, Birdy?"

"Yeah, I'm fine."

"That's what you said after you fell off the gas tank. You sure you're OK?"

"Sure I'm sure. When you only weigh ninety-three pounds, you don't fall very fast; especially if you have as much air surface as I did. I didn't come down fast at all."

Birdy just isn't real. He climbs out of the water, adjusts a few vanes that'd gotten bent and wants to try again. I tell him he's going to get himself killed and I don't want any part of it.

We scramble up the side of the dump hill, more ashes in the old shoes, dragging the wings with us. We get up there and Birdy tries to show me, drawing it out with a stick in the ashes on his runway, how with his light weight, accelerating at thirty-two feet per second per second, after he's fallen twenty feet or so, his downward velocity isn't going to increase. He tells me he's already learned to jump from a twenty-foot height by collapsing his legs and rolling. He gets the wind knocked out of him, but that's all. He's actually convinced himself he can jump off any height and not hurt himself. Now, that's really nuts.

He tells me to look at newsreels of people falling off high places or jumping into firemen's nets. They start accelerating fast at first but then they reach a certain speed and seem to float. He says you can throw a cat out a three- or four-story window and it can land fine and that's like a twenty- or thirty-story window for a person. It's all dependent on weight and surface and density he says, and more than that, knowing you can do it. I ask him why it is they die when they hit the ground; people, that is. He says you can fall off a curb and kill yourself if you don't know what you're doing.

While we're hassling this out, we haul the wings and the bike back to Birdy's yard and put them in the garage. We take out a little time to look around for the baseballs but don't find anything. She's got to be selling them. Birdy shows me where he has his freaky pigeon suit hidden. I ask him if, when he learns to fly, he's going to start wearing it, like Clark Kent slipping into his Superman costume.

Birdy's not fighting me anymore about taking another flight right away. He's decided he needs to do some more work on the wings and strengthen his arms. He wants to practice gliding before he tries flying again. He says he has to arch his back while he's flapping. He'd done all his working out on the sawhorse and forgotten he needs to keep his body out stiff in the air. I try once more to talk him out of the whole cockeyed business but he's not listening to me. He's planning some kind of brace to go under his stomach that he can arch against.

He's already talking up those three or four seconds when he seemed to be flying so you'd think he'd flown around the world a couple times.

When we get home he shows me how he can jump off his back porch roof without hurting himself. You wouldn't believe it. He hunches himself down, springs out like a diver with his arms spread, then, in midair, pulls himself together, pushes his feet in front of him, just before he reaches the ground, then collapses both against the direction of his jump and the vertical drop. He says the more horizontal movement you can develop, the easier it is to absorb the vertical force.

He takes me upstairs to show me his drawings and calculations on this. He's talking vectors and points of impact and trying to make it clear to me. I can't believe this is the same Birdy in Algebra with me who's having a hard time pulling B's.

We sit around in his room for a while and he makes me watch his birds through the binoculars. He's really built a great little aviary under his bed. I don't know how the hell he talked his old lady into it. My mother'd skin my ass. Birdy wants me to watch how the birds take off and land. He's convinced the birds are in the air before they even use their wings. I can't see it. Birdy has quick eyes and he's been watching the birds a lot. I can't even pick up what he's talking about.

He's named this one skinny bird Alfonso, after me. It looks like a mad, hungry sparrow. I tell Birdy it's OK so long as he spells it with a "ph." I'm the one and only Alfonso with an "f" around here. Birdy says it doesn't matter because that isn't his real name anyway, it's only what he calls him. I ask, "What is the secret name?" Birdy says he doesn't know. He tells me he doesn't know enough canary talk to ask him yet. Yet! he say and he doesn't blink, just wiggles his crazy eyes. He isn't smiling and I know he's not kidding.

It's hard to figure if somebody like Birdy is crazy or not.

$\mathcal{N}$ext morning I decide to take the risk. I open the door to Birdie's cage. Then I go out of the aviary and sit behind my binoculars. I can always go in and rescue her if it gets too bad.

Birdie hops out right away. Alfonso is up on the top perch. Birdie sees I've put in new bath water, so, after a few inquisitive queeps, she hops down to take her bath. She's completely ignoring him. He stands up there on his perch menacing. I'm expecting any minute he'll swoop down.

Birdie goes through her whole bath routine but he doesn't move; he doesn't take his eyes off her, either. It's the last thing I expected. Birdie flies up to the top of her little cage and starts preening her feathers.

After some minutes of watching her, the dive-bomber zooms down, has himself a few seeds and a little drink. He hop-flies around the wet places from Birdie's bath. He hops up onto the edge of the bath, wiggles his face around in it as if he's going to take a bath himself, then decides against it. He goes over and has a few more seeds. I'd put in some treat food too, and he gobbles some of that.

Then he does his straight-up jump and with a few wing flips re-establishes himself at the top of the aviary. He perches there and stretches his wings a couple times, trying to look bored. He wipes his beak about ten times on the perch to show what a big shot he is, then does that kind of bird gargle where they open their beaks wide and wiggle their tongues around. He flips his tail up and takes a couple quick pecks at his asshole. I'm getting bored myself, especially when I'd been expecting an attempted murder, at least.

Then, seemingly for no reason, he starts to sing. He starts quietly enough, going through a few bars just slightly more powerful than before, but gradually increasing the volume and the emotional content. A certain harshness begins to dominate. Meanwhile, he's started rocking back and forth on his thin legs and agitatedly moving the length of the perch. He sings leaning forward with his throat fully extended. His wings are slightly lifted from his body and his stomach is pulled taut. Altogether he's damned impressive. He impresses me, that is, but apparently not Birdie. She's just finishing off the last little soft feathers on her back.

Now, Alfonso starts holding notes. He holds the same note till I think he's going to fall off the perch. It seems as if he doesn't breathe. He's in a regular frenzy. Suddenly, he pounces down to where Birdie is basking. He lands about a foot from her, continuing his song during the drop and while he's standing there. Birdie looks over at him. He begins his pursuit immediately. Birdie jumps up and flies to the perch he's just abandoned. He's right after her, in full song. His whole body is quivering.

It gets to be a regular WWI dogfight with Birdie finding no place she can land without his swarming all over her. He even manages somehow to harry her in midflight. It's obvious he wants to mate but equally obvious that Birdie is totally unprepared for his cave-bird tactics. At last, she makes the mistake of flying into her cage. He goes right in after her and there's such a scramble, I hurry into the aviary and put my hand in the cage to rescue Birdie. He's got her trapped so she can't escape. She doesn't resist but I get a few good pecks on the back of my hand from the tiger himself. I intend to close the door and keep him in there, but before I can do it, he's flown out and is up on the highest perch menacing me, with his wings lifted and his beak open.

I go out of the aviary and close the door to keep him in there, at least. I let Birdie loose. She flares her feathers, gives me a queep, a QReep and a couple peeps, then flies over to the wire of the aviary. Now, she's flirting. She knows she's safe so she's going to tease him.

She flies to one spot and Alfonso, singing madly, swoops over to her, then she flies a foot or so away from the wire and lands in another place. He flies to meet her there. This goes on for about five minutes. Then he flies up to his perch again. I guess he's pooped or maybe he's tired of having her make fun of him. Birdie hangs on the wire and queeps at him, very plaintive, very demanding.

After a few minutes, he starts singing in a normal tone. We listen. He really can sing. Then, gradually, he gets all worked up again; it's as if his own singing turns him on. This time he flies down to the floor. He stands there on the floor and sings up to where Birdie's hanging. He looks like an opera singer; standing in the light on the white sand, turning left and right and taking short steps backwards and forwards as he sings. It's the first time I've ever seen a canary do something like walking.

Birdie flies down to the floor on the outside of the aviary and looks through the wire at him. He keeps singing and slowly struts over to her, giving her the full tenor treatment. She doesn't move. He gets to the edge of the wire and they aren't an inch apart. He's singing wildly. Birdie looks and listens then starts giving her little whimpering "feed-me" signal. She squats and flips her wings quickly, opening her mouth and pressing it through the wires.

Alfonso stops singing and looks at her. He can't seem to figure what this is all about. He cocks his head and looks down into her mouth, listens to her and starts singing again. Poor Birdie. He begins rocking back and forth, leaning down till his throat is touching the floor. He lifts his head up and down with the power of his passion. When, at last, he can't bear it anymore, he throws himself against the bars of the aviary.

This frightens Birdie and she flies away. He climbs up the bars of the aviary trying to watch her. She flies over to the mirror on the dresser and looks at herself. He hangs there for a while, then flies down onto the floor again and takes a drink. All that passion must've made him thirsty.

This whole ritual happens over and over, all day long. At the critical moment, Birdie wants to be fed and Alfonso can't bring himself to do it or doesn't know how. Frustrated, I put Birdie back in her cage and leave the room.

That evening, I let Birdie out while I'm drawing a new design for my wing. I'm at my desk, my desk lamp is the only light and it's practically dark in the aviary. Still, there's enough light so I can see Alfonso hanging on the side of the cage. He starts singing, low, smoothly. When he stops, Birdie begins whimpering again, fanning her wings. At last he does it. He feeds her through the bars. It sounds so satisfying. He throws back his head to bring up food from his crop, then gently puts it into her open beak. With each beakful, there's a rise in tiny peeps from Birdie, and then, a moment's pause while she swallows. He keeps it up till he's given all he has. Birdie continues her insistent peeping and shimmying around so he flies down for more food. He comes back and does it all again.

After this, he flies onto the top of her cage and sings. He sings as if he's trying to say something. There's all of asking in his voice and not the "Come here, Baby" sound he'd been giving us up till now. Birdie sits perfectly still and listens. I do too. There's tremendous variety in the paths of his singing. There are certain kinds of things he does well; these he repeats but at different volumes or different tones and in all kinds of variations.

There's open air in his song, the power of wings and the softness of feathers. He's telling how it will be if she'll only let him put his little dong into her little hole. It's clear as any love song. He sings of things he could never have seen or known in the aviary at Mr. Lincoln's. These things must be memories in his blood carried through in his song. There's the song of rivers and the sound of water and the song of fields and seeds in their natural places. It's a song I'll never forget. It's with this song I began to understand something of canary. Canary isn't a language like ours with individual words, or words put into sentences. In the singing, you let your mind go, not think, and it comes to you, clearer than words. It comes as if you'd thought it yourself. Canary is much more feeling, more abstract than any language. Listening to Alfonso that night I found out things I knew must be but I'd never known. It was the song of someone who knows how to fly.

The next day's Sunday and after mass I let Birdie into the aviary. She glides down and hops over to the food. Alfonso sees her and swoops down immediately. I think it's going to start all over again, but he stands on the other side of the food dish and eats a few seeds. Birdie hops to the bath and starts her morning ablutions. Alfonso stands nearby to watch and when she sprinkles water she showers him. He flies up to the first perch, then flies down again. He hops to the bath dish and jumps in. He really splashes, scattering water all over the aviary, tossing it up over his back with his beak in a way Birdie'd never done. Then, they get in the water together, in and out, until there's no water left in the dish. They both fly around the aviary wildly, drying off. Birdie's entered into the spirit of this frantic bathing style. The feathers around Alfonso's beak are ruffled and you can barely see his eyes. He's gotten himself so wet, his feathers are heavy, hanging from his body. He looks really bedraggled. He keeps flying back and forth long after Birdie's quit and is cleaning up. He rubs his wet face against the perch and against the bars of the cage. He flies down and rubs his face on the wall, of all things. It's obvious he doesn't bathe often and doesn't like it when he does.

At last he's clean and dry. They both eat again and she starts whimpering and giving her "feed-me" signal. He starts to feed her but this gets him so excited he begins singing and then goes into a little dance. He dances around in circles beside her while he holds a single note. He dips his head up and down, stomping his feet to some hidden rhythm. I figure, here we go again.

While he's doing this, Birdie begins her own little dance. She's squatting, whimpering, twisting around to keep lined up with him while he dances. All in one movement, Alfonso flies up over her and hovers while he lowers his dong under her upraised tail and into her hole. It lasts only a few seconds and he's hovering in the air all the time. The only real point of contact is where he fits in.

When he's finished, he lands beside her, squats and starts giving the "feed-me" signal himself. They twirl beside each other for half a minute alternately feeding and being fed. Then he does it again. This time he doesn't sing and there's only the pleased whimpering of Birdie and the sounds of his wings as he pumps the air to hold himself over her. Her wings beat in a counterpoint to his and there's a great trembling of air. It's something to think how much a bird can flap its wings without moving an inch and how, when he wants to fly, the quickest, simplest flick of wings transports him straight up, twenty, thirty times his length. Flying is much more than flapping wings.

Now Birdie goes berserk. She flies around the cage, peeping little peeps and flapping her wings as if she can't stand still. She seems too excited even to eat properly. She goes down, eats one seed, then, looking as if she's forgotten something, flies madly all over again. She ducks into the old cage about every five minutes, inspecting and making sure. Then she starts tearing paper up from the bottom of the cage and carrying pieces of it around. She begins storing these pieces of paper in the corners of the aviary and in her cage. Every half hour or so, Alfonso recovers enough to chase after Birdie, feed her and they do it again. It's a hectic Sunday afternoon.

The next day, Monday, I buy a wire strainer without a handle, about four inches in diameter at the top. I wire this into the small cage. All the books say this makes the best kind of nest because it doesn't harbor lice. Then I scissor off the top of a burlap bag, cut it into squares about two inches each way and shred it into two-inch length strings. I put bunches of this stuff in different corners of the aviary. Birdie attacks this new challenge with vigor. She starts by scattering it all over the aviary, then she picks up a piece and flies back and forth till she forgets she has it in her beak and drops it. She seems to think it's some kind of new game. She's interested but has no idea what practical use she can make of it.

Two days pass and I begin to get worried. Usually, the egg will be laid within four days of fertilization. I'd read about birds who lay their eggs on the floor; all kinds of crazy things. Birds, like people, have been living in cages so long they've forgotten many things they should do naturally.

On the third day Alfonso takes over. For the first time he picks up a piece of burlap. He flies straight to the nest and drops it in. Birdie watches with obvious incomprehension. Then Alfonso jumps into the strainer-nest and wiggles himself around as if he's taking a bath. He jumps out. Birdie's followed him into the cage. She has a piece of burlap in her beak. Alfonso jumps into the nest and demonstrates again. Birdie jumps into the nest holding the string in her beak. She jumps out again. Alfonso pulls the string out of her beak and drops it into the nest. Birdie looks at him as if he's some kind of nut and flies out of the small cage to play with the strings again. Alfonso gets into the nest and waits for her. Birdie comes back with two pieces in her beak. Alfonso gets out of the nest and Birdie jumps in. Alfonso jumps on top of Birdie and starts singing, pumping and pecking her on the neck. Birdie varies between whimpering and trying to escape. Alfonso gets off, squats and feeds Birdie in the nest. Then he sings to her. Birdie tries to get up on the edge of the nest but Alfonso forces her back and does the whole singing, pumping, pecking routine again. He flies down to get more burlap.

Birdie finally gets the idea. She jumps up on the edge of the nest, then back in again. She snuggles down in it. She jumps out again, then back in. By this time, Alfonso's arrived. She takes the burlap from his beak and drops the pieces into the nest. She jumps in on top of them and wiggles around. I hope that at last we're on our way.

That night, after chow, I meet the CO who's the orderly on Birdy's floor. We get to talking. He tells me his name is Phil Renaldi; he's Italian but not Sicilian. His grandparents came from around Napoli. He invites me over to eat some fruitcake he just got from home. I'm still not sure if he's queer or not but I go. What should I care if he's queer; I'm not all that sure about myself. Maybe I'll get a chance to ask him about what it is to be crazy.

He's got a great place. It's a little squad room, walled off and independent. It's like the platoon sergeant's room at Jackson. He has it all to himself. Renaldi's got this room fixed up almost like home. He has a record player on a table at the end of his bed and another table in the center of the room. He's rigged a light with a lamp shade hanging from the ceiling over the table. He even has a little hot plate and a tea kettle.

One of the things I've never gotten used to in the army is bare light bulbs. At home, my mother has all the lamps covered with colored lamp shades. It gives our house a good Italian look; a place to eat fettucini or zeppoli. The army has bare light bulbs high up in the ceilings. They flatten everything out and make it even more depressing than it is.

Renaldi's made his lamp shade out of some orange paper. It gives the place a warm, civilian look. He brings down the fruitcake and it turns out his girlfriend, not his mother, sent it. He comes from a place called Steubenville, Ohio. His girl is there and writes him every day. He shows me bundles of letters, enough to fill a mail bag. He has them stored in boxes under his bed. He shows me some pictures of her; Italian girl, going to get fat with the first baby.

I don't know how to bring up the idea of what it is that makes somebody crazy. I'm fishing around and somehow we get sidetracked on the whole CO business. I'm ready to listen. I tell him I joined the State Guard and then enlisted. I can hardly believe it myself, now. He's curious about why. He's not being hot-shit or anything, he's just honest-to-God interested. Like I said, I'm ready to listen but this guy's a champion listener. He's really interested.

Not many people are interested in what somebody else is thinking, or what they have to say. The best you can hope for is they'll listen to you just so you'll have to listen to them. Everybody's loading shit on everybody else. Sometimes, somebody'll act like they're listening, but they're only waiting back in their minds for you to say something, something they can jump on or kick off on themselves. For me, conversation's usually a bore.

Renaldi is truly listening. He wants to hear. You get the feeling you're doing him a favor by telling him things. He listens as if what you're saying is interesting to him and he asks the questions you want asked exactly when the right time comes. This Renaldi is some kind of mental enema. I come close to spilling it all. I manage to hold back at the last minute. Maybe he seems this way because I need somebody to talk to.

Renaldi starts by telling me how hard it is for his parents. He's their only son and the only one in his neighborhood who went CO. His mother doesn't get to hang a blue star in her window. Some ladies in the neighborhood sent her a blue banner with a yellow star on it. This was yellow, not gold. If you're lucky enough to have a son or husband or brother killed in the war, you get to hang a gold star in your window and you're a "gold-star mother/sister/father/wife." These ladies call Renaldi's mother the "yellow-star mother." She writes Renaldi about things like this or how she found shit on the porch or spread on the doorknob. Renaldi tells how, a couple times he's almost given in. His girlfriend keeps it secret that she writes to him and he writes her care of General Delivery.

We agree the only crazy thing is wars. That's where I should've gotten him off onto the crazy business but I missed it. Renaldi turns on the hot plate and pours some water into the tea kettle from a jerry can. We talk some more.

Renaldi's twenty-five and was taking his master's in philosophy at Columbia when they tried to draft him. He has the idea you can only stop things like wars one person at a time. He says, nobody's going to outlaw them. He asks me if most of the guys in my outfit wanted to fight. I couldn't think of one who was charging in there for the old war after the first artillery came in. He wants to know how it was back in the States before we went over. To be perfectly honest, the only person I could think of who wanted to get into combat was me.

Then, we get on the atom bomb they've just dropped. This is something Renaldi's all hung up on. To me, it's what ended the Japanese war; probably one of the best things that ever happened. I couldn't care less how many Japs got killed, or whether it was one at a time or a couple thousand. The best and easiest way as far as I'm concerned.

"Yes, but think of it, Al. They bombed women and children who weren't involved in the war at all!"

"So what's the difference, they're all Japs. If we're fighting Japs, we kill Japs."

"OK, Al, but soldiers choose to fight; these were innocent victims."

I tell him I can't buy that. Sure, kill off nuts like me, hostile assholes looking for trouble, but most guys don't want to fight any war; they're victims like everybody else. They're out there carrying guns because of how old they are and the kind of plumbing they have. Women, old men and even kids make wars happen as much as anybody. Everybody isn't like Renaldi and Birdy; and they even got Birdy. You can't build a world around them either, they're too rare.

Renaldi's still giving me a fishy stare, so I decide to tell about Birdy and my old man. That's a story I hope will give some idea what I'm talking about. Probably I could just recite the multiplication tables and Renaldi'd eat it up.

He cuts us each a piece of fruitcake and pours out some more tea. Can you beat it? Tea! Six months ago, nobody could've convinced me this guy wasn't queer.

There was a used car lot on the way up Long Lane to Sixty-ninth Street. Every Friday evening, when we took our books back to the library, Birdy and I used to stop by there to look at the cars. We were both motor freaks. The cars themselves didn't interest us much—in fact, Birdy swore he'd never drive a car—but the way motors worked did. We'd already played around with small airplane motors, and the motor from a bombed-out motor scooter, and we fixed Mr. Harding's lawn mower.

My old man bought a new car every year and kept it parked in front of our house to show what a big shot he was. I had to wash and simonize the beast once a week; Birdy used to help. We'd read all the manuals that came with these cars. My father bought De Sotos because the mob had an agency in Philly, so with the trade-in, he got them for practically nothing. My mother's brother is one of the big capos in Philly and he's the one who arranged it. We were the only ones on the block who had anything like a new car. Birdy's mother and father didn't even know how to drive. Birdy's father rode to school on the school bus.

Anyway, we used to clean the sparks, check the timing, clean the points, adjust the carburetor more than those cars ever needed. We kept that motor looking as if it'd never left the showroom floor.

Birdy and I were always shopping cars. We knew all the horsepowers and gear ratios, length of piston stroke and cylinder dimensions. Either of us could tell almost any car just by listening to the motor, not seeing the car at all.

One Friday evening we were nosing around in the car lot, looking at the new trade-ins, and there was a fantastic car. It was a 1915 Stutz Bearcat. We couldn't figure how it got there.

It didn't run at all and the tires were flat. Schwartz, that's the name of the guy who ran the lot, said he had to tow it in. He gave twenty-five bucks on it to somebody who bought a 1938 Dodge. Birdy and I couldn't keep our hands or minds off that automobile. It had an eight-cylinder engine and the frame was in perfect condition. We negotiated around for two weeks and got it for thirty dollars; it cost another three dollars having it towed to our garage. The old man said we could use the garage till winter came and it got too cold to leave his car outside.

We worked like fiends on that machine. We tore the motor all the way down. The pistons were frozen in the cylinders. We unfroze them and milled out the cylinders. We put in new rings and rockers. Birdy tooled replacement pieces for ones we couldn't buy. He did it in the machine shop at school where he made his wings. We took off all the paint, pounded out the dents and cleaned up the chrome. It had solid chrome, not plate. We got new inner tubes and inflated the tires; there were genuine wooden spoked wheels.

After a thousand tries we got the motor to turn over. The clutch, transmission, everything else, were in great condition. We tuned that motor to perfection. We patched up, cleaned, and Neetsfoot-oiled all the upholstery and refurbished the wooden dash with sandpaper and varnish. God, it was beautiful. We sanded it down to the metal, then painted it silver-gray. We worked on it for three months.

When we cranked her up, she made tremendous resonant, deep motor sounds; the whole garage vibrated. We rolled her out and drove her up and down the alley. Neither one of us had a driver's license. The car wasn't registered and didn't have an inspection sticker. It was strictly illegal. We knew we had something valuable but we didn't want to sell it. We loved that car.

I used to dream about it; I still do sometimes. I dream we're touring it through a beautiful warm landscape, maybe in some foreign country like France. There're no billboards and the road is lined with trees and the fields are full of flowers.

We decide to get it past the Pennsylvania state inspection and get it registered so we can have a license. My old man says he'll take it down and go through the inspection for us. We're too young to own a car. The car gets passed and put in my old man's name. I remember the license number: QRT 645.

While Birdy is over at his place that spring, taking care of the birds, I'm either in the garage with the car or down in the cellar working out with weights. I can already press over a hundred fifty pounds. I'm working on muscle control, too. I can make a rope with my stomach and twist it from one side to the other. I keep asking Birdy to punch me hard in the stomach so he can test me, but he won't do it.

About two months after we have it registered and licensed, I go down to the garage after school to put on a new steering wheel cover. The car is gone! I'm sure somebody stole it! I run upstairs and the old man is sitting in the living room reading the paper. He sits there with his legs crossed. They're so short and thick at the thigh that the leg on top sticks straight out. He's wearing black low shoes and white silk socks. He has something against colored or woolen socks.

"Somebody stole the car!"

"Nobody stole it. I sold it."

He doesn't even look up from the newspaper.

"Aw, come on! Quit kidding! You didn't sell it! Who'd you sell it to?"

"Your Uncle Nicky came over with one of his 'friends' and the friend wanted the car; he thought it'd be a real gag and offered me a C note. What'd ya think I'm gonna do anyhow; get myself in trouble over some junk heap of a car?"

He looks up at me for the last part, then he turns his paper again, bangs on it to straighten it, and looks away. Uncle Nicky is my mother's capo brother. I turn to her.

"Is that really true? Did he actually sell our car to one of Uncle Nicky's gangster friends?"

My mother's ironing in the doorway between the kitchen and dining room. I don't know why she always irons there. She couldn't be more in the way. Come to think of it; I do know why. She wants to keep an eye on the cooking and at the same time be able to talk with the old man.

She starts talking in Italian, actually in Credenzia, the Sicilian dialect. She always does this when she has something private she wants to say. It's stupid because I understand everything she says. I can't talk the stuff, but I understand. They know that. She tells my father to give me the money.

"He don't know what to do with no hundred dollars. He'll just get in trouble again. I'll put it in the bank. When he wants money he can ask me for it. I don't want no more of this running away stuff."

He crosses his legs the other way at the same time he opens and closes the newspaper again. He reads a newspaper folded in quarters like he's riding in a subway or something and doesn't want to take up too much space.

"Half of it isn't even my money. Half of that car belongs to Birdy."

He doesn't look up at me. My mother comes in from the ironing board.

"Give him the money, Vittorio. It's stealing to take somebody else's money."

This is in Credenzia again. The old man looks up at my mother. He's enjoying being the big shit.

"I don't have to give him or anybody nothin'. That car is mine; it's in my name. I can sell it to anybody I want."

He pauses to let that sink in. Then he shifts his weight and pulls out his roll. He keeps his money like that, in a hard roll in his side pocket, big bills on top. He peels off five tens. He has that hundred dollar bill on the outside, but he pulls the tens off from underneath. He has a piece of elastic, not a rubber band, he keeps it wrapped in. It's the kind of elastic my mother makes her garters with. He holds out the fifty bucks to me.

"Here, give this to that wiggle-eyed friend of yours. I'm warnin' ya, he's gonna get you in trouble yet. That kid ain't right in the head."

I hold back. What a shitty thing to do. He re-rolls his roll, slips the elastic over it, tilts and slides it back in his pocket. He's holding out those curled bills in his hand. I don't want to take them. I stand there. My mother turns away; she's done all she can and she knows it. My old man'll bop anybody if he takes a mind to it. He looks at me hard. He's not really mad yet but he's annoyed.

"Ya don't want it? Well, don't tell your friend I didn't try to give him something for his share of that junk heap."

He's shifting to reach into his pocket. I know if he puts it back on the roll and in his pocket I'll never see it again. I reach out and take the fifty bucks. He doesn't even pay attention, just grunts like I'm robbing him and goes back to reading.

I take off for Birdy's. When I tell him, he asks me to tell the whole thing again. He keeps making me repeat parts. His eyes are wiggling like crazy. I try to give him the money but he'll only take half. He actually takes twenty, tells me to get the ten changed and he'll get the other five then. He's thinking about something else.

Then he asks me if I can find out who it is who bought our car. I tell him there's no chance; if this guy's in the mob, we'll never find him. Birdy says he's going to come and talk to my father. This is suicide; I try to stop him. There's nothing he can do. My father'll kill him; he doesn't like Birdy anyway. But, there's no way to stop Birdy. I tell him he's going alone, I'm not going to get all splattered with his blood. Birdy's not listening, he's on his way.

Well, my mother comes to the door. She never shows much on her face but she doesn't smile. I'm hanging back on the porch step. Birdy asks if he can talk to my father. My mother lets him in. I run around the block to the back and let myself in by the cellar. I come up through the kitchen. My mother's still ironing in the doorway. I can hear them in the living room.

"Whaddaya mean you want your car back?"

"You had no right to sell that car, Mr. Columbato. That car belongs to Al and me. We did not want to sell it. It is worth much more than a hundred dollars."

"Get outta here, kid; that car was in my name and I could sell it to anybody I want. Go 'way. I'm tryin' ta read my paper."

Birdy doesn't move. I can tell my old man is getting mad. He's jiggling the top leg he has crossed. That's a bad sign, like a cat twitching its tail. My mother stands the iron up on end and watches.

"Mr. Columbato, would you tell me the name of the man who thinks he bought our car?"

My old man just ignores him. His leg keeps jiggling. Birdy stands there. I'm expecting all hell to break loose. My mother turns and tells me to get Birdy out before my father does something. I can't move. Birdy keeps standing there. My old man, without looking up, says, "Look kid. You'd better get outta here or I'm gonna call the cops!"

"Thank you, Mr. Columbato. I was going to do that myself. I want to report a stolen car."

That does it! The old man throws the paper down and jumps up! Birdy doesn't back off an inch. The old man isn't very tall, not much taller than Birdy, but he's at least twice as thick. He shakes his fist in front of Birdy's face. He shakes so hard, his hair, which is slicked back with Wildroot, jumps up and down in back.

"You callin' me a crook? You sayin' I stole that junk heap?"

Birdy looks him in the eyes, right through that fist. I wonder if my father can hit him. Birdy isn't even moving. He stands there like a stuck feather.

"I think you made a mistake, Mr. Columbato. You sold a car that wasn't yours. You didn't understand. If you will tell me the name of the man you sold it to, I can tell him what happened and give him his money back."

For a minute, my old man can't say anything. His eyes are bulging. I know he wants to pick Birdy up and throw him out the door but he's beginning to get suspicious.

"I'm tellin' ya, kid. The guy that bought that car ain't never goin' to give it back. You give him any trouble and you'll wind up in a concrete shirt at the bottom of a river somewhere."

Birdy acts as if he doesn't even hear him.

"If you would just give me his name, Mr. Columbato, I can contact him directly and I won't have to go to the police."

My father starts his jabbing routine. He can hit so hard with the point of his middle finger just on the soft part under the collar bone, it's like a bullet going through you. Birdy stands there taking it. He doesn't move. I can't believe the old man's using his full force. He stops and stares at Birdy; I can see he has his hand down at his side now itching to give one to Birdy. I'm beginning to think it'll be the old immovable object and the irresistible force.

"You see, Mr. Columbato, Al and I have a signed receipt of purchase for that car from Mr. Schwartz. It is officially our property."

This is pure bullshit. We don't have anything from Schwartz.

"You agreed to have the automobile officially inspected and registered, so it's in your name, but you are not the official owner; you have no evidence of purchase from us. It is still our property. Now, if you will just tell me the name of the man who bought the car, I can explain this to him."

The old man sits down. I can't believe it. Birdy's still standing there.

"I'm sure the man who bought the car would rather not have the police investigating this. It could be embarrassing for everybody."

The old man is actually breaking out in a sweat. There are beads of water across his forehead and over his lips.

"Why you want to be such a hard nose, kid? Look, I'll do you a favor." He tilts, reaches into his pocket and pulls out the roll. He peels off another fifty bucks and holds it out to Birdy. Birdy doesn't move. The old man waves the money.

"That's all I got for it, kid. Take it and get outta here. Leave me alone, huh?"

My mother's moved into the room. She takes the money from my father and grabs hold of Birdy's arm. He comes with her and she leads him back to the kitchen. Birdy's face is chalk white, his lips are blue, and his whole body is shaking. My mother talks English to Birdy.

"Boy, you take the money. I get more from Al's uncle, my brother. Don't make trouble. How much money you want?"

Birdy looks at her. Tears are coming into his eyes. He takes the money from her and hands it to me. He shakes his head and goes down the cellar steps, then on out the back. I try to follow him but my mother stops me.

When I finish telling this story to Renaldi he sits there, looking straight into me, listening. All along he's nodded his head or let me know other ways that he's listening and interested. I find it hard to go on with the story sometimes because I fill up. My nerves still aren't quite right.

So, my mother gives me another hundred dollars about a week later. She really forces me to take it and swears she got it from her brother. Her brother'd give her ten thousand dollars if she asked for it and he wouldn't even ask what for.

I give it all to Birdy and tell him Nicky'd kicked in with two hundred. You see, Birdy's still sore. He figures the car is worth at least three hundred and he's been checking things out to find who bought the car and he's going to call the cops. He's even written to the department of motor vehicles to find out what name the car is registered in. I tell him they'll kill him but he couldn't care less. When Birdy's got his mind on something, especially when he's pissed like that, it's hard to turn him off.

It must be almost three weeks later when I go over to his place and he's working out with his wings, flapping in his back yard. I see giant black and blue marks on his chest. It takes me a few seconds to realize that's where the old man gave him those finger pokes. The old man wasn't holding back; Birdy was just pushing forward on each poke. He was probably practically breaking the old man's finger.

I stop. I'm tired of telling about it. I don't think Renaldi's getting what I'm talking about anyway. I'm not even so sure myself.

"Gee, Al. You really ought to tell Weiss this stuff. Maybe

he could understand some and be able to help Birdy. I don't think Weiss even knows he's called Birdy. That should mean something to him. You owe it to Birdy."

"Not me. Don't you tell him either! I'd rather Birdy stay crazy than have a shit like Weiss bring him back. If I came back from being crazy and saw somebody like Weiss standing there in front of me, I'd probably cry the rest of my life."

That's where I should've asked about "being crazy" but I didn't. I figure Renaldi doesn't know any more than I do. We all have our own private kinds of craziness. If it gets in the way of enough people, they call you crazy. Sometimes you just can't take it anymore yourself, so you tell somebody else you're crazy and they agree to take care of you.

Since the mating, Alfonso is less hostile toward me. I wouldn't say he's friendly, but there's a form of truce. Actually, to be honest, he more or less ignores me. I don't know what Birdie told him, or how much canaries can get across that kind of thought, but he accepts the idea I'm not going to hurt him.

The nest building proceeds quickly now. They're up and down, in and out, all day. Alfonso is allowed to help with the carrying but he isn't to put anything in the nest. Birdie has definite ideas about how things should be done. He'll come up with some burlap and she'll take it out of his beak. Apparently, Alfonso only has the concept, he doesn't have the skills to build.

When I come in to peer at the nest, Birdie makes no fuss and seems proud of herself. She isn't exactly weaving the little strings, but she's overlapping them carefully in such a way that it makes a compact, formed mass. Alfonso isn't so happy about me sticking my nose into things. He stands on top of the cage while I peer in, and gives me his most threatening look. Birdie's shaping the nest as a deep hole somewhat smaller than her breast dimension and turning it in slightly to close at the top. The inside is shaped like the hole for a small vase. Tuesday night I can see it's finished.

On Wednesday, when I come home from school, I'm

shocked to see the entire nest torn apart and strewn over the floor of the aviary. *Holy God, what next! it's enough to drive a person batty.* The new nest is under construction. She's more frantic this time. *I think if Alfonso didn't feed her once in a while she'd starve.* It's up and down, back and forth; carefully picking the right pieces out of the piles; flying up; placing them even more carefully in the nest. Each time she takes a moment's snuggling to check dimensions and then goes out again. *I can't even guess what could've been wrong with the first nest.* She makes poor Alfonso work like a slave. He's getting no creative satisfaction out of the thing but she forces him. He's playing hod carrier to her bricklayer. Twice, I see him fly up to his favorite top perch to do a little singing and take a rest. Birdie chases after him and forces him back to the grind.

This time, as she comes to finishing the nest, she starts fraying the individual threads into light brown fuzz. With this she lines the bottom of the nest and the upper ramparts. It's beautiful. Then, apparently, even this isn't soft enough, so she starts chasing Alfonso around the cage, snitching feathers from his breast. The first few times he lets her get away with it, but then he's had enough. When she makes another pass at him, he gives her a couple good pecks on the head and chases her around the aviary till she flies back into the small cage and settles onto the nest. He flies in after her, goes over and feeds her on the nest. She stays there while he sings the soft, tender song he sang the first night I heard him. I know from the song that the nest is finished.

Canaries living in a cage are like human beings in that they're not living a completely natural life. They have a life which is safer than natural life would be. For this reason, they don't get enough physical challenge and experience in survival. Also, birds, which in nature would die, are kept alive by the bird breeder because he has other interests than survival, such as color or song or special shape or something else. Gradually, the cage bird loses much of its vitality, its capacity to survive.

For example: in nature, a bird lays her first egg and is so busy providing herself with food and protecting her territory, she usually doesn't start sitting the egg right away. She waits until she has a full clutch before she begins bearing down and really brooding. A cage bird, however, has a different situation. She's so anxious and so confined to the area of the nest, she starts sitting tight as soon as an egg is laid. This means, if there are four eggs laid, the first bird is hatched four days before the last. Four days is a big difference in baby birds and the big one gets all the food and stomps over the little ones, so they don't have much chance. For this reason, the bird breeder removes the eggs as they are laid. He puts them back when the whole clutch is finished. He puts a fake egg, or a marble, in as a replacement for each egg taken, so the bird doesn't get discouraged and abandon the nest.

I have my fake eggs ready on Thursday morning. Birdie'd slept in the nest the past two nights and this is supposed to be a sure sign. I have oil and cotton ready in case she gets egg bound. The books say sometimes a young female can't pass her egg easily and tenses so the egg can't get out. This can kill the bird. When this happens, you drop warm olive oil on the vent and massage it gently with a cotton swab until the muscles relax and the egg is delivered.

That morning I put fresh food and egg mash on the floor of the aviary. I'd been feeding them egg mash since the mating. It's made of hard-boiled egg mashed in with pablum. Both Birdie and Alfonso really like it. As soon as she smells it, Birdie comes down for some. I go into the aviary and look into the nest. There's an egg. I'm so nervous I'm afraid to take it out. I take deep breaths to calm myself. I have a teaspoon ready and I reach in carefully to slip it under the egg. I lift it out rolling, my hand shaking, and lower it onto a cotton nest

I've made in a small dish. I quickly put the fake egg in the nest. I've been keeping it in my hand to warm it. I know Birdie is too smart to be fooled by a cold marble.

Birdie has flown up to the nest while I'm doing all this. She's watching me suspiciously. She queeps her most plaintive queep and that doesn't help my nerves at all. After I've put the fake egg in, she hops on the edge of the nest, seems satisfied and lowers herself over it. My forehead and hands are covered with sweat. I carry the dish with the egg in it carefully out of the aviary.

The egg is beautiful. I put the dish on the window sill and look at it. The shell is a pale blue-green and there are tiny reddish-brown spots. The spots aren't blood marks, they're real spots. The spots aren't dark, more like pale freckles. Against the light, I can see through the shell and pick out the outline of the yolk. It's amazing to think there's a beginning bird in there; that the feathers and the beak and the flying are in the egg. I wish I could be in there myself and be born again as a bird. I wish I could live in that nest and be warmed under Birdie's feathers and be fed by her and snuggle with my brothers and sisters, feeling my wings getting stronger and my feathers growing.

Birdie doesn't sit tight on the first egg, but she sticks close to the nest and Alfonso spends a good part of his time with her in the cage. The next morning there's a second egg. It's a slightly darker blue than the first one. Now, Birdie settles in. The whole of the next afternoon she only gets off the nest once. Alfonso brings food to her but her body needs calcium to develop the new eggs so she flies down and nibbles on the cuttlebone. Alfonso not only feeds her, he stands beside the nest and sings to her. Now and then he fucks her on the nest. I'm not sure if this is going to hurt the eggs she's carrying or not. I consider closing the cage door, with Birdie in it, to keep Alfonso away but decide against it.

The next morning there's a third egg. It looks more like the first one but has fewer spots. It's longer and thinner, too. Each time, I put in a false egg. The book says one is enough to keep a hen on the nest but I'm sure either Birdie or Alfonso can count to four. Now, when Birdie flies down to eat or exercise, Alfonso sits on the eggs. First, I see him standing on the edge of the nest looking in when Birdie's away and I'm afraid he's going to lean in and try eating the eggs. This is not completely uncommon with canary birds. I'm feeding them hen eggs and there isn't that much difference. The book says that if by some chance an egg gets broken, it should be removed at once, to keep the birds from eating it. Once a bird starts eating eggs, it's useless for breeding.

After the fourth egg, I put the whole clutch back in and mark it on my calendar. The eggs are supposed to hatch thirteen days after I put them in. The next morning I'm surprised to see Birdie's laid a fifth egg. Usually a canary only lays from two to four eggs, especially a young female like Birdie.

Now begins the long wait. I think the two weeks will never pass. I begin to get jumpy and nervous about noises. The book says sudden noises or shocks can stop the development of the embryo, or frighten the female so she'll abandon the nest. I put little rubber bumpers on the door to my room so there's no danger of it slamming. I make a sign and put it on my door saying QUIET PLEASE. My mother is working up a mad and is about to explode. Luckily I bring home a good report card just then, good for me, that is; still she mumbles away about smells and mice. I'm afraid she'll walk in and open the window or the aviary door, or both. I don't know why she's like that.

Alfonso gets to sitting right beside Birdie on the nest. He feeds her and she feeds him. It's hard to believe he's the same bird. He's almost friendly with me, just so long as I don't get too close to the nest.

I go see Mr. Lincoln one Saturday to visit his family and

get some ideas about what to do next. I tell Mr. Lincoln about Alfonso and he shakes his head and says I must have a way with birds. He says to watch out Birdie doesn't sit too tightly and get the sweats. Sometimes a young hen will get so nervous and anxious about her eggs she'll generate too much heat in her brooding and start sweating. This uses up her energy and makes her nervous and she's liable to accidentally spike an egg with a claw or even abandon the nest. He says I should stop feeding them egg food or treat food or any kind of greens, especially no dandelion. I shouldn't give anymore until the day the eggs are to hatch. This way they won't get their blood all enrichened up. Mr. Lincoln should write his own book about birds. He's better than any book.

On the twelfth day, Birdie comes off the nest and takes a bath in the drinking dish. It seems like such a crazy thing to do, I'm sure she's abandoning the nest at the last minute. Even though it's a school night, I pedal over to Mr. Lincoln's. He laughs and says Birdie is a smart bird. He says sometimes a female is like that, and either by counting or feeling the little ones moving inside the egg, she knows they're about ready to hatch and she'll come out to bathe and then go back on the nest while she's still damp. The water softens the shells so the babies can work themselves out easier.

I don't get back home till after seven o'clock, and I've missed dinner. My mother's mad and my father's quiet. My parents are strict about my not being out in the dark on school days. I say I've gone to ask Mr. Lincoln about the birds. It would be a sad scene if they ever find out Mr. Lincoln is black. My parents are peculiar that way.

The fourteenth morning is a Saturday, so I can listen and watch all day. I'm still in bed and just awake when I hear the tiny peep-peep of the first bird being born. I already have egg and pablum in the cage. I get down from the bed carefully and look in the aviary. Alfonso is getting some egg food.

Birdie is sitting tight on the nest. I can see into the floor of the cage and there's an eggshell. In about an hour, a second bird is born. I watch Birdie reach under her breast and help it. She pulls the shell out and drops it on the floor. I can't tell if she's feeding the babies or not. I have to go down to breakfast, and when I get back, another one is hatched. I can't tell if it's one or two more. The tiny peep-peep-peep-peeps overlap so I can't be sure.

I watch all day and Birdie isn't feeding. I begin to worry. As I said, canaries are like human beings; they're not in a natural state so they do some stupid things. Besides eating the eggs, sometimes they won't sit on them or won't feed the babies when they're born. Sometimes the babies will be born and the female will be so frightened she'll jump off the nest and won't go near it. Nice smooth eggs are all right but wiggling baby birds are too much. It isn't because a bird like that is mean or anything, it just doesn't know or remember what to do. Some human mothers and fathers abandon the nest, too, for the same kinds of reasons.

At about three o'clock in the afternoon, Birdie gets off the nest and flies down to eat. Alfonso flies up. He stands over the nest looking in, then reaches his head into the nest. I'm afraid he might be going to throw the babies out; this happens sometimes, too. Then I see him lift up his head to bring more food from his craw and I know he's feeding them. I'm so excited I want to run around the room. When Birdie comes back, he's still doing it. I can hear the increased sound of peeps each time he leans his head in. I try everything to get up high enough to see the babies. I even climb up on the bed and hang my head over the edge but it's impossible. Birdie, after watching for a minute, slides down over her babies and ends the session. I begin to worry again. Can Alfonso take care of all the feeding? Won't Birdie ever get the idea?

It isn't till late in the afternoon of Sunday when I finally see Birdie feed her babies. I don't think she ever would've started if it hadn't been for Alfonso. He's forced her off the nest twice so he can feed. She's bewildered by it all and doesn't know what to do except sit tight and hope things will work out. The last egg is hatched that day, too. I see another shell on the floor or I wouldn't have known. The baby birds keep up a continuous peep-peep-peep-peep-peep, overlapping, irregular, changing and passing each other because they peep at slightly different intervals. I can't distinguish one from the other.

In school the next day, I'm completely out of it. I catch myself sitting still and holding in, hatching eggs. I keep trying to think what the birds look like. Are they dark or light, would there be one like Alfonso, are they males or females? Would Birdie keep feeding them? How will Alfonso act when they come out of the nest? Would they be mean birds and attack each other in the nest? I can't wait to get home.

That night I take the chance when Birdie goes down to eat. I go right into the aviary and beat Alfonso to the nest. There's still one unhatched egg. That means there're four birds. It's just a mass of slightly fuzzy flesh in the bottom of the nest. Then, Alfonso brazens it out and flies to the edge of the nest. As soon as his feet hit, four tiny heads poke waveringly up out of the naked flesh. Soft-looking beaks open searchingly between closed eyes. He feeds them, as if unaware of my close watching. There's one that's completely dark-skinned; probably will be as dark as Alfonso. There're two light ones and one that seems spotted. I decide I'll wait another day before I take out the egg. The birds all look the same size so I can't tell which one was born a day after the others or if that's the egg that hasn't hatched.

Birdie flies up to the nest and joins Alfonso in the feeding. The little heads reach up greedily and the adults almost take the small heads into their mouths to force the food into the throats. Alfonso flies down for more food but before he gets back, Birdie decides they've had enough and settles onto the nest.

The next morning I reach in among the warm squirming bodies and lift out the egg. I hold it up against the light and see that it's clear. I hold it up closely in front of a light bulb and there's nothing there. Somehow it didn't get fertilized; it's sterile. It seems amazing with all that fucking going on. I can't throw it out, so I keep it in a little box with cotton in a drawer with my socks. It's probably just as well it didn't hatch; four is enough of a crowd in a nest.

The next day I have my morning session with Weiss. I'm wondering if Renaldi has told him anything. I don't think he would, but you never know. He could be some kind of trained fink Weiss uses.

He's definitely the psychiatrist this morning. His coat is clean white and starched, his glasses have been shined so you can only just see his eyes. He has his hands folded, fingers tucked in on the desk in front of him. He has on his best smile, calm, loving, brotherhood-of-man-and-ain't-life-awful-but-we-can-make-it-together kind of smile. His thick thumbs give him away; they're taking turns slipping over each other. There's so much pressure you can almost hear the fingerprints rubbing together.

I stand, holding the salute, and he smiles at me. Then he gives up and makes a sloppy salute ending with one of his fat hands pointing; all fingers out, thumb lightly folded in, at the chair in front of the desk.

"Have a seat, Alfonso."

Alfonso! Shit! Nobody, not even my mother, calls me Alfonso. I wish the fuck I knew his first name. All it has is Maj. S. O. Weiss on the black tag in the corner of his desk. I'm tempted to ask what the "S." stands for, besides Shitface, but there's no use looking for trouble. He's only doing his job. I just wish he did it better.

Hell, no good psychiatrist would be working for the stinking army. If he were even average, he'd be in the air corps. I'll bet any half-baked air corps psychiatrist would be better for Birdy. It'd be a real twist. All day long they're dealing with guys who don't want to fly and here's one guy who *wants* to; without an airplane, yet.

He's still smiling at me. I wonder if he practices in a mirror. OK, if that's the way we're going to play. He hasn't had much experience with Sicilians. Sicilians can sit at a table all day long smiling at each other, talking about the weather, telling each other how wonderful they are. At the same time, they know there's poison in the glass of wine in front of the other guy; they have a knife open and ready under the table; and three friends have shotguns pointed at the other guy's head. They can do this when they know the other guy has all these things on them, too. There's something crazy in most Sicilians, probably has to do with all those generations of sun and then mixing the Phoenicians, the Greeks, and the Romans. It's a bad combination. We wound up with the sneaky qualities of the Phoenicians, the cleverness of the Greeks, and the meanness of the Romans. I go into the routine. I'm smiling my ears off but with the bandages he can't get the full effect. I figure I'll go for openers.

"What made you decide to be a psychiatrist, sir?"

Not a move. He could be a Jewish Sicilian.

"I mean, sir, did you know when you were in high school or did it slip up on you the way things do, sir?"

Weiss grunts in his throat. These are fair questions. He leans forward on the desk, still holding himself down with his hands.

"Well, Alfonso; it was in medical school, actually. You know the old joke about, 'What makes a psychiatrist?' "

I know it but I'm going to make him say it. I smile back. "No, sir."

"Well, they say a psychiatrist is a Jewish doctor who can't stand the sight of blood."

Oh, great. I don't know what he expects me to do but I laugh. I laugh just a bit too long. Most Sicilians have a built-in fake laugh they can bring out for any occasion. They can laugh at their own funeral if it's to their advantage. It's a laugh that can fool anybody except another Sicilian.

"That's a good one, sir." I'm not going to cut and fill for him either. "But, seriously, sir. How did you get interested in dealing with crazies and loons as a profession?"

"Well, Alfonso, all my work isn't with abnormals you know. Many people will have some little thing that's bothering them and I can help them work it out and make their lives better."

"The army pays for this, sir?"

He's moving in fast for the kill. He's a smooth son-of-a-bitch all right. He's just itching to get inside my head somehow.

"The army isn't all bad, Sergeant. Fighting wars is never pleasant under any conditions, but the army takes care of its own."

"It's certainly taken care of me, sir." I give this to him straight on. He's good. He just smiles back at me.

"Alfonso, tell me something. What was your father like?"

"My father's still alive, sir."

He looks down at the pile of papers under his hands. There can't be anything there, not about my old man anyway. He's acting psychiatrist again. "Oh, yes. I mean, what is he like; how do you get along with him?"

"Oh, he's a great guy, sir. We were always like buddies. He used to take me out on camping trips and we made model airplanes together; things like that. He's really a great guy; wonderful to my mother, too. She's the best mother in the world."

Maybe a few verses of "Jack Armstrong, the All-American Boy" would fit in here.

"Ah, yes. And what does your father do for a living, Alfonso?"

"He cleans out sewers for the city, sir. He calls himself a plumber but what he actually does is shovel shit all day. He comes in the back way nights, takes a shower in the cellar and scrubs himself with a big laundry scrub brush. He keeps his fingernails cut so short, you'd think he bit them. That's to keep the shit out from under them, sir. When he comes up to eat dinner, you'd never know he'd been standing in shit all day. He's just a great guy, sir. I've never heard him complain even once and he gives everything he earns to my mother. We're poor but we're clean and honest, sir. We're glad to have a chance in this great country of ours."

Right here a quick "And Who Do You See, It's Little Orphan Annie" would be good. Should I tell him I have a strange dog with holes instead of eyes?

I'm keeping my face straight through all this. That Sicilian blood is coming through. Uncle Nicky would be proud of me. Uncle Nicky's making a fortune from the war. He sells certification of allergy from legitimate doctors at fifteen hundred bucks. He's clearing a grand each. One of those certificates is a sure 4-F. He's got another racket going, too. He's opened "clinics" where you can go and have your arm broken. Guys at the end of their furloughs go in and he breaks their arms for a price. Then they don't get shipped overseas with their outfits. You go to him, he gives you an anaesthetic and he has a little machine like a guillotine, only instead of a blade it has a heavy blunt piece of lead. Clump! You wake up and your arm's already in a cast and in a sling. You have X-rays and a doctor's signature, the whole thing. He does legs too, but that's more complicated and more dangerous. He's better at arms. If they'd ever've let me come home before the fucking war was over I was going to have myself done. Nicky'd've done it for free. Krauts beat him to it; didn't charge me either, and I'll get a pension on top. I wonder if Weiss'd believe all this if I told him.

He's ruffling through the papers some more.

"Sergeant, can you give me any information about the patient? You were close to him. Was there ever anything you observed that would give a hint to explain this sudden, complete catatonic state and the bizarre cringing positions he gets into?"

We're back to Sergeant again. I can't believe it! Weiss

still hasn't caught on that Birdy thinks he's a canary! Dumb shit!

"He was always perfectly normal, sir. Like me, poor but from a nice family. He lived in a big three-story house with lots of grounds around it. He was good in school, not a genius, sir, but he was in the academic curriculum and usually got B's. Could you tell me, sir; what happened to him? It must've been something awful to make him like this."

Let's see him squirm out of it this time. He lifts the papers one at a time. I don't think he's looking at them, reading anything, I mean; he's stalling for time. Maybe he's hoping my question will go away. He might know something and not want to tell me, or, more likely, he doesn't know any more than Renaldi.

"I've spoken to his mother and father. They came down to verify the identification. He'd been reported as missing for over a month. They recognized him but there was no recognition from the patient. At that time, if anyone came near he would go into frantic jumping and twisting activity, falling to the floor. It was almost as if he were trying to escape."

"That doesn't sound like him at all, sir."

He can't be that stupid. He'll catch onto the bird business soon. I wonder if Birdy's old lady and old man told about Birdy raising the canaries. They probably wouldn't think it meant anything. But they'd sure as hell tell about Birdy and me running away that time.

"Sir, perhaps I should tell you, it might be important; the patient and I ran away. It was when we were thirteen; we went to Atlantic City and then to Wildwood in New Jersey."

"Yes."

Yes, yes, yes. Yes, fathead, we did it all right. He's interested now. I figure I'll feed him a bit at a time. He looks down at his papers. He's reading something from a yellow sheet.

"Yes, Sergeant, I have that right here. There's a police report as well. It says here you were accused of stealing some bicycles."

Now isn't that the shits. There's no sense saying anything about it. Fatass Weiss isn't going to believe anything I say. After all, he has it right there before him in black and yellow.

He leans across the desk toward me now. He's wiped the smile off his face. He's practicing his concerned look. I lean forward, too, and try to look as if I'm sorry for being alive. That's not too far from the truth.

"Tell me Alfonso. Just between us, do you often get the feeling that people aren't being fair to you? Do you think people are out to 'get' you?"

What is this creep, a fucking mind reader? He looks down at his papers again, then looks up at me, stern, serious but very understanding.

"This report on that incident at New Cumberland indicates you were in the army only five days at the time; is that true?"

"Yes, sir."

"It says you knocked out eight of the non-commissioned officer's teeth and broke his nose."

I keep my mouth shut. What the fuck's this got to do with Birdy?

"Was he being unfair to you, Alfonso? You're a noncom yourself now. Looking back on it, do you think you might have been overreacting? Would you do the same thing now in the same conditions?"

I stick with my "bad little doggy" routine. "We all make mistakes, sir. He was probably only trying to do his job like the rest of us."

I didn't know I could be such a good bullshitter. Maybe I'll be a used car salesman. I'm enjoying fooling this asshole. It's something like making some big bastard cry when you're hurting him only it doesn't take so much effort.

He's catching on. His eyes disappear behind the clean glasses. He takes the papers, stands them up on end, bangs them edgewise against the desk a few times, then gets the folder and slips all the papers into it. He sits back.

"Well, Sergeant. I guess it can't hurt if you spend another day with the patient. It could happen all at once. Do you have any other ideas; anything you can remember about the past? If you do, let me know."

That's when I bring up the baseballs. I can never just let things go.

"Sir, there's one thing. Maybe it sounds crazy but it's something I know has always bothered the patient. You see, he lived just over the left-center field fence of our local baseball park. Whenever anybody hit a ball over that fence for a home run, his mother used to keep the balls; wouldn't give them up. Everybody hated her for it. The patient felt terrible about this. He used to apologize to everybody and swear he'd get the balls back. He kept lists of all the people his mother had taken balls from. He promised to get them back for everybody someday. He spent hours looking for them in his house, in the attic and in the garage, everywhere. Maybe if you could get his mother to send those balls down here it would help. I know it would take a big load off his mind and it might be just the thing to help him remember."

Weiss is looking at me as if I'm completely bananas. Then he realizes I couldn't make up a thing like that. Sergeants are notorious for being unimaginative. He takes the folder back out. He starts writing in it. He looks up.

"How long ago was this, Sergeant?"

"Oh, it went on for years, sir. Seven years at least. There must be an awful lot of baseballs in that collection, sir."

He's writing and mumbling to himself. I'm biting my tongue to keep from laughing.

"All right, Sergeant. If you come up with any more ideas like this be sure and report them to me. If you notice anything in his behavior here at the hospital you think I ought to know about, tell me that, too. In general, keep talking to him about the past. You might hit on something that'll bring it all back."

This time there's no kidding around with the psychiatrist shit. He stands up. I stand up, too, and salute. He gives me a fair enough salute; I spin around and walk out, past spitface and outside into the sunlight.

I'm actually anxious to get back with Birdy. I'm beginning to feel he knows I'm there. Talking about all this stuff with him helps me more than anything. I'm wishing Birdy'd come back and we could have fun working over Weiss together. Weiss is the kind of person brings out the worst in me. I should be around him some more and try practicing self-control. It's either that or I'll wind up one of the meanest shits in the world, myself.

I walk across the hospital grounds and into the building where Birdy is. I'm still laughing to myself about the baseballs. I'll shit my pants if she still does have those balls and ships them down here. I can just imagine Weiss's telegram:

PLEASE SEND ALL THE BASEBALLS. STOP. NEED THEM IN TREATMENT FOR YOUR SON. STOP. MAJOR WEISS.

I can see it, two hundred used baseballs in a big box being shipped air freight, maybe even on a special military plane. Birdy'd love this.

I see Renaldi and tell him about the session with Weiss. He laughs when I tell him about the baseballs. I have to tell somebody. He says Weiss will sure as hell send for them.

Renaldi opens the outer door. Birdy swings around and looks at me when he hears the noise. I get my chair from out in the corridor and set myself up. Renaldi says he'll see me at lunch.

I sit there for a while trying to think of something to say. Then I remember.

—Hey Birdy! How 'bout that time we went ice skating up the creek? Remember? The time they closed the school 'cause all the pipes froze up. Remember?

I know he's listening now. He looks at me sometimes and he gives the old Birdy spaced-out smile there once. I keep on talking.

It was about zero degrees and when we got to school they sent us all back home. Even the water in the toilets was frozen. Five of us walked home from school together and decided we'd go ice skating. We said we'll meet down at the edge of the dump, where the railroad track crosses the road.

There's Jim Maloney, Bill Prentice, Ray Connors, Birdy and myself. We're all there except Prentice when Birdy says how if you put your tongue onto a frozen railroad track it'll stick so you can't get it loose. Jim Maloney says he's full of shit. We get to arguing back and forth; Maloney says he'll stick his tongue onto the track; Birdy tries to talk him out of it, but Maloney's a smart-ass Irish bastard. He kneels down and puts his warm tongue flat on the track. Naturally it sticks there. He tries to pull it off but it's really stuck. We're all laughing and Maloney's making noises and starting to cry. It's really a bitchin' cold day.

Connors starts yelling he can hear a train coming. We all begin running up and down the track yelling and pretending a train's coming. Connors runs, actually pretends he's running, and says he'll try to flag down the train and stop it. He takes a stick and starts pounding on the track Maloney's stuck to, like the sound of a train going over rail junctions. Maloney's bawling his eyes out. He's screaming, "Heh ee! Heh ee!" Birdy says the only thing that'll help is some warm water. We're a couple blocks from the nearest house. Connors comes running back yelling he can't stop the train. We tell Maloney the only warm water we can think of is piss so we all whip out and start peeing on his tongue. What a crazy scene. Connors is actually peeing in Maloney's ear. I'm laughing so hard I can hardly make it go. Birdy's only pretending.

Maybe it's the pee or maybe Maloney just got mad enough, but he rips his tongue off the track. It's bleeding and stays flat, frozen. He can't get it back in his mouth. He starts laying out after all of us. We run in every direction, my feet are so numb it hurts to run. We can't understand Maloney but he's crying and cursing, trying to see his tongue. He keeps pulling at rocks to throw at us but they're all frozen to the ground. Finally, he drops on his knees and cries. Connors says he'll take him home; they live near each other on Clinton Road. He says it's too cold to go skating anyway.

Birdy and I wait a couple more minutes, but Prentice doesn't show up. We start walking along the track up toward Marshall Road where the old mill and the dam are. In some places there's ice frozen on the rails of the track. Birdy tries balancing on the icy rails.

First thing when we get to the mill pond, we build a fire. We kick out some rotten timbers in the mill and there's an old can of practically frozen motor oil. We pour it over the wood to get it burning. When our feet are warm enough, we put on our ice skates.

The ice froze so fast it's perfectly clear, what we call black ice. It's so invisible it's like walking on water. We can see catfish swimming on the bottom. They jump when we go over them and make little explosions of mud.

We skate around and play one-on-one hockey with some sticks and a stone. We get the idea to skate upstream as far as we can. First, we throw some big pieces of wood on the fire to keep it burning, hide our shoes near it, then start out.

It's terrific fun skating around stones in the creek. Some of them are four feet across. Sometimes, there're only narrow ice ways between sand bars and other times the creek widens till it's almost as wide as the pond.

Birdy's really good on ice skates. He can jump turn and land on either foot. It comes from all the practicing he does getting himself ready to fly. We get up speed and jump over some of the rocks. Of course, Birdy can jump over rocks twice as high as I'll even try. I measure the distance he goes and he's going over twenty feet on those jumps. Think of what he could do broad jumping!

We skate all the way through the golf course, under the little bridges, then behind a factory and along the edge of Sixty-third Street. We hear the el go by once. We're having such a great time we aren't even cold. The other guys were jerks not to come with us; but we're not missing them. Birdy and I already know we're making a little bit more of our own personal history. We'll have fun telling about it when we get back to school. We'll lie about it some to make it sound better and we'll add things each time we tell it. It's something

Birdy and I do automatically without even talking about it beforehand. Birdy makes up the lying part and I back him up with details to make it seem real. What a team.

About three miles up the creek we come to a frozen waterfall. The fall is formed by a wall at an angle. In summer, water trickles over the wall and it's covered with moss. At the bottom there's a good place to fish. The ice has formed great rounded white balls all down the sides of the wall. The balls are perfectly smooth and you can see through some of them.

We want to see if we can climb to the top. There's a good-sized pond up there that ought to be great skating. We could've just walked in our skates around the falls, but climbing up a frozen waterfall sounds like something Richard Halliburton would do. Birdy and I are both big fans of Halliburton. We think his was the greatest message ever sent. It was from a Chinese junk as he was trying to cross the China Sea: "Having a wonderful time, wish you were here, instead of me." It's the last word ever heard from him.

The wall of the waterfall must be about fifteen or twenty feet high. We use our skate points to dig in and we push our butts out for balance while our hands and face are against the ice. Birdy gets to the top first.

I'm at the top and Al scrambles to the edge near me. The ice over the edge of the dam is smooth as glass. There's nothing to get hold of. When I lean forward across the ice I lose grip with the skates. Al says he'll give me a push. He reaches under my skate and pushes me up over the brink. I hear him tumbling down the side of the wall to the bottom. I look back and he's turning and spinning as he goes, thumping over the ice bumps. Then he slides across the ice at the bottom.

The pond up there is beautiful; bigger than the millpond, and there are no reeds growing through the ice. I stand up and look down at Al. He's standing, brushing himself off. He says he's fine. He's going to try climbing the wall again. I get down on my stomach to lean out and give him a hand when he gets close.

Al works his way to the edge and I grab him. I start pulling him slowly, my clothing is just warm enough to stick to the ice. We're almost there, when Al pulls a bit too hard and unsticks me. We both begin sliding over the edge. There's nothing we can do and we start laughing. For a few seconds we're balanced, then down we go. I'm going headfirst and Al turns onto his back. The bumping isn't as bad as it looks because we have on heavy coats. When we hit bottom there's too much weight and we go through the ice.

I go completely under, headfirst, and come up under the ice. I bump my head against the ice and can't break it. There's an air space and I can see up through but the water's freezing cold. Al breaks ice over to me and pulls me up and out. The water at the bottom of the fall there must be seven or eight feet deep. I've swallowed a lung full and can't get my breath. Al spreads me on the side bank and pumps water out of me. When I sit up I'm surprised I don't feel cold, only limp and tired.

Al's jumping up and down and pulling off his wet clothes. He says we have to get them off and wrung out so we can skate back to the fire before we freeze. I start getting undressed and trying to jog in place but my legs are numb. Al wrings out the clothes as we take them off and then we put them back on. They're already freezing. Then we make the mistake of taking off our skates to wring out our socks. We can't get the skates back on because our feet are swollen and our hands are too cold. The matches are soaked so there's no way to build a fire. Al ties the skates around his neck somehow and says we'll have to run back down the creek bed.

We start running and that's when I find out I can't breathe right. Whenever I breathe deeply I cough and can't get my breath. Spots come before my eyes; black dots against the snow. I want to stop and rest. I'm not so much cold as tired and I can't breathe. I stop and sit down on the ice. Al comes back and I can't even talk. I don't have enough breath. My ears feel like they're filled with snow.

Al picks me up and throws me over his back in a fireman's carry. I have no energy, to resist. Al goes jogging along down the center of the creek. He can't go fast because it's slippery. He puts me down once and throws the ice skates under a tree growing over the ice. That's the last I remember.

It's a good three miles we'd skated up that creek. While I'm running along, I'm keeping my eyes open for somebody up in the old factory or on the golf course who can help us. Birdy's passed out. I decide against trying to get up the side of the hill to Sixty-third Street. I could never make it. I'm to the point where I'm going on automatically. If I stop for anything, I'm finished.

When we get to the fire, it's almost burned out. I put Birdy down beside it and throw on some more wood. Birdy's gone all right. I slap him a few times to bring him around. It's like he's in a deep sleep. He's breathing shallow, noisy gulps of air. I'm not cold at all myself; I'm sweating, but I'm dead tired. I lift Birdy up and walk him around to force some circulation into his legs. The fire starts burning fine but it's not giving off enough heat. I know I have to get Birdy home. I can't squeeze our shoes on either of us, so I string them around my neck and pick up Birdy again. This time I carry him piggyback. I hate to face his bitchin' old lady.

I trot up out of the woods and across the fields along the railroad tracks. I take the back way up to Birdy's house past the Cosgrove place. The last part is uphill and I'm about pooped. I get him to his gate and put him down on his feet so it won't look so bad. He can walk a bit now.

Lucky nobody's home. Birdy has a key. I get him upstairs and run some water in the bathtub. Birdy can't get his buttons undone, so I undress him and get him into the tub. I sit on the john and watch to see if he's OK. I'm starting to get cold myself; my clothes are starting to thaw in the warm house and I'm sopping wet. The sweat is turning cold, too. The bath brings Birdy around fine. In fifteen minutes he's almost good as new. I take off for my place.

When I get home, I jump into the tub. I throw my wet clothes into the hamper. I lie in that hot water for at least half an hour. My feet are bruised and cut. As the hot water starts to defrost them they begin to hurt. When I was running I couldn't feel a thing.

Next day, school is still closed. Birdy and I go up the creek to get the skates. We find them OK. In this weather, nobody's sneaking around stealing ice skates. We go on up to the place where we went in. It's frozen over again. We check the ice and it's more than three inches thick already. If Birdy'd been alone he'd never've been able to break his way through.

We pace it off on the way back and it's over three miles from the falls to the fire. Then, another mile to his house.

Birdy comes out without even a cold but I practically get pneumonia. I have to stay home from school for three weeks; lose ten pounds. Birdy doesn't tell anybody about it till I get there and we have the fun of telling it together.

It's amazing how fast they grow. By the end of one week their eyes are open and they begin laying their heads on the edge of the nest. Birdie doesn't sit on them nearly as much and spends most of her time hauling food.

At the end of two weeks they've developed pin feathers and feathers over their backs. Their eyes are bright, wide open, and they cower down in the nest when I come in to look at them. Little tail feathers have started and stick out about half an inch. They're beginning to look like birds. I even think I can tell the males from the females. I decide there are three males and one female. The dark one is definitely a male and one of the yellow ones. The spotted one is probably a male too. I judge this partly from the shape of their heads and the look in their eyes but more from the way they act in the nest. All the males keep away from the door and the wire of the cage and the little yellow one I figure for a female is less afraid. It's this bravery which almost does her in.

By now, the nest is beginning to get messy. At the beginning, Birdie took their droppings in her mouth; then, by the time they're a week old she has them trained to shove their butts up over the edge of the nest. Still, it doesn't always clear the edge and the outside of the nest is covered with bird droppings. There's so much crap I change the paper under the nest every day.

About halfway into the third week, this little yellow female starts climbing up on the rampart of the nest to get a breath of fresh air and look around. I can see she's going to be the same sort of curious type as Birdie. She's just a little over two weeks old when she falls out the first time. This means she falls about eight times her own height to the bottom of the cage. There are practically no feathers on her wings, so it's a free fall. It's like me falling off the top of our house. Weight or density has a lot to do with falling. Baby birds even fall out of trees and survive.

I don't see her fall but I look in and there she is, trying to stand on the flat surface at the bottom of the cage. Alfonso is hopping around in total confusion. He feeds her and there's nothing else he can do. Birdie peers down over the edge of the nest. That baby bird'll freeze if she has to stay out there all night. She doesn't have enough feathers.

I reach in, pick her up and put her back in the nest. She has virtually no feathers along her breast or along her thighs. Also, her head is very thinly feathered. She snuggles back into the nest with the others and I think that's the end of it.

The next day I come home from school and she's on the floor again. Alfonso and Birdie are frantic. I have the feeling she's been out quite a while. When I pick her up she feels cool. I hold her in my hand to warm her, then put her back in the nest and hope for the best. Birdie feeds all of them and when I go down to dinner, everything seems in order.

After dinner, she's out of the nest again. I put her back in and wonder what I can do. I watch to see what's happening. Birdie might've taken a dislike to her and is throwing her out, or maybe feels that since she left the nest voluntarily, she shouldn't be allowed back in. Who knows what goes through a canary's mind? In about an hour, the yellow one's climbed up on the rampart. She looks over the edge and out into the aviary where Alfonso is flying. She stands up on her thin, barethighed legs and flaps her slightly feathered stubs of wings. She tumbles forward and almost off the nest. In about two minutes she does the same thing again and falls. The only solution is to make sure she's in the nest before I turn out the lights.

During the next week, all of them start standing on the edge of the nest. It becomes the thing to do. You can see they're preparing themselves for flight. There's much stretching of wings; they stand up high, stretch straight out and flap their wing stumps at faster than flight speeds. I wonder if they're getting any lift from this flapping. I try it myself with my own arms as fast as I can but I can't feel anything. You have to have feathers. I feel if I could only flap down without having to flap up again, I'd definitely get some lift. When I went off the gas tank, it was mostly falling.

By the end of three weeks they're all standing on the edge of the nest, even at night, and Birdie isn't sitting them anymore. She's beginning to carry around pieces of burlap so I put in a new nest on the other side of the cage. Between feedings now, she begins to build again. Alfonso is more and more the main feeder of the babies. They've started mating again, too, and I figure it won't be long before Birdie lays another batch of eggs.

Twice, Birdie comes over and snitches soft feathers from one or another of the babies. I've read how sometimes a female will pluck a whole nest of young naked to feather her new nest. This can cause all the babies to die from pain and cold. This is another one of those things that happens because canaries have been in cages so long. I wonder if it ever happens with wild birds.

The third time Birdie comes over to take a pass at one of the young for some soft down to line the new nest, Alfonso pounces on her and chases her out into the aviary. She comes back twice more and each time it's Alfonso to the rescue. For the next few days he sits beside the nest on guard. There are so many things that can go wrong.

Finally, Birdie is finished with her new nest. In the meantime, I've had great fun watching the young make their first flights. The yellow female keeps falling out till she's figured it by trial and error. I begin to think she likes falling. I'm beginning to like it myself, jumping, not falling, but free falling as far as possible. I can already jump from eight feet without hurting myself.

The first male to make the flight out of the nest definitely decides to do it. It's the yellow one. He's too careful to let himself fall and he's almost too careful to fly. He spends a lot of time on the edge of the nest tottering. He flaps his wings madly there, standing high, and nothing happening. It doesn't look as if he's getting any more lift than I do with my arms. It's like somebody thrashing their arms and legs about in the water when they don't know how to swim. You have to feel that air has substance and can hold you up. It's mostly a matter of confidence. This yellow male can't seem to work up enough confidence in the air to shove off. I watch him for hours, days I become that bird. I know I can feel what he's thinking, when he almost gets himself to do it, when he backs off.

By now, each of them looks almost like a real canary. Their tails are still short and the soft flesh around the corners of their beaks hasn't hardened; they still have little fluffy antenna-like hairs sticking out over their eyes. Other than that they look like canaries, only half-size.

This yellow male finally makes the decision. Still, after he's committed, he tries to go back, but it's too late, he flutters down in a half glide to the far corner of the breeding cage. He slips and has a hard time standing on the slippery newspaper and gravel in the bottom of the cage. He starts hopping after Alfonso for something to eat.

Now, sometimes a male won't feed the babies unless

they're in the nest, but Alfonso seems prepared to accept the inevitable. For the next while, he'll be the prime parent for the baby birds. He feeds both of the escapees, the new yellow male and the yellow female who's been out for a day. It's while he's feeding these two that the dark male, out of pure greed, having nothing to do with flight or wanting to escape from the nest, comes flying down with a bump near Alfonso and starts begging to be fed. Here he's made one of the most important moves of his life, his first flight, and all he can think of is food. He couldn't stand to be up there in the nest while feeding was going on down on the floor. It's easy to miss the important things in life.

The last one, the spotted one, jumps later the same day. He's a really timid one. He climbs out of the nest onto the perch and only winds up on the bottom because he can't balance himself.

They all huddle on the floor in a corner, trying to recapture the warmth and security of the nest. Whenever Alfonso comes into the cage, they chase after him and practically hound him to death with a continuous feed-me pleading. Alfonso's very good with them and ferries food back and forth. I feel sorry for him and put a good supply of egg food in the bottom of the breeding cage.

Now is the time I've been waiting for. I want to watch carefully to see how the babies learn to fly. At this point, they haven't flown much more than I have.

I watch them do all kinds of feather cleaning and wing stretching. They're still so unsure of their footing they'll almost fall over when they try to stretch a wing with a foot. They still can't sleep on one foot.

They've been getting a good deal of wing exercise during the feeding process. Probably without realizing it, this flapping of wings while being fed is flight preparation. I can't see any other function for it except to attract the attention of the mother or father bird. They're flapping those stumps long before there are any feathers on them. I determine to flap my arms at least an hour every day. It seems as good a place to start as any. It's where birds start. I flap for ten minutes that first night when the babies are out of the nest and I can't go on. In the morning my shoulder muscles are so stiff I can barely lift my arms. My chest muscles are so sore I can't touch them.

The first flights they make are up onto the lowest perch by the feed dish and water cup. It's about the same kind of jump if I were to jump up onto a table. These baby birds are already trying to separate themselves from the ground. They seem to know that their place is in the air. At night, they struggle to get up onto that first little perch and somehow balance themselves. When you see their courage and determination, it's easy to know why people can't fly; they don't want to hard enough.

Most of the times when the babies make that first jump up onto the feeding perch they swing right on over and off the other side; they can generate enough spring with their legs and frantic wing flapping to get up there, but they haven't learned to use their tails yet to stop themselves and balance.

If these babies look at Alfonso and Birdie moving so easily from perch to perch, twisting, hopping along, without a thought, without an effort, it must be discouraging. Something like flying isn't easy even for birds; it takes practice and effort. I don't see anything of Alfonso or Birdie trying to teach them, the babies have to work it out for themselves. I notice, though, that when one baby has figured something out, the others pick it up quickly. They seem to be learning from each other.

The next day, in the back yard, I use the old saw horses and a four-by-four as a perch to practice with. I put my perch up three feet and take a running jump flapping my arms. I realize how much spring those baby birds have in their legs already. If the spring in the legs develops in comparative strength the same as the wings, a grown bird must be able to hop, even without wings, almost as well as a frog. It would be interesting to see how a bird growing up without wings would behave. I don't mean a penguin or something that gave up flying to be able to swim, but a bird who naturally would fly but doesn't have wings.

That night my arms are deadly sore from flapping, but I keep it up. If those little birds can do it, I can, too. I get so I can jump up on the perch and stay there. My main problem is the same one they have, that is, stopping my forward motion and not going over the other side of the perch. I flap my arms to keep myself balanced.

What I need is a tail. I could put some cloth sewn to my trousers between my legs, but that wouldn't help. The tail has to be completely independent of the legs and controllable. Already those babies can tilt their tail up and down and spread the feathers. They got practice at this shitting from the nest. I'm still keeping up with them but already I can see that I don't have a chance without mechanical help. The one thing I know is I don't want a motor or anything like that. If I can't fly on my own power, then I don't want it.

It's the dark male who makes the first up-flight successfully. Alfonso'd flown onto a higher perch to get away from them after he'd finished feeding and this one flies right up after him. I don't think he even thought about this flight either. Maybe that's part of flying; you can't think about it too much. I don't know how I can stop myself from thinking about it.

The dark male lands on the perch beside Alfonso and then, in the violence of his wing flapping for feeding, facing Alfonso sideways, gets unbalanced and tumbles off the perch. He catches himself midway and glides more than falls into the food dish on the side of the cage.

The baby birds seem able to take an awful beating with their falling around, and not show any sign of it. This jump of the dark male was up at least four times his outstretched height; for me this would be like jumping up onto the roof of our house. I can't even jump down that far without hurting myself, and he isn't a month old yet. It's discouraging, but I'll watch more closely and practice. I know I want to fly at least as much as any canary. I don't have to fly anything as well as a canary; gliding down from high places with arm control might be enough.

Birdie has laid a new egg and we're off on the second nest. I take it out the same as last time and put in a marble. She doesn't sit too tightly on this first egg but she stays by the nest to protect it from the young birds. She gives off the feeling she's finished with them and wishes they'd get out of the breeding cage. It's a bit like some parents with teen-agers. She puts up with them and she'll feed them if they insist but her mind is elsewhere.

In a few more days they're all capable of flying up to any perch, or the nest, and are beginning to have fun trying out their wings. Birdie starts sitting tight on the nest as soon as she's laid her third egg. I think she's more afraid of the babies doing the eggs harm than anything else.

All of the babies have started picking at the egg food when I put it in the bottom of the cage. The way they get started is by smearing it on themselves accidentally while jumping around Alfonso when he's eating. They're hopping in and out of the dish full of egg food and then, more by chance than anything, discover they can go directly to the source. This is a critical moment. I decide to leave the door of the breeding cage open and watch what happens.

As soon as it's open, of course, Alfonso takes off out into the aviary. He's been locked in with those babies for five days and is showing signs of going stir crazy. He flies about madly, checking all his systems and giving the old wings a workout. It's almost as much fun for me watching him through the binoculars as it must be for him. It isn't long before the little yellow bird who kept falling out of the nest is on the edge of the cage door looking into the aviary. I can almost feel her mind trying to work it out. There's a perch in front of her and slightly down, about twice as far as she's ever jumped before. She cocks her head this way and that trying to figure the distance. Birds don't have stereoscopic vision, and have some difficulty judging distances. She takes off for it after about three minutes pondering and makes a perfect landing. Now, she really looks little. Alfonso, almost as if he's rewarding her, comes over and feeds her.

It's exciting, for me watching, as each of the young birds comes out into the aviary. At first, each flight from one perch to another is a major adventure, there's lots of falling and fluttering to the bottom. Once they're on the bottom, it's a major project flying back up to the lowest perch. This perch is at least two feet from the ground. They all work it out though and in a few days are making experimental test flights. They seem to enjoy fluttering down from one perch to a lower one, more than struggling their way up. It's a couple of weeks before they catch onto gliding.

This is the opposite of the way I'll have to do it. From what I know now, I think I'll have to be satisfied with gliding first, then work my way to some kind of flapping.

It's several days after they've left the breeding cage before one of them, the dark one, finds his way back. Birdie has finished laying her fifth egg again and I've put all the eggs in the nest. These days, Alfonso has been able to fly into the cage from the aviary and feed Birdie or sit on the eggs when she wants to go out to feed or take some exercise. Now, this young bird comes over to the nest and starts giving the feed-me signal. Birdie hunches down deeper on the nest and ignores him. I'm wondering if I'll have to lock Birdie in the breeding cage, leaving Alfonso out, something I'd hate to do. Then Alfonso takes care of things himself. It's almost as if he'd figured it out.

He flies into the breeding cage and chases that baby bird

out. When the baby, all confused at this hostile act from the ever-loving father, is outside, Alfonso feeds him. In this way, he trains all the young birds to stay away from Birdie on the nest.

But it's no real problem. They're all beginning to have such fun flying, they don't do much of anything but eat and fly all day long. They practice different flying tricks. Now, I'm sure they're watching Alfonso to learn how to do some things. It would be interesting to see how quickly a bird would learn to fly if it never saw any other bird flying. I decide to try that one out when I have enough birds.

I'm keeping a notebook of all the things I see. I'm doing a lot of drawings and I write down my observations and thoughts. I'm also writing down all the different experiments I want to try so I can figure out what flying is and how birds learn. I take ten pages of notes alone on how a bird learns to turn around on a perch. It's definitely something they have to practice; they don't know how to do it for almost a week after they're out of the nest. Out in the back yard I'm working on that trick myself and it is not an easy thing to learn.

Birdie seems happy and well. She's extraordinary, laying a second clutch of five eggs. The book says a female can have three nests a year without hurting, if she's in good health. Birdie looks fine to me and as the young birds get more and more independent with their feeding, Alfonso gives her more help. He brings food up to feed her on the nest and sits when she flies out to eat. She takes long exercise periods, completely ignoring the baby birds; they ignore her too. It seems that after baby birds leave a nest, the mother bird just forgets them. At least, that's Birdie's way. The weather is getting warmer now, so Birdie isn't so passionate at sitting as the first time. Sometimes she'll take as much as fifteen minutes off the nest to preen her feathers. With Alfonso up there anyway, hovering over the nest, there's no real danger. I don't think Alfonso really sits on the eggs, not the way Birdie does.

He spreads his legs and straddles the eggs, more like he's protecting them than as if he's trying to brood. If Birdie abandoned the nest or died, I don't think Alfonso could hatch the eggs.

The babies are growing fast. The growth of their tails seems to be stimulated by flight, or maybe it's the other way around. By the time they're five weeks old, I can scarcely tell them from grown birds. Some have started cracking seed already. Until all of them can do that, they aren't really safe. The book says the real test is when they molt their baby feathers and grow in the first adult feathers. I'm not worried too much; they look so healthy.

It occurs to me one evening as I'm feeding the birds that all I did was put two birds in the aviary, some food and water and nothing else and now there are six of them. I know this is perfectly natural, it's one of the things life is all about, but to have it happen in my bedroom, under my own eyes, is magic.

My aviary begins to look and sound like the real thing. There is the continual fluttering of wings, the sounds of birds calling to each other and the sounds of beaks being wiped on perches. My mother, who hasn't been paying too much attention, accuses me one night at dinner of having bought more birds. I explain they're the babies of my first two. She goes Harumph, sneaks a look at my father, who's putting a piece of baked potato in his mouth, then says they're beginning to stink up the whole house. It scares me when she talks like that. She has so much power over my life and the world of birds in my bedroom.

The next day I buy some stuff in a bottle that makes everything smell like pine trees. I put it around in all the corners of my room but not in the cage. My room begins to smell like a fake forest. It's such a terrific thing having birds, I'll do anything to keep them.

That afternoon, I stay on again to watch Birdy being fed. I ask Renaldi if I can come in. He says it's against the rules but it's OK with him. He opens the door with his keys and I push the cart in behind him.

Birdy's squatting there watching us; he's watching me more than anything. I'm convinced he's bullshitting me now. Maybe he wasn't before, but now he is. I push the tray to the side and stand in front of Birdy. Renaldi goes around the cart and lifts covers off the food.

"Well, Birdy; I'm here. This is Al and you know it, you bastard. Are you really going to squat there flapping your arms like a baby canary while this guy feeds you?"

I say this to him in a quiet voice while Renaldi tinkers with the food. Birdy is looking at me full face, no shifting from eye to eye, none of that bird business. He's looking at me; his eyes aren't even wiggling. I can't say he shows any signs of recognition but he's definitely looking me over, seeing if he can trust me. It's Birdy all right, but he's different. This isn't the old Birdy who used to believe everything; he looks as if he can't believe anything anymore. He doesn't look as if he can't even believe in himself.

Renaldi signals with some cereal and a spoon to me that I can feed him if I want. I reach over and take the bowl and spoon from Renaldi. He's checking the doors to see if anybody's looking in. What're they going to do, fire him? They aren't paying him or anything; they tried putting him in the army, that didn't work. They can't kill him. It's stupid how most of us get in the habit, looking all the time to see if somebody's watching us, as if they're going to catch us doing something wrong. Somewhere, when we're kids, our parents and the shits at school get us all feeling guilty about almost everything.

I hold the food and the spoon out in front of Birdy's face. He keeps looking at my eyes, not at the food.

"All right now, Birdy. It's time to start flipping your wings and peeping. I don't believe it."

He doesn't move.

"OK. I'll feed you anyway. This is all ridiculous. If you could see yourself squatting there on the floor and me shoveling this crap down your throat, you'd probably laugh yourself to death."

I push the food toward his mouth. He keeps his mouth closed and turns his head.

"Come on, Birdy; open up! Let mommy put some mush down your throat. It's good for you."

He turns his head the other way. Renaldi is beginning to come around the cart. I give him a hard look to keep him away.

"Look, Birdy. This guy's giving me a special chance to feed you. Open up! I know the whole thing is damned undignified but what's the difference? Either he feeds you or I feed you. If you're going to pretend you're a stupid bird, at least be consistent. You know you don't crap like a bird. You can jump around all you want, but you'll never fly out of here. They're going to keep you in this cage the rest of your life!"

Birdy stares at me. He's pissed. It's hard to get Birdy mad. He doesn't usually care enough about most things. What I've heard him say more than anything else is, "It doesn't matter." According to him, nothing matters. I'd be burned up about something, at school, or his mother, or my father, and he'd say, "It doesn't matter."

Then, I notice his wings, I mean arms, coming away from his sides. For a minute, I think he's going to spring at me like some crazed bat but he brings them around slowly in front of his face and looks down at them. He turns them around, un-curls his fists, and feebly wiggles the fingers. He looks at me and reaches for the bowl and spoon. I put them in his hands. He doesn't look down, his eyes are still burning into mine. Mad! I'm not sure he isn't going to pitch the mess at my head, but I keep my eyes on his. There's something going on and I'm not sure what it is.

After about two minutes of boring into me, he looks down at the bowl and then at the spoon. He shifts the spoon a few times in his hand as if trying to remember how to hold it. I want to reach out and help but I don't. I'm knowing, for the first time, just how far away Birdy's been. It's a long way back, a long way for him to come. He gets the spoon almost right and starts moving it and the bowl together. He misses twice, then gets the spoon into the mush and stirs it. He stirs for at least three minutes. I'm beginning to ache in the back of my legs from squatting. I'm wishing I didn't have the bandages on my face so it would be easier for Birdy to see me and recog-nize me.

Finally, he lifts the spoon out of the dish with some mush in it and puts it into his mouth. He has a hard time getting the spoon out of his mouth because he bites down on it. It's like watching a baby learning to eat; he has his elbow sticking way up in the air. He probably thinks he's a bird imitating a human being now. Maybe he is.

It takes more than an hour, but Birdy gets a fair amount of food down. He gets to where he's spearing some of the meat with a fork. He lets me take the bowls and fork or plates from him but there's no reaction. His face could be a beak for all the movement it makes. He looks as if he has a mask on, with his eyes glittering out from behind it.

We get outside and Renaldi's all excited. He says this is a big breakthrough; we've got to tell Weiss. I ask him what the hell Weiss will do except write it in his papers or have the T-4 type it out so he can spit on it; can't we keep it to ourselves? Renaldi listens to me. He doesn't want to, but in the end he's willing to go along. I ask him what good is it if Weiss is going to come watch Birdy feed himself. What good is that going to do?

Renaldi leaves and I take my place in the chair between the doors. Renaldi says there's no way he can leave me in the cage with Birdy.

I sit there for a long while watching. I think Birdy's beginning to feel silly squatting all the time. Twice he stretches out one leg or the other. He hasn't done that before. He goes over to the toilet to take a leak. Instead of squatting on the crapper, the way he usually does, he half straightens himself up so he's leaning across the john, opens up his pajamas with one hand and uses the other hand to support himself against the wall. Probably he hasn't straightened out his back that much in months. I don't think he can stand up anymore. Renaldi tells me Birdy sleeps in a squat; won't use the bed. He says sometimes Birdy leans against a wall and sleeps standing on one foot. You'd know Birdy would carry it too far.

When he finishes pissing, Birdy takes a few hunched over steps toward the middle of the floor, like a skinny hunchback of Notre Dame or something, then he goes back to the old squat.

"Nobody's watching now, Birdy. Stand up like a human being. I won't tell anybody. This is Al, you can trust me."

He looks straight into my eyes. I still have the feeling he's mad at me and this is really rare. Like I said, it's hard to get Birdy mad. Even with my old man and the car that time, Birdy wasn't so much mad as discouraged. He couldn't get himself to believe anybody'd do a shitty thing like that. He was sure there'd been some kind of misunderstanding and when he could talk to the person who bought the car he could make it all right again.

There was only one time I can remember Birdy actually getting mad. That's the first time I realized what it would be like when a crazy, trapdoor-minded person like Birdy got mad. I knew then I'd never actually been mad in my life; I'd been pissed or angry, but mad is like crazy.

"Birdy. How about the time that O'Neill kid stole your bicycle. I really think you'd've killed him."

It wasn't too long after Birdy and I'd met each other. We were still going to Saint Alice's Elementary School. We were taught by sisters and it was enough to ruin anybody's life. I'd sit in the back row and think about the nuns menstruating away under those long black, hot costumes. Habits they called them, the costumes I mean.

There was always a plaster statue of the "Blessed Mother" up at the front of the room dressed in light blue, flowing, plaster robes with a snake and flowers crushed under her feet. I used to wonder if she had tits under all that. There were girls in our classes, but it was boys on one side and girls on the other. The girls all wore these crappy dark blue uniforms. I was really glad when I got to the junior high school.

This is just when we're building the new loft in the trees down in the woods; before the gas tank. We're stealing all the wood, but we need money for the wire screen and hinges and things.

The third floor of St. Alice's is the auditorium. They serve lunches up there and every Friday afternoon they have a movie at ten cents a head. Anybody who doesn't go to that movie is a real pauper and doesn't love God either. This church has more damned ways to gouge the last dime out of poor people.

Anyway, up on the third floor they also have a beat-up old piano. Half the keys don't work and there's practically no ivory left on them so it looks as if the piano has most of its teeth knocked out.

The church got a "donation" of another piano and they want this old one taken away. The guys who brought up the new piano say it'll cost five dollars to haul this beat up one down but Father O'Leary, the pastor, says that's too much, so it sits up there. Everybody thumps or bangs on the piano when they go by. The other piano has a key to lock the keyboard and the music sister keeps it locked. She gives piano lessons, at another twenty cents a head, on the new piano.

Birdy tells Father O'Leary he'll get the old piano down out of there for two dollars. O'Leary tries to talk Birdy into "donating" his work for the "love of God," but Birdy holds out for cash. He tells me about the project and we go into it together. Birdy's plan is to chop up the piano and throw it out the window into the school yard after school when everybody's gone.

So, one day after school, Birdy gets the ax and sledgehammer from his garage and we set ourselves to hammering and hacking away at that piano. The real reason we're doing it is for the metal. The sounding board is mounted in cast iron which is worth at least five dollars at the junk dealer's in Greenwood. This is 1939 and everybody's selling scrap metal to the Japs to help along their war effort.

The job goes fast. I'm thumping away and Birdy's chucking huge hunks out the window. We're having a fine time. The damned piano is making great slunking, thonking noises as I swing away at it. Terrific workout. I get all the strings vibrating by hitting them with the sledgehammer and it sounds like heaven. They make a swell sound when I slice through them with the ax, too. We've got an OK to burn the wood in the incinerator and we'll haul away the metal.

Now, Birdy used to ride his bike to school even then. This is the bike the cops stole from us later in Wildwood. He'd lock it to the fence outside the back gate to the play yard. We can see it from up where we are. Birdy'd made the trip right after school, to get the ax and sledgehammer, and then parked the bike in his usual place. I didn't know it, but he didn't lock it when he came back.

We're just about finished with the job and the two of us are pushing a huge hunk of cast metal up onto the edge of the window, when we look down and see a kid getting on Birdy's bike.

Birdy doesn't say anything, he takes off across the auditorium and down the stairs. I hold onto the hunk of metal and yell down to the kid, "Leave that bike alone, you bastard." I can see who it is. It's one of the stupidest kids in the school, Jimmy O'Neill. There are six O'Neill kids going to the school, one stupider than the other. There can't be one complete brain in all of them put together. This Jimmy O'Neill is in the seventh grade but he's sixteen years old. He's short, with bunched muscles. He thinks he's pretty tough. I never remember him except with snot running down his lip and with frayed, torn snot-stiff sweater sleeves. He's a great one for beating up on sixth- and seventh-graders at recess. I've knocked the shit out of him twice already but I don't think he remembers from one time to the next. The last time, he picked up a horse turd and threw it at me. You wouldn't believe a kid that stupid would be allowed to walk around, let alone go to school. He still can't read.

He knows I see him but he rolls off on the bicycle. He's so stupid he can hardly ride the thing. He goes across the sidewalk, wobbling, and turns up Clarke Avenue. He's getting it straightened and is starting to pump away. About half a minute later, Birdy comes running out. I yell, "He went up Clarke! It's Jimmy O'Neill!"

Birdy takes off. I want him to know what he's going to run into when he catches the bike, if there's any chance he can catch a bike by running after it.

I lower the big piece of cast metal onto the floor and take off down the steps myself. I figure Birdy's going to get his block knocked off if he catches O'Neill. I'm looking forward to knocking O'Neill's teeth in. This time I'll have an excuse and no shitface sister or priest to butt in and save his white Irish ass.

When I get to the corner of Clarke Avenue and Franklin Boulevard, I look up and down. Way at the end of Franklin, I see the bike on the ground; Birdy and O'Neill are having at it. I start running that way and I'm surprised when O'Neill breaks away and starts running in my direction. Birdy's right after him. O'Neill looks up, sees me, and turns back.

I wouldn't believe it if I didn't see it. Birdy leaps into the air, at least five or six feet, and lands on O'Neill's shoulders. O'Neill keeps running and Birdy is kicking at him with his feet and punching him in the face and on the side of the head.

O'Neill goes down. He shakes Birdy off and stands up. His face is bloody. He takes a shortcut through a yard and back toward the church. The church is next to the school. Birdy's right after him. I slow down. I'm bushed from running and now I want to see what Birdy's going to do. He's left the bike lying in the street up there on Franklin Boulevard.

Now, this is something to be surprised at, considering the way Birdy is about that bike. Birdy bought it with his own money when he was only about ten years old. It's an old-time bike with giant wheels and old-time thin tubeless tires. Everybody else is getting balloon tires with coaster brakes, but Birdy wouldn't have balloon tires with mere twenty-eight-inch wheels. He keeps his tires pumped up till they're about to explode and tools that bike around at tremendous speeds. He can balance himself on it standing still, only twisting his front wheel once in a while. I've seen him sit that way five or ten minutes, watching something or somebody, then wheel off without ever putting his feet to the ground. He has a way of turning around by lifting up the front wheel and twisting like a horse in a rodeo. He keeps it clean so the spokes and rims shine like new. Birdy practically lives on that bike.

After I get to know him, I really begin to use my bike more, too. Saturdays we'd go on all kinds of trips. There isn't any place within fifty miles of where we live that Birdy hasn't pedaled to at one time or another. He keeps a big map on the wall in his room with the trips he's made marked on it. Birdy'd say, "Let's take a ride to Abington" and we'd be off.

Once Birdy said that when a person is on a bicycle, he's almost totally separated from the earth, practically free from gravity and friction. Birdy is always worried about being held down.

So, I'm really surprised when he leaves the bike and takes off after O'Neill. Maybe he saw me coming and knew I'd move the bike out of the street, but I think he was so mad he didn't see anything and didn't care. I go over and put the bike on the curb leaning against a tree.

I go after Birdy and O'Neill. I'm about to believe they've

run off to hell or disappeared in the ground somehow, when I hear this godawful yell from inside the church. I dash in the back door and Birdy has O'Neill on the floor at the top of the aisle, between his legs, and he's pounding him in the face as O'Neill twists right and left trying to get away. Birdy is all over him, not saying anything, just pumping them in, left, right, left. I run up the aisle. O'Neill's squealing like a stuck pig. Somebody's going to hear him for sure and come in. The rectory and the convent are right next to the school and church.

I have to actually pull Birdy off. He looks at me the same way he just looked at me here over that bowl of mush; like he doesn't know me and might just take a poke at me. His eyes are black and the irises are completely open. He looks crazymad.

"Leave him alone, Birdy! For Christ's sake, let's get the hell out of here before somebody comes!"

Birdy looks at O'Neill as if he doesn't know him either or how he got there. He doesn't say anything, then turns and starts walking down the aisle of the church. I lean over O'Neill. His eyes are puffed up and he's missing teeth. No great loss, his teeth were all bucked and crooked anyway.

"Look, shithead! You tell anybody who beat you up and I'll kill you myself. Nobody'd believe it anyway."

He looks up at me from the floor. He reaches and feels the spaces and loose teeth in his mouth. His mouth is a bloody hole. Then he rolls over onto his knees with his head toward the altar. He kneels there on his hands and knees and cries and bleeds. I figure it's better than being eaten by lions; maybe a little praying will do some good.

I go back to Franklin Boulevard and Birdy is up checking his bicycle over. There are a few bent spokes and some scratches across the top of the handlebars. The front wheel is out of line, too, but we straighten that out OK. I look at Birdy and there's not a mark on him, not even a red mark or a scratch. O'Neill must've been getting nothing but air with those big fists of his. He probably figured he was fighting a ghost or one of the little people, maybe.

Birdy gives the bike a test ride and says it's OK but it'll never really be the same. He's like an old-fashioned Sicilian whose wife has been raped. Even if he knows it isn't her fault, even if she's beaten up from fighting back, he can never be the same toward her. Birdy's like that about the bike. It's one of the reasons he's willing to sell it in Wildwood and why he never got a decent bike again after that. He loved that bike and after it was violated he didn't want another one. Somebody with a mind like that is hard to deal with.

I look at Birdy there, squatting, watching me, open, soft, empty-eyed. I begin to realize he's been violated himself somehow. And now he doesn't want himself anymore.

*A*lfonso's been too busy to do much singing, but now with Birdie on the new eggs and the babies feeding themselves, he begins again.

The first time, he sings lightly, up on the top perch. I'm doing my homework and it's dark in the room. It's great to hear him. He's singing without passion, with a feeling of description, as if he's trying to tell his children about the world outside the cage.

The next morning he sings just as I'm waking up. I lie in bed above him and try to hear what he's saying. I know if I can only open myself to him, I'll understand what canaries can tell me. I lie there with my eyes shut and try to be Alfonso, to feel as if it's me singing. It is coming. I have some knowing, but I can't put it into thoughts or words.

The little dark one, and the yellow one, the one I'd thought was a female, start making chirping bubbling noises along with Alfonso. This is a good sign that they're males. After a few more days listening to Alfonso's songs, all of them sing at one time or another. I can't believe it's possible but it looks as if the whole first nest is male.

At school, I carry in my mind the songs and notes Alfonso sings. There's no way I can imitate them with my big throat and soft mouth, but I have them memorized. It's like knowing music you've heard played with instruments. You carry more than the melody, but also the sounds of the instruments and their blends too. It's the way Alfonso's music is in my head.

I start training the baby birds not to be afraid of me. I go into the aviary with treat food or dandelion greens or apple, things they like. I put these on my knee or on the toe of my shoe and sit down to wait. Birdie comes down, usually, to say hello and eat. The little ones are shy at first but gradually come over and start to eat cautiously. I get the dark one and the spotted one to sit on my finger after a week. Even Alfonso eats off my shoe and once off my knee. He sure is a suspicious bird.

Birdie doesn't like me to pick her up anymore. She gets nervous and jumps away when I put my hand over her. It probably has to do with nesting. Her responsibility as a mother bird is too much for her to take those kinds of chances.

The Alfonso meanness seems directly tied to the dark color. The dark baby is already pushing his nest mates around. The only one who gives him any fight is the spotted one. The little yellow babies just good-naturedly move away or wait their turn.

One time, the dark one forgets himself and tries to push Alfonso off the perch. Alfonso flies away the first time. The little dark one follows him. When Alfonso realizes what's going on, he rears up and gives that baby one sharp rap on the skull. The poor thing plummets to the floor of the aviary and walks around in circles, stunned. Alfonso goes about his business, without following up, and that's the end of it.

The new babies are born all in one morning. There're four of them. They all look dark, no pure yellow ones. Birdie and Alfonso start their routine. They seem to have made a rule that the babies of the first nest aren't allowed in the breeding cage. Alfonso enforces this. It doesn't take many bops on the head or Alfonso growls for the young ones to get the idea.

I've taken out the old nest holder and removed the nest. I've also cleaned up that corner of the cage where it was caked with crap. The new babies grow fast. In almost no time they're teetering on the edge of the nest. I've given up trying to guess sex. There are two completely dark like Alfonso and two with light breasts and dark wings. One of these has a dark head, too. The other has a spot over the left eye. They're almost three weeks old when it happens.

One of the spotted ones, the one with the dark head, has already fallen out of the nest several times. I've put it back every night before I turn off the light. One morning, I go in and find this one has fallen out during the night. I pick it up and it's stiff, legs straight out, and ice cold. I hold it in my hands hoping the warmth might revive it, but it doesn't move. I put it in warm water. I hold it in the water with the head out, but there's nothing to do. The poor thing froze in the night; it's dead. I'm sorry for Birdie and Alfonso. I watch but they keep on feeding the other birds and don't seem to notice one is missing. I don't know what I expect them to do. Birds can't cry. I guess the only animals that can cry, laugh, and lie are people. We're probably the only ones who have some idea about being dead, too. Most animals try to keep from being dead but I don't think they make much of it.

There's something I want to know about birds that I haven't been able to find anywhere; the density, how much it weighs in relation to its volume. I can figure it out with this dead young one. I didn't want to try it with a live bird.

First I fill a glass of water to the very top, put the glass in a saucer and put the dead bird into the glass. I push the bird until all of it is under. The excess water flows up over the side and is caught by the saucer. I pour that water into a jar to take to school to measure it accurately. I wrap the bird in a piece of cloth and put both the jar and the bird in my lunch bag.

My homeroom is in the science lab and there's all the equipment I need to measure and weigh. I weigh the bird and divide the weight by the volume of the displaced water. I'm amazed at how light a bird is.

The next day I do somewhat the same thing on myself. I half fill the bathtub, mark how high the water is, then climb in, get completely underwater, and mark how high the water rises. I measure this rise and all the dimensions of the tub. With this I figure my volume. I weigh myself accurately and do the dividing. I'm one hell of a lot denser than a bird. That's something I have to get around somehow.

That night I put the baby bird in a bottle of alcohol I snitched from school, and hide it with the sterile egg under my socks. Later I want to cut the bird open and look at the bones. I read that the bones are hollow and I want to see what they're like. There are also supposed to be air sacs in a bird, like in a fish. I want to see if I can find them, too. I can't do it yet, I couldn't get myself to face Birdie if I did.

The other birds get out of the nest without any trouble and go through the same business of learning to fly. I watch them by the hour. I sit outside the aviary mostly and watch through the binoculars. I have the binoculars tied to the back of a chair and I kneel down to keep my back from breaking. I must look like a very religious character praying all day long.

With the binoculars I can concentrate on one bird and watch it. I'm trying to find out what it's thinking. I can get the feeling I'm a bird after a while. After two or three hours like that, when I look around my room and at myself and it all looks strange. Everything's huge, exaggerated, and falling over. It takes me several minutes to come back inside myself.

The babies are easy to watch because they don't fly around so fast. I'm still trying to see the difference between the way they flap their wings when they fly and when they're being fed. For one thing, when they're being fed, they squat, pushing against the floor and curving their backs in. The wings flap without any pull from the breast muscles. When they try to fly, it's the opposite. They hunch forward with their shoulders thrust ahead and give a quick powerful push down and back. It's as if they're pulling themselves up a wall. I practice running around the yard doing this.

It helps considerably in jumping up to the perch. Now, I can do it without falling. I can jump up, turn around in mid-air, and come down facing the other way. I can also get into a squatting position on the perch with my arms held down at my sides like wings. Squatting, I get the feeling of being a bird.

I practice out in the yard doing these things for about an hour every night and I flap a half hour in the morning and another half hour before I go to bed at night. I close my eyes when I flap and try to imagine I'm flying. I'm trying to get the rhythm of it across my shoulders. If I can just loosen the scapula and open up the accrumen process at the shoulder some and then develop the trapezius, deltoid, and triceps muscles, I could build up a lot of flapping power. I practice jumping with each flap so I'll get a smooth movement.

In my room, I take off my shoes and double up the carpet so my mother won't hear me. She's already asking questions about my perch exercises but I tell her it's something we do in gym class at school. I have the feeling she's looking for something. I'll have to figure some way to get her to go along with the idea of the birds.

As soon as the second bunch is out of the nest, Birdie is off and building her third. I put back the strainer from the first nest and more burlap. Alfonso has to dash around protecting all the birds from her feather-snitching. The first bunch is fast enough now so they can get away, but the little ones are easy victims. I wonder how many feathers she'd really pull out if Alfonso didn't fly to the rescue. I hate to think she'd strip them bare. It seems so crazy.

As soon as this nest is finished, she starts laying eggs. She lays five, again. The entire cycle is started. It's May now and she'll just finish her third nest before the hot summer comes on.

The second nest has worked their way out into the big

aviary. They still like to be fed and they chase their older brothers and sisters around. These fly away, except for one I'm calling Alfonso II, that's the dark bird. He usually gives them a quick clout on the head or neck.

Alfonso I is being run to death by the babies. He flies up to hide on the top perch whenever he can. Gradually they all learn to eat egg food, and some of them even start experimenting with seeds. The first nest is onto the system of cracking seed and spend all their time chasing each other or practicing singing. They make quite a racket when they get started.

One of the dark birds in the second nest has already made half an attempt at singing and could be a male, too. Now there are nine birds in the aviary. When I come in the room, there's a rush of wings as they all take off up to a high perch. I spend much time with them and they're all tame. I clean out the aviary every day. The birds don't mind me at all and will land on my head or shoulders. It's only if I make a fast move that they get scared and fly away.

The feed bills are mounting up. I search around downtown by the central market till I find a big seed store where I can buy birdseed roller mix by the hundred-pound sack. It costs eighteen dollars, but that's less than a third what I've been paying. They say they'll deliver right to my house.

When it comes, I put the sack out in the garage inside an old oil can I found down at the dump and cleaned out. With birdseed you really have to watch for mice. In the dusk or early morning, it's hard for a bird to tell between a piece of mouse shit and a seed. Mouse shit is poisonous for birds.

Speaking of mice, my mother is sure the birds are going to bring mice into the house. She has a regular passion against mice. One morning I catch one on the floor of the aviary. He was probably already in the house anyway, but I could never convince my mother of that. I put it in a small box and let it free near school. If she ever finds this out, I've had it. Birds, cages, everything, out the window. She's liable to do it any day anyway. I half expect it every time I come home from school and go up to my room.

Every bird hatches in the third nest; five of them. When I look in, I see that most of them are light this time. There's such a crush in the bottom of the nest you can't be sure of anything. It's warmer now, so Birdie doesn't sit as tight. She mostly spreads her legs over the nest and hovers. The young birds get to be such pests, I close the cage door to keep them out. I put feed in for her during the day while I'm gone. As soon as I come home, I open it and Alfonso dashes up to help with the evening feeding. Birdie has developed into a wonderful little mother.

In the warm weather and with the increase in birds, even I have to admit the room definitely smells "birdey." I'm using a dozen eggs and a package of pablum a week making egg food. I'm also soaking regular birdseed and mixing it with egg food to start the young ones cracking seed. I feed in the morning when I wake up, just before I leave for school, when I come back, and then again before night. They eat tremendous quantities. Buying seed and eggs has almost used up my bankroll. I'm going to have to find some way to make money over the summer.

It seems no time at all before the third nest is ready to jump. There are three yellow ones like Birdie. Two of these have marks on the head, one a dash over the left eye, and the other a black cap, slightly off center to the right. There is one Alfonso-dark, and another dark-winged and light-breasted with a pure yellow head. It really makes a crowd. Birdie is a heroine, hauling up food, keeping the nest clean, and mothering the whole batch. There isn't enough room for all of them on the edge of the nest and they start pushing each other off. Luckily it's much warmer now and there's no danger they'll freeze. At three weeks, all five of them are out of the nest and on the floor.

It's right here I make my mistake. I should've taken

Alfonso out of the aviary and put him in a separate cage. Before I know what's happening, Birdie is building another nest. I haven't put in a new strainer but she's building in a corner at the back of the cage, wedged between a perch and the wall of the cage. Alfonso's done his trick and she's heavy with eggs and no place to go. I pull the nest apart but she frantically puts it together again. I take all the nesting material out of the cage, but she starts attacking the babies and pulling feathers out till it looks like it's snowing yellow. Several of the babies begin to look bare around the thighs and under the breast. I give in. She seems in good condition so I clean out the nest, wash it, and put it back with some nesting material. She finishes it in one day and the first egg is laid that night.

She lays five eggs again. She sits this clutch rather lightly and I'm half hoping they won't hatch. I watch Birdie carefully for signs of fatigue but she peeps at me friendlily and, despite a certain frantic air, appears happy and content with her lot. I wonder if she realizes that the whole aviary full of singing, screeching, scrambling birds, with the exception of Alfonso, came out of her somehow. It's as if it all came out of nowhere. I still can't believe it.

The whole clutch hatches again. I have to leave the doors open all the time so Alfonso can help with the feeding. I don't think Birdie could make it without him. Alfonso keeps the other babies out of the breeding cage and stays with Birdie in the cage most of the day and all of the night. I'm getting so I hate to open the boiled eggs in the morning and smash them into the pablum. The smell of the two, mixed with the smell of the fork I mash with, is too much.

This nest is very dark. There are three as dark as Alfonso and two light ones with head markings. They have the same crowded nest conditions and it's even hotter. I take Alfonso out as soon as the first bird climbs up to the edge of the nest. I find an old cage at the dump and fix it up. I don't want to scare him by catching him. I'd certainly lose any points I have if I chase him around the aviary and grab him with my hands. He'd probably bite and give me blood poisoning. So, I put the cage in the aviary with some egg food in it, wait till he goes in on his own, then jump up and close the door.

I take the cage out of the aviary and hang it over my desk by the window. There's all kinds of peeping and queeping back and forth. Alfonso is sure I've finally shown my true colors. I wonder what he's telling Birdie about the situation. She's torn between abandoning the nest for Alfonso and taking care of the babies. She flies over to the screen of the aviary and looks across at him. Alfonso breaks into a song of great bravado. I feel terrible. I hate it when people tell me they're doing something for my own good, and here I am doing it to Birdie and Alfonso. I'm almost ready to put Alfonso back in the cage and take the chance. But, I know, they'd have another nest and it'd probably kill Birdie. It's getting time for both of them to go into the yearly molt and they shouldn't be having babies during this time. It's a tremendous strain on birds when they molt and change their feathers.

Birdie finally resigns herself to the fates, that is, me. She goes back to feeding the babies till they get out of the cage. As soon as they're all down on the floor, I take out the nest. This time, Birdie shows no signs of nesting again. She goes out in the aviary and flies around.

As soon as the birds are feeding themselves, I remove Birdie from the aviary and take out the breeding cage. I put Alfonso back in with the young ones. I want Birdie to have a complete rest. Anytime I'm in the room, I let her fly free. It's like old times. She sleeps in the cage up on the shelf above my bed where it used to be.

Al and I take the job dogcatching and I make enough money to pay my feed bills. I spend all my free time watching the birds. I'm trying to figure what's the next thing to do.

When I go for my session with Weiss, I can smell right away he's going to work on me. I know for sure I'm not going to tell him anything; I'm certainly not going to tell anything about Birdy. I don't want him to find out about Birdy feeding himself or standing up and walking around. I'm convinced Weiss can't do Birdy any good. If only I can stay a little longer maybe Birdy'll come around.

We salute and he leans back, crosses his hands over his fat stomach and smiles at me. He's got the folder open on his desk. He has another folder there, too. I'm willing to bet it's my records from Dix. He's working himself up a thing OK. There's nothing I can do but play it by ear. I try to get myself into a good Sicilian mood. I pretend we're sitting at a cafe in Cambria with sunshine streaming down on us. Weiss is a tribal chieftain from the other side of the hills.

"Well, Sergeant. How did it go yesterday?"

"Fine, sir. I talked to the patient about how we used to ice skate in the winter sometimes. I think he might have been listening to me, sir."

"What made you think he was listening, Sergeant?"

"Just the way he was sitting, sir. He seemed to be watching me."

I'll have to be careful here. Whatever happens, I don't want Weiss charging into the ward. Birdy'd be sure I'm working against him. I back off some.

"How is your jaw coming along, Sergeant? I have your

papers here and you seem to have had a rather serious injury there. How long is it before you have another operation scheduled?"

He's the psychiatrist this morning, all right. He couldn't care less about me. He's working up to something.

"It's fine, sir. Next week I have the final work done. They'll put on the last layers and finish it off."

Weiss leans forward and pulls my folder in front of him. He flips open the cover. It's my records all right; I see my name.

"Sergeant, would you mind going into more detail about this court-martial you had at Fort Cumberland? What actually happened?"

"I don't see what that has to do with the patient, sir. It all happened a long time ago."

"Let me decide that, Sergeant."

Son-of-a-bitch!

"Well, sir, if you think it might help, I'll tell you all I can remember."

Some way I have to keep this shit away from Birdy. He's sitting there smiling at me over his folded hands. I smile back, a Sicilian smile, the Southern smile which says, "You and I know all this is so much horseshit, let's get on with it."

He leans back in his chair, exhales a deep sigh, closes his eyes behind his glasses while picking up a yellow pencil from the desk. He starts putting the pencil on its point, sliding his fingers down the pencil, then turning the pencil around so the eraser is on the desk, and sliding down again. He's sort of subtly jacking off on the pencil. I consider sneaking away; I don't want to talk about Cumberland. Boy, Birdy, the crap I'm putting up with for you.

"Well, sir, I was in the Pennsylvania State Guard and in December they sent me to Fort Cumberland for induction and reassignment into the regular army."

I even have to show those assholes at Cumberland how to hook bayonet scabbards to the webbing equipment. There's a hunky T-5 in charge, but he sits in the squad room all day long topping up his load. Hell, I'm taking over the barracks, going to make general in six months.

The third morning, we're called out and lined up in the company street. It's so cold that when I spit it freezes before I can smear it with my foot. A second lieutenant and a Sergeant come out from a shed on the other side of the street. The Sergeant calls us to attention and there's mail call. My feet are freezing, my nose is about to drop off, my fingers are stiff in the gloves. None of us is going to get any mail. Then, the Sergeant calls us to attention again and the lieutenant starts.

"All right, men. After this, you'll be dismissed to quarters. Chow at twelve hundred. First, Corporal Lumbowski will choose men for details."

The hunky T-5 starts walking down the line. He stops every once in a while and points. He comes to me, points and says, "Coal." Would you believe it, I'm proud I've been chosen. The rest are dismissed and about fifteen of us stay.

Weiss is still lying back with a smile on his face, his eyes closed behind his glasses. I almost expect him to snore but he isn't asleep at all. I'm wondering how much I can bullshit this without making him open his eyes.

The T-5 calls us together. He's a chunky bastard, not tall but square, true hunky type, reminds me of a Cheltenham Polack I pinned in the District finals. Pinned him first period; strong but dumb. The stupid shit cries while I'm pinning him. Tears are running down his red face while I'm tightening a half nelson and jacking up a crotch hold. The T-5 tells the coal detail to report to him at the shed next morning at oh-five-hundred. There are four of us.

Back in the barracks it looks as if the shit hit the fan. Everybody's thrown all their gear on the floor and crowded around the stove. I start high-kneeing up and down the barracks, jumping and dodging all the crap on the floor. I hate to think of going into combat with fuck-offs like these.

Next morning, a PFC flunky wakes me and I get down to the kitchen for chow. I'm the first one there and I even made up my bunk before I left. The kitchen is warm and steamy. I eat while the rest of the detail comes straggling in.

After that, we stand for ten minutes in the dark on the company street, waiting. I'm wearing two pairs of socks, but my feet are already cold. My arms are stiff from the shots. I jog in place and windmill my arms. The other three jerks are hunched inside themselves, smoking.

Finally, the T-5 comes out. He doesn't look up or count us. Maybe he can't count to four. We follow him to the motor pool where a truck is waiting. There are two jigs in the cabin. I smile at them but they ignore me. The T-5 pulls down the tailgate.

"OK, up you go, shitheads."

I muscle up and swing into the truck first. Two guys can't make it so I give them a hand. The back of the truck is sheet metal, wet, slick and black with damp coal dust. Shovels are leaning against the front wall of the truck bed. There are no seats. The damned coal dust is going to get all over the new overcoats. I go and squat beside the shovels. The other farts line up on both sides of me. Nobody's saying anything. We're not even looking at each other.

The truck starts with a lurch and swings hard out of the motor pool. We're all thrown on our asses and slip across the truck bed. We can hear the sons-of-bitches laughing in the cabin. The T-5 looks back at the fun through the cabin window. We barrel along a dirt road, falling all over each other, till we get on the main road to Harrisburg. Our knees are black from sliding around, and Christ it's cold! There's nothing to block the wind. My face and ears have turned numb. After about half an hour, we pull up to some coal piles near the river. The truck stops and the T-5 comes around to open the tailgate.

I guess I've stopped talking and I'm only thinking because Weiss opens his eyes and says, "Go on, Sergeant, tell me about the incident that related to the court-martial. Tell me everything you can remember."

"Well, sir. They transported us by military transport to

Harrisburg. There was a corporal in charge, Corporal Lumbowski, the non-commissioned officer I was accused of attacking. There were also two PFCs driving the truck and four of us on the detail."

I'm running my mind a mile a minute trying to give Weiss enough to keep him interested but not too much. I'm hoping I can tell this without sounding like a homicidal maniac.

I jump off the truck first and my legs buckle. I can't feel a thing. One guy takes a header and cuts his hand on the gravel. The T-5 is standing, pointing into the truck. He's wearing thick leather mittens.

"Stupid basturds; ya fergot the fuggin' shovels. Ya wanna shovel tha' coal whit yer han's dat's OK whit me. You!"

He points at me.

"Yeah, you, musclehead. Jump up deah an' git dem gahdamn shovels an' make it fast! We ain' gaht awh fuggin' day!"

I do a quick, one-handed hurdle up onto the truck bed. The moron didn't expect that. I grab the shovels. I stand with them at the tail of the truck. I motion to one of the guys on the detail.

"Here, you; catch!"

I throw him a shovel. The asshole not only misses; he ducks!

"Cut dat shit, fuck-off! Jiis' han' 'em down. Dem's guvment isshew. Ya wanna make outta fuggin' Stamenttachaages, huh?"

I jump down and pass out the shovels. The jigs back the truck close to a huge pile of coal. The T-5 takes my shovel.

"Naow, disheah's ah shovel, an' disheah's de wokkin' en'. Disheah's de hannel. Ya take-a-hold by de hannel an' push de flaht paht unnder de coal deah and lif' up an trowh de coal inna truck. See? Unnerstan?"

So fuckin' stupid. We all start shoveling. The coal's frozen so hard we almost can't get the shovels in for the first few bites; we have to kick them in. We're all getting in each other's way. The T-5 goes up to sit in the cab with the jigs. They keep the motor running so the cab'll stay warm. All we're getting is carbon monoxide out the back. Nobody's talking; none of us is much at shoveling; we're all hurting from the shots and binding tight in the new overcoats. It's going to be one long morning filling that truck.

"Well, sir, we work for about two hours shoveling coal into the truck. None of us had had much experience and the noncom in charge, Corporal Lumbowski, was getting impatient. He had a job to get done and we were way behind schedule."

Weiss nods and gives a few hmms to show he's listening. I think he really likes hearing this kind of crap. Maybe psychiatrists get into it because they like freaky stories.

I'm just getting up a sweat, when the moron T-5 jumps down from the cab, puts out his cigarette and comes back. I can see the jigs looking through the cab window over the coal we've piled up. The T-5 has promised them some kind of show. I'm expecting the worst. The T-5 stands watching half a minute, then comes over to me. He grabs my shovel and pushes me aside.

"Dat ain' no way ta shovel, musclehead. Do it lak dis heah!"

He drives the shovel into the coal, tilts and swings it over his shoulder in one movement. He does another. They gave this fart the coal detail for good reason, he's got to be some kind of coal miner in civilian life. The other guys have stopped to watch. He pushes the shovel back at me.

"Naoull, gitto it. Stop de fuggin' golbricken'!"

He goes back. The cab door opens and they're laughing; deep, inside, nigger laughing. That laughing sounds warm. I'm so frozen, even my Sicilian laugh wouldn't work. I start shoveling.

About five minutes later, he's there again. He stands watching, banging his mittens together, stamping his feet. I'm trying to show the bastard up; digging in hard, tilting up a full shovel load, and really swinging back to get it all in the truck.

No fartface, hunky, coal miner's going to outdo Al Columbato. He comes over to me.

"Foah chrissake, musclehead; yer trowin' haf de coal unner de fuggin' truck. Giddown deah an' scrape it all ou' an' trah ta aim atta gawhdamn truck instead'a all oveah de yahd."

Five days in the regular army and I've already found somebody to kill. I lean under the truck and scrape out the coal. There's not half a shoveful. I start shoveling again. After about two shovelsful, he grabs me by the arm and reaches for the shovel. I pull the shovel away.

"Keep your fuckin' hunky hands off my shovel, shithead."

Everything stops; nobody's shoveling. The T-5 stares; there's no going back, now. I'm not going to let myself be pawed over by a dumb shit like him, stripes or not.

Weiss has stopped jacking off his pencil; he's tense behind those glasses. He's practically holding his breath, waiting for a violence scene. The trouble is, I want to shock the shit out of him. What the hell, the war's over. They can't lock me up. I'm ready to be discharged. I have more than enough points with the Purple Heart and everything.

The T-5 takes a step toward me and sticks his ugly face out.

"What'd yoou say, soldjur?!"

"You heard me, asshole. Keep your filthy hands off my shovel. I've got work to do."

I start shoveling again.

"Oh yeah? Oh Yeah?! Yore in big trubble, soldjur. Gimme dat shovel. Ahm takin' yoou off deetail naull an' turnin' yoou in!"

He reaches for the shovel.

I step back about two steps to the edge of the coal pile and swing from the hips! God, I've got to say, it feels good! I catch him flush in the face, straight on, flat out!!!

Weiss is breathing hard; maybe he'll have an orgasm.

The T-5's feet go out from under him and he's on his back in the coal pile. He starts to get up, then falls back again.

His face looks blurred, as if somebody'd pulled a silk stocking over it. At first, it's white, then the blood starts.

The jigs have both jumped out of the truck. Blood's really flowing now. The T-5 begins spitting teeth. The jig holds the hunky's head up so the blood can come out. It's dark, thick blood and there's not a tooth left across the front of his mouth.

The other jig is holding a pistol on me with both hands. He's shaking and he has his finger on the trigger. I can't tell if the safety is on or not. He's staring, wild-eyed, down that gun at me.

"Man, you done it. The fuckin' ahmy's gwine'a kill you!"

I try to stare it out with him. What else can I do? He's liable to kill me as not.

"Put down that gun, nigger. I'm not gwine'a kill you, not yet!"

I'm feeling cold inside. The jig lowers the gun but keeps it in his hand. The hunky is sitting up. He still doesn't know what happened.

Weiss is leaning forward, his eyes open. His mouth has dropped but he's not drooling yet.

"Well, sir, after I hit him, I was confined to quarters and three days later I had a summary court-martial. I was reprimanded, it was written into my service record, and they shipped me out to Benning for Infantry basic. It wasn't much of a way to begin an army career, sir."

So, General Columbato was court-martialed and broken to private after only five days in the regular army. The whole thing was a farce. I'm confined to quarters for the rest of the time I'm at Cumberland; this meant no details, no standing around in the cold. They also take half my first six months' pay. Big deal, half of fifty-four dollars a month. After the sentencing, the captain who's in charge sees I'm not hurting. I'm trying my damnedest not to smile about the whole thing. He leans toward me.

"Soldier, I also command you to visit Corporal Lumbowski in the hospital!"

"I can't do that, sir."

He stands up and leans farther forward, vested authority pouring from his eyes.

"And why not, soldier. That's a direct order!"

"I'm confined to quarters, sir."

I keep my face straight and he's pissed. Maybe I'll get a second court-martial for insulting a commissioned officer. I'm working my way up.

The captain keeps his eye on me and pulls out a drawer from the desk. He writes on a pad of paper. He hands the paper across to me. I take it without looking at it.

"That'll get you to the hospital, private."

"Thank you, sir."

I take the chance; give him a fancy salute, sharp one, he returns it. I spin on my heels and leave. I walk through the orderly room, down the steps, across the company street and into the barracks. I flop out on my bunk the way the rest of the slobs do. I borrow a comic book from the bunk next to me, Captain Marvel. The bunk's covered with comic books. Five days and about a hundred comic books later, I get orders for Benning. I never do get to see that T-5.

I'm finished and Weiss is wanting more. We sit there quiet for a couple minutes.

"And that's the whole story, Sergeant?"

"Yes, sir."

"And you don't feel you'd do anything like that again?"

"No, sir. I learned my lesson."

"Did you ever hit or use violence on the patient?"

Finally, he asks the jackpot question!

"No, sir. We were friends."

He pushes the pencil up and down a few more times.

"Do you have any idea, Alfonso, why you've been victim to these aggressive, hostile impulses? Did your father ever beat you excessively? Do you have some deep feeling of being hurt?"

Son-of-a-bitch!! He fooled me with all the fat and the

smiles and glasses. He knows. I'm beginning to know, too.
I'm stuck with some crazy things, like Popeye.

> I yam what I yam
> And that's what I yam;
> I'm Popeye the sailor man:
>   Toot!!! Toot!!!
> I eat all my spinach and
> Fight to the finish.
> I'm Popeye the sailor man;
>   Toot!!! Toot!!!

Bullshit!!!!

$\mathcal{I}$ spend all that summer, when I'm not catching dogs, watching the birds. There are eighteen young birds besides Birdie and Alfonso. We get through the molt without losing a single young one. I'm really enjoying learning their different flying styles. Each bird has its own way. The flying is what interests me most. The way Mr. Lincoln is interested in color, I'm interested in flying. I could watch all the time; it's almost like flying myself.

With the warm weather, my room is definitely beginning to smell "birdey." My mother keeps sticking her head into the room and sniffing. I've got to do something before she goes over the edge.

In the meantime, I'm doing experiments with the young birds. I want to know exactly how much weight a canary can carry and still fly. I also want to know how important wings are to flying. Would a bird without wings keep trying to fly? I take one of the young birds from the last nest and pull out its flight feathers as they grow in. It does everything the other birds do, except when it jumps out of the nest it can't fly. It hops around the bottom of the cage. The others grow and are out flying in the aviary while it's still bound to the bottom of the cage. However, when its flight feathers do grow in, it catches up with the others and is soon flying as well as they are.

I choose some of the best flying young birds and put

weights on their legs. For weights I make little bands from solder. I increase these weights a bit at a time, putting on more and more bands. My calculations show that, with my volume, to equal the density of a bird, I'd have to weigh less than fifty pounds. I can never make that and live. I'm hoping that birds can still fly when they have a higher density.

The way I weigh the birds is to put our kitchen platform scale in the aviary. I spread some feed on the platform and wait. When one of the birds lands to eat, I read the scale. That way I get the weights of all the birds. The birds all weigh almost the same; there's less than a few grams separating the heaviest from the lightest. It's hard to believe they're so light. I don't put any weights on Alfonso or Birdie; I figure they've already worked enough.

I keep increasing the weights until a bird refuses to fly. There's quite a difference in endurance. Some birds quit after I've only put two bands on each leg. They just sit on the floor of the cage puffed up and pretend they're asleep. It seems that when a bird thinks it can't fly, it gives up. I have to take the weights off these birds or they won't even eat.

In the end, there are two of the young males who keep flying, without giving up, even when I've more than doubled their weight. They can struggle their way up to the highest perches in the aviary. These two young ones take some hard bumps before I remove the weights. Still, now, if I get myself down to below a hundred pounds and can keep my strength up, I have a chance.

One night, after dinner, my mother starts in about the birds. There's only one thing to do and that's let her go on. My father and I sit and wait till she winds down. My father looks at me once but I can't tell anything.

My mother complains about the smell, the mess, the noise, the mice, the fact that I'm spending all my time with the birds and don't even have any friends except for that wop up on

Radburn Road. That's Alfonso. I really don't know what I could do with my life that would make her happy. When she seems to be finished, I wait a few seconds, enough to make sure she's finished and not so long that my father is going to have to say something. I know he hates this kind of thing.

It's too bad my parents didn't have more children. My mother says it's because my father chose the wrong trade and the depression came at the wrong time and my father was out of work for four years. He did his apprenticeship making wicker chairs, the kind people have on porches. It used to be high-class to have those kinds of chairs and they were hand-made. We have a porch around two sides of the house, and my father made our chairs. There are all kinds, some rocking chairs and some with high fancy backs. It's fun to watch him. He keeps the wicker lengths in water and weaves them into the forms of chairs with his hands and a few simple tools. It's like watching Birdie build her nest. His hands move fast and automatically. He served a six-year apprenticeship and has his master's papers. It's hard to be so good at something nobody wants anymore.

I start telling him my idea. I explain how this year alone with only two birds I've raised eighteen young birds. The males are worth eight dollars apiece on the wholesale market. I can sell off the females and pay my feed bills. That means a profit of almost ninety dollars. That's a month's salary for my father, working at the high school. I point out how most canaries in the United States are imported from Germany and Japan. Now that we're at war, these sources are drying up. Raising canaries could be a good business.

I'm talking fast. I've got to convince him. I take out my calculations and show how much money I could make if I had fifteen breeding couples. If they all only produced an average of ten birds, and half of them males, I'd make fifty dollars on each breeding pair, that would make seven hundred and fifty dollars. The chances are the price for canaries is going up, too.

My mother says she isn't going to have hundreds of birds stinking up the house no matter how much money I say I can make. I tell my father I want to build an aviary in back of the garage where I used to have my pigeon loft. I tell him I have enough money saved to build the whole thing.

My father sits with his elbows on the table and his hands in a double fist in front of his mouth. He has his thumbnail jammed between his teeth while I talk. My mother stands up and starts taking the dishes off the table. She's making a lot of noise doing it. My father doesn't look at her.

"You say you think you can make seven hundred and fifty dollars a year raising canaries?"

"That's right."

"That's almost as much as I make, working a full year, day in and day out. Are you sure of that?"

"Yes, I'm sure. I know I can do it."

He sits with his thumbnail still between his teeth. He only takes it out to talk. It's then I notice how thin and thin-skinned he looks. If you didn't know, you'd think he was sick. His veins show on his hands and on the side of his head. He looks dead next to my mother, who's so thick, round and pink. My father is ten years older than my mother.

"What would you do with all this money?"

"I'll do whatever you say."

He looks straight at me. It's as if he's seeing me, too. I'm glad my mother is in the kitchen.

"All right. But you give the money to me. I'll put it in the bank so you can go to college. I don't want you working all your life for a lousy twenty dollars a week."

So, that's how it is. My mother won't talk to me but there's nothing she can do.

I start building my aviary on the back wall of the garage. It's away from the ball field so nobody can see it unless they come into our yard. Still, it isn't too visible from the house, either. It's the perfect place.

I get most of the wood the same way I got it before. I buy the wire mesh, nails, hinges, paint, and things like that. I have over a hundred dollars from the dogcatching. I only told my parents about the dollar an hour, not about the dog money. I gave them all the actual salary but I kept the dog money for myself and hid it with my pigeon suit.

I build the frame with two-by-fours. The whole exterior dimension is twelve feet wide by six feet deep. It's six feet high at the front and seven feet where it butts against the garage wall. I cover the roof with small, dark blue composition shingles. Inside, I divide the aviary into three parts. The center part has the outside door opening onto it. That's where I'm going to have my breeding cages. It's exactly six feet by six feet. On either side, and opening onto the center section are the flight cages. These are three feet by six feet and the whole height of the aviary.

I stretch the wire mesh over the framework and nail it in place. The mesh has quarter-inch square holes. I put sand in the bottom of the flight cages and then move all the birds except Birdie down from my room. I put the females in the left cage and the males in the right. They zoom around like crazies checking everything out. They fly against the wire of the cage to look at the outside. It's the first time the babies have seen the sky. Their world is expanded a million times. Still, the actual flying space is about the same. Sometimes, wild birds come up against the outside wire of the cage to look in. Alfonso, with some of the young, fights them off. I wish I could find a way so my birds could fly free like pigeons. It'd be great to have them loop and fly all over, singing and roosting in the trees; then come when I called them into the cage.

I paint the outside gray and white. When I'm finished it looks like a true little house. While the birds are in the flight cages I start building the breeding cages. I've decided to breed one male to a female. I'm not really in business. The males can help with the babies and it's too confusing with two females.

I build five rows of cages, three cages in a row; one on top of the other, going from the floor to the roof on the back wall of the center room. Each cage has two parts with a sliding door between. That way, I can separate the male or the young ones, or both, from the female, when she's started a new nest. I work out automatic feeders and waterers and build sliding trays in the bottoms of the cages for easy cleaning. It's really fun building the cages; like making my own nest.

I get tremendous advice from Mr. Lincoln. He builds his cages himself and has some great ideas that I use. He's really a genius with birds. I tell him my idea about breeding canaries for flying. He laughs in a circle around his aviary. Tears come into his eyes. When he stops, he says nobody's going to buy my canaries. He says if I can breed up a canary that can't fly at all, then I'd really have something. People could keep them on a stick without a cage, like parrots. He says cats'd like my non-flying canaries, too.

I finish the breeding cages before Christmas. The males in the flight cages are singing their heads off. Almost anything is music to a canary. They sing when I hammer or saw or when I run water. The wind blowing is a symphonic concert to a canary.

While I'm working, I keep watching them fly. Alfonso is still the star, but there're two or three others who have all his tricks; dive-bombing, jumping straight up, turning sharp in midair. One of them even has a new trick. He dive-bombs, then instead of landing, turns just above the ground and shoots straight up again. Somehow, he uses his downspeed to turn up. I watch it a hundred times but can't figure how he does it. I can see he tilts his body so he's practically standing on his tail with wings full out at the split second when he pulls out of

his dive, then, he hunches his shoulders over and traps the fast
air under his wings to give him the thrust up. This bird is yellow like Birdie but has all the hawk look of Alfonso. He's not as
mean as some of the dark birds, but he fights if anybody
pushes too hard. Most times he just moves away to another
perch. He's one of the ones who flew with all the weight.

Alfonso II, from the first nest, is almost as mean as old
Alfonso himself. The two of them get into some awful battles.
Alfonso has a hard time finding any place in the aviary where he
isn't invading the territory of number-one son.

I still haven't lost any birds. Mr. Lincoln gives me some
great ideas for tonics. I soak seed and mix it with egg food and
cereal. I give them apples, lettuce, and dandelion leaves.

Counting Alfonso and Birdie, there are twenty birds—
twelve males and eight females. The only sure breeding pair I
have is Alfonso and Birdie. I could line-breed to Alfonso with
one of the females but he's so good with Birdie, I hate to break
it up. It's hard to do, but I decide to sell, or trade off, all the
females. I need new blood; I can't breed brother to sister. Some
of these females are beautiful, and I hate to sell them. I feel
like a slave trader.

I'm going to run fifteen breeding couples, so I need three
more males as well as the females. I hunt around for two
months before I find the kind of males I want. The trouble
is it's hard to see how well they fly, even in flight cages. The
birds can't get up any real speed.

One male I buy is what's called a cinnamon. He's sort of a
golden-brown color. He's long and slim like Alfonso, but his
song type is what is called Saxon; sort of half roller.

Another male is yellow except for a black head and a topknot. A topknot has his hair parted and combed out from
the center of his head. He looks as if he's wearing a hat. This
one looks almost like a clown. If you breed two topknots together you get a bald-headed bird. Mr. Lincoln is disgusted that

I'd buy a topknot. He doesn't like any of the fancy birds. But this topknot can really fly. Also, he's incredibly good at hovering. Canaries don't hover much but this topknot can hover around the top of an aviary like a hawk hunting. He can also do a fair glide. Finches generally aren't much for gliding, so, I have to have him.

The last one I get from Mr. Lincoln. Mr. Lincoln gives me the bird for nothing. He's convinced this bird's crazy. It keeps flying into the sides of the aviary. Most birds learn fast just what a cage is and how wire is. They get so they fly up against the cage but swing their feet up and grab hold. Only a baby bird will actually butt its head against the wire of a cage.

Now, this bird won't recognize the cage. It's full-grown but he'll fly head-on against the wire as if it isn't there. As a result he spends a fair amount of time on the bottom of the cage recovering from crashes. Mr. Lincoln says he's born stubborn dumb. I try to trade one of my dark females for him but Mr. Lincoln doesn't even want that. He says he thought of me as soon as he noticed this stupid bird.

I trade away the females one for one. Mrs. Prevost takes most of them and gives me the pick of hers. She's glad I'm going to breed one male to a female. I spend two weeks in her cages trying to pick her best flying females. I work out a system. I borrow a stopwatch from school and watch a particular bird for five minutes. I only count the time the bird is actually in the air. I want my birds to like flying. I check each bird three times then add in such things as gracefulness and speed of flight. When I'm finished I have all the birds ranked on a flying scale. I'm also trying to avoid birds who are plain clumsy. This type will come in for a landing and stumble or crash into other birds. They'll do a lot of crazy fluttering when they try to land on a perch in a tight space between other birds. I'm also avoiding any female who sings or fights. All the books say these are bad signs for a breeding bird. Singing females have a tendency to abandon the nest. I get my lists finished and give them to Mrs. Prevost. There're a few of her best breeders on the list and she won't sell or trade those, but I get most of what I want.

When I have all these birds in my flight cages it's beautiful. It's great to see a cage full of fine flying birds. These females fly much more than the males.

There're still two months before the breeding season starts, so I continue with my flying experiments. It's cold out in the aviary now, so I dress up in all my warm clothes when I go out to watch. I've got my mother convinced it's all part of raising canaries.

Now that the birds are full-grown, I experiment with flight feathers. A feather, if you look at it carefully, is incredible. It's designed so that when pressure is put under it, no air can pass through. At the same time, air can pass through from the top easily. The feather has a hollow shaft with feeders for circulation of blood. On each side of the shaft grow out branches called barbs. These branch again into things called barbules which have little barbicles with hooks on the end. They all interlock and can be pulled apart or put together like a complicated fine-tooled zipper. The feather can be zipped and unzipped by the bird with its beak. This is what birds are doing when they run their feathers through their beaks; rezipping feathers that've come apart.

Also, the feathers rotate on an axis, so they can be vertical on the upswing and horizontal on the down. All this complication is built into something weighing practically nothing; light as a feather. The feather is the thing I'm up against. Either I have to make something like it or learn to do without.

I start pulling flight feathers from my hero birds, the ones who flew with their own weight hanging on their legs. I put the weights back on and pull one flight feather out from each wing. One gives up immediately. All that weight and now this.

He sits on the bottom of the cage and tries to sleep. I take the weights off and let him free. He flies without trouble after a few minutes. Apparently, missing two flight feathers isn't much to a canary if he isn't weighted down. The other one manages flight of a sort. It's a desperate frantic flight but he gets off the ground and makes it up to some of the first perches. I decide to leave the weights on and see how he compensates.

At the end of a week there's definite improvement. He gets so he can struggle his way to the top perch of the aviary. He stays up there most of the time and his flights down are hellish. They're hardly flight, more plummeting nose dives. He spins down, missing all the perches, flapping his wings frantically. Still, he survives and manages the tough flight up again. I figure he's suffered enough for science and take off the weights.

In the meantime, I'm working nights on designs for mechanical feathers. I'm using designs like Venetian blinds, pivoting on pins. They close on the downstroke and open on the up. I use a bent driveshaft run by a rubber-band motor to make them flap. I'm making models in both balsa wood and thin aluminum. It's going to take a tremendous amount of strength to activate enough flapping power in wings large enough to lift me. One big trouble is that birds flap their wings by pulling them forward on the upstroke and pushing back at the same time they flap down. It's almost like a butterfly breaststroke in swimming. They trap air under the wings and push against it. The joint of a bird's wing moves in a circle, clockwise into the direction of flight. It's hard to work this out with a rubber-band motor. I get some of my models to fly but they won't take off, they only fly when I launch them by hand. If I can't get these little models to fly, I don't have a chance.

I'm still doing my exercises. I flap an hour in the morning and an hour at night. I try to twist my shoulders in circles, grabbing air under my armpits. That's the way birds seem to do it. I'm flapping with weights in my hands now. My shoulders and neck are beginning to get bumpy. If I'm not careful, I walk around with my head sticking out in front of me.

I work in the afternoons on the cages. It's really great seeing them, all painted, with feed cups attached. I've painted the insides of the cages light blue. I have everything ready, newspaper in the floor of each cage and gravel on the newspaper. I'll have to change all that about once a week. The nests are in place and there's cuttlebone for each cage. I have feed in the seed cups and water in the automatic watering trough.

The breeding lists are worked out and I have my pairs decided upon. It was fun doing all the matching. I'll be at school and I'll get a new breeding idea. I've watched all the birds until I know every one of them and they all know me. I've made out breeding books to keep track of the young and I've bought bands to put on their legs for identification. With any luck, I could wind up with a hundred and fifty young birds. I'm ready.

Jesus, the next day Renaldi tells me the baseballs have actually arrived. They were shipped down on a military plane. The box was opened by the T-4 slob. He's the one who tells Renaldi. He probably thinks they've been shipped down so he can practice his spitball.

Renaldi tells me the T-4's name is Ronsky and he keeps spitting because he always has a bad taste in his mouth. He hit the beaches at Normandy and flipped on D plus 3. He was in the wards here for months and used to keep spitting so much his room was soaking wet all the time. They couldn't keep him from dehydrating.

Before you know it, if you're not careful, you can get to feeling sorry for everybody and there's nobody left to hate.

I never really thought the balls would actually come. I wonder if Birdy's old lady has been stashing those baseballs away all these years or if she went out and bought a lot of old balls to ship down.

"I'd like two hundred used baseballs, sir, so I can ship them down to the loony bin and help my crazy little boy who thinks he's a canary."

Renaldi says they're mostly a motley collection of baseballs. They go all the way from some that are almost new to some that are just black-taped. He says they're covered with mold. These must be the original balls and she's kept them all this time.

What the hell could she've been thinking of? Keeping baseballs wasn't going to make the ball field go away. She wasn't making anything out of it, stealing all those balls, except enemies. It doesn't make sense. Hardly anything seems to make sense anymore.

Why the hell is Birdy in there trying to grow feathers and I'm hiding behind these bandages. I'm beginning to know I don't want to come out, barefaced, into the open. It's not because of the way I'll look, either. The docs at Dix say everything's fine. I'll look OK, hardly any scars even.

But, I have this crazy idea in the back of my mind that I'm going to come out of the bandages like a butterfly when I used to be a caterpillar. I'm still not finished being a caterpillar. I know I'm really a butterfly now and all the caterpillar part is finished, but I'm not ready to come out.

I'll have the one more operation, then a month of bandages, then I'll be discharged. I'll have to go back to the old neighborhood. Everybody will see me. They tell me I'll get thirty or forty percent disability. I'll be eligible for Public Law 16. This means I can rake in the dough just by going to school. I have no idea what to study. The only thing I was ever good at in school was PE. Maybe I'll be a PE teacher. That sounds like as dumb a way as any to spend the rest of my life.

Or, maybe I'll start wearing a mask and cape like Zorro and charge up and down the street. I'll challenge all the kids under twelve to duels with plastic swords. That way I can work up the disability to ninety or a hundred percent. The mask part sounds good anyway.

After breakfast, I walk over to Birdy. I pull my chair into place and make myself comfortable. Birdy turns around when I sit down. He's still squatting flat-footed, but instead of his arms at his sides, he has them folded across his chest. He feeds himself completely now. There's no trouble with it at all. He takes the dishes and shovels it in.

I try to look into his eyes. He isn't more than two paces from me. It's like looking into the eyes of a dog or a baby.

After a while, you can't do it anymore because you know you're hurting them, burning holes in their souls. They don't know enough to turn away, but they're scared. I look away.

"You know, Birdy, this is really a fucked-over situation. Who the hell would've thought we'd wind up like this? What went wrong? I have the feeling we haven't had anything to do with making our own lives; we're just examples of the way we're supposed to be. We're a little bit different, but in the end, we were as usable as everybody else. You might be the nut and I'm the bolt but we're all part of the plan, and it's all worked out before we have anything to say about it."

I was always so damned sure about being myself and how nobody was going to make me be, or do, anything I didn't want; now here I am. I'm not much different from my old man when you come to think about it. There's nobody original and there's nothing left so we can even fool ourselves.

"You know, Birdy, it wouldn't matter if I hadn't been doing such a good job kidding myself all those years. I wouldn't care so much; but I feel like such a jerk. You're the same, you know. It's terrible to see how easy it is for them to make us like everybody else. They put some clothes on us, give us a rifle, teach us some tricks and then we're just names on a company roster, somebody to schedule for K.P. or guard duty or a patrol. They finish us off with a discharge or put us on a casualty list or whatever happens and it doesn't matter who we are or were."

It's going to take me a long time to convince myself that Alfonso Columbato is anything but another piece of moving meat with a fancy electronic control system. It'll be hard for me to believe in myself as something separate again.

"And what the hell does any of it matter? Where's it all leading to anyhow? Look at you! Either you stay like this and they feed you and keep you warm all your life or you get better; join the human race again. If you stay back there in that fake birdbrain of yours, they have it all worked out, you'll be written into some budget as a loss. If you come back, so you go to school, or take a job, or start raising canaries again; it doesn't matter. Everything's been arranged for. You'll be fit in before you can think about it.

"Even if you could reach down and bite your own jugular vein, they have a whole system with forms to fill out and everything; it's just another kind of thing they expect. I don't even know who *they* are except all other human beings, including us."

I stop. What's the use talking about it. I only want Birdy to know he's not alone thinking the world is shitty. Maybe if he knows I'm with him, that he's not the only one who knows, it might help.

"Look, Birdy. I'm going to have another operation on my face next week. That means I'll have to leave here. I'll only be staying around another day or two. If I stay any longer, they'll probably lock me up in one of these rooms. That shit, Weiss, is getting close. I don't know what he'll think if he ever gets a really good look into my head.

"You watch out for him, Birdy, he's one smart son-of-a-bitch. He gets inside when you aren't expecting it. He's got you figured for at least one paper at the next psychiatric convention. He doesn't want to cure you, he wants to keep you just like this. Your advantage is, he doesn't know you're a bird. When he figures that one out, you're in trouble.

"He'll probably have some kind of giant bird cage made for you, with perches, feeding cups, and everything. He'll search out that old pigeon suit of yours and have you shipped air freight at army expense to the big conference. He'll keep you in this cage and lecture on the 'bird boy.' When he's finished with you he'll probably sell you to a circus.

"I can see it all. There's the blare of trumpets and an elephant, all dressed in sequins, pulling a little cart. The cart is painted red and black; on top is a golden bird cage. The circus orchestra is playing 'He's Only a Bird in a Gilded Cage,' and there you are, all decked out in a bird costume, only this time it's a canary costume. Ten thousand canaries will have been defeathered to make this costume. You'll hop from perch to perch, do some peeping and maybe warble a few songs for the people. They'll have a giant-sized nest and you'll jump into it and try hatching some eggs the size of medicine balls. As a finale, a dwarf clown jumps out of one of these balls, dressed like a miniature bird, and thumps you on the head with a rubber worm. You'll be an international success, Birdy. You'll get all the birdseed you can eat."

I'm winding down but Birdy is definitely smiling.

"You know, Birdy; your old lady actually sent all those baseballs here? Having them sent was my idea; I hope you don't mind. I told Weiss it might help you come around. Now I don't know what the hell to tell him. He's liable to put those baseballs and you together and figure it out.

"Think of it. She had those balls all the time. Renaldi says they're moldy, so she must've had them buried. Maybe she had them buried down where we hunted for the treasure. Maybe she ran down just before us and dug them up. It'd explain the depression in the ground."

Birdy's watching me. He's giving me his "you must be crazy" look. I'm beginning to believe he's been right about that all the time. I can see them sending Birdy up to Dix in about two weeks. There I am hunkering around in the "altogether," throwing shit at anybody who comes near me. He's sitting with a garbage lid for a shield talking to me about raising pigeons and running away to Wildwood, and ice skating, all that crap.

God, it'd be great; just to let go and stop pretending; to let it all out; holler, scream, give Tarzan yells, run up walls or punch them; to spit or piss or shit at anybody who comes near! God, that'd be good! What keeps me from doing it? I've been hurt enough; I could do it if I really wanted to. Nobody could blame me.

$\mathcal{J}$ don't know how long I was dreaming the dream before I began to know. It's hard to know you're dreaming unless you catch yourself doing it.

I was working in one of the flight cages when it first came to me. I'd put all the birds into the breeding cages and there were already eleven nests built and over thirty eggs had been laid. There were eggs being brooded under four of the females. Everything was going beautifully.

I'd decided that sand in the bottom of the flight cages wasn't such a good idea. The bird shit sank into it and got smelly. Also, the seeds and shells of seeds fell into the sand and rotted. I was designing a slanted concrete floor I could hose out easily through the wire.

So, there I was, sitting in the bottom of the cage, smoothing cement, when it came to me. I realized I'd been in this cage. Now, this shouldn't have surprised me, except my feeling was that the cage had seemed larger, much larger. My view of the inside of the cage was different; it was the view of a bird.

I searched my mind. The only thing I could think of was that I'd dreamed about being inside this cage and was remembering the dream. The next two days I concentrated, trying to remember the dream. I was getting more and more sure I'd dreamed it and was somehow being stopped from remembering. It's hard to catch a dream.

First, I set an alarm clock under my pillow so I'd wake up dreaming. I did this three nights in a row with the alarm set for different times. Each time I woke up, but by the time I shut off the alarm, the dream was gone. I'd lie there in the dark trying to make my mind go back. I'd almost make it sometimes, but then it'd slip away. I began to wonder if I wasn't going to start making up a dream that didn't happen.

Then, one afternoon, I was painting the new cement floor of the flight cage with waterproof green paint, when it came back all of a sudden. I remembered being in the cage as a bird. I had to have been dreaming it. The dream came to me while I was in that open-minded non-thinking state you get into sometimes when you're doing something easy and concentrated, like painting. At first, it was as if I were thinking it, daydreaming, then I knew I was remembering the dream. I kept painting, trying to keep it happening. I felt that if I turned my mind onto the dream too much, it'd go away.

I could remember many nights of dreaming; it seemed to go back a long time. This could be because it was a dream. Dream time is different. In my dream, I'd been living in this flight cage with the other males. Alfonso, the bird, was here, and all his male children, along with the cinnamon, the topknot, and the crazy who kept flying into the sides of the cage. I could talk to them. I heard them speak in my mind in human language, in English, but they sounded like birds. I was a bird myself; I made sounds like a bird. I couldn't remember in the dream how I looked. I didn't look down at myself, but the other birds treated me as a bird, or almost like a bird.

I ate seed, watching them eat and imitating. I was like a baby bird learning, and they all helped me. I could feel myself standing on a perch with my feet. I didn't look down at my feet but they were bird feet, not human feet, and were wrapped around the perch.

I flew with the other birds! The flying was wonderful. I'd

flap my wings and soar from perch to perch. It wasn't so easy. The other birds flew beside me and taught me what to do. I was learning about flying. Alfonso flew with me to the top of the cage and made me look down at the bottom. I had no fear of flying at all. I felt like a bird. I felt I couldn't be hurt by falling. Going up was harder, took a little more effort, than going down; that was all.

I looked through the cage to the outside. I saw the houses and knew what they were. I could see the wall and the gate and knew what they were for and what was behind them. I remembered all the spaces around that I couldn't see. I knew all kinds of things a bird couldn't know. I looked out at the trees in the yard and wished I were flying there.

In my dream, in the cage, I learned to fly the way I've always wanted to fly.

That night, as I'm going to sleep, I force myself not to think of anything but the dream. I go over all the details I can remember. I don't want to think of anything else between being awake and going to sleep. I go to sleep and dream. When I wake in the morning, I remember everything. I've "caught hold" of the dream.

After breakfast, I go to feed and take care of the birds. It's a school day so I do everything in a hurry. There are eight new eggs. I take them out of the nests and put eggs into three other nests. There are ten birds now sitting eggs. The first eggs should start hatching in another week. I look into the flight cage where I fly at night. I wish I could be in the dream, flying there, instead of outside, getting ready for school.

All day I wait to get back to my birds, even more, to get back into the dream. The day at school is more like a dream than the dream. I'm turned upside down. The realest thing is the dream and the next real thing is watching my birds. Going to school, writing English papers, doing geometry, studying

Biology or talking to people isn't real at all. The things that are happening in the days of my life are now the way the dream used to be. I know they're happening, but I don't care enough to remember.

The days and nights go on. Babies begin hatching in the nests. More eggs are laid. Every pair is well on the way. There is an average of better than four eggs per nest. All the birds look healthy.

Because I talk to them in my dreams, I feel very close to the birds, especially the males; because I'm still flying in the male cage. I wonder what will happen when the dream catches up with the day and I'm left alone in the flight cage. Or maybe I'll be with a female in one of the breeding cages, except there're no extra females. I don't have any control of the dream; I can only wait and see what happens.

In the day I try talking to the males, the ones I talk to in my dreams, especially Alfonso; but they ignore me. They don't recognize me at all, except as Birdy, the boy. It makes me feel rejected, alone. I spend my days watching different birds with the binoculars because it gets me close, blocks out everything else; the birds fill my whole vision. They're the way they are in my dreams, real, my size. I feel physically close to them and they're not just little feathered animals. I'm getting to hate taking my eyes from the binoculars and looking at myself and everything around me. My hands, my feet, are grotesque. I'm becoming a stranger in myself, in my own cages, with my own birds.

I stop doing the flying exercises. If I can fly in my dreams, I don't need to fly in the real world. I'm ready to accept the fact that there's most likely no way I can actually get myself off the ground, anyway. I could probably manage an extended glide, but I wouldn't fly. I'm also finding it isn't so much the flying I want, not as a boy flapping heavy wings; I want to be a bird. In my dreams I am a bird and that's all that matters.

I'm making egg food three times a day. I'm using almost a dozen eggs a day now. There are young in all the nests. It isn't nearly as much fun having so many birds. When you get too far away from anything and there's too much of it, the outside is all you see and it becomes work like anything else. It's also hard for me to handle the birds. I feel like an awkward giant; the bird is only a bit of feathers beating and struggling in my hand. It takes the wonderful part away.

Then, I have something new happen in the dream. I'm in the flight cage as usual; the other males are still with me. I'm flying up and over a perch without landing on it. It's a trick Alfonso has been teaching me. Alfonso watches for a while, then suggests we go down and have a few seeds. I fly down with him and land on the perch by the seed cup. It's late afternoon and there's sun on the new aviary floor. I look out of the cage into the part of the aviary with the breeding cages.

I see myself sitting on a chair with the binoculars! I can't see my face, only my jacket and my legs with the pants I'd been wearing that day. I fly over to the wire and look carefully. I peep to myself but I don't turn around. I can look at myself all I want. It's me. I'm even wearing my red woolen cap. I can see my own hand over the edge of the chair steadying the binoculars. It's like looking at myself dead. Me, out there, doesn't seem to know about me in the cage, hanging on the wire. I'm afraid to look down to see if I have a bird body; I'm afraid I'll end the dream. How can I see myself in two places at once? That's too much even for a dream.

If I'm out there, gigantic, looking through binoculars, then where am I really, what am I? I don't look down. I fly over to Alfonso.

"Al, who's that outside the cage?"

Alfonso casually looks through the wire of the flight cage. He cracks another seed and swallows it.

"He's the one who keeps us here, he feeds us, he moves

us. He brought me here once. He brought Birdie here, too. Everybody knows about him."

"Yes, but what is he?"

I want to find out what Alfonso knows. I want to know how much Alfonso is only me in the dream.

"I don't know. It's better not to ask. He's just there. Without him there would be nothing."

I fly up again to the perch. In my dream, Alfonso doesn't know, only I know. I'm confused and this time I'm not sure I'm dreaming. The dream is changing. It's the first time I'm two separate beings. Time is catching up with the dream, too.

When I wake up, I stay in bed a long time; it's Saturday. I have to clean all the breeding cages. I have to put in new feed, clean water troughs, make egg food, wash out all the egg cups. Do the birds ever think about where the food comes from? None of these seeds would grow within hundreds of miles of here. It's all so artificial, make-believe. Their lives go on because I want them to.

Probably our world is the same. At breakfast I put butter on my toast. I don't know how to make either butter or bread. I don't know how to raise a cow or milk it. I don't know how to plant wheat, harvest it, remove the grain, mill it, bake it. The Little Red Hen has it all over me.

—Who wins? What's winning? The sure way to lose is to have to win.

One thing I know. You sure as hell can't pin life.

I'm getting so the dream holds together. It stops for the days but I can't remember that it stops. Another thing is I can't remember the beginning of what I'm calling the dream no matter how hard I try. In my dream, I'm convinced I've always been there, and the dream has no beginning.

When I go out to the aviary, I do not feel strange. I know I exist as me in this aviary in the dream. I know I have my things to do and the birds expect me to do them. I'm Birdy, the boy, who makes it all possible. Without me there would be nothing. I belong here; I'm part.

I sit watching the birds and thinking. One side of me wants to know and another side wants to let it all just happen. I get a pencil and a piece of paper. I write myself a message and put it on the floor of the aviary. How much of what happens in the daytime has anything to do with the dream? Can I reach myself this way?

That night I'm alone in the aviary. It is as empty as it is in the day. The dream has caught up. I can hear the males in the breeding cages just as they are in the real world. I go down to eat some of the egg food and some dandelion leaves. The paper with the note is on the floor.

"Birdy is a bird is a Birdie."

That's what I'd written. I fly to a top perch. I feel terribly cut off; I'm even cut off from the other birds. I peep and call out to them but they do not answer. I call for Alfonso. Nothing! I'm alone but I can fly.

I practice flying and trying to feel exactly what it's like. I had the wrong idea when I built my models. Flying isn't like swimming. It isn't all pushing down, catching air under the wings and pushing against it. There's a feeling of being lifted from the top, of moving up into an emptiness. Also, my flight feathers twist and pull on the air, pulling back, so I go forward. There was nothing in my models to keep me going forward. Reaching ahead with the wings and pulling back isn't enough. The flight feathers work like the propeller of an airplane.

I get the courage to look down. I am a bird. I look exactly like a canary. I look like Birdie. I fly all over the cage; I try to watch myself fly. It's a marvelous feeling, more wonderful than I could possibly have expected. I look outside and wish again I could fly free. There are so many places I'd like to fly. It's so natural to fly and so unnatural not having anyplace to fly to.

The next day, I think more about my message. It actually didn't prove anything because I already knew what was written. I went into the dream with it in my head and so I was seeing something I already knew.

When I finish feeding and checking nests, I take five pieces of paper and write five different messages. I turn them upside down and shuffle them completely. I take one at random and put it on the bottom of the flight cage, face up, without looking at it. I also put some seed, egg food, and water in the empty cage. This doesn't make sense because there was always something to eat when the other males were there, even though the cage'd been empty for two weeks and I hadn't been putting in any food. But now, the dream is caught up and I don't want to take any chance of starving myself to death. I suspect there's the possibility I could get caught in the dream for several days, even in one night.

In my dream that night, I'm alone again. There's the piece of paper on the floor. I fly down to read it. All five messages are on the one sheet of paper. I go over to eat some egg food and drink a drop of water. I look at the paper again. This time there's nothing on it.

I'm beginning to know what I'm doing. I'm at the edge of where you have things happen to you or you make them happen. The dream is mine and it's as real as anything but it's mostly a matter of what I want. Usually I don't know what I want, so it's hard to control the dream. Also, things that happen outside the dream come into the dream on their own. I can't make anything happen in the dream without something like it happening in the daytime world. I still don't understand but I'm not frightened.

After that, I get so I can talk to the other birds in the breeding cages. I've never talked to them from the big aviary flight cage before, or looked at them from there, so I have to wish it on purpose for it to happen. I know the birds, I know where they are and I've talked to them before. I put these things together to make it happen.

I talk to Alfonso first and then to Birdie. It's good talking to her. I know her so well but we've never been able to speak to each other. She's very excited about her new babies and she's glad I'm in the dream. She doesn't call it "in the dream," she says "with us." I talk to almost all the other birds. By looking through the binoculars I know what each cage looks like from the inside and which bird is in which cage. I know who I'm talking to without seeing them. I don't feel so alone.

Another way I'm not like a bird is I look at things with both eyes, straight on. I can't get myself to see the way a bird does. In every way, when I don't look down at myself, I feel like me, Birdy, the boy.

In the morning, before I leave for school, I go out to put in new egg food and generally check around. I look at the note on the floor and it's still there, but just one message. The egg food is untouched. All day long in school, I think about it. I dream the things I know. That's why I'm Birdie; I know Birdie best. I wonder if I'm a female. Birdie's a female but I was in the male cage. I'd like to find out which I am. I don't want to make myself one or the other, I only want to know.

—Sex, age, races, all that bullshit keeps everybody apart. Competition gets to be the only link we've got. But, if you've got to "beat" somebody then you're more alone.

Games are something we've made up to help us forget we've forgotten how to play. Playing is doing something for itself; Birdy and I played a lot.

Birdy really smiled at me there, a true vintage "It doesn't matter" smile. He could be putting this whole thing on. That's OK, too.

I'll try singing in my dream tonight; that should settle it for me. In Plane Geometry that afternoon, I get into an argument with Mr. Shull, the teacher, about parallel lines. I say they have to meet. I'm beginning to think everything comes together somewhere.

In the dream, I sing. I can never remember singing as a boy, but singing as a bird is completely different from anything I've ever known. It isn't what I expected at all. I sound like a roller canary singing, but the words I'm hearing are in English and sound almost like poetry. I'm hearing myself simultaneously as bird and as boy speaking words. I'm singing the thoughts I've had about flying combined with the feeling I'm having as a bird.

One of the first songs I sing sounds like this: There is nothing of fright when one flies free. There's only the taste of air and touching nowhere. I see the earth below and it's down the way the sky is up when you look from the ground. Everything is out or away and the play of gravity is like sand.

Now, I know I'm not Birdie completely. I can hear Birdie from the breeding cage. She wants me to sing more but the singing is still hard for me. Alfonso starts singing to Birdie. I can understand his whole song for the first time. He sings this: Come fly with me; dry thistles sliding through a crystal sky, you and I. Below, mountains hump and clouds hover while cows slumber seven stomachs deep in clover. We glide together in twisting currents of air, caring for nothing. We are each other and we take wing to find fertile fields and silent beaches.

I listen and know Alfonso couldn't sing that song. A bird can know nothing about cows' stomachs. I've just learned about them in biology class. Alfonso has never flown over mountains or clouds; these are my ideas. Alfonso is singing and I'm hearing his song with my mind, in my dream. Can Alfonso really talk, or is it all just me? I can't believe that.

Alfonso's taught me things about flying I could not know myself. I can't put this together in my dream. During this night, I know I'm dreaming all during the dream.

There's one thing I'm sure of. Singing is like flying. When I sing, I close my eyes and see myself flying through and over trees. I'm sure that's why canaries sing. They were put in cages because they sang and now they sing because they're in cages.

Canaries have been in cages for over four hundred years. A canary generation, the time from birth till breeding, is less than a year. A human generation is about twenty years. Therefore, birds have been in cages for a time that for humans would be eight thousand years. In fact, canaries and humans have been in cages the same number of generations.

I begin to wonder what men do that's the same as canary singing. It's probably thinking. We built this cage, civilization, because we could think and now we have to think because we're caught in our cage. I'm sure there's a real world still there if I can only get out of the cage. But, would my canaries sing as much if they could live in the open and fly freely? I don't know. I hope some day to find out.

The breeding cages are going at a great rate. I already have birds out of the nest. Soon, I'm going to have some ready to put in the flight cages. I don't know whether to put them in the cage where I am in my dream or in the other one. I'm still trying to decide this when I start dreaming of Perta.

When I say dreaming, I don't mean I'm dreaming of Perta the way I'm dreaming the rest of the dream. I'm dreaming of Perta in my dream. I'm sleeping in my dream on one foot as a bird and I'm dreaming of Perta.

Perta is smaller than most female canaries. She has a light green head blushing back to a lighter yellow-green on her breast, then darker green on her back. Her wings vary from layer to layer of her feathers. This gives a variegated surface like a blue check pigeon, only in shades of green. She has white bars on the outside of her wings because her last two flight feathers on each wing are white. Her shape is roundish and she flies with small movements, fast flapping but great grace and speed. She has markings over her eyes almost like eyebrows. Her beak and legs aren't as dark as Alfonso, nor as light pink as Birdie.

In my dream, I'm sleeping on the top perch of the aviary and dreaming. I'm lonely and tired; I'm sleepy and sleeping in my own dream. I know this much. It's several nights before I realize I'm dream-dreaming Perta.

In the dream-dream, I'm alone in the flight cage and look down to see someone at the food dish. I know immediately it's a female. She either doesn't know I'm up on the top perch or she's ignoring me. I stay still, watching her, enjoying her movements. I watch her closely the way I watch the birds with my binoculars as a boy.

Her flying is not exceptional in terms of power or thrust but she's very light in the air. I feel she loves flying and flies for pleasure. I watch her practice different landings and banking maneuvers. She integrates the movement of her tail, the tilting of her wings and the shifting of her body as if she's dancing in the air. I'm falling in love with her in the dream the way I fell in love with Birdie, but it's so much more real.

In my dream, I sing to her the songs I know and some I didn't know I knew. When I wake in my bed, I can't remember the songs I've sung. It's too far inside. As a boy, I decide to put some water in the flight cage so Perta can bathe. I want it to be something special. When my mother isn't in the kitchen, I take the cut glass butter dish she got when her mother died. We never use it except for company so I'm sure she won't notice if it's missing one night. I put the dish in the bottom of the cage that afternoon after I've fed all the birds.

I move two nests of young birds into the other flight cage; they're eating egg food and starting to crack seed. I'm saving the male flight cage for Perta and myself. I call her Perta because that's the closest word I can think of for the sound I know her by.

So, now I'm getting into the dream, and in the dream I'm forcing myself to sleep again so I can dream.

Perta comes in the dream-dream. The water is on the floor, in the late afternoon sunlight, just as it was when I left it that afternoon. The light is going through the cut glass and making rainbows on the floor and on the back wall. I wait patiently, on my perch in the upper, darker part of the aviary. I know I'm making it happen, I'm controlling the dream in the dream but I also know I have feelings and knowings beyond myself, that I can't know what will happen. I'm into the furthest back parts of my mind.

Perta hops onto the side of the dish and puts her beak into the clear, cold water. She lets it roll back down her throat, tipping her head back and thrusting her breast forward, stretching upward on her thin legs. She does this again. I watch. Then, she pushes her face into the water and splashes back under her wings. She flaps her wings to capture the cold water under the warmest parts of her wings, inside where the down of softest feathers is. She does this two or three times before she lightly springs into the water, arches her back, tilts her head and starts throwing the clean water onto the feathers between her wings on her back.

I can see all this with unnatural clarity. It's as if I'm beside her. I see each drop remain intact and roll off the soft feathers. I can slow down the rapid movements of her bath and see them happen slowly, unfolding with infinite grace.

Then, I start to sing. I'm singing, and I've made no conscious decision to do this. Perta has flown onto a perch and is preening herself. She doesn't seem to hear me. I'm excited.

I feel hot blood rushing through me. All my muscles are con-
tracted and my wings are lifted in tension. I've pulled myself
tall on my legs and I'm rocking back and forth with my song;
dancing to my own rhythm, aiming all of me toward Perta. I
feel a sense of haste, of need, of desire for completion. Perta
continues her preening.

I fly down next to her. I land beside her on the perch and
increase the strength and desire of my song. Perta pays no
attention. She doesn't turn her head or move. I edge toward
her. She doesn't move away. I'm prepared to have her fly
from me; I want to chase her, to sing to her in flight. I come
closer. She reaches back with her beak and pulls out, straightens the feathers on her back. There's only one thing to do; I
feel it inside myself. I fly over Perta and lower myself onto
her. I'm turgid with passion.

There's nothing! I come down on the place where Perta
was and there's nothing at all. I'm alone! I find myself falling, not from the perch but from the dreams. I fall out of my
dream-dream into my dream; know myself for a second, alone,
asleep on the top perch, then I fall again out of the dream
and into my bed in my room.

I wake up. It's the first time I've had a wet dream. I've
kept hearing about wet dreams but never had one. I go into
the bathroom and wash myself off. I bring back the washcloth
and wipe up the sheets.

I lie back and feel as if I've fallen from a far place. I'm
terribly alone again.

That weekend I go looking for her. I know she has to be
somewhere. I must've seen her and not known it. I couldn't
make her up completely. Instinctively, I go to Mr. Lincoln's
first. His cages are in full breeding. He shows me his new
young birds. He has two very dark ones. He tells me he thinks
he'll have his pure black canary in only about ten more years

if he keeps going at the rate he's going. He's worked out a chart on a curving graph. He says the getting darker tapers off as you get closer. The difference looks less and you're always having regressions. He calculates he's ninety percent of the way; it's going to take ten more years to get to 99.96 percent black. He points to himself and says, "I ain't even ninety percent black myself, not by a long shot."

I ask him if he has any females he's not using. I want to see if she's there. She isn't in any of the breeding cages. I knew she wouldn't be. He points to the cover over his flight cage on the left. He says he keeps it covered because these free females will flirt with the males in the breeding cages and those males'll sing back, and sometimes a female on a nest will get so mad, she'll abandon the nest. I'd never thought about that. He tells me he's going to sell off these females; most of them are sterile, or lay an egg or two per nest, and none of them are important on his breeding charts.

I look into the cage and there are about ten females. I see her right away. It's Perta exactly. Some part of me, the bird part, remembered her. I'm in love with her as a boy. I fell in love with her in my dream as a bird but it's come through to my life as a boy. I have to have her; I turn to Mr. Lincoln and point her out. It seems so strange to see her as a bird when I'm a boy; I feel as if I'm spying on her. It's as if I'm looking through a keyhole and seeing something I'm not supposed to see.

"You mean that one there?"

He's pointing. I nod.

"She's not going to do you much good. I've had her for two years now and she hasn't had a fertile egg yet. I've tried three different males on her. The last one was the most ruttinest buck of a bird you can imagine. She just has a regular four clear eggs every time. I'm sure she's been bred, but there's something wrong with her."

Mr. Lincoln watches her with me. She's moving side-ways, back and forth on the perch. She's seeing me. I know it.

"I don't know anybody I hate enough to sell her off to. I should wring her neck but she's such a pretty little thing I can't get myself to do it. Still, there's no good in a female who won't give off a fertile egg. I'm sure she'd make a great little mother, too. You should see the fine nest she builds; and she sits it tight and brave as you could like, all for nothing."

"I want to buy her."

I get it out. I'm watching her and I know she's watching me. She never looked at me in the dream-dream. Would she look at me now?

"I won't sell her. I'll give her to you. Save me having to wring her neck. All she does is eat seed."

I really don't want to buy her. I'm glad Mr. Lincoln is giving her to me. It's as if he's her father and he's giving me permission to marry his daughter. I can't say anything so I put out my hand to shake with Mr. Lincoln. He doesn't know what to do for a minute but then he sees I'm serious. He reaches out and takes my hand in both his. He looks into my eyes. My eyes are filling with water, not that I'm about to cry, I'm excited and happy.

"Are you all right, boy? Have you been sick or something?"

I shake my head. I don't want to talk. When you've been a bird, talking seems crude as grunting. Mr. Lincoln knows somehow, turns away and goes into the flight cage. He has no trouble catching her; he just goes over and picks her off the perch. She wants to be caught. I know that. He takes her out in his hand, turns her upside down and blows away the feathers around her vent.

"See? She's right ready. You'd thing she'd be a perfect breeder."

I close my eyes and don't look. Mr. Lincoln doesn't

notice. He turns Perta around and rubs his fingers over the top of her head.

"See? She has little eyebrow markings over each eye, almost like human eyebrows. I never seen that on a bird before."

I nod my head. He hands her to me. I feel her heart beating against my hand. Mr. Lincoln goes to get a small carrying box for me but I say I'll carry her in my hand. I have a terrible advantage.

I'd come over through the park instead of on my bike. I try to thank Mr. Lincoln but I really only want to get away, take Perta back with me.

I put her in the flight cage and watch her all the rest of the day through my binoculars. It's exactly like the dream-dream. This is the first time something that started in the dream is happening afterward in my boy life.

When I look into the breeding cages and clean the floors I feel part of the other birds. I'm not alone even when I'm only a boy; I have my female, too. She's with me in my boy life and in the dream-dream, too. I'm hoping she'll be in the real dream tonight. I'm even more excited about it than flying.

That night in the dream I don't sleep. I'm up on the highest perch and I see her on the bottom of the cage eating seed just as she was the first time in the dream-dream. I know enough to know I'm dreaming and to know why she's there, but those ideas are only like dreams themselves. She's most real here in my dream.

I watch her for a while. The butter dish is filled with water, and she takes a bath just as she did in the dream-dream. I'd forgotten to put the dish in the cage before I went to sleep; this is how the dream can have its own life. The dream me knows what I want more than I do myself.

*I watch her bathe as I did before. Till now, she still hasn't
seen me in the top of the cage. I sing to her. I sing:*

How is it I know you, strange one?
In what untrammeled sky did we fly?
Perhaps I was the air and you
the bird. Did you fly through me?
Why are we not mated? Give me
a sign; will you be mine?
Do you see me, feel my desire?
Or are you already tired of my song?

*When I'm finished, I fly down to her. She sees me. She
hears me. The wall between us is gone.*

"Hello. I didn't know there was another bird in this
cage. I thought I was alone. Have you been here long?"

*I don't want to lie to her but I also want her to think of
me only as a bird. I answer.*

"Yes, I've been here all the time."

"I like your song. You sing very well. Do you have a
female?"

"No. I am alone."

"Were you serious in your song? Did you sing what you
mean? Or were you only singing?"

"I was serious. I sang what I mean."

"I have no male now. I have had no babies. I have had
many eggs but no babies. I would like to be your female, but
you should know this."

"Yes. I would like that."

"Do you understand?"

*I cannot answer her. I've never talked to anyone who
spoke and thought so directly. Her ideas, her ways, are clear
and straight as clean water. There is a natural flow between
us that I've never known. I feel myself going out into her
and she coming into me. I start to sing:*

I bring unweathered seeds of joy,
an endless coming together. Let
us fly. Our time grows from
yesterday's tomorrows; we glide
gently to our private past.
Let us fly.

"That was lovely, even stronger than the first song. You
have thoughts in your songs I've not heard before. It is as if
you are more than a bird, have seen beyond the cage."

"Thank you. But if you are a bird, there is nothing more
or beyond. Let us fly together."

We fly over all the cage that night. I show her things
Alfonso taught me and she shows me how to do her quick
turns and slow graceful hovering landings. She has a fine way
of using the air as a hold and not sliding on it. It's like tread-
ing water. She teaches me how to do it without thrashing or
fighting the air.

The next night when I dream, it is early afternoon. It is
earlier in the day than it's ever been before in the dream. The
bath water is there and it's fresh. I did remember to put it in
this time.

Perta is there. She is waiting and welcomes me by flying
up before I fly down to her. She looks me in the eyes, straight
on, very unbirdlike. As I remember this, she shifts her head
and looks at me, bird-style. We shift our heads back and forth,
looking into each other; my left to her left, right to right, my
left to her right, her left to my right. I don't remember birds
doing this. Then, she flies to the perch below.

"Come, Birdy, let us bathe together."

I didn't tell her my name.

I follow her down, wondering how she knows my name;
it makes a big hole in the dream. I don't understand. Is the
Perta here totally separated from the Perta in the flight cage?

Do I completely make her up? Does she know my name because I know it? I fly down with her to the water. She is standing on the lip of the dish waiting. I stand beside her. She dips her bill into the water and throws some onto me. I've never taken a bath as a bird. I don't quite know how to go about it. I dip my bill into the water and throw some onto Perta. I'm awkward. Perta looks at me intently. She throws water on me again. I throw some water on her. I'm better the second time. I have a terrible fear Perta will discover I'm not a bird, that I'm the boy and she'll become frightened of me. This guilt, this fear, is coming between us. Perta feels it. She looks at me, then lowers herself into the water. The sunshine is again broken into pieces of colored light. I'm bathing in the light as she throws beads of water around me. Then, I'm in the bath myself, fluttering, losing myself in the light, in the water, in Perta. It is like floating in music. I want to sing but I wait. I follow everything Perta does. We dance to our own music. I do not need to sing. I realize then that, as all male canaries sing, Perta dances, probably all female canaries dance. It is something you cannot know unless you are a bird; female canaries dance.

When we are completely wet, when the bath is finished, we fly together over all the cage. Our feathers are wet and we are heavy. We fly in the air with the same feeling a boy knows when he swims in the water. We go slowly. We must struggle for space, for distance. We shake the water from our feathers, sprinkle each other. I'm still following Perta, watching her move. It continues as dance, a dance in slow movements, but a dance. Perta watches me watch her. From her eyes, I can see the questioning. Perhaps birds never watch each other the way I'm watching her. I'm watching her because of the pleasure it gives me, also to learn how to take a bath as a bird.

When, at last, we are dry, we sit on a perch beside each

other and preen our feathers. It is a wonderful feeling to pull
the slightly wet feather through my beak, feeling the individual branchings and lining them up. It is like carefully combing
wet hair, but a thousand times more satisfying. There is a
right way, no other, for feathers to be. When they are that
way it gives a feeling of being finished, of having things done
correctly. I want very much to do a most unbirdlike thing; to
preen Perta's feathers. I've never seen birds do this. Except for
feeding, singing, peep-peep-peeping, and fucking, birds show
no other signs of affection I've ever seen. I want to caress Perta
the way a boy would caress a girl, but I have only my beak and
my feet. It would seem so natural to take one of her feathers
into my mouth and straighten it with the tender edges of my
beak. This is a place where the bird and the boy are different.
I decide to ask her about my name.

"Perta, how did you know my name?"

She looks at me, surprised. She stops preening.

"I do not know your name. You have not told me."

"But when you invited me to bathe, you called me Birdy."

"Yes. But Birdy isn't a name."

"What is it, then?"

"It's Birdy; what you call a bird when you don't know his
name. Birdy is anybird. Every bird knows that."

How can I explain I didn't know it? How does all this fit
in the dream? This is one of the nights I know all the time
that I'm dreaming. It's one of the last nights like that. Perta
looks at me.

"How did you know my name? I did not tell you."

Perta in the dream-dream had a name and it was Perta.
She did not tell me; I made it up. How could I know her
name? I have to lie again.

"You told me the first night when we were flying."

Perta ruffles her feathers and takes half a minute before
answering.

"No. I did not tell you. Why do you lie to me? There is no reason for us to lie to each other. Each time we cannot be true, it is something between us. There must be truth or there is nothing."

"I do not know what is true, Perta. I know your name by ways I cannot tell you about. That is not a lie."

"It is not the truth either. When one knows and one does not tell, that is not truth."

Perta flies down and eats some seed. I fly down beside her. We eat together for a while. I am very much in love with her. It is so strange to find such a hard stone of purity in so much softness. It is like the pit in the center of a peach.

During the days, I can think of nothing but Perta. It is spring and I'm in my junior year in high school. Everybody's all excited about the Junior Prom. My mother asks me who I'm taking. I'm not taking anybody. The girls at the school all look like overgrown, awkward cows to me. They move as if their feet grow right into the ground. My eyes are tuned to the fine, delicate movements of birds.

Al is taking one of the cheerleaders. He has his letters in football and wrestling. He'll probably take another letter in track for throwing the discus. These are all varsity letters. He's going to be the only junior three-letter man in the school.

Al practices with the discus out in center field just over our fence. I go out sometimes and throw the discus back to him. It's one thing I can do as a boy which isn't completely boring and doesn't have to do with my birds. Making a discus go a long way is as much a matter of getting it off at the right angle to catch the air under it, with the least air resistance, as it is strength. Throwing it back to Al, I keep experimenting and once in a while I throw it farther than Al does himself. Of course, I have a strange strength advantage. I'm unnaturally strong in the deltoids, triceps, and latissimus dorsii muscles from all the wing-flapping.

Now, Al wants me to go out for track and throw the discus. He keeps measuring my distances. I like throwing the discus but I don't like the measuring. I try to explain this to Al but I don't get anywhere. I think people lose the real fun in things by measuring, scoring, wanting to win.

Al keeps bugging me to take some girl or another to the prom. Through his girlfriend, the cheerleader, he knows about twenty girls who want to go to the prom but have nobody stupid enough to take them. My mother is getting absolutely hysterical. It's some kind of personal insult to her that I don't want to go out and rent a tux for five dollars, buy an orchid for a dollar and a half to pin on some girl I hardly know, and pay two dollars for prom tickets. I hate to dance and the whole thing'd be a waste of time for everybody.

It's three days before the prom and I think I'm home free when Al comes over to our house one evening. I've finished with the birds and I'm looking forward to the dream that night. Perta and I are getting very close and I miss her terribly during the day. Al tells me, right in front of my mother, how he knows a girl named Doris Robinson who asked him to ask me if I'd take her to the prom. She has the tickets and will buy her own corsage. She drives and can get her father's car. All I have to do is rent the tux.

Jesus, I could kill Al! My mother starts all over again about how there's only one Junior Prom in your life and how if she'd had the chance to go to high school she would have considered it a high point in her life and how I don't appreciate how lucky I am. My father reaches in his pocket and pulls out five dollars. He says I can have it to rent the tux. I'm cornered, what can I do? I say I'll go. I know I'm feeling guilty about Perta. I want to tell her. I want her to know this is happening to me and how I don't want it to. I can feel another whole non-truth area opening between us.

The night of the prom comes at the worst time, right in

the middle of things. Perta has asked me if I want to start a nest. She's been flitting her wings when we've been together, so I'm not surprised. Perta in the day has been flitting her wings, too. This is a big decision for me and I want time to think it out. Instead, I have to go through all this Junior Prom thing.

Al takes me to the tux place and tries to talk up Doris to me. He talks about what great legs she has. I've tried watching girls' legs to find out what the excitement is about, but they all look the same to me. One has a bit more flesh here or there, one has more wrinkly knees than another, or the ankle bones stick out more or less, but, so what?

And women's asses. They're just flesh around an asshole like everybody else. It's only an overdevelopment of the gluteus maximus, to make it possible for people to walk on two legs, and sit down. To me, anything sitting down is ugly. A bird usually stands when it isn't flying. It never sits except to hatch eggs. That's beauty.

Then, tits. What a dumb development for feeding babies. Women have to carry them around all their lives, flopping, getting in the way, right under their noses, and they're only used for about two or three years at the most. I've watched lots of tits and Al has tried to show me the difference between good tits and poor tits. It's mostly a difference in volume and pointedness. Looking in the National Geographics, I can see they're not much different from what a goat or a cow has; just a bit more inconvenient.

All the way back from the tux rental place, Al is raving on. He knows I can "make" this girl. He means he thinks she'll let me fuck her. He knows two guys who "had" her. That's supposed to be exciting. I know Doris Robinson. She's an ordinary girl with regular legs, regular ass, and slightly more than regular tits. Doris doesn't look as if she could ever fly under any conditions. She's a small to medium size reddish-colored cinnamon with freckles. My mother would like to see me going to the Junior Prom with a girl who looks like Doris. Al wants to see me go to the Prom with Doris. Al wants me to get fucked. I don't know what my mother wants.

Dressed up in the tux, I look like one of Mr. Lincoln's black birds. I feel like a freak taking the bus to where Doris lives. Thank God, I'm not carrying any crappy orchid. All evening long I'm going to have to dance with an orchid under my nose. Orchids smell like death to me. There's a moldy, mushroomy, damp smell like an old coffin; and on top, there's a soft perfumy smell. Together, it's the smell of an embalmed corpse.

I think I'm going to have that orchid under my nose all night, but that's not the way it turns out. When I get to Doris's address, it's a big single house in the fancy part of Girard Hill. I walk up the driveway and knock. Her mother opens the door. I introduce myself and she lets me in. Who the hell else was she expecting to walk up the driveway in a penguin costume? Mrs. Robinson is all dressed up and wearing so much perfume I think for a minute she's the one I'm dragging to the prom.

"Doris will be right down. Won't you sit over here, please?"

She practically pushes me into a chair just inside the living room at the bottom of the stairs and then leaves the room. I've been ushered into my seat for the grand entrance. I wait. I start thinking of Perta. I'd love to tell her about all this. It's too bad this is so far from anything she knows. She'd never understand. Even if she could understand, she wouldn't believe it.

Then Doris comes down the stairs. It's Gone With the Wind again. She comes down three steps, then pauses when she sees me. She looks at the chair where I'm sitting, smiles an Olivia de Havilland–Melanie smile, then comes down the rest of the stairs quickly, without bouncing, like she's on a sliding board. I get up.

She's twisting her hips back and forth to make the dress stand out. It makes a stiff crackling pigeon noise. Then her mother comes back into the room. She's carrying the box with the orchid in it. She tells me it's been in the refrigerator to keep it fresh. That's as good a place as any for something that smells dead. I begin to realize they probably bought this house for that staircase so Doris could come sliding down it on occasion.

The mother is holding up the orchid for me to admire. It's big as a pigeon and shaped like a pigeon, too, a pigeon taking a dust bath. She hands me the flower and a long pin. They're both ice cold. I'm supposed to pin this flower on Doris.

Right here I notice there's no place under my nose to pin this thing. That is, if I'm not going to pin it through bare, raw, freckled flesh.

I stand there, holding the pin in one hand and the flower in the other. I could stick it right through what looks like it might be one of her nipples but what I think is a piece of rubber. Doris has big tits but in this dress they bulge out past her elbows. There's such a space between them, I know if I get the right angle I can see through to the floor.

Apparently, pinning is one detail they hadn't worked out. The mother starts giggling. Doris turns a sort of salmon color and the freckles get darker. The mother moves in and pins the flower on her waist. Now it looks as if she has a monster vine creeping up on her from behind. I wonder where I'm supposed to put my hand when we dance.

Now, the father comes in. He's a pale, tired-looking man. He puts a silk cape over Doris's shoulders and gives her the keys to the car. He also gives all kinds of advice about locking, turning off the lights and not going over thirty-five. He kisses her on the cheek. Her mother kisses her on the cheek, too. The father turns around and shakes my hand.

"Have a good time, son; but be sure to have her in by two o'clock."

Son! Holy mackerel, they've got me married to her already. The dance is over at twelve-thirty. What am I supposed to do with her till two o'clock? What will Perta think if I don't come into the dream? This whole business is getting to be more of a catastrophe every minute.

At the dance, I have to move the flower from her waist to her wrist. She wants it on her left wrist so I tie it to her wristwatch with a rubber band I have in my pocket. It sits on top of her wrist so she looks as if she's going falconing. The hand is perched on top of my shoulders while we're dancing so the damned orchid keeps tickling the back of my neck and ears. It sends chills up and down my spine. This way I can smell it without seeing it. I keep being reminded of the rotten horse meat smell at the place Joe Sagessa took us.

This smell combined with all the sweating bodies around us and the sound of the music brings me to the very edge of what I can bear. To take my mind off it, I keep trying to think forward to the dream when I get home to my bed. Doris is saying things to me about the music or asking where I live. She knows my father works here as a janitor but she doesn't say anything about that.

I see my father twice. He's acting as a sort of bouncer-janitor combined. He keeps track of those who go into the boys' toilets. His job is to slow down the drinking and help clean up the vomit if anybody gets sick. He gets five extra dollars for the night; just enough to pay for my stupid tux. I wouldn't go through another night like this for fifty dollars.

I see Al swinging and dancing around with his cheerleader. He isn't much of a dancer, but she's one of those girls who could dance with a buffalo and make it look graceful. Al dances one-two-three-four at the same beat to any music. He doesn't even listen to it. With the tux on, he looks like a gangster in a movie. He's wearing a white carnation but still he could be Brian Donlevy playing Heliotrope Harry.

Doris asks me about the birds. That's something I don't want to talk about. If I really thought she was interested I'd tell her. I'd stop the stupid dancing, sit down and tell her about it. I look to check; but all she's doing is making dance conversation. Sometimes it seems humans can only play games; all kinds of complicated games. Going to the Junior Prom is another game with a whole set of rules. Talking while you're dancing is one of the rules.

I don't have a watch and I can't see Doris's with the big orchid draped all over it, but there are clocks at each end of the gym. They have wire mesh over the face to keep them from getting broken by stray basketballs, but you can still read the time if you get the right angle. The time is crawling by. I'm pooped. It's past eleven o'clock and I'm usually in bed by ten for the dream. My arm is tired from holding up Doris's arm. I try letting my arm down sometimes, taking the weight off my shoulder muscle, but she doesn't pick up the load at all, just lets both arms drop. Finally, when I can't keep them up any longer, we leave the arms down and she snuggles in closer to me with her head tucked under my chin. Now I've got her hair tickling my nose, while the flower is tickling me on the back of the neck. Both my hands are occupied. Besides that, Doris's big tits are pressed against me, they're about the consistency of blown-up inner tubes. From all my flapping exercises, my sternum has a tendency to stick out more than most people's; so her tits fit on both sides of it. We make a beautiful couple. We fit together like tongue-in-groove flooring.

At last it's over. I take Doris over to get her cape; we go outside. Everybody's slamming car doors in the dark and laughing. I help her into her side of the car. She asks me if I want to drive. That's wild. Nobody drives in our family; we've never had a car; never will. My father won't even ride in an automobile.

When I tell her "no," she sticks the key into the ignition and turns it on. The car's a Buick, the last model they made before the war. The motor is eight-cylinder, loaded with power, but it's all pissed away in this car with something they call Dynaflow. This is a way you get to drive a car without knowing how to shift. My father says soon they'll have cars you won't have to steer. People'll go around killing each other without knowing it.

Doris turns to me. Her face is soft as a baby bird with just the lights from the dashboard. Her cape is pulled back and she looks almost naked. She reaches over and turns on the radio. She must've had the dial set beforehand, maybe even called up the radio station to have the right music played. They come on with Glen Miller's "Sunrise Serenade." It's one piece of music I really like; it has the inside completeness of a good canary song.

"Let's go for a little ride out to Media."

It doesn't matter what I say, we're going to Media. She's most likely already gone out and mapped the route. I settle back to relax and let it all happen. This is probably the night I get fucked. She has to be back by two o'clock. The clock glowing green in the dark dash says quarter to one. How much can actually happen in an hour?

Doris isn't paying too much attention to what her father said. We're whipping around these tight curves, on roads one car wide, through the heavy green overhanging trees of Media, at about fifty. There's a straightaway under the high stone arched railway overpass and she gets it to almost seventy. She's so little, she's peering up over the edge of the dash. I scrunch down and concentrate on those tiny silver shoes pushing on the accelerator and brake. I wonder what Perta's doing. What would happen to the dream if I wind up welded into that dashboard in front of me, with an eight-cylinder engine hot in what's left of my lap.

She has the place picked out. We swing off the macadam road and along a dirt road so small, the branches on both sides are scraping the edges of the car. She isn't saying anything, just driving, peering up to avoid potholes. We're following through. Doris is going to have her Junior Prom with all the trimmings. I feel like a candle on the cake that's about to be blown out.

We cross a little stream with that monster car and the road turns into nothing but rocks. Finally, she stops, turns off the motor, pulls on the emergency and puts out the lights. She turns the ignition so the dash and radio stay on. This car has everything. It gets about nine miles to the gallon but they have a B-ration sticker, so what the hell.

At first, she sits there holding onto the wheel of the car, like a kid pretending to drive while the car's sitting in a driveway. I unscrunch myself and sit up. I turn toward her and pull my inside leg bent up on the seat. Anything can happen. I know it's going to be embarrassing.

Doris climbs up onto her knees. In the darkness I see she's left her shoes down there by the accelerator. She holds out her wrist with the orchid on it for me to take off.

"I'd like to keep it as a souvenir."

She says this as I try to untwist the rubber band in the dark. She's wiggling the end of her hand at the wrist like a snake. When I get it off, she takes it from me and puts it on the shelf over the dash. In the dark, with the magnified reflection from the curved windshield, it's frightening. The whole car is filled with the smell.

I'm expecting we're going to have one of those great conversations which start with "Don't you like me?" or "Why is it you don't like me?" I've already had several of those. There's practically no answer you can give that isn't either insulting or a lie. I'm all ready to lie for the illusion of the great

Junior Prom but I don't have to. Doris starts humming to the music and somehow she's leaning on me, rocking back and forth as if we're dancing; dancing in a Buick Dynaflow! I put my arms around her and try to keep up my end. Maybe if I fuck Doris it'll help the dream with Perta. The dream is made out of things I know.

Doris lifts her face and we start kissing. We get to kissing along and I'm having a hard time keeping my nose out of the way. Then, she starts opening her lips so I open mine too. I'm doing my best. Next, she's breathing into my mouth and sucking in! I feel the air being pulled in through my nostrils! Holy God! Is this kissing or is good old Doris Robinson some kind of vampire who gets you by stealing your breath. I'm thinking this when, suddenly, she sticks her whole tongue into my mouth! It's like sucking a bubble gum wad in. I can't breathe at all except through my nose. And, I can't believe it; I'm getting a hard-on! All this crazy stuff and it goes straight to the old dong. I try to cross my legs, to hide it, maybe to crank it down, but there's no fooling Doris. She's shoving her stomach right into it! She moans and pushes her tongue in deeper. She takes her arms from around me and I think maybe we've done our share for the Prom and it's all over, but she's pulling down the top of that dress and those tits pop out. They stick more to the outside now that they're loose. They look better than the ones in the National Geographic.

She leans back and I stare at them. There aren't any freckles on them, at least not by the dash light.

It's then I know I could do it. I not only could, I want to do it. I want to fuck Doris. At the same time, I start thinking of Perta. I want to do it the first time with Perta. I want to do it the first time with my wife, not with Doris. Doris could never be a wife to me, all I'd be doing is fucking Doris's tits, her tongue, her cunt.

Doris keeps trying but I'm finished. I go on kissing her and I hold her tits in my hands, and stroke them a bit. Doris breathes hard and cries but we don't say anything. At last, she sits up, and tucks the tits back into her dress. It's getting on to two o'clock. We've been kissing away for almost an hour.

We have one hell of a time turning that car around. I get out to direct her. There's no room, and Doris isn't much good at backing up. We get stuck twice before we get out. We drive up her driveway at two-thirty. Was that pale, gray man going to shoot me for almost fucking his daughter and keeping her out late? The car is probably all scratched up from brambles and branches, too.

We kiss an ordinary non-vampire good-night kiss before we get out of the car. Doris asks "if she'll see me again." I say, "Sure. I'll see you at school." I see her every day there. We're in the same Geometry class.

She has a key and lets herself in. Her mother is still up and says she'll drive me home. All the streetcars and buses are shut down. I tell her I don't live far and I'll walk home. She doesn't insist too much. She wants to get all the details from Doris. I wonder how much Doris tells her. You never know with rich people like that.

I'm glad to have the four-mile walk. It gives me time to think. I hope I didn't hurt Doris's feelings, but I'm glad I didn't fuck her. I want to get into my dream with Perta. I sneak up the back stairs without waking anybody. It's four o'clock when I last look at the clock by my bed.

When I come into the dream, it's late. The sun is setting. Perta is flying from one of the two middle perches to the other. I watch her a minute, then fly down to her.

"I've been looking for you, Birdy. Where have you been? How is it you are here sometimes and sometimes you are not? I do not understand. Do you go outside the cage? Do you fly alone out there? Aren't you afraid? Couldn't you take me with you?"

"No, Perta. I do not fly out there."

I can't answer the rest of her questions. She looks so beautiful to me. She's against the light so I see the lovely curve of her breast and back. Inside myself, I can feel the restlessness arising.

I approach and Perta squats on the perch and starts peep-peep-peeping to me. Her wings are fluttering in expectation. It's time for me to feed her. I'm the same as Alfonso; I can't do it. I want to, but I can't bring food up into my mouth. I've always hated to vomit. The boy is getting in the way of the bird.

Perta stays there, patiently, waiting to be fed. I try once more and it comes. The bird gains control and it's as easy as flying or singing. I give her food and Perta is happy. She peep-peep-peeps some more. I give her more food. I sing and approach her. She squats down further. I'm not ready yet. I feed her again. Partly it's wanting to make it last as long as possible. Perta doesn't say anything and we fly together all the night long. I sing and feed her till the morning when I wake up.

The next day, I'm tired from being out so late. My mother keeps asking questions but I don't tell her much. I'm cleaning the cages when Al comes over. I've put twelve more young birds in the other flight cage. I still haven't lost any of the young ones. The breeding cages are in full swing. With the sound of babies hollering to be fed, and the males singing, it makes quite a racket. Perta is flying back and forth alone in the flight cage.

Al starts pumping me about how it was with Doris. I tell him I didn't fuck her, but he won't believe me. He says Doris is one of the hottest firecrackers in the whole school; she'd fuck a horse if she could get it to stand still. I tell him I believe it but she didn't fuck me.

My father testifies to my mother that I danced every

dance. My mother wants to know where we went after the dance. I tell her we went to Don's in Yeadon; that's a milk-shake bar, the kind of place my mother would like me to go after a dance. I tell her I had a good time. My mother goes over the tux and brushes it off. I pulled all the leaves and stickers out of it before I went to bed. She'd really flip if she found jit smeared along the inside of the pants.

Al looks the birds over but he doesn't have much interest in canaries. What he does understand is that I've got a regular bird factory going. He asks me about feed costs and how many birds per nest and works out how much money I can make.

"Jesus, Birdy, you're going to be a fucking millionaire! King of the Canaries. You'll be voted most likely to suck seed."

Al thinks that's funny. He manages to get it in the year-book under my picture. There's nothing else there; no clubs, no honor rolls, no sports, no offices. It just says "Nickname Birdy." "Voted most likely to suck seed."

Al notices Perta flying all alone in the flight cage and asks about her. He wonders why I don't put some of the young birds in there. I tell him she's a special pet of mine. She's a spare female.

"Don't tell me she's like the pigeon witch we used to have."

I tell him, "Yeah, she's something like that, only she doesn't bring back any fancy birds."

"Does she eat out of your mouth the way the freaky witch did?"

For a minute I have the feeling Al can see into the dream. If anybody could, it would be Al. Then I remember. I laugh and tell him that canaries are harder to train than pigeons.

We go out and throw the discus for a while, then Al goes home. I go to the aviary and watch Perta with my binoculars.

I'm trying to decide how to tell her what I am. I'm trying to decide what I am, too.

That night, in the dream, I know I must tell Perta about myself. As boy, I've decided this and it's come through to me as Birdy in the dream.

First, Perta and I fly together in a new dance. In the dance, we fly over each other, then drop on the other side, so the first flies over the one who has dropped. It's beautiful, but hard to do in the small space of the cage. It would be so terrific if we could fly free.

When we're finished, she squats and peep-peep-peeps to me and I feed her easily. It is time to mate with her and she's waiting. I know the beginning egg is inside her waiting for my seed. I want to put my seed into her, to know it is buried warmly in her egg.

"Birdy, what are you afraid of? Do you want to have a nest with me? I feel we could have such wonderful babies, that we would be together in them, that for the first time, my eggs would be filled with life; with our life. Why are you afraid?"

I look at her. I love her so. What she is saying is what I've been thinking, dreaming, singing. It is more than flying.

"Perta, there are things I must tell you first."

"Do you have another female, another nest, somewhere?"

"No. Nothing so simple as that, Perta."

"That is not so simple."

"Listen carefully, Perta. Listen to the way I tell this as much as to what I tell. I want you to know I speak the truth. I want you to know what I am, so we can truly be together."

"Say it, Birdy. Tell me."

"Perta, all this we have together is not real."

Perta shifts from her left to her right eye but remains quiet.

"In reality, I am the boy out there."

I point to myself as boy in the aviary. I'm out there filling feed dishes, changing water.

"This, here, that we have together, is just a dream. I dreamed you in my dream. I wanted you to be, so I dreamed you."

I wait. Perta says nothing. She shifts eyes twice more; flips her wings once. Can she possibly understand?

"Perta, I went out, as boy, in the real world and you were given to me. I carried you here to the cage."

I wait for some sign that she is with me, that she understands. If I only understood it better myself, I could explain it better. Perta looks at me closely.

"Go on, Birdy. I'm listening."

"You see, Perta, we are here together because of two things, the dream I dreamed in my dream and then the bird I carried back with me, who flies alone here in the cage during the day. You are the bird in my dream-dream and you are the bird I love as a boy but cannot know. You are here in the dream between those two. I am here in my dream because I want to be here. I want to be with you and so it is so."

I stop. I can't understand what I'm saying myself. I'm too much of a bird to understand. My boy brain makes up the ideas, the words, but my bird brain can't understand them. I'm seeing Perta not as a bird but as another creature like myself with whom I'm in love. What I'm saying sounds like crazy talk. How can I expect Perta to understand, to believe, when I cannot do so myself? I stop.

"Go on, Birdy. Tell me more."

"That's the most of it, Perta. As a boy out there, in reality, when the dream is over, I own all the birds. I bought Birdie, Alfonso. I raised all of them in my bedroom in another place. I built this cage where we fly now. I go places when I am a boy that you cannot see from here. I live with other beings like myself, as a boy. I am but a young creature in that world, not capable of taking care of myself. I have a mother and father with whom I live. My house is out there, out of the cage. If I do not come here, take care, feed all the birds, this whole life would stop, it would all end. Do you understand?"

"Of course not, Birdy. You know I cannot. I am a bird; those things mean nothing to me."

"But do you believe me, Perta? Do you think I lie when I tell all this?"

"No, Birdy. You are telling me your truth."

"Can't it be your truth, too, Perta? I want it to be your truth. I want you to know me truly."

Perta looks at me straight on, very unbirdlike.

"No, Birdy. I am a bird. Your truth cannot be mine."

I don't know why I want her to know. Is it because I think that if she knows, believes, then the dream will be more real. But how can a dream be more real? It is like making a zero more zero by writing zero ten thousand times in a line. It is still zero.

"Perta, do you realize that what I am saying is that you do not exist at all; that you are only a part of my dream?"

"What is a dream, Birdy?"

I'm stopped. I hadn't thought of that. If birds do not dream, there's no way. Still, this is my dream. I can have birds dream or not in my dream, as I want. I can make it to fit my dream.

"Perta, when you sleep, do you not have thoughts, images, visions, feelings that are not true, that come from inside you, that you only imagine?"

"No. When I sleep I am giving myself strength. I give myself force to fly, to have babies. It is the great unbeing. It is when we build our feathers, harden our beaks, unbecome."

This is beyond me. I cannot make birds dream, even in my own dream. I know then that the boy does not really want Perta to know. I must live my bird life as a bird only. I must surrender myself. It is a relief, a wonderful feeling to know this.

A great peace comes into me. I feel my strength as a bird spreading through me. The blood is circulated in warmth out to the tips of my feathers, to the ends of my toenails.

Perta is watching me. She is telling me that I am a bird; that I am to forget all this nonsense of the boy. She wants me as her mate. These things I have been telling her are only the ravings of a maniac, a fever. It is clear to her I am a bird. If I can see myself with her eyes, then I am a bird in her world. I let go. I settle deeply into the life I've always wanted. I become, re-become, a bird in this world of the dream.

I start to sing. Perta is alive to me. There is a transfer of feeling, knowing, one to the other from us that I have never known, never dreamed of dreaming. Perta starts to fly in a complex dance. I fly after her, singing. She flies, dances to my song and I sing, dance, to her dance. It's not a chase but mutual following. We speak in language beyond words. Our every movement magnifies the tension of our merging identity. Then, Perta stops, waits for me. I approach, in deepest passion, maximum awareness, to her. She waits, cups herself to receive me. I hover, then lower myself into her. My penetration is engulfed by her whole being. For just that moment I am not alone, not separate. I pass through the illusion of identity into a depth of shared reality.

When I wake that morning, I've done it again. I'm covered with jit, my sheets, my pajamas. I wash everything so my mother won't find out. I've got to do something.

I go down to Cobb's Creek with a long stick. They're floating by in that creek all the time. There must be toilets flushing into the creek, there just couldn't be that many lovers along the banks. I get one in good shape, wash it out in the creek first, then take it home and wash it again. I turn it inside out. I slip it on and when it's on, I can hardly feel it. After that, I sleep with that condom on. I fill it almost every night during those first mad weeks when Perta and I are so deeply involved with each other, when all the dreams are devoted to passionate flight, singing, dancing, and overwhelming culminations.

Now, I'm separating the dream from the day better. Especially in the dream, I hardly remember that I am a boy. I am almost completely bird. As boy I've wired a nest into the cage with Perta the daytime bird. In the night, Perta and I are building our nest. Strangely enough, Perta, alone, in the days shows interest in the nest also. I give her burlap and she starts building. This isn't uncommon. Sometimes a female without a male will build a nest during the nesting season.

In the dream it is such fun building the nest. Perta does most of the work and she's a fine engineer. It's a combination of weaving or knitting and construction work. Mostly I'm bringing up materials. Perta is meticulous and ingenious with her nest building. I admire it even more as bird than I did as a boy.

Every day when I go out to feed and take care of the birds, I check on the nest Perta is building in the flight cage. It's exactly like the nest Perta is building in the dream, except the dream nest seems to be slightly more advanced than the nest in the cage. Could the dream be getting ahead of real life? I'm beginning to think I don't know what's real anymore.

When the nest is finished, Perta tells me she thinks she is going to lay the egg that night. For me as boy, the dream nights are the day. In the real day the thinking of the dream dominates me. I'm thinking all the time of our egg to come. It's hard for me to realize that Perta the bird is asleep while I'm dreaming, and Perta the dream is awake while Perta sleeps. Are they dreams to each other? Is Perta right? Do birds not dream? Don't they ever dream themselves out of the cage?

That night the egg is laid. I sit beside Perta. She tells me she can feel the egg becoming inside her, how the shell is hardening and starting to move out into the world.

She asks me to sing to her so the egg will come more easily. I begin to sing softly, absently, not knowing what my song will be. I sing about how we are there, together, living as one, in life just begun. Being the father of an egg is so far from what being a boy is.

The sky is just lighting in the morning when Perta tells me the egg has come into the nest. She lifts herself carefully so I can see. It is beautiful. She leaves the nest and I lower myself slowly over it. The warmth of Perta's body comes from the egg, from the nest, through my feathers to my breast. I hold myself still and this warmth goes through me. I try to feel what Perta has felt, is feeling. Perta leans over the nest and feeds me. Then she squats beside the nest and cups herself to receive me.

Both Perta in the dream and Perta in the cage lay four eggs. Perta's eggs in the cage are as lovely as ours. I leave the eggs in the nest with Perta the bird. I don't want to take any chance that the eggs in my dream will turn into marbles and also I know that Perta the bird's eggs must be sterile. If I know they must be sterile, there is no reason to take them out.

I worry, as boy, that the eggs in the dream will be sterile, too. In the dream I don't worry about this at all. I ask Perta why she has had only sterile eggs before and she tells me she was never properly fertilized. This is what I want to believe.

Mostly, I want our eggs to be fertile. I wish it as hard as I can. With my binoculars, I watch the birds in the breeding cages as the eggs are hatched. I get it deeply printed into my mind. I want to know exactly what to do as a bird. I want to power my babies into this life.

The other flight cage is getting filled with young birds. From the warbling going on all the time, it seems there's a good proportion of males.

I watch poor Perta in her cage with her sterile eggs. It doesn't seem fair for her to do all that sitting for nothing. When she's been sitting on them for seven days, halfway through the brooding period, I take them out one at a time and hold them up to a light. They're all sterile.

I decide to do something about it. There are three hens who have nests due to hatch within a day or two of Perta's. One has five eggs and the others have four each. I take two eggs from the nest of five and one from each of the others. Three birds in a nest is a good number, not too crowded, and the young have a better chance for survival.

I give these four eggs to Perta as substitutes for the sterile ones. I feel much better. I'm sure Perta will be a good mother. Two of the eggs came from Birdie and Alfonso. I don't think Birdie minded my taking them. Perta doesn't seem to notice the substitution and accepts the new eggs without trouble. I check each egg before I put it in the nest with her and they're all fertile. I use a small hand flashlight to check the eggs. A fertile egg of seven days has opacity and small red veins running through it.

In the dream I look into the nest of our eggs but there is no change I can see. Changing Perta's eggs in the cage has not changed our eggs. I'm hoping it will give our eggs a better chance to be fertile. I'm feeling a strong desire to be a father. I want to be able to feed my own babies. I often feed Perta on the nest and sing to her. Being a father, knowing I'm there in the new babies, will be more proof that I am. I feel that I'll be more, not only as bird but as boy. Knowing he's a father is one of the only proofs a male has that he is.

On the night when the babies are to hatch, when Perta tells me she can feel the babies moving in the shell, I sit on the eggs while she takes a bath to help the babies by softening the shell. I feel them moving. I can feel movement in each egg. They will all hatch in the morning. I know it. When

Perta comes back to the nest, I sing her this song. I'm sure the babies are mature enough to hear me now. The shell of the egg is so thin.

Become now,
Tap through the shell
Of being and taste the
Soft air of your beginning
This is yours, the safe
Surrounding blanket
Of new life.

The day the birds are to hatch is a school day. I play hooky for the first time in my life. I know they're bound to catch me. I usually eat lunch with my father down in the boiler room; he'll know I'm not there. I don't care. I can't hang around the aviary or my mother would catch me. Instead, I go down to the woods and climb a favorite tree, not far from where we had the pigeon loft. I wedge myself into a fork near the top, high over the bank of a hill.

I spend the day up there. I can't keep myself from thinking about my babies trying to hatch from the eggs. I can feel their struggle. I lie back on the length of the branch and try to put myself into the dream. I can't do it. I know also, in my deepest part, it would be dangerous to enter the dream in the daytime. I'm not sure what would happen, whether it would break the dream or I would not be able to come out and back to life as a boy, but I know it would be dangerous to do.

While I'm up in the tree, I think of myself trying to teach my babies to fly. I look down from the tree and wish I could fly here and have them fly with me in the open. It's that day in the tree when I decide how to do it. I make all the plans and I'm so full of them, I hardly pay attention when my father and mother holler at me during dinner about cutting school. They keep wanting to know where I was. I tell them I was up in a tree but they won't believe me. I don't know where it is they wanted me to be.

After my parents finally settle down, I go out to the cage and listen, but none of Perta's birds have hatched. I wonder if the birds in the dream will hatch if hers haven't. It's hard to tell which is in front anymore, the dream or real life. I go to sleep not knowing what will be.

When I arrive in the dream, Perta is excited. She tells me one of the babies is cutting the shell with its beak. She stands high on her legs so I can look in. One of the eggs is opening. Perta reaches in and carefully pulls off part of a loose shell with her beak. We can see a dark eye and moistened head. I'm nervous but Perta is serene and happy. I do some of my best flying around the cage to calm myself.

Within two hours, all the babies are hatched. I help Perta take the shells out of the nest. I can see that two of the young ones are dark and two of them are light. Perta tells me there are two males and two females. Both the males are dark and the females are light. I'm a father! Perta lets me feed them and it's such a wonderful feeling to put the small bits of food into their mouths. The little cries of demand and delight are a special bird song.

The next morning before breakfast, when I go out to the aviary, I check Perta. She has eggshells under her nest. I put some egg food in the bottom of the cage and she comes down immediately. I look and there are four little babies, two light and two dark, the same. When I go out she flies up and starts feeding. I wish I could help her, too. I feel I'm using her, having her live without a male. I'm afraid to put a male in with her because of the dream. I might be jealous, too.

During the days, I do everything I'm supposed to. I go to school, do my work, help at home and do some designing on my bird models. I'm trying to use things I've learned as a bird to improve the models. It also helps the days go by. It's not so much I want to fly or make a model I can fly; I'm only trying to bring some of the dream into my life.

During the course of the breeding season, Perta and I have three nests. For each nest we have, I take eggs from other nests and give them to Perta in the daytime cage. I'm afraid not to. We have twelve babies but one of them, a young male, dies. Perta says she could tell from the first that it wasn't meant to live or fly, there was nothing of the sky in its eyes. In my dreams, birds have a kind of knowing humans don't. I don't know why this is. I'm only human, so I suffer very much at the loss of this young one. It is five weeks old when it dies. In bird time, it was in Scheen.

Birds don't have any kind of time except in relation to themselves. The movement of the sun or the earth doesn't mean much to them. They have two kinds of time. First, they have the time which is one year or breeding period. It begins with Ohnme. This is the period after the molt and before breeding. Then, there is Sachen, the time of courtship, till the first egg is laid. Kharst is the fourteen days of sitting on the eggs. The next time is from when the young hatch till they leave the nest; this is Flangst. After this is Scheen, which is until the young can crack seed on their own and live without their parents. It is in Scheen when our son dies. Then, there is the first molt period of young birds; this is called Smoor. The molt time for older birds is called Smoorer. After Smoorer the adult birds go into Ohnme again. So, the bird year has six different periods. The longest is Ohnme and the shortest is Kharst. Kharst, Flangst, and Scheen are repeated three times in the typical bird year.

The other kind of time birds have is related to the in-dividual bird and not so much to the mating-molting season. The whole first year before breeding is called Tangen. The years of breeding are called Pleen and the last days before death are called Echen. Sometimes in old age or illness a bird goes into Echen. It is a time when a bird does not want to fly or eat. The birds have no word for death. As far as I can tell, Echen includes our idea of being dead. When Perta told me our son had gone into Echen, I went down to help him; he was not dead yet but there was nothing I could do. He was in Echen. When he finally died I told Perta and she only said:

"Yes, he is in Echen."

The strange thing is that on the same day our son dies, one of the young birds in Perta's nest in the cage also dies. It has the same markings as our son. I take it from the bottom of the cage and in the dream our son's body disappears. I tell Perta this but she doesn't want to listen. She never talks of him again. When I try to speak of him, of his death, of my sadness, she only gives the same response; "Yes. He is in Echen."

All these words are the closest I can come to what I'm hearing in canary. I have no way to know if they are bird ideas or Birdy ideas. In my dream I've begun to hear the bird sounds as words like these, although to my ear, as a bird, they sound like bird sounds. I don't know how this is happening. No bird word sounds in itself like any English word, but the birds sound to me as if they're talking English. I'm converting the sounds as I'm hearing them and I'm only hearing my own conversions.

At the end of the breeding season, Perta and I have eleven wonderful children. There are seven females and four males. The remarkable thing is that the young in Perta's cage have the same markings as my children in the dream, and as far as I can tell, they are also the same sex. I can understand that I might have structured the birds in my dream to resemble the birds in Perta's cage, but I knew the sex of Perta's daytime young before I could know them in reality. Perta in the dream told me. This is something I can't put together.

I try talking to Perta, the bird in the cage, in sounds I remember from the dream but she doesn't respond. However, if I peep or queep in the ways I used to do with Birdie, she'll peep or queep back enthusiastically. She wants me to stay as a boy. My dream has nothing to do with her reality. Still, her babies are the same as mine in the dream. I'm getting so I can't tell which reality is making the other. It must be that I'm tailoring the dream in some way to the things that happen, but sometimes it seems the other way around. It's easy to fool yourself.

The other flight cage is so full I have to do something. I've gotten three nests from almost every breeding couple. I need to separate the young males from the females and take the breeding birds apart. The season is over and the adult birds will be going into their molt soon. I need more space.

To solve this, I divide off a part of the male cage for my project. I build in a new floor about one third down from the top of the aviary. Above this I put Perta and her young. The bottom part I use for the adult and young males. There are eighty-five young males and eighty-two young females. Now I'll feed them and give them tonic to get through the molt and ready for the market. I hate to think about selling them, especially the children of Birdie and Alfonso. Still, making money is the excuse I have for keeping my birds. It's the way I can hold onto the world which makes my dream possible.

The reason I build off the special cage is so I can live privately with Perta and my children in the dream. The very night the partition is finished, it's that way in the dream. We don't have as much space to fly, but this will be all right after I get my plan going.

My plan is to work out a way for free flying with my family. It is the idea I developed up in the tree.

In the dream, I'm happy as husband and father. I spend wonderful hours teaching my children to fly, to crack seed, to eat. We bathe together and I teach the young males to sing.

We start with simple songs about flying, without any difficult parts, and move on to harder songs. One of the children's songs is:

Down is up.
Up is sky.
Sing a song
Don't ask why.

Another is:

Touch the air
Hold it tight.
Stroke the wind
Ride the light.

When I sell the young birds, I sell off three of my breeding females and one of my breeding males. I replace them with some of the best of the new young birds. I replace the three females because they aren't good breeders. One only laid two eggs each nest and raised a total of five birds. Another laid eggs but consistently pulled the nest apart scattering the eggs on the floor. The third abandoned each of her nests when the babies were less than a week old. I saved the babies by distributing them to other nests, but she has to go. The male I sell because he's developed the habit of egg-eating.

All of these young birds are even better fliers than their parents. It's a pleasure to watch them. The rustling sounds of their wings is musical. Because they fly so much and so well, they are all trim and longer-legged than ordinary canaries. I wish I could have Mr. Lincoln come see my aviary and birds. I think about it often but I could never explain it to my parents. I wish people could be more like canaries.

During the day, I spend hours watching the birds fly. The more I watch, the stronger, truer, my dreams are. I'm getting so much inside the bird world, my dream seems completely independent of the day. I don't even know what I know anymore. I can't know all the time why things are in the dreams or how they're going to be. The dreams have gotten so complicated they're at least as real as the day.

I don't do any flying experiments with the birds. I know all of them too well from my dreams. I'm not really that interested in flying anymore; at least not as a boy. It's better to watch a bird fly naturally than to watch one with weights or with feathers missing. Flying is something practically impossible to take apart. You have to learn it all at once; it can't be seen in pieces.

The price of birds does go up and I sell my birds to a wholesaler from Philadelphia for even more than I thought I would. At the end of the year there's over a thousand dollars profit. My mother can't believe it and wants me to pay board. She says I live in the house and I'm making almost as much money as my father so I ought to pay. I don't care. I'm not keeping canaries for the money. My father says no; he's going to put the money in the bank for my college education. It doesn't mean anything to me. I'm not going to college anyway. I only want to raise my birds and fly with them at night. I can do that anywhere; I don't have to go to college for that.

The thing I'm more worried about is getting drafted when I'm eighteen. There's nothing I can do about this. The army isn't going to let me keep canaries, that's for sure. I wonder if the dream would continue then if I didn't have any birds to watch. The army will probably take one look at me with my pointed chest and mark me off as 4-F anyway. I hope so.

My father is great about my birdkeeping. He's proud of the canaries and begins to talk about them, and the money I'm making, to the people at school. Everybody there knows I'm crazy with birds but they didn't know about the moneymaking part.

I demonstrate one of my ornithopters in physics class and

they put it in a glass case in the hall. This kind of clinches it for me as Birdy the bird freak; "most likely to suck seed." I don't care much; I'm happy doing what I have to do. Sometimes I wish I could tell Al about my dream. I know he wouldn't understand; he's so real. He'd just think I'd finally flipped and that was it. Also, I'm afraid the dream might stop if I tell somebody else about it.

During that winter I spend hours training Perta's young birds in the cage. In the night I play and fly with my own children and then in the day I play with them as a boy. The personalities of the two sets of birds is exactly the same, so it's easy for me to train Perta's birds. I know them as my own children.

I train all of her birds and Perta, too, to come when I whistle. This whistle is the closest sound I make as a boy to the bird sound for food. I go over it with them thousands of times. I give the signal and they fly directly to my finger to be fed. They eat from my finger or my lips or out of my hand. In the end, none of them has any more fear of me than Birdie had. They are really my children, even during the day.

I'm in my senior year in high school now. I ride my bike to school rather than take the school bus. I stay mostly apart. Al and I see each other some but he's all involved in sports. He's trying that winter to win the District Championship in wrestling. He does it and then goes on to be State Champion at a hundred sixty-five pounds. I'm at the Districts to watch, but there's no way for me to get to Harrisburg for the State finals. He wins the finals with a first-period pin.

It's on a warm day in the end of February when I decide to make the big test. I choose a little female who is the closest to me. She's exactly like one of my daughters from our last nest. I take her out of the aviary on my finger. When we get outside, I check the sky for hawks and the yard for cats. It's all clear. I throw her up in the air from my finger the way I've done it in the aviary. I've been practicing with the birds in the center part where the breeding cages are. The door to their flight cage opens onto this part. I throw her up into the sky the way you would a pigeon or a falconing hawk.

First she flies up and lands on the roof of the garage. Her flight, which looked so competent in the cage, seems awkward here in the open air. She hops along the edge and peeps down at me. She looks so small against the sky, so yellow and vulnerable in the immensity of blue. I give my whistle and hold out my finger. She flies immediately back down to me and takes a bit of treat food from my lips. I stroke her on the head. She fluffs her feathers and peeps. It's a peep lost in the air. She's a beautiful lemon yellow, yellower than Birdie. She looks so pure and clean in the winter sunshine.

I throw her up in the air again and this time she stretches her wings and flies across our yard onto our porch roof where the pigeons used to roost. I almost swallow my heart. She's so beautiful flying, but so far away. My mouth gets dry and I have a hard time whistling but I manage. She flies straight back to me and makes a cocky, wings-down, no-flutter landing on my finger.

Over the next days, I practice with the rest of Perta's young ones. I throw them up one at a time and they all fly back to me. It's much more fun than pigeons. It's better than trying to fly model airplanes. I know these birds are flying for me.

I wait every night but I still don't fly outside the cage myself. This I can't understand. My own children have started flying outside in the dream. I can see them flying but I'm caught in the cage.

After a week, I try throwing up two birds together. I'm worried they might not pay attention to my whistle, but it's fine. They come directly to me. I leave them flying for longer and longer periods before I whistle them back. One pair I leave out flying for fifteen minutes. Once I even go over and sit on the porch steps to watch them, instead of standing in front of the aviary. They both come in when I whistle; no trouble. Still, I'm not flying myself; I'm confined to the cage.

In my dream, I look more and more outside the cage and want to fly there. I talk to my children and they tell me it is a completely different thing. It's not just flying to get food, or from one perch to another, but flying for the flying itself, flying free of everything.

One day one of the young males sings from the tree hanging over our house. Hearing that beautiful song in the free air is a wonderful thing. The singing has all of space in it ringing out to the open sky.

Next I throw all the birds up at the same time. With a rush of wings, they take off in every direction. Most of them fly back to places they've been before. It's lovely to see sparkles of yellow and green on the roof and in the trees. The trees are coming on with new leaves. One yellow male is singing up on the chimney of the house. The yellow against the blue sky is sharp and clear.

I'm concerned about how far they will fly. If they fly too far they couldn't hear my whistle. Canaries don't have homing instincts or capacities like pigeons. In fact, for free flying, canaries don't have many skills left at all.

After five minutes, I whistle and seven of the twelve come right down to me. They come swooping in and land on my fingers, my hands, my arms. I walk into the aviary with them hanging onto me, give each some treat food, and put them in the cage. When I go out, the other five have flown to the top of the aviary. When I whistle again, they come down and jump on my fingers. It's all gone well. I wonder what would happen if a cat or a hawk dispersed them. Would they still remember to come when I whistle or would they panic? I'm sure I'll fly free in my dream that night, but it isn't so. Even with all of them flying, I still don't fly outside the aviary.

As spring arrives, I take the birds out every day. They come to know and expect what's going to happen. The other birds, the ones I'm saving for breeding, don't seem to know what's going on. In my dream I tend not to communicate with them; probably I'm feeling guilty.

My fliers come to the door when I open it and jump onto my finger even before I whistle. I walk out of the aviary with them on my arms and shoulders and stand there in the open. I don't want them to fly till I toss them up in the air. If one takes off by itself, I whistle it back. Soon they all know this rule. It's like the starting of a track meet with false starts. The birds are between the pleasure of flying and the safety of what they know.

After a month, I can leave all twelve of them, including Perta, out flying free for as long as an hour. The yard is their territory and nobody flies too far away. Once in a while, one will swoop over the fence out into the outfield of the baseball field, but there're no trees to land on so they return. One bird ventures downhill toward the burnt-out Cosgrove barn but comes right back. They're all learning the details of the territory and the landmarks for the aviary. I'm getting convinced you can train canaries to live in the open, like pigeons, and have an open aviary. I'm still not flying free in my dream and I'm beginning to know what's wrong. I'm getting in my own way.

All the free flying, so far, has depended on me, Birdy, the boy. I'm the one who takes the birds out on my finger to fly. However, in my dream, it's impossible to contact myself as boy. I can see myself, but I can't get my attention and so I don't exist. Therefore, there's no way for me to be whistled to or be taken out. In my dream there's no other way to get out of the aviary. I can't just wish myself out; it isn't enough.

I work out a new idea. I design a pigeon-type outside door entry to the cage. I do this with thin wires hanging freely from the top of an outside opening, overlapping the inside of the cage. I build a landing board just outside the opening. This way a bird can land on the board outside and go into the aviary by pushing aside the wires. He then can't go outside again because the dangling wires will have fallen back into place. The question is, can I train my birds to use this kind of an entrance?

When I get it finished I take the birds out of the aviary the same as usual, throwing them up to fly. When I want them back in the aviary, I stick my hand through their cage and out the opening so it rests on the landing board. I whistle. One at a time the birds come and land on my finger. I pull them through the door into the cage. When they're inside I give them treat food. I do this several times.

Next, instead of taking them out the usual door and carrying them on my fingers, I pull back the dangling wires so the opening is free, then stand outside the aviary where they can see me, put my finger on the landing board, and whistle. They quickly learn to fly out the door onto my finger. As they come out I give each of them a toss into the air. We practice this several times until it's automatic. After that I can stand outside the door, whistle, and they come out. It isn't long before they come out when I pull aside the wires on the door. They can now go outside of the cage to fly on their own whenever I make it possible by clearing the opening.

I regularly reinforce their coming to me with the whistle and then throwing them up again. I try changing the whistle for each bird, so I'll have a way to call in a particular bird, but they're spoiled with the one whistle. You can't ask too much of a canary. Once, I cut one of the dead birds open in biology class and saw how little the brain is; in fact, the eyes of a canary weigh more than its brain. I can't ask them to learn too many complicated things.

It takes a long time for the birds to get used to flying into the aviary on their own. First, I put treat food inside the door and whistle them in. I also put them on the landing board, but they don't want to push aside the wires. I think canaries are more sensitive to touch than pigeons. I begin leaving the wires pulled back and then they go in for the treat food. Finally, one at a time, they get the courage to push aside the wires to go in on their own. It's done. They can practically live the life of a free-flying pigeon. They've become amazingly quick and agile fliers so that, even after three hundred generations living in cages, I'm not much worried about cats or hawks.

In my dream one night, I look up and see the opening; the wires are pulled back. I fly onto the edge of the opening and hop out onto the landing platform. The dream of my dream is coming true. I'm going to fly free.

I fly up onto the top of the aviary. I hop along the roof edge, look down at the ground, then across the yard to the roof of our house. It's a beautiful day, the spring leaves are open, there are huge, soft, white clouds drifting in the sky. I spring. I loop-swing through the air, feeling the fullness of the wind in the pits of my wings. I look down and the yard gets smaller. I circle once, then land on the rain gutter. The world is bigger and smaller at the same time. Bigger because I can see farther, and smaller because I'm looking down on it and know it's mine, more than ever before.

I fly from the roof almost straight up; straight as I can, not flying to anywhere, just feeling the sky. Then, I fold my wings and let myself drop until my feathers begin to flutter in the wind. I open my wings, catch myself, and fly straight up again, stalling, looping a long lingering loop. I look down.

Below is my yard, all in one piece. I can see all of it without turning my head. I can see the whole baseball field and out along Church Lane to the cemetery. I'm directly over the tree in the corner of our yard. I come down in slow circles looking for a branch on which to land. I find one just on the yard side of the top of the tree. I land and fluff out my feathers. I feel all together. I feel like me to the very tips of myself.

I look over to the aviary. Perta is coming out, standing on the landing board. On top of the aviary are two of my sons and one of my daughters. I think of peeping to tell them where I am but decide to sing. I start to sing in the sunshine and my song goes out into the blue air. I have a sense of drifting into the sky with my notes. I feel I'm a part of everything my song touches. While I'm singing, Perta flies up, and joins me on the branch. She feels what I'm feeling and asks me to feed her. I feed her and sing some more, then feed her again. I fly up over her and in. It's more than it ever was before. I spring away and fly small circles over Perta. I sing while I'm flying. I'm forgetting I'm Birdy; I'm a real bird and it isn't a dream.

I fly all through the night and can go everywhere my birds have gone in the day. There are other places I want to fly to, like over the gas tank or to the mill pond, or down where we used to have the pigeon coop in the tree, but I can't do it.

In the days, I think about flying all the time. It's all so real in the dream that the things I do in the day are harder and harder to believe.

It's time to start breeding for the new year. I clean out all the cages and get them in shape. I've already decided who the breeding pairs will be and I've been giving them egg food and dandelion to get them in breeding condition. When I put the breeding birds in the cage, I'll take out the dividing floor and use the whole flight cage for my family.

Early in April, I put the breeding pairs together. In the dream that night, Perta and I fly to the edges of the places we can go. We chase each other in the air and sometimes brush wings as we come close. I'm tempted to turn over in the air like a tumbler pigeon, but a canary can't do that.

Perta says she doesn't want to build our nest in the aviary; she wants to build it in the tree. It's my dream so I thought this up, but I'm surprised in the dream. If Perta builds her nest in the tree in the dream, will it be there in the daytime, too?

The next day I'm busy feeding and watering the birds in the breeding cages and watching to see how the mating is proceeding. More than half the pairs have mated before, so they should get started quickly enough.

I've already opened the door to my flying family and they're out flying in the open. After I'm finished with the breeding cages, and before I go in for dinner, I whistle for them to come back into the cage. Everybody comes in but Perta. I'd trained her later than the others so I whistle again. She comes to the landing board and when I put out my finger she comes onto it. She has something in her mouth; it's a piece of dry grass.

That night, Perta and I search all over the tree for a right meeting of branches where we can build our nest. I think about climbing the tree in the day and putting a nest holder up there for us, but decide against it.

The next afternoon, Perta doesn't come when I call. I know she's building a nest outside somewhere. This is another thing that began in the dream and now is happening in the day. I put some seed and water on the roof of the aviary where she'll be safe from cats, and hope for the best.

Perta and I spend many hours building the nest. It's much harder without a container and without shredded burlap. We gather pieces of dried grass and bits of wood from every direction. There's an old straw chair in the garage my father made years ago, before I was born. We tear out pieces and shred it to line the nest. It's a beautiful construction. I can only do what Perta tells me and her instincts are coming on strong. We get it finished two days before the first egg comes.

It's a terrific nest. I fly to different branches so I can look down on it. The place we chose can't be seen from the air, or from the ground either. No hawk or cat would ever even know it's there. Perta lays her usual four eggs and she's very happy. I sing to her from different parts of the tree and go down to the seed and water on top of the aviary to get food for her.

In the daytime I find immediately where Perta has built her nest. It's exactly where we've built our nest in the dream. Perta could have fertile eggs this time, fertilized by one of the young from her last year's nest. I hope Perta's eggs will be fertile. Some of the other fliers are beginning to build nests, too. Most of them, like pigeons, are building in the security of the flight cage. One, like Perta, is building outside. It's the little yellow one, the one I first took out. She's building in the tree overhanging the roof of our house. Because of cats, this worries me. I don't know whether I should try to move the nest or not. I decide to leave it alone and hope for the best.

—I've got to learn to live with myself the way I am. The trouble is there are whole parts of me I don't know. All my life, I've been building a personal picture of myself like body building in *Strength and Health*. Only I didn't build from the inside, I built from the outside, to protect myself against things.

Now, a big part of this crazy structure is torn apart. I have to start all over, looking inside to find what's really there. I don't know if I can do it. I'll probably wind up putting together the old Al with some pieces missing and plaster it over somehow.

I've got to learn how to live with fear. It's built in and there's no sense fighting it. Without fear we wouldn't be successful animals. Fear's nothing to be ashamed of. Just like play or pain it's natural and necessary. I've got to live with this.

In the dream, all four of Perta's eggs hatch. There are three darks and one yellow. Perta says the yellow one is female and the darks male. I still can't tell; I'll probably never make it as a bird. In the daytime, up in the tree, Perta's eggs hatch; so she wasn't sterile after all. It makes me feel better about my Perta.

The birds in the breeding cages are going at it like mad. There are eight nests of five. As they're ready to leave the breeding cages, I'll put them all in the female cage so the male flight cage can be kept for the fliers. The fliers have begun to fill their cage with young ones too. The nests are built with materials they've scavenged from outside. They're in and out of the aviary all day like pigeons. I leave the wire gate open for them. The opening's too small and the landing platform too high and too narrow for a cat to get in.

I'm not sure what I'll do when their babies begin to fly around the flight cage. The problem is whether to leave the outside entrance open or not. These young birds won't have been trained to come to me when I whistle or to come back to the aviary at all. Would the parents teach them? Would they realize that the only food for them is in the cage? I decide to take the chance and leave the cage open. As long as they're being fed by the parents, they'll come back to the cage. That way they'll get the habit. When they've started cracking seed for themselves will be the time when I'll know if it's all possible. Can they be free and still be part of the aviary community?

In my dream, life is really a dream. I fly and sing and help feed the babies. Then when they come out of the nest, I teach them to fly. Teaching them to fly in the open air is almost as much fun as flying itself. Teaching flying is always the best part of flight dreams. Perta is happy and is already sitting on a new nest of babies. They're a week old. I fly with the first nest to all my favorite places. Some of my children from last year fly with us, especially the males who aren't tied down to the nest. These birds are something between brothers and uncles to the new ones, and help with the teaching. Being a father and grandfather at the same time is a tremendous experience. I feel like a brother to my own children. It's too bad people are so old when they get to be grandparents.

The other female who built outside the cage in the daytime hatches her birds, too. I think there are three of them. I can't see the nest where Perta has built very well because it's so high. I wouldn't know her birds are hatched except I hear them peeping to be fed. In my dream, there is no other bird besides Perta and myself who builds outside the cage.

The way my canaries have adapted to natural life is almost proof that a canary keeps many of its natural skills even after centuries of being in cages and generations of interbreeding with other types of birds. I feel that if my canaries could find proper food, they would probably survive alone, without me.

The birds from the nest built in the tree over the roof are just getting up onto the edge of the nest and tottering when one day I notice a beat-up tomcat sitting on the porch roof and staring up at them. I'm not sure he can jump from the porch roof to the roof of the house, but I throw some stones at him till he goes away. It'll really be dangerous when those young ones are starting to fly and flutter to the ground. I can't think of any way to keep that cat out of the yard.

The female flight cage has sixty-two young birds in it already and the new nests are filling. It looks like even more birds than the year before, and that's not counting the babies of my fliers. The feed bills are enormous, but I have enough money. I just tell my father how much I need and he gives it to me.

Those babies of the fliers are flying in and out of the aviary on their own. There doesn't seem to be any trouble. They all come into the aviary to eat and roost at night. The mothers are generally onto second nests but the males fly with the young. Some of the young males have already started with their burbling, warbling songs. The father males still come when I whistle but the young don't pay any attention to me at all. It's marvelous that they're so free; practically no strings tying them to the cage. Most of the females don't go out much because they're busy with the nests. I can still whistle down the one female who built her nest in the tree over the house. She'll come for a brief minute and eat from my finger, but then fly back to her nest. It's good to see how conscientious the birds are with their babies.

The young ones are very much like wild birds. They've never known what it is to be closed in a cage. They fly farther from the yard than the others; they also tend to flock more than the parent birds. The parents don't seem to have any instinct for flocking left, whereas these young ones flock almost like pigeons. They're much more easily frightened and will spook up in a flock to the tops of the trees.

All the birds have started eating the food I leave outside for Perta and the other young female. I decide to move that food inside. The only power I have left to bring them into the cages at night now is the food. After my evening feeding of the breeding cages I drop the wires of the outside door so when the birds come in to eat they can't go out again. This way I can keep some count of them. As far as I can tell, there are already about twenty flier babies. The rate of reproduction is nothing like those in the breeding cages. There are more losses all along. For one thing, I don't take out the eggs as they're hatched. This means none of the nests have more than three or four birds.

I don't like it when the young fliers treat me as any other enemy. They're almost like my own grandchildren, but they don't recognize me. My dream is built on them but they are completely separate from it; they're practically wild birds.

—I probably built myself mostly to "beat" my father; not just "beat him up," but to be better at being what I thought he was. So, I became like him. We become like the people with whom we compete. It's like cannibals eating part of an enemy warrior to absorb his courage. Crazy stuff!

Then it happens. I've just come out to the morning feeding when I look up at the nest in the tree over the house. There's that cat on the roof and he has one of the young birds in his mouth. He's reaching out to knock down another of the young birds roosting on a branch just below the nest. The mother bird is frantic. She's flying at the cat and the cat swings at her. I don't see the other young one.

I pick up stones and start throwing them. I yell, but he ducks and keeps pawing at the branch, or, when the mother bird comes near enough, bats at her.

I whistle for the mother to come to me and she flies down to my finger but jumps away again before I can catch her. She flies back up to the tree. I run into the garage and get out the ladder. My father comes out. He helps me put the ladder so I can climb onto the porch roof. My mother comes out. She's worried I'll fall and that my father will be late for work.

I climb up onto the roof. The cat is holding his ground but backs off a little when I stand and start reaching out for him. Now I'm up there, the mother bird is even braver in her attack on the cat. He still holds the body of the young bird in his mouth. The young one he's been trying to reach has backed up the branch toward the nest where the other baby is looking over the side.

I'm just scrambling onto the roof when the cat knocks down the mother bird with a swing of one paw. I jump to get there ahead of the cat but he gets her first. He drops the young bird and grabs her with his teeth before I can do anything. I catch hold of the cat by the front leg. He scratches at me while I shift my hold and get him around the neck. I pry open his mouth to get out the mother bird. It's too late. She's dead. I pick up the little dead baby bird. I've let go of the cat and it slinks back across the roof, then drops to the porch roof. My father is standing with a stick by the rain barrel. The cat leaps off the roof and past him. He swings at it with the stick but doesn't hit it.

I climb down and inspect the two birds. Both their spines are broken at the neck. A cat knows what it's doing when it comes to killing a bird.

Before we take down the ladder, I go up and get the two baby birds out of the nest. It isn't hard to catch them, they can't fly. I take them into the fliers' cage with the other young ones. Maybe one of the males will adopt them. I stuff them with food before I go to school and hope for the best.

When I come home, they seem all right and I give them another feeding. I'm sure somebody is feeding them. The fathers can't remember all the birds, and one of them is father to these birds anyway.

That night in the dream, I'm afraid for what will happen, but everything goes all right. Perta's nest is fine and there's no sign of a cat. The nest we have is too high up in the tree for a cat to see. I talk to Perta and try to tell her about the danger of cats, but she's never seen one and can't know what I mean. I almost want to move our nest back into the cage. I wonder what would happen if I climbed up into the tree in the daytime as boy and moved the nest. Would Perta abandon it in the dream? Would it stay in the same place? It's too big a risk. I feel confident that if I'm careful nothing will happen. The dream doesn't have everything happen that happens in the day. The nest of the little yellow bird isn't even in my dream.

It's a week later and I'm feeling it's all going to pass over, when, in the dream, I see the same cat climbing our tree. I'm perched just above and behind our nest where Perta is sitting. That day our babies have started standing on the edge of the nest. It's what had to come about. The babies were too young before; now they're old enough. It can happen.

Perta still hasn't seen the cat. Our first nest of babies for this year, all four of them, are off flying with their older brothers down where we used to have the pigeon coop in the tree. There's nothing I can think to do. I wait and watch the cat. I see him very clearly. He has one ear partly torn off, a ragged dog-ear of a cat's ear. I can see all the details of this cat. I didn't know I'd seen him so well. I was so busy thinking and doing things I didn't notice myself seeing the cat.

What I must do is break the dream. I have to wake up. I need to become Birdy the boy and somehow work it out with this cat in daytime life. I can't. I can't make myself move out of the dream. I'm on the wrong side of the door; the key is in the other side. It's like when you wake up and you're not sure you can move your body and you're afraid to try. I can't make myself try. The bird in me is too strong. The bird doesn't know it can make it all stop by going away. The bird is too afraid of the cat to get any distance. The bird has to stay and protect Perta and the babies. It won't believe the other thing, the other existence. Yet the boy knows a canary cannot fight a cat.

I give in. I wait and watch as the cat scratches his way up the tree. Everything of my body wants to fly away. My bird-boy brain has to stay. I try to think out how the dream will happen. Must Perta be killed? If she sees the cat, will she fly at him or fly away?

I hop down to the nest.

"Look Perta, why don't you take a little fly for yourself. I'll sit the nest."

Perta looks at me. She's tired but she doesn't want to

leave. She senses my fear; it's impossible to lie to her. I'm thinking maybe if she's out of the dream I can wake up. I say again that I want her to take a rest; I want a chance to be with the young ones alone.

Perta knows something is peculiar, but she eases herself off the nest. The young ones are disturbed and make feed-me noises. I get on the nest and they settle down.

"Go on, Perta. Take a fly. The young ones are in the woods. Go see what they're doing. They're flying around by the ruined house in the tree. You know where that is. It'll do you good."

Perta looks at me once more, then flies off. She doesn't see the cat. She isn't looking for it. The cat is pressed against the trunk of the tree. He's already halfway up. I'm sure he heard the babies peeping, but that doesn't matter now. At least Perta is away. Now if I can only control the dream; stop it from happening. I try once more to concentrate, stop the dream, but I'm still too much inside it. I tell all the babies to stay down deep in the nest. It's a hot day; the nest is tight and smelly. They don't want to. It's almost time for them to fly out; they want to sit or stand on the edge of the nest, stretch their wings. I make them stay down.

Now, I leave the nest myself. I fly to a higher part of the tree. The cat doesn't see me. He's concentrating in that maniac cat way on the nest. He's already tasting the feathers and blood.

My only chance is to scare him somehow or hurt him. I think of getting my father to help me but my father is never in the dream. I think of trying to get myself to help. I can see me in the aviary across the yard, but that's impossible too. I never pay any attention to myself as bird. I must do it alone. The only chance is to hurt the cat. I must somehow get to his eyes by diving down directly from above without making noise.

The cat has climbed higher into the tree. I fly out and

hover in the air. I'm afraid. The bird in me is panicked by the cat. I think if I fly into my bedroom to a place I haven't been as a bird, a place where I am as boy, that the dream might end. I know there isn't enough time for that.

I start my dive. I dive between the branches and come fast down onto the cat's head. I drive my beak straight toward his eye. The eye, yellow-green, black-slitted, concentrated on my babies. Then, I'm falling, my wings won't work; I have no breath; I hurt. The cat has swept me out of the air with a quick stroke of his paw. I hit the ground and cannot move. My eyes are open, but I'm paralyzed. I'm lying on my side and looking up into the tree. I close my eyes again and try to make the dream stop. I open my eyes; I'm still there on the ground. The cat is looking down at me from the tree. Now he's distracted from the nest.

I struggle to get my legs under me but nothing moves. The cat is turning his head over his shoulder and backing down the tree. He scrambles and slips, then jumps the final few feet from the tree to the ground. I'm still there. The cat stands still watching me. I don't move; I can't. The cat is crouched ready to pounce. I look into his eyes, I try to make him see the boy in me, not just the bird. The slits in his eyes are opening and closing. His eyes are crossed in concentration. He is rocking his head slowly back and forth in anticipation. I try to hold him, stop him with my eyes. I try again to break the dream. I feel I can do it if I close my eyes. I know if I close my eyes the cat will pounce. I close my eyes and then, as before the dream ends, I hear a sound and the cat screams.

I wake in bed shaking and sweating. My heart is pounding. I can scarcely walk to the bathroom for a drink of water. One side of my body is numb and sore. I look in the mirror but there's nothing, no redness, no cut. I'm pale and my hair is matted with sweat.

I go back to my bedroom and get out another pair of pajamas. I hang the first pair over the radiator to dry. I'm so sore I can hardly get them on. I fall back into bed and stare at the ceiling. I don't know if I should go to sleep again. I'm tired but I'm afraid of the dream. Is it still possible to sleep without dreaming? If I dream again, what will be happening? I make my mind go over what's happening in the dream; try to make it come out right.

The cat was screaming. Why? Was it just the scream before he pounced on me and began ripping me to pieces? If I go into the dream, will I be dead? If I'm dead in the dream, will the dream be ended? If I'm dead in the dream, will I die as a boy?

I feel I'm almost dead lying in bed. I know I could die very easily. It's only a matter of not trying. I can't stop myself and I go to sleep.

I come into the dream with my eyes closed. I'm still there, not dead. I open my eyes and the cat is leaping and jumping in a circle. He's screaming and there's blood. One eye is closed and leaking fluid. The cat runs off with a final yowling scream. I look, and on the ground beside me is Perta!

—Jesus! Now Birdy's crying. What the hell can be the matter? What's he crying about? Maybe everything. If he can cry, let him. It's not so easy to do even when you want to.

I close my eyes again. I want to end the dream. I must end it. The babies are alone; Perta is dead. I know she is dead not only from the way she is lying but because it is still my dream. I close my eyes and concentrate on ending the dream. Finally, it slides from under me, the dream stops and I stay asleep. I know that sleeping without dreaming is being dead.

When I awake in the morning I can't move. I'm surprised to find myself alive. I don't want to cry out, I don't want to move. My mind has lost control of my body. I feel totally separate. I watch as my mother comes in, talks to me, gets mad, then looks at me, shouts at me, and runs out of the room. I feel in another place.

I'm watching all the things as if I'm watching the birds through binoculars. I watch the doctor. I watch them taking me to the hospital. I open or close my eyes according to how much I want to see. I feel that I'll never sleep again, never dream again, never move again. I don't care too much. All I can do is watch; I'm enjoying watching. They lift my legs in the air. They lift my arms. They ask me questions. I don't answer. I don't want to answer. I'm not sure I can answer. Even my voice isn't mine anymore. I'm between me and something else. Then I do sleep. It is the same kind of dead sleep.

It's as if there is no tie between before I go into that sleep and when I wake up. I wake up in the hospital. I'm hungry. I eat and I can move. I'm back with people. Perhaps the dream is gone forever. I don't know how I feel about this. I'm like a small child; all there is, is me, feeding me, looking at things around, smelling things, tasting things, hearing things. I move my hand and watch it. It is all new.

Three days later, they take me out of the hospital and I go home. I stay another week in my bed just enjoying being me. My father says he's taking care of the birds. He tells me how many new birds he's put into the breeding cages and what nests have been laid with how many eggs. I don't care. All that is finished. I'm frightened; I don't want to go back. He asks me what I'm going to do about the free-flying birds. He wants to lock them in the cage. He says he's counted at least fifteen young males singing in the trees and there're probably twice that many. That's more than three hundred dollars flying around in the trees. I don't want to talk about it.

It's the third day after I've started school when it starts

again. I have all kinds of final examinations coming up and I can't get myself to study for them. I'm enjoying riding my bicycle and watching people. I've never looked at people much before. They're as interesting as birds if you really look. I go to a track meet and I'm all caught up watching people run, jump, throw things. Al wins the discus with a throw of a hundred and seventy-two feet. I have my binoculars with me and I can see all that's happening with close eyes.

It might be the watching with the binoculars that brings it back. In my sleep that night, I wake in the dream. I'm still on the ground under the tree. I get onto my feet. I stretch my wings. I hop over to Perta. She is dead. Her neck is broken the way I was afraid Birdie's would be when she flew into the window, the way the little yellow female's was; there's nothing I can do. I do not know I'm in the dream. I am completely bird. I have no arms with which to lift her from the ground. Still, I'm not bird enough to accept Echen and leave her there. I want to move her, to take her to some place where the cat won't be able to eat her. I look around; the cat is not in the yard. I can't leave Perta on the ground like that. I fly up into the tree to see our babies. They're scrunched down in the nest, frightened. I feed them and tell them I'll be back. I'm feeling stretched out. I'm confused about time. I fly back to Perta.

Then I see me coming out of the aviary. I'm walking across the yard toward me. I stand there on the ground as bird and wait. I know there is a new hole in the dream. I can feel the mixing of the waves of two places, like an undertow. Two places are pulling at once.

I do not see me. This is as usual. Then I lean down and pick up Perta. There is great unhappiness on my face. It is the unhappiness of a boy; birds' faces show nothing. I pick up Perta and walk back toward the aviary. I fly painfully after me

to the edge of the aviary roof. I watch myself come back out
again with a small spoon and a matchbox. It's one of the
kitchen matchboxes in which I keep the eggs. I put Perta carefully into the box and close it. I dig a hole in the back of the
aviary beside the wall and bury the box. I go back into the
aviary.

I hop from the top of the aviary and stand by Perta's
grave. I'm glad she's safe from the cat. I know I must go to my
babies but I don't want to leave Perta.

Then I see myself come out of the aviary again. I have
a popsicle stick with me. I push the stick into the ground over
the space where the matchbox is buried. I hop close and read
the writing.

MY WIFE, PERTA.

I wake up.

That next day at school I know all the things that have to
happen. I'm not too frightened by the strange way the real
world has to follow the dream. I'm sorry for Perta and I think
of locking her into the flight cage but then her baby birds
would starve. I could put those babies under other birds but
this whole thing is something that has to happen. If it doesn't
happen as it must, then my Perta will never be really dead, I
can never be free as a boy again.

After school I'm working in the aviary when I hear the cat
scream. I walk across the yard and over under the tree. She's
there exactly in the spot where I look for her. I look, but know
I cannot see myself. I pick Perta up and her neck is broken.
There is no other mark on her body.

I carry her across the yard to the aviary and do the things
I'm supposed to do. I'm feeling very calm inside myself. More
than ever I feel that I am together. As boy I'm doing exactly
what must be. I almost feel myself fitting into the space I occupied in the dream. I put Perta in the box and go out to the
place beside the wall. There's a slight depression in the

ground. I dig the hole half-looking, expecting a matchbox to be there. Al will never know about the treasure we didn't find. In some way it was there, there, in the power of our dream.

There's no matchbox and I put my matchbox with Perta into the hole. I cover it over and look for myself up on top of the aviary. I'm not there. I go back into the aviary and take the popsicle stick I use for scraping out the corners of the cages. I clean it off and print the message on it with a dark pencil. I go out and push it into the ground over the grave. There are no bird tracks. I wake up.

During the day I can't keep my thoughts from the dream. My throat hurts because I'm not crying when I should. We're having final exams so no one notices me much.

That night I'm still standing by Perta's grave. The dream has become more like a dream. Things don't happen the way they used to. I don't see any of the other birds. When I fly, I fly in slow motion. It's like a dream.

I fly up to the babies and feed them. I tell them their mother won't be coming back but I will take care of them. I spend all that day and night sitting on the edge of the nest, feeding them when they're hungry and remembering Perta. I know they will not remember her. To them, she's in Echen and that's all there is to it. It's not worth thinking about; it doesn't matter.

In my dream, over the next weeks, I bring the young birds up till they can fly from the nest and join the others. They are free, they can fly where they want to. My babies are completely bird. I do not show them where Perta is buried, it would mean nothing. I'm getting more and more boy in my dream, the bird in me is fading. The dream is becoming less and less real.

As boy, I'm not as interested in the breeding of birds either. I'm seeing them for what they are, canaries. Everything in the aviary seems so automatic. The young birds all look

alike. I can't tell them from last year's birds anymore. I can feel
it all coming to an end. Something is finished.

I build a feeding platform on top of the aviary. I build a
roof over it to keep off the rain. I build perches for the feeders
so the flying birds can feed up high away from cats. When it's
done, I let all the birds out of the new flying cage. Some few
females are still sitting on nests, so I allow them to stay in the
cage.

When the last nest is finished, I put the floor back in the
cage to separate the upper part from the lower. I begin to select
out the singing males from the female flight cage, and put them
in the lower cage. As the breeding birds finish up their third
nests, I move them into the flight cages, too. Birdie is tired but
as friendly as ever and I take her out for a free flight. I take
Alfonso out too and it's the first free flying for him. His flight
is weak from the long time in a small cage but he quickly finds
his wings and takes long flights to the tree and the house. I'm
not sure he'll come back to the cage but he does. I decide to
leave Alfonso and Birdie out with the free fliers. They deserve it.

The free fliers are now totally out of the cages. They sleep
in the tree or on the house. I leave the cage door open but they
don't come in. There are about sixty birds out flying free. It
makes me proud to see them. I feel I've helped put them back
in the air where they belong. I wonder if they'll stay close to
the house now when they don't sleep in the cages. At the end
of summer will be the time for northern hemisphere finches
to migrate. What will these birds do? Will this instinct take
them off and in which direction? Will Birdie and Alfonso
leave and fly with them? How far can a finch fly without eating? There's no way I can think of for them to get to Africa,
their original habitat. Will they learn to live on the grains
and fruits our finches live on here? Will they interbreed with
other finches or stay apart? It doesn't matter. It's so great to
see them flying free.

There are over two hundred birds in the flight cages. More than half are males. The price of birds is astronomical. I'll be glad when the birds are old enough to sell. I don't want to keep birds in cages anymore. I'd really like to set all of them free but these young birds without free flight experience could never make it. Also, my father is very happy thinking of the money we will get when we sell them. He's kept my mother off my back, so I can't let him down. He'd like to get all the free fliers into the cage and sell them, too. He keeps listening to them and has all the males identified. He's up to thirty-five males.

I'm dreaming again, but in my dreams I'm always alone. I see the other birds flying but I stay away. I fly all the night alone. I fly to every place I've ever been. I fly over the rooftops and trees or sometimes high in the sky. It seems so easy and I'm more me, not so much a bird. It's me, a boy, flying. I'm flapping my arms like wings and it's easy. It's just knowing I can do it that makes me fly. In my dreams I'm always wanting someone else so I can show them how to do it. It would be such fun to teach Al or my father how to fly. When you can do it, it seems so incredibly easy.

The wholesale man comes and buys all the birds. We get nine dollars apiece for the males and three dollars for the females. The total check is for over fifteen hundred dollars. My father doesn't understand why I'm selling the breeding birds, too. He still wants to trap the flying birds and sell them, but I put him off. They are my birds. I let him think I'm going to use them for breeding the next year.

It's quiet in the aviary now. I clean it all up and cover the breeding cages with newspapers. At night, in my dream, I begin to sense a strange restlessness in myself. Even when I'm flying, I'm thinking of something else and I don't know what it is. Then I know. I'm feeling the urge to flock and migrate. Is it in the other birds or is it only me? Is it in the dream birds, too?

Daytimes I watch the birds and I'm sure they're preparing to leave. There is much flocking and random flight. They have increased their eating and fly further distances from the yard. Sometimes there will be no birds at all in the yard for as long as two or three hours.

My mother is starting to complain about the bird shit on things and the noise. The noise she's talking about is the singing. My father says they're all going to freeze in the winter cold. He says it'd be cruel to leave them out, and we have to get them back into the flight cages. Most of them have never lived in a cage.

He opens up the door to the flight cage and moves the feeders inside. The birds start coming into the flight cage to eat, then they come in to sleep at night. A few of them, like Alfonso, still sleep out in the tree, but most times they all come in. I know the time is coming when my father will close the door and lock them in.

In my dream I go to the birds. I tell them it is time to leave. I tell them if they go into the cage to sleep they will be closed in the cage and put into small cages. At first, they do not understand me, then they do not believe me. Alfonso speaks; he says he knows what I say is true, that I have never lied to the birds. It is time to leave. He says he knows how to go, that it is a long flight and some will die, but he is going, so is Birdie, and they are leaving in the early morning. I listen and I'm sad. The birds are excited.

At dawn, all are ready; we go up in a single movement. Alfonso is at the head of the flock. We fly straight south, over the top of the gas tank, over Lansdowne, down over Chester and I am with them. I'm wondering what is happening with my life. Will I ever wake up in my own bed again?

Then, somehow I am not with them. I am in the sky, flying, watching them go. I cannot keep up; they are leaving me. I see myself as bird, with them, flying, up behind Alfonso and Birdie. I know I will be with them wherever they go. I watch from my place in the sky as they, we, become small spots getting smaller until there is only sky. I find myself getting heavier, falling, gliding down to the earth only a little slower than I fell off the gas tank. I flap my arms as I fall and I just manage to get back into my sleep under the empty sky.

In the morning there are no birds. My father is angry. I feel very lonesome. We wait all day for the birds to come back. It is Saturday and I spend the day watching the sky, trying to keep it empty.

The next day I go out and take apart the aviary. I store the wood behind the garage. I do it quietly so no one will know what I'm doing. Things come apart much easier than they go together. The aviary is down and gone when I go inside to bed.

That night I do not dream.

The days pass slowly. I feel terribly alone. I'm worried about telling my father I'm not going to college. I'm also worried about being drafted. All this works itself out; it's decided for me.

In September, I get a letter from the army saying I've been selected to study engineering with the ASTP, the Army Specialized Training Program. They've assigned me to the University of Florida in Gainsville. I'd taken the test for the ASTP at school in February and forgotten about it completely.

It seems like the perfect solution. I can get away from everything and it's something I can live with. They tell us we're being trained as engineers to help with the rebuilding of Europe and Japan after the war. My parents are happy, they think I'm going to be an officer, and that impresses them.

I enlist at the end of the month. I'm sent to Florida for a semester, then they dissolve the ASTP. I'm sent to Fort Benning for basic training, then to the South Pacific as an infantry replacement.

I think often about the birds, about Perta, and my children, but I don't dream about them.

The next day, when I go see Birdy, I swear he smiles at me. I fit the chair between the doors and wait till Renaldi is gone.

"Hi, Birdy, this is your old pal, Al. How about it? You ready to talk yet? Remember who I am?"

He's squatting and watching me. His arms are crossed over his knees; his chin is resting on his arms. His eyes are on me but there's no answer in them. He's watching me the way he used to watch birds. His eyes are flitting back and forth but somehow staying concentrated on me. It's a creepy feeling but I know for sure that he's there.

I begin talking some more about the old things we did but I'm boring myself. Birdy and I spent a lot of time together, walking on Sixty-ninth Street or going to the Municipal Library for books on Friday night, but those things aren't worth talking about. I start with the old high school and the crummy little locker we lived out of, but that doesn't go anywhere either. I'm getting the feeling he knows all that stuff and doesn't want to hear it anymore. I know he wants to hear about me but can't ask.

I'm ready to talk, to tell him. I didn't know how much I needed to tell somebody. If not Birdy, who else?

After basic they send me to Europe as a replacement with the Eighty-seventh Division. I start telling Birdy some of the good parts; the funny things; riding in trucks in fine weather behind tanks. Then, all the French girls and after that the mud in the Saar. Then, I tell about Metz and the Twenty-eighth charging up that stupid hill at Fort Jeanne d'Arc and how Joe Higgins got it there. Higg played left tackle beside me at U.M. I'm having a tough time getting to the real part.

By the time we go into Germany and are up against the Siegfried Line, I've actually gotten to be a sergeant all right. It's not because I'm any hell-fire soldier, but there just isn't much of anybody else left. One thing I didn't know about myself is I'm lucky. That's not the only thing I didn't know about Al Columbato either.

I find out I get more scared than most people do of things I can't do anything about; things like artillery. Little punks, guys afraid to look anybody in the eye, guys I could wipe out with my left hand; can sit under fire in a hole with the sides falling in and eat chocolate bars or make jokes. They're scared but they can live with it. I don't know how to be scared with any dignity. I'm scared deep into my bones about being mangled. I see gore, my gore, in a thousand different ways. My fucking love for my own body wipes me out. I get to a point where I'm even scared of being scared. I'm scared I'll take off and run sometime, and it takes all my nerve just to stay, even when nothing's happening. Everybody gets to know I'm the tough wop with no balls.

There's a little Jew-boy, not big enough to wrestle bantam and he gets to be squad leader. He deserves it. He always knows when to move, when to stay; he's thinking all the time. That's what a real soldier does. Big-shot Al is spending his time trying not to crap his pants, literally. I'm breathing deeply in and out, trying not to stutter it, trying not to hotfoot it back to the kitchen truck.

And every time I get up enough nerve to turn myself in, go psycho, take my section eight; we're taken off the line and I try to put myself together again. I'm not sleeping much; I've got the GI's all the time. My hands shake so much I can hardly load a clip. This is all the time, not just when things are tough. It's like my freaking body has some kind of controls all its own. My mind, my brain, has nothing to do with it.

Lewis and Brenner, Brenner's the Jew-boy, get it at the crossroads in Ohmsdorf. There's nobody left from the old group so they make me assistant to Richards. Richards came in as a replacement in the Saar. I sew on the stripes while we're in battalion reserve. I sew them on with big easy stitches. I don't figure I'll have them for long; they're bound to find me out.

I'm bunking with Harrington. Harrington's ex-ASTP and got trench foot in the Ardennes in the snow. He came back two weeks ago. He's smart and knows I'm about to crack. Just before we came off the line he took one of Morgan's stupid patrols for me. There's no greater gift than taking another guy's patrol. Harrington comes from California. I never knew anybody with the kind of nerves he's got. He'd sure as hell be squad leader if he hadn't gotten trench foot.

I shit bricks day after day in reserve, waiting, thanking God for every extra day. Then we get the word we're going up to relieve the first battalion in a town called Neuendorf. We're smack against the Siegfried Line there.

We go in around the edges of hills under a barrage at night, about two hours before dawn. The first battalion passes us going the other way. They're giving out with all kinds of cheery messages like "Good luck, fuckers, you're going to need it," or "Welcome to eighty-eight alley." Really great for the old morale; I can feel my stomach turning sour. Three or four eighty-eights and mortars hit near us on the way in. They're near enough so we have to hit the dirt. Shrapnel is flying. Even in the dark we can see the dark places where they hit. They dig up clods of pasture and scatter them thumping around like cow flop.

We get into the town and there's not a building standing. It must've been bombed; artillery alone couldn't flatten a town like that. We're herded into the cellar of what used to be a house. It's beside the church. The church has a front wall almost intact, the rest is rubble.

Lieutenant Wall, the liaison officer from the first battalion is still there. Richards and I go over to talk with him. He tells us there's a town called Reuth on the other side of the valley. It's starting to get light and he points to some white dots near the horizon about a mile and a half away. Reuth is supposed to be a communications center for this section of the line. The krauts are defending it like crazy men. There've been at least ten tiger tanks in and out of the town. There's been all kinds of patrolling. He says his outfit's been here in Neuendorf for ten days and has had twenty-seven casualties. He shows us the outposts for our platoon. He tells us we'll probably have to attack Reuth; the whole division's being held up here.

When I get back to the cellar, my insides are churning up. When I get scared, my infield gets loose and my head feels empty. I'm already shaking inside. Christ, I'm going to make one crappy assistant squad leader. The only way I can see to get out of all this is to get hit.

The cellar is smoky, smelly but warm. The squad is stretched out sleeping in sacks against the back wall. The fire's built into an arched hole near the door. It might've been used to store potatoes once. There's no flue so the smoke goes up to the ceiling of the cellar, drifts to the door and up the cellar steps. The smoke comes down to about four feet from the floor and you have to stoop over to breathe or find your way around. There's a blanket over the doorway, and the only light is the fire. The room smells of smoke, farts, and feet.

I go out again to find the latrine, it's against what's left of the back wall of the church. There's a little path worn through the rubble. The morning light is coming on stronger and taking some of the bite out of the cold. Kohler and Schneider are on post; I can see them standing in the hole out on a small knoll. Christ, I hope there aren't any patrols. There'll have to be though if there's going to be an attack.

I squat and let fly. I'll probably never take a normal crap again. My asshole hasn't felt anything solid slide past it in three months. The toilet paper is hung on the handle of an entrenching tool. I wipe about five times to get it all, stand up, button up, then throw a few shovelfuls of dirt over the mess. The latrine's still deep; should last till the attack anyway.

The next week and a half aren't actually too bad. We don't get any of the patrols and we only have the one outpost to man. I get plenty of sleep. I'm hiding in my fart sack in the cellar. The only way they can hurt me is with a direct hit. It's not likely at a mile and a half. I'm feeling safe but dreading the attack.

When we do go out, it's four in the morning. We make a long dogleg to the left and into a forest. It's a pine forest and has a narrow point going over the edge of a hill and part way down the other side in the direction of Reuth. It's the closest we can get without going through open country.

We sneak all the way there and to the front edge of the forest without anything coming in. Richards tells us to dig in. It's about five o'clock and the attack is for seven. Our artillery barrage is going to start at six-thirty. So, here it is, the whole thing over again. The first times, you don't really believe it's going to happen. Then, when it is happening, it's so real, you can't think of it ever stopping. Now, I know it's going to happen; pure fear has me tight by the balls.

Harrington and I are down by the point of the forest. As the light comes up, we can see the houses of Reuth. They can't be more than three or four hundred yards away. Harrington says maybe they've pulled out. How the hell can they pull out of a communications center unless they figure on abandoning this whole section of the line? I can't see the krauts doing a thing like that. Maybe being brave is not thinking too much; or at least being able to fool yourself.

It's cold and there's no smoking. Richards has me going around checking to see if everybody has their weapons in order, bandoliers, grenades, stuff like that. I don't think anybody's as scared as I am, not even the two new replacements. How the hell can they know? I'm glad to get back to our hole, jump in, and snuggle deep. It feels good to have solid earth against my back. There's practically nothing smells or feels so comforting as deep earth when you're scared. No wonder men lived in caves.

We stay down there during the barrage. The heavy stuff is flying over our heads like freight trains. I huddle deeper; I've got a real thing about shorts. I can't stop myself thinking of all the stupid civilians making those shells and then the morons back at corps shooting them off.

At seven we're up out of the holes. It's just our luck; we're the point squad of the point platoon of the point company; probably the point battalion of the point regiment of the point division of the whole pointed American army. Harrington's first scout and Richards is with him. I'm bringing up the rear. This is where I'm supposed to be. It also happens to be where I want to be. That's not quite true. I want to be almost anywhere else but out on this slanted field.

We go down the field in close order route march. We look like mad golfers hunched over our clubs, not running, walking fast, everything pulled in, waiting for it. There's a ground mist coming up from the field and a fog hanging from above. We walk halfway down the hill, too far now to go back. If they see us, now's the time to do it. I'm hoping Harrington's right and I keep swallowing to hold back my coffee. My ears are thumping. The cold sweat is sticking on the hollow of my back. I have a phosphorous grenade on the end of my rifle and the tear-shaped, dark green, bulbous tip looms in front of me. In my fear, the whole field and the edges of the houses glow in rainbow colors.

Then it starts. It's burp guns and some kind of heavy caliber machine gun; then mortars. The tanks must not be there yet. We break into a run. Somebody drops. It's not Harrington or Richards. It's Collins. I run past and he's holding his left shoulder with his right hand. There's blood. I keep running. One of the replacements falls. He has his hands over his face and he's rolling down the hill. Then his hands come loose from his face and his arms flop out till they stop his roll. He's not getting up. I sprint ahead of Morris. Shit, this is going to be a morning! I catch up to Richards and Harrington.

They're hunkered down in a gully where the two hills meet, the one we've just come down and the one going up to Reuth. There's water running along the gully. There're flakes of ice on the mud and sticking to the grass. Richards is looking up over the edge of the hill and Harrington looks around at me. I point back.

"Collins and one of the replacements got it!"

"Shit!"

Richards doesn't look back.

"Fuckin' hill's covered with fuckin' mines. Goddamned mashers with wires strung out and shoe mines, too, I'll bet. Sons-a-bitches!"

There's tracers flying over, singing like mad bees. Five stingers you can't see for every buzzer you can. The rest of the squad's squatting along the gully now. I look back and see the platoon coming over the hill. It's going to be a real massacre, the crossroads all over again. We've got to do something; mortar's going to start coming in any minute; we're for sure under direct observation and when those tanks come up, we're had. We've got to break out; get past the mine field and to the top of the hill. Over the top like WWI, wiping out machine gun nests! I'm thinking all this but I can't move. I can't talk. I'm squatting deep in the mud; the cold wetness is cooling where I'm chafed between my legs. I'm shaking and letting myself sink deeper in the mud. I can't get myself to look around anymore. Harrington stands up.

"The only way is to work up gradually, not go directly through the mines. They're strung so we'll trip 'em if we go straight up. It's the only way!"

"Yeah."

Richards doesn't move. He's stuck there too. Harrington begins to crawl along the ditch.

"Come on, Al. Let's you and me try it. We can't stay here! Shit, we're all going to get killed!"

He moves off and I hate him. I follow him. I keep my eyes on the ground looking for mines. Twice, I step over thin wires between mines. I see one of the little pegs for a shoe mine. I get the shakes so bad, I'm stopped in my tracks. I can't go on. I'm in the open and I can't make myself go either way. It's like on top of the gas tank; I'm paralyzed numb. Harrington is picking his way along. I don't call out. I look back and Richards is gone. I feel alone. I can't see anybody and I hope nobody can see me. I sink slowly to the ground.

I don't know how long I stay like that. I know I should get out my entrenching tool and dig but I can't make myself do it.

Then, I see somebody coming over the brow of the hill toward me. I scrunch lower. At first it's just silhouettes, then I see the field green of a kraut soldier. Shaking, I bring my rifle to my cheek and feel for the trigger through my gloves. I pull and nothing happens. They keep coming. I push off the safety and pull again. There's a tremendous kick. Only then, I remember I still have that phosphorous grenade on the rifle. It hits one of the soldiers and explodes with a flash.

"Who the hell is that? Hold your fuckin' fire."

It's Richards and he's brushing madly at a kraut. I rush up the hill, forgetting the mines. I get there and help brush phosphorous off the kraut. He's sitting on the ground. The phosphorous is like pieces of fire that burn through everything. The kraut is screaming and we brush madly to get all the pieces off. He peels off his overcoat and jacket, there's a dark red spot on his side where the grenade hit.

"What the fuck you doing back here? You're supposed to be with Harrington. I'm using this fucker to pick a path through these fuckin' mines for the rest of the platoon to get through. You get your ass after Harrington. Tell him to meet up with us at the pine trees just over the hill."

I start going around the hill in the direction Harrington was going. Now, some mortar is coming in. I think one hits just over the hill in front of me, but then from the flash, I know it isn't mortar. I start hurrying. I'm stepping over mine wires and past shoe mine triggers like I'm playing hopscotch. I don't get it. A few minutes ago I couldn't make myself move.

Harrington's sitting on the ground. He's holding onto his knee and rocking back and forth. His rifle's on the ground beside him. He's screaming!

"My God, my God! Mother of God! Mother! My leg!! Oh my God!"

I drop beside him. His face is green. Blood is spurting out between his hands from his knee! I almost vomit when I see it. The bottom part of his leg, below the knee, is hanging by a piece of flesh. Jagged bones stick out from shrunken flesh. The other leg has fragments of shrapnel sticking through the cloth, through the boot, into the flesh. Harrington looks at me and his eyes are black holes.

"Holy God! I'm bleeding to death! Stop it! Help me, Al! Jesus Christ, help me!"

My hands are shaking but I get my belt off. I wrap it tight where Harrington's squeezing. I pull it taut and try to make it hold. My fingers are slippery with blood. I get the friction bar of the brass buckle to catch. Harrington lets go with his hands and there's only a trickle. I take off my aid kit and pull out the bandage. I put the pad over the stump end and wrap the strings above the belt. I take out my canteen and make Harrington take the wound tablets. I'd forgotten the sulfa and try lifting the bandage to scatter it inside. Somehow, I'm making it. Harrington is leaning back on his hands and looking down at his leg hanging there cocked sidewise. The shoe's been completely blown off and you can see the bones where the flesh is flayed away.

I'm afraid to pull any of the shrapnel pieces out of the other leg. Harrington's sinking into shock fast. His face is completely white and he's crying. The hell with Richards; I'm going after a medic. They're probably all hanging back in the woods. I still haven't said anything to Harrington. I try to steady my voice.

"Don't move! I'll go get a medic!"

Harrington nods his head. He's biting his lower lip and holding onto the leg that isn't blown off. I carefully prop the stump of his other leg onto his helmet. I drive his rifle, barrel first, into the ground so the medics can find him. I look once more at Harrington and start back down the hill.

Jesus, the whole field is solid mines! I'm going against the lines of mines and stepping over one wire after another. I'm amazed I can do it. Maybe I've gotten past something in myself. About twenty yards down the hill, I look around to orient myself for bringing the medics back. Harrington lifts one hand; he's been watching me. I wave and start down the hill again. I haven't gone three steps when there's a tremendous explosion. I look back and see Harrington's limp body in the air. It twists once, then hits the ground with a bounce. I run back, jumping over mines and wires.

He's torn in half. I can see through his stomach. There's not a mark on his face and he's already dead. His intestines glisten and slide in the last gushings of blood. I turn my head and throw up.

There's no excuse to go back now. I get down on my knees carefully. Harrington must've had a shoe mine behind him, between his arms, all the time. He probably just lay back on it. I'm absolutely gripped with fear again.

I don't know how long I stay there beside Harrington. It could've been two minutes or even twenty. My mind is going back and forth, not wanting to work. I know I'm crying; I'm not making it at all.

It begins getting lighter; the fog is lifting; the sun is orange over Reuth. I have to do something. I stand up and start working my way up the hill. I'm walking over mines like walking over cracks in the sidewalk; I know I'm not being careful enough. I'm numb in my mind. I get to the top of the hill.

There's a grove of trees over to the right. The whole platoon is there. I see Richards. They're all digging in like crazy. Richards comes running to me.

"Where the fuck've you been? We're going to be pulling out of here and going into the town in a couple minutes! There're tanks up there! Who the hell has the tank grenades?"

"Harrington got it back there; shoe mine."

"Shit! Christ, we've got to get outta here. Who the hell's got the tank grenades?"

"One of the replacements had them. He's back on the hill."

"Christ! What a fucking mess! We need bazookas! Mortars getting closer and we're fucked if those tanks find us! Where-in-hell's the Lieutenant?"

Richards is dashing back and forth saying these things. He's at least as scared as I am but he thinks of things to do. He runs back to the others. I flop on the ground there and hold onto it. I'm going to stay right here. I'm ready to take it all, whatever comes. Let the tanks blast away; let the krauts take me prisoner; give me a court-martial, dishonorable discharge. I'm ready for it all. I'm dead; out of it. I'm not thinking these things out loud but that's the way it is. I'm past even being scared; past everything. I only want it all to stop.

Then Richards stands up and waves his arms in the "let's go" signal. Everybody stops digging and gets up. I watch myself get up with them. I'm not thinking anymore. I'm just doing it. I'd make a great lemming. They start over the ridge, Richards first, then Vance and Scanlan, then the other replacement, then me. There are other guys who fall in behind. The whole thing is screwed up.

We go about fifty yards and one of the mortars comes in close. We all hit the ground. When we get up, the replacement turns, looks back, then runs past me down the hill. He's going to hit a mine for sure.

We go on some more. Still no tanks. Maybe Richards is wrong. My mind is starting to work again. Then it comes fast, no sound. Direct fire, eighty-eight. I'm on the ground; the ground socks my guts. I don't even hear the motors. Dirt is coming down everywhere. I put up my head and it comes again. The ground thumps under me but I'm still all right. I'm enjoying not caring much; it makes it all so much easier. I feel separate, like at a movie of a war.

Somebody's yelling he's hit. It's Vance. He runs past holding his helmet out in his hand. Blood's flowing. A piece of shrapnel has pinned his hand onto his helmet. I hear a moan in front of me. I look. Scanlan turns his face to me. He's screaming. It doesn't look like Scanlan, it's a death head; bare skull starting to ooze blood.

"I'm hit! My eyes! I can't see! Help me, somebody!"

He stands up and wobbles toward me. He can't see because his whole face's been wiped off and pulled to one side like a mask. The flesh is hanging over one eye and the other eye is hanging over the bone socket onto his cheek. His nose and upper lip are gone; I can see his teeth sticking into his gums. Some of the teeth are broken and pushed in. I crawl up to him, grab him by the legs and pull him down.

"Don't touch your face! You're hit in the face!"

Scanlan sits on the ground, still holding onto his rifle. I squat in front of him, grab the skin of his face and try to wrap it across into place again. It feels like rubber and is shrunken so it doesn't fit. I get the nose centered and tell Scanlan to hold onto the end of the flap while I undo my aid kit. For a second, I actually don't know where my aid kit is. I'm yelling for help but nobody's behind me anymore and Richards is still on the ground up ahead. I yell again but he doesn't move.

I take off Scanlan's aid kit and get out the bandage. I'm scared more stuff is going to come in, but my hands are steady. I wrap the bandage tight around Scanlan's head and tie it in the back. Scanlan's having a hard time breathing. He keeps swallowing the blood but more and more blood is leaking out everywhere. The hell with the wound tablets; I'm getting Scanlan back and turning myself in! My mind is working slowly but clearly; I don't feel like me.

I tell Scanlan to drop his rifle. He isn't talking anymore, only moaning deeply. He takes off his left glove and there are two fingers in the middle missing. Blood's pumping out of there, too. I grab his wrist tight, pull him to his feet and start running him back. He's going to pass out soon and I can't carry him. I might pass out myself any minute. I'm feeling very empty-eared. Scanlan pulls away from me. He goes back and picks up the glove he just pulled off, the one with the fingers in it. He holds it with his good hand. Jesus Christ! What's he thinking of?!

Somehow, we get through the mines. This time I go around farther to the right. I only see two masher wires. I'm having a hard time believing in mines anyway. When Harrington got it, it's as if he defused all of them for me. I have the feeling I could even step on one and it wouldn't go off. That's how far gone I am.

We get back to the edge of the wood and there's Lucessi, the first sergeant. He yells at me.

"Who is that? Where the hell're you going?"

I stop and turn Scanlan toward him. He's my ticket out of hell. It's lousy, but that's the way it is. I'm trying to ride Scanlan all the way back to a medic tent.

"I'm taking Scanlan back, Sarge. He's hurt bad!"

Lucessi can see that. He can also see I'm scared shitless. He knows what I'm doing. Why the hell should I care what Lucessi thinks anyway? He's just another fucking wop, even if he is first sergeant. Lucessi is checking Scanlan. I'm wondering if I shouldn't maybe just make a run for it up to the woods. Lucessi isn't going to shoot me or anything.

"Where's Richards? Where's the second platoon? Where's your squad? What the fuck's going on up there?"

"Richards says tanks are coming up. He needs bazookas. There're no anti-tank grenades."

"Yeah, and where in hell's Richards?"

Lucessi is trying to pull the bandage smooth over Scanlan's face. I'm still holding onto Scanlan's wrist.

"He's up there past the trees. He's on the ground there where Scanlan got hit. I yelled but he didn't answer or move."

That's how my mind's working. It's only then I let myself know that Richards is hit. Richards has had it. Richards got it. I don't even like Richards, but the shakes start coming. I want to get away, anywhere away. I'm not only running back now; I'm running away. I have a hard time keeping my feet still. But, I'm afraid of Lucessi. I could probably beat the shit out of him one-handed; but I'm afraid. I'm waiting for a chance to run away, hide in the ground, starve to death, anything, just disappear, be alone. I'm still holding onto Scanlan's wrist to stop the bleeding and he's fucking around with the glove in his other hand. He pulls something out of the glove and wipes it on his pants. It's a wedding ring. He puts it in his pocket. Lucessi's watching me.

"You get the hell back there, Columbato. If Richards is hit, you're in charge of the squad. The way things're going, maybe the whole damned platoon. What a fuck-up. I'll take Scanlan. I'll get the bazooka and anti-tank grenades sent up. Now, you haul ass up there!"

He's already redoing the company organization chart. He's moving slips of colored paper around in his mind. I hand Scanlan to him and he squeezes the wrist. Blood is dripping from Scanlan's face all over his field jacket. Lucessi turns and runs Scanlan back toward the woods.

I'm alone again. I know I'm only going up to the trees and hide. I'll jump in one of those slit trenches the squad was digging. I'll lie up there and wait till things settle down. Then, maybe I'll sneak my way back into France, travel at night, find some French family I can hide with. I'm quietly going crazy right out there in the open.

I get across the field again, hopping over wires, trying not to look across to where Harrington is. I make it up to the trees and hide myself in a hollowed-out bit of a hole. I don't want to dig.

Then it starts. It's one-five-five; ours. Somebody must've given these trees as coordinates and called in division or corps artillery. I jump up and start running madly along the hill toward Reuth. The ground is bouncing and pieces of dirt fly around and thump into me. It's hitting me in the face as I run, like running through a hailstorm or riding a bicycle behind a truckload of gravel. Then I feel something pull on my left arm and spin me around. I look down and there's a small hole, shaped like an acorn, on the right side of my left wrist. A drop of blood is oozing slowly out of the hole. It's dark red. I stop in the middle of the field and stare at it. I close my fist and the little finger stays stiff out. I turn over my hand and there's no exit hole on the other side. Something breaks inside me and

I'm crying. I can go back. I can go to a hospital and be operated on! I can talk to doctors, tell them I'm finished! The war is over!

Another shell hits to the left and I'm knocked down. My ears are ringing and when I wipe my face, my hand comes away wet with blood. I feel all over my face but there's nothing except where the dirt and pebbles have made little cuts. I start running again. I run till I come to a road on the outskirts of Reuth. I still haven't seen anybody. I can hear small arms fire up ahead in the town. I see a hole dug on the side of the road. I'll climb in there and wait till some medic comes for me. I have all the time in the world; the war's over. Alfonso Columbato is going home as a wounded war hero. I hear another shell coming so I run forward and jump in the hole.

The war isn't over! There're two krauts in the hole! I land right on top of them! They struggle out from under me and put their hands on top of their heads. I lean back in the hole and try to cover them with my rifle. I'm scared shitless and they're smiling at me. The whole thing is crazy. They want me to end the war for them, too. Here we are, three guys in a hole, bucking for civilian.

One's an old guy, over forty; the other can't be sixteen. Neither of them has a helmet, just field caps. They keep smiling at me. They're glad I'm not killing them. I'm glad they're there, now I have two excuses to go back. I'll be the wounded war hero coming in with prisoners captured in hand-to-hand combat. Maybe this is the way all heroes are made.

Then the stomping one-five-five starts creeping up the hill. Somebody's changing the coordinates and marching it right up. The whole world seems to be coming down on us. One hits less than ten yards away and the walls of the hole begin crumbling. I feel panic. Here I am so close and now I'm going to get killed for nothing. I lean back and point my rifle at the krauts. I signal them to get up out of the hole. They're not smiling now, they don't want to go. I'm getting out of there and I'm taking them with me. I want to end the war for them and I'm going to be a big war hero on top of it all.

They won't move. I drive my rifle barrel into the ribs of the older guy and yell at him to get out. He jabbers away but he starts climbing and the young one follows him. They leave their rifles and keep their hands on top of their heads. I point with my rifle toward the trees. If anybody were actually looking, it really would look like some kind of war scene with the bloody hero forcing his prisoners back to the lines. I smile to show them that I'm on their side but I'm too scared to bring off a real smile. They have to trust me; we can't hole up there with that heavy stuff coming in.

We go about thirty yards down the road toward the trees when all sorts of shit comes down on us. This time it's kraut artillery, not tanks; this is big. The two krauts hit the dirt, still with their hands on top of their heads. I'm sprawled behind them. The whole world is rocking. We've got to get the hell down to the woods and in a hurry. We're going to be massacred if we stay out here in the open. I'm yelling for them to get up and get moving. They can't hear me, they can't understand me, and they wouldn't move if they did. They push their heads deeper into the dirt. I could've just left them there and I should've. But I've got myself convinced I want these prisoners and I also think I know what's best for them.

I squeeze off a shot over the head of the older guy. He turns around and looks at me. There's fear in his eyes all right. I give him the "get up" signal with my rifle. He jumps up, then the young one, and they both start running with their hands still on top of their heads. I'm pushing myself up with the butt of my rifle when, BAM, it happens.

I come to, covered with blood and gore. My rifle stock's broken in two. I try to get up but I pass out again. When I come to a second time, I'm bleary-eyed, my ears are ringing, and my nose and mouth are full of blood. I spit and look up. The two krauts are on the ground in front of me. The shell hit between them and dug a huge hole there, at least one-five-five. I start checking myself out. Most of the gore is from the krauts. I feel a soggy soft spot in my groin, but it doesn't hurt.

I try to stand and I can't. My head buzzes and I fall over.

My leg won't work. I crawl up to the two krauts and they're both dead. I don't know how long I was out but it was enough time for them to die; long enough for flies to find them. The sun is up full and it's a sunny day. It's the first sun we've had in two weeks. There's no artillery. The world looks new. There's no sound of fighting from Reuth. It all seems so quiet, I think I might be deaf. I try to say something to hear myself, but there's something wrong with my jaw. I hear myself moaning as the blackness flows over me. It's more like going to sleep when you're really tired. As I pass out, I know that at least I'm not deaf; I heard myself moan.

The next time I come to, I begin crawling toward the woods. I should just stay there and wait till somebody comes but I'm not thinking. I want to get off the road, out of the open, and into a shady place. I want to get away from the krauts. I hold my hand over the soggy spot and I can feel my intestines bulging against my hand when I move. I don't have any bandage to put over it so I keep my hand there. It isn't bleeding much. My head is getting clear. I'm thinking things out, trying to save my ass.

I crawl down the field to where Richards is still stretched out. I crawl up to him and there's no blood at all. I have just a minute when I think he might be "dogging it," letting the war go by him, the way I am. His eyes are open and his mouth. He's dead. I see the piece of shrapnel sticking out the side of his neck. It's a long thin piece and it's sticking out like a pen in a pen holder. The skin of his neck is bent in to fit around the rough edges of the cast metal. I'm seeing very clearly in the morning sunlight. I pull out the piece of shrapnel with my good hand. It comes out easily and there's a short gush of blood. Richards' neck bends so his face is against the ground. His eyes stay open.

That's when I begin cracking up seriously. I hear myself muttering "Richards is dead" over and over like a prayer; it hurts and I can't stop myself. I lie there beside Richards and can't move.

Next thing I remember, De John the medic is over me.

He's asking what's the matter, where it hurts, but I keep muttering and crying. My jaw hurts up into my ears. Harrington is dead and I'm crying about Richards. Even while I'm crying I know it doesn't make sense, but I can't stop. De John tapes in my gut and puts on sulfa but doesn't give me wound tablets. He looks at my face and pulls another bandage out of his kit. He starts wrapping up the bottom of my face and jaw down to the neck. I can see in his eyes that it's bad and I'm glad. I'm glad for anything that'll keep me out of combat. I know I'm even trying to section eight it now. I'm keeping on about Richards when it doesn't make any sense at all. I'm trying to hold onto whatever advantage I've got. I don't have any pride or honor or anything left. I just have a need to go on living.

They get a litter to me, carry me back, and then there's a ride on top of a jeep and into the field hospital. They put me down on a bloody cement floor. I see the dead ones piled in the corner, covered with blankets, boots sticking out. I look for Harrington, but all of them have two boots.

Now I begin to get the idea that I'm not hurt enough, they're going to send me back. A T-5 medic squats beside me. He asks me my outfit, name. It hurts too much to talk. I shake my head. He pulls out my dog tags and checks. He looks under the bandages. I feel myself sinking. I'm ready to cry again, to beg them not to send me back. This T-5 is being cheery and telling me it's not too bad and I'll be up and around in no time. I'm hating him. He makes out a ticket and wires it to my field jacket. That must mean something. I begin to relax. I'm a package now to be handled by other people. I don't have a rifle, I don't have a helmet. I'm not a soldier anymore. I'm a sick person. Somebody else comes over, rolls up my sleeve, and gives me a shot. I feel myself slipping away.

The next thing I'm being jiggled and moved from the litter onto a black operating table. A doctor smiles down at me with clean hands, a clean white coat and splatters of blood on his glasses. He looks at my tag, then starts to scissor off my clothes down to where I'm hit at the top of my leg, in the groin. He cuts off the bandage and I can feel him pressing with his hands. Somebody else is cutting and pulling off my boots and the rest of my clothes. I feel like a little boy. Nobody's undressed me since I was four years old. The doctor turns to me and smiles. He's tired. It's been a red-letter day for surgeons.

"We're going to put you to sleep now and clean this up a bit. Don't be scared, it'll be all right."

Hell, I'm not scared; I want to be put to sleep. I want the whole medical corps to come and try themselves out on me. I want them to keep me in hospitals to practice on for five years, or however long it takes to get the crazy war over. I'll do anything to keep people from knowing what I know. I'll do anything to keep out of combat; if it means getting cut up by doctors in hospitals, that's great with me.

When I come to, I'm on another litter, a padded one, and I'm covered with a blanket. My face is practically smothered in bandages, my whole hand and wrist are bandaged. I reach down with my good hand and feel that I'm bandaged from my belly button down, but my cock and balls are still there, squeezed out between the bandages. There's a tube coming out of the end of my cock. I lie back and relax. They're not going to be able to give me a rifle for a while anyway.

I feel like I'm on a moving stairway, an escalator. Even the smell of ether is good to me, a smell of security, of calm and of peace. I look around and realize I'm not in the field hospital anymore. There are rows of us and we're in a big room. I lift my head to look around and I can't believe what I see. There's a woman in a uniform and she's coming over to me. I haven't seen a real woman in months. I'd forgotten how good they look. Think of it, I'm going to be able to go home where there are women and I'm not going to have a dishonorable discharge. I'll probably even get a pension and people who don't know will think I'm a hero. I'll be able to fuck all the women I want. The lady stops and squats beside my litter.

"Are you all right there, soldier?"

I see the lieutenant's bar on her cap. I can't open my jaw and I talk through my teeth.

"Yes, sir. Where am I?"

"You're at division headquarters and we're waiting for an ambulance to take you back.

"Where will I go back to?"

"Probably to the hospital in Metz."

I lie back. They haven't found me out yet. If I can get as far as Metz, they'll never get me in combat again.

"Would you like a cup of coffee?"

As she says this, she's looking at the tag pinned to me. It's longer and more official-looking; I'm special delivery now. I wonder if it's still the same day. It seems like weeks since we left the forest and went down that slanted field toward Reuth. For just a minute I think of the war still going on. Who's head of the squad now? I could've made staff if I'd stayed on. Did they finally take Reuth? I stop thinking about it. I'm rear echelon now; let the boys at the front do the fighting. The lady lieutenant is finished reading my delivery ticket.

"Oh, I'm sorry. It says here you have a stomach wound. You can't have any liquids. I saw your face and I thought that was all of it. I'm sorry."

This must be the first time I've ever had a lieutenant sorry for me. I pull my bandaged hand out from under the blankets to drum up a little more sympathy, but she's already on to somebody else. If she can't serve me coffee, she doesn't want anything to do with me.

I lay my head back and try to remember the reality. I want to remember how lousy a soldier I really am. I don't mind fooling everybody else but I don't want to fool myself. It's been a hard lesson to learn. I can already see how easy it's going to be for me to make myself out the big hero. I've got to take what I know about myself now and plan my life around that. I pass out while I'm thinking about it.

The hospital at Metz is a real hospital. I mean it isn't a school converted into a hospital or a barracks made into a hospital; it was a hospital in the first place.

I have my first operation two days after I get there. It's the operation on my stomach. Actually it isn't my stomach. It's an instant rupture I've got down there. They give me the piece of shrapnel afterwards. It looks about like one of the pennies we used to mash on the tracks of the trains at the terminal on Sixty-ninth Street. The doctor says I'm lucky I wagged when I could've wigged because it just missed cutting the sperm cord. He says the shrapnel looks like American one-five-five. Maybe he thinks I'm a kraut who snuck in here to get some free treatment.

I couldn't care whose side I'm on. I don't even care who wins anymore. I'm out of it. I lie there in bed all day just enjoying the quiet, the normalness of things. My insides are gradually settling down. I'm happier than I can ever remember. When I wake up in the morning, before the nurse comes around to wake everybody up and wash them, before the orange juice, I lie there with my eyes closed, listening, thinking about how I'm out of it. I'm out of everything, not just the war. I'm captured; the world's prisoner. I'm not fighting anymore. It's a great feeling, everything seems so unimportant.

Every morning they throw a pack of cigarettes on my bed. Free cigarettes. "Another carton of cigarettes for the boys overseas." I start smoking. Hell, I'm not trying to be the world's strongest man anymore. I'm just trying to get through without making too much of a disgrace of myself. I lie there on the white bed, moving nothing but my good hand; a clean, clean hand, washed every day by clean hands. I put the white cigarette in my mouth and blow smoke through my bandages. I'm not really smoking, I'm blowing smoke and watching it. I practice blowing smoke rings. Uncle Caesar used to do it for me so I know all the moves. The air in the room is still and after a few days I get so I can blow perfect rings. I'm saving inhaling for another time. It still hurts to take a deep breath, and coughing is a misery.

I blow away twenty cigarettes worth of smoke rings every day. I allow myself one cigarette each half hour. There's a clock on the wall and I hold onto every minute I can. Time never seemed so sweet. I don't think I ever actually lived in the present before. Now, I'm forgetting everything that happened and not thinking more than half an hour ahead. Each of those half hours has more in it than most days in my life.

There are other guys in the ward, but they're mostly other gut wounds and are more serious than I am. All of them are on intravenous. I only have the peeing tube hooked to me, so I'm practically a free man.

They change the bandage on my hand every three or four days and the big operation is looked at every other day. They put clean bandages on my face but it's two weeks before they do anything except clean it. One day a doctor wheels me into a room and unwraps the face bandages. He takes little scissors and scissors away some pieces. He tapes it up and says I'm going to need plastic surgery. They don't have any facilities to do it in this hospital. He tells me the jaw is dislocated and shattered in the joint. They'll have to work on that first.

I don't care. I'm beginning to like operations. The nurses keep telling me how brave I am. Bullshit! Nobody's ever going to fool me there. They can keep me in the hospital and cut me up a little at a time; only no pain, please. Take my lovely, muscular body and hack away. But no shocks, no sudden pain, no dirt, no attacks, no patrols; I can't take it.

I'm just able to sit up again when they tell me I'm being shipped back to the States. I'm being shipped to Fort Dix because it's the military hospital nearest my home. Christ, I'm beginning to feel like a civilian already. A few pieces of metal cut into me and everything changed. I don't even think about the squad, the platoon, none of it anymore. I read the *Stars and Stripes* every day to see how the old war's going. The Russians are sweeping across Russia, Poland, Germany. Everybody's squeezing the Nazis. Then, Hitler puts a bullet through his head. It's like reading a novel; it doesn't seem real to me. It's as if everything went from super real to mushroom soup in one morning. I'm not complaining. I can't even get myself to worry much about being a coward either. I'll make new tracks. I'll find something to do so nobody will ever know.

Maybe I'll open a pizza parlor or a hoagie shop. "ALFONSO'S," great name for that kind of place.

It's hard for me not to put on the tough guy thing with the nurses and the doctors. They want me to, I can tell. That heroic shit is hard to stop.

By this time, the whole side of my mouth is twisting to one side. It's getting hard to open my mouth at all. The doctors decide I'm an emergency case and put me in an airplane. I've never been in an airplane before; I'm wishing Birdy could be with me. He'd love it.

I'm in America almost without knowing it. A hospital is a hospital. I'm rolled off the plane in a stretcher and into an ambulance. We go through New York with the siren blowing. I'm playing poker with another guy in the bottom bunk as we go. The nurses at Dix are different, older and very sympathetic. Everybody seems guilty. They're practically crying over us. I'm feeling about seven years old now; great feeling. I'm turning into a great baby. Maybe I'll win a prize in the war baby beauty contest.

I have two days of X-rays with all kinds of doctors fingering my face flaps. Then they put me under anaesthetic and do the first operation. I still haven't seen my face; it's always bandaged up. I don't really want to see it. I can see enough of what it looks like from other people's faces when they look at it. I know I'm not as bad as Scanlan. I'll bet he was a nightmare for some plastic surgeon.

I'm still just relaxing and letting things happen. They call my parents and tell them I'm in the hospital. They come tooling up in the De Soto. I can't say I'm sorry to see them, except my old lady keeps staring at the bandages on my face and crying. The old man looks tired, much older, and for the first time I realize I'm his kid and he does care. Only he can't allow himself to show anything. He's standing pale and scared there trying to be the Sicilian big shot. His face lights up when I tell him I made sergeant. It's a dumb sad life most men live.

When they go home I turn back into my private world. My body is still my ticket. Come on, doctors, punch holes in it. Punch all the holes you want, it's gotten me this far, all the way back to America. Punch away.

Now, I start hurting from that first operation. I'm put on intravenous for a week and then I'm fed with a tube. I feel like a baby pigeon being fed regurgitated food. I don't care; take care of me, world. It's two weeks before I can even drink thin soup. I can't chew at all, even on the good side. The doctor tells me how they've put in a metal plate and pins to hold my jaw. They have to get the jaw straightened before they can start any plastic surgery. He tells me I'll have a slight malocclusion anyway. I don't know what that is so I ask one of the nurses. I have to ask her through my teeth. She says it means my jaw won't come together quite right. I can live with that. The doctor also tells me he's going to bring some skin from my ass and put it on my chin. Got a match? Yeah, my face and my ass. That's when I find out, too, I won't be able to grow a beard. I've got enough hair on my ass, more hair than most people have on their faces, but it won't help. They're taking very thin layers.

"I'm just finished with the third operation when they tell me about you, Birdy. They say you're down in Kentucky and they want me to go talk to you. Even your shit old lady comes over to our house and asks me to go down. I don't want to go. I don't want to see anybody who knew me the way I used to be. I know I'm not me anymore and I don't want any more pretending than I have to. We were too close, Birdy; we were too much to each other. But I can't say this to your old lady; she's crying all over my mother. The crummy pigeon poisoner and baseball crook is crying. I tell her I'll go.

"I come down and talk to fatface Weiss, here, and then I start talking to you, Birdy, about how it was with us with the pigeons and all that shit. You're some kind of freaky bird looking out the window, crouching on the floor, not paying any attention to me.

"Hell, you're not even listening now. We're both impossibly screwed-up, Birdy. I think maybe we put off growing up a little too long."

I stop talking. What's the use? What's the use of anything? Nobody really talks to anybody else anyway, even if they aren't crazy. Everybody's only strutting around, pecking and picking.

I close my eyes, put my elbows on my knees, and lean forward with my head in my hands. I still can't put any pressure on the left side. I figure this is the last time I'll see Birdy. I can't take it anymore myself. Old Weiss's going to figure it out and lock me in one of these bins soon.

I open my eyes and Birdy's standing up against the bars. He has a big grin on his face and he's looking straight at me; his eyes aren't even wiggling.

"Well, Al, you're just as full of shit as ever."

Holy Christ! Is that you, Birdy?!! Are you there?!"

I can't believe it! He's leaning against the bars, his face sticking through. He's so thin he could turn sidewise and walk on out of the place. While he was squatting or sitting, you couldn't tell how thin he really is. He's taller, too. He was always a runt but now he's taller than I am. I stand up and go close.

"It's really you, Birdy. You're OK?"

"Well, Al, I'm not OK, but it's me."

It's Birdy all right, but he sounds different.

"How about all the bird shit, then? Don't tell me you've been pretending all this time. If you've been sitting there listening and laughing, I'll kill you barehanded!"

"That's right, Al. I was pretending. I pretended I was a bird; now I'm pretending I'm me. I figured it out while you were talking. I think I'm me now. That's not completely true either. I don't know who I am, but I'm not a bird."

"Holy shit! I can't believe it. You mean you remember everything; you're not a loon anymore?"

"I'm not so sure about that either, Al."

Al's heavier. He'd have to wrestle heavyweight all the time, now. He must be a hundred eighty, at least. He looks like the invisible man from the movie with all the bandages over the bottom of his face. He has the same eyes, deep, dangerous, but softer, worried-looking. You feel he'll jump away if you make a fast move.

"OK, Al, so here we are. Birdboy meets Superboy. How're we going to work our way out of this one? Can we possibly kid ourselves into thinking all this makes sense, has some reason?"

Birdy laughs quietly and settles into a squat in front of the bars. This is his normal squat, the way he used to squat in the pigeon coop or watch pigeons in the street. He's squatting flat-footed with his arms out over his knees, straight out, with the palms up. He cocks his head to the side while he listens. There's still a lot of bird there.

I watch Al. He's having a hard time deciding whether to talk to me as a patient, the loon in the loony bin, or to me, as myself, Birdy.

"OK, Birdy, so what do we do? I'm stuck. I can't seem to make myself different and I can never go back to fooling myself the old ways. I know it; I'm finished. The old Al isn't there anymore!"

"You don't really know that, Al. You just want to think you know it. It's the easy way, quiet, bloodless, deathless suicide. I'll tell you, Al, I've been thinking. Maybe crazy people are the ones who see things clear but work out a way to live with it."

Birdy takes a long staggering breath. He talks slowly, not much like Birdy; Birdy always talked five miles a minute.

"Look, Al, you and I had a going concern. We could take almost anything that happened and turn it into a personal adventure, like comic book characters. Birdboy and Superboy playing at life. We just Halliburtonized our way through everything. Nothing could really touch us. That's something special, you know. We were so good at playing we didn't need to make up games. We were the game."

"OK, great, so now we've been shot down."

"It's not that bad, Al. We're still here. I know I can't fly and I don't even want to anymore. You know you can't chew nails and spit tacks; but so what. We can still go on trying to put things together, shifting, arranging, so things come out right."

"What's that mean, Birdy? You going back to squatting there in your cage, letting people feed you and I go back to leg pressing a thousand pounds and running around catching people so I can hold their shoulders to the ground for three seconds? I don't see it."

"Listen, Al. I think what I'm trying to say is, we really are loons. We're crazy because we can't accept the idea that things happen for no reason at all and that it doesn't mean anything. We can't see life as just a row of hurdles we have to get over somehow. It looks to me as if everybody who isn't crazy just keeps hacking away to get through. They live it out day by day because each day is there and then when they run out of days they close their eyes and call themselves dead."

Al looks straight into my eyes. He's still not sure if I'm talking sense. I think I am, but I've been wrong so often lately. I can't hold back a smile.

"Aw, come on, Birdy. Let me tell you something first. You're going to have one hell of a time just getting out of this place. Your psychiatrist, that fat slob Weiss, has you pegged for a once-in-a-lifetime case. He's never going to let you go."

"He's OK, Al. He brought you down here and I'm fine now. You've got to admit he did the right thing. I'm not a bird and when I decide to get out of here, I'll go. I'm not ready yet, but when I decide to leave, I'll go. I just need more time to put it together, to figure out what I can do so my life will be some fun and I can stay alive."

"You don't seem to get it, Birdy. You're locked in here. You can't walk out just like that."

"I'm not worried, Al. I'll get out. That's not the problem."

"OK, Birdy, OK. Then we con Weiss into giving you walking papers. You get a pension and live a life of luxury with nobody on your ass. How's that?"

"It's not enough, Al. That's just hurdling, getting through, leaning back. We can do better than that."

"But you have no idea, Birdy. This place is a regular prison. First, there's these two doors; we can manage that, OK; but then there's the door to the ward. I think Renaldi'd help us there. But there's a fifteen-foot wall all around this place with guards at the gate. If you think you can fly over that, then you're still a loon."

I stare at him. I don't want to hurt Birdy, but I've got to know.

"Tell me, Birdy. What the hell happened to you? How'd you wind up here anyway?"

Al's embarrassed asking. I know I have to tell him something.

"Well, Al, it's like everything else, it just happened. Would you believe I got hit going into Waiheke Island off New Guinea? I think it was one of those little Japanese twenty-five-caliber machine guns.

"I come to in a hot tent with the sun making everything yellow. I'm connected up with tubes and pipes. I'm on my back and can't move. There are long rows of cots and hanging bottles of blood and water. I pass out.

"I wake up again and there's a lot of noise. People run past the cot; I hear rifle fire. It's either morning or evening. There's a noise at the far end of the tent. It's a Japanese soldier cutting through with a bayonet. He goes down the line of cots. There's no screaming, only the thump of his rifle and the tear of the cot when his bayonet stabs through each time.

"I rip off the tubes, crawl under the edge of the tent, and start to run. Then, I begin to fly. I fly past the Japanese, over the tent, and into the jungle. I look back and see the tent on the edge of the sand and the water glistening. The next thing I'm here listening to you talk about pigeons.

"Would you believe that, Al? It's what I remember."

"Shit, Birdy. That's crazy! Nobody can fly! What do you think really happened?"

"That's what happened, Al."

"Jesus!"

Al's backing off again. I didn't want to lie to him, but now he's worried.

"All right, Al. So everything is crazy. Maybe without knowing it, I'm making up the whole flying part; but here we are now, let's find some endings we can live with. Let's get the old combination going."

We sit quiet for several minutes. It's so wild I'm afraid to bring it up, especially after the "flying story" he just told me. Birdy's liable to wind up squatting in the middle of the room again. But, I can't help myself; I've got to tell him. "I got an idea in sort of a dream, Birdy. It was a terrific dream after the other ones. I woke myself up laughing out loud.

"You know, Birdy, I asked Weiss to ship all those base-balls down here, the ones your old lady used to steal."

"Yeah. I remember. You told me."

"I didn't know you heard."

I can't believe my mother kept those balls all these years. There's no end to the absurd things people will do trying to make life mean something.

"Well, those balls tripped off this dream. I woke up in the middle of it and then kept it going, the way you do with dreams when they're good. If we could pull this off we'd out-crazy Weiss in spades. The fucking army'll give you a hundred and fifty percent disability just so they won't ever have to see or hear from you again.

"First, I'll give Weiss a full load of bullshit about how you seem to be coming along and how when I talk about those baseballs you perk up. I'll work up a sob story about your mother taking the balls, making you feel guilty. I might even tell him something about you wanting to fly, and balls flying through the air. I'll give him the super dramatic version of you flying off the gas tank.

"Now, here's where I bring up the suggestion of bringing the balls into your cage here and watching what happens. He'll fall for it. I can see it all."

Weiss starts *hmming* and *hummming*. A few times he strokes his chin, then tries to wrap one arm across his fat chest so he can rest his elbow on it. He's almost too fat to pull it off. How can you be a psychiatrist if you can't fold one arm across your chest, rest the other elbow on it and stroke your beard with your hand? It must be terrible to be a psychiatrist in the army and have no beard to stroke. Poor bastards go to school ten years practicing beard stroking and proper *hmming* and they zip the beard right out from under them. Weiss would look better with a beard, a nice black beard to hide extra chins.

So, the next morning, early, we march down the corridor, the three of us, Weiss, Renaldi, and me. Renaldi's proof you don't have to actually be in the army to hate it.

Weiss's in the lead with his clipboard and fresh note paper. Renaldi's behind him, acting very serious and professional. I bring up the rear with the box of balls. They smell moldy and are a mixed bunch, nobody could've bought them anywhere. These are the original baseballs, the real thing, stolen one at a time from live baseball players. This is one of the great collections in the world. Birdy's mother, the left-center field ball hawk; burier of lost baseballs.

We get to the cell and Weiss steps aside for Renaldi to open the door. He stands there, rocking up and down from his toes to his heels, back and forth, rocking his whole body like he's fucking the air. He has his head tilted up, looking at the ceiling of the corridor. He's like a monster choirboy; there's something eunuchoid in his smooth-skinned face. A nice bushy mustache might help. I can just hear him breaking out with a quick Gregorian *Kyrie eleison* in high C. I stand there sniffing the baseballs and trying to hold myself in.

I'm really into the story now and Birdy's laughing. God, it's good to hear him laugh.

Renaldi gets the door open and Birdy comes hopping on over to us. He's flapping his wings to be fed. Weiss jerks out of his choirboy position and stares. He whips his clipboard into place and starts scrawling away. Renaldi gets the second door open.

"Birdy, you start jumping up and down now, flapping your arms and running around the room bouncing against the walls with those tremendous leaps you can do. We'd need one of your greatest bird imitations. You finish off by leaping up and perching on the edge of the toilet."

Weiss is stunned. He's standing there, leaning forward till he's almost falling over. His hands are hanging at his side, pen in one hand, clipboard in the other. I give him a shove with the ball box to get him all the way into the room. Renaldi locks the door.

I walk past Weiss toward Birdy. Birdy hops off the toilet and over to me. He starts giving me the feed-me signal. I put the box beside him.

'Here, Birdy. These are the baseballs your mother took from all the baseball players. You don't have to worry about them anymore.'

I back off to where Weiss and Renaldi are standing. I know if I look at either one, I'll break up.

Birdy hops around the box. He keeps his hands at his sides like wings and sticks his head into the box. He starts moving the balls around with his nose. He starts sniffing as if he's a dog. Then he makes the big move. He spreads his legs over the box and lowers his butt on top of them, just the way a hen would lower herself onto a nest. He settles himself in and a slow smile spreads over his face.

Weiss is a little recovered, his forehead is sweating and he's scribbling away. Birdy sits there. Then, he lifts himself slightly off the nest. He looks down. His legs are straddling the box, more the way a male hovers over a nest than the way a female sits. Birdy reaches into the box with one of his hands and pulls out a baseball. It's one of the better ones with the stitching still intact and almost white.

He holds this ball up against the light. He peers into the light, through the ball. After somewhere between five seconds and five minutes, he stands up straight, still straddling the box of balls. 'Sterile!' he yells.

"And then, Birdy, you throw the ball straight at Weiss's head!"

It's a perfect bean ball! His glasses go flying! He turns and looks at me bare-eyed. 'My God, Sergeant, the patient's turned violent! Let's get out of here. Where are my glasses?!'

I pick up his glasses and hand them to him. The lenses are OK but the frame is bent out of line so they sit cockeyed on his face. He's trying to get them on right when we hear the yell again.

'Sterile!'

Weiss is bopped again right on the forehead. He goes down backwards like he's been pole-axed. His glasses are hanging by one ear. He gets on his knees with his back to Birdy and looks at Renaldi. 'Open the door and get me out of here!'

Weiss's struggling to his feet when Renaldi picks up one of the balls and throws it toward the toilet.

'Pick-off play at first!'

There's another yell.

'Sterile!'

Weiss is hit on the right cheek of his ass this time. The ball bounces toward me. I throw it up at the window, the one Birdy's been staring out of all these days.

'Foul ball, strike two!'

Weiss looks over at me. He's still on his knees and trying to hook his glasses over his ears. Birdy has another ball out of the box. He doesn't look at it this time. He just throws it.

'Sterile!'

At the word, Weiss gives up on the glasses and huddles close to the floor with his hands over his head. A fat man down on the floor like that would bring out the worst in anybody. I know how lions must feel when they've brought down a water buffalo or some other big, dangerous animal. Birdy misses with this one but gets another one off right away. Before Weiss can move, it nips him on the back. The ball rebounds and Renaldi catches it on the fly.

'Pick-off play at second!'

He throws the ball past Birdy's head to the far corner. Balls are bouncing all over the room now. Weiss keeps down, hunched, trying to get his glasses hooked back onto his face. He's yelling. He wants Renaldi to open the door; he wants me to get the keys from Renaldi. We're ignoring him. He's threatening me with a court-martial; he should know better than that. He's yelling for somebody to come save him. Nobody can hear much of anything through the two doors. They're designed that way.

We're having a great time throwing the balls. Sometimes we throw them to each other, sometimes up at the ceiling trying to break the light bulb, or sometimes at Weiss when he looks as if he might be trying to get up. Every time we throw a ball, we yell out something basebally.

'Cut him off at home!'

'Squeeze play! Run him down!'

'Double him off at third!'

'Watch out for the steal!'

'Sacrifice!!!'

'Texas leaguer!'

'Cut down the lead-off man!'

We're throwing balls every which way. We're running around the room now. The balls are bouncing off the padded walls. We're completely out of hand. I keep trying to throw one through that high window. We're all getting hit by baseballs now. It's like a free-for-all snowball fight. I'm almost wishing Weiss would get up off the floor and join in.

We start running around the bases. We're throwing balls and catching them or picking them up as we run. We keep up our wild yelling. The toilet is first base, the back corner is second, Birdy's sleeping mat is third, and Weiss is home. We're running round and round. We're tagging Weiss with our foot each time.

Then the playing starts turning into a game. Each of us

stops to throw when we're at home plate, that is, Weiss. We're all throwing up at that window now. The window has bars on it and must be fifteen feet high. The bars are set so there's enough space for a ball to get through if it hits right. Three or four times we hit the bars and Renaldi yells, 'Ground rule double!'

We get going faster. I'm running out of breath and I'm afraid one of those balls is going to hit me on the jaw. I can see myself trying to explain to the doctor at Dix how I hurt it playing baseball in a padded cell.

"Then, suddenly, you stop at home plate, Birdy. You put up both hands like an umpire calling time out and you walk forward a step. I almost expect you to take out a little whisk broom and brush off old Weiss."

Birdy says, 'Pinch hitter!'

'Two men on base!'

'Two outs!'

'We're behind by two!'

'Last of the ninth!'

'Batter up!'

We stop on the bases to watch. Birdy has three balls. The first misses the window to the right. The second is a little low. The third goes through the bars, there's the sound of broken glass and the glass falls down the wall. Renaldi's at third, standing on Birdy's bed. I'm straddling the toilet at first. Renaldi yells. 'It's a home run, a case of Wheaties! Clear the bases!'

He runs toward Weiss who's stuck his head up at the sudden quiet and the sound of broken glass. Renaldi races home. He tags up, then goes over to the door and opens it. I'm rounding second. Weiss's ducked his head back down as I come on home. Renaldi gets over in time to shake my hand. Birdy's just behind me and we both shake his hand and pat him on the back as he goes by us. Weiss is pushing himself up and Birdy hurdles clear over him. The height he jumps, he could've gone over Weiss if he'd been standing full up.

"Then, Birdy, we run out the door and lock Weiss in there."

Birdy's been listening and laughing through the whole story. He even puts in some parts the way it always happens with us. We keep interrupting and correcting each other to make it better and then agreeing that's the way it really is. I stop and Birdy stares at me. We're winding down.

"Honest, Al. How many times are you going to have to pin your old man? Jesus Christ, I'm not throwing baseballs at Weiss for you. It doesn't make sense anymore. God, we're practically grown men. If you don't watch it you'll be taking it out on your kids, making them into wrestlers or football players or something so you can convince yourself that you really did pin old Vittorio. The whole thing has to end somewhere. Don't you know, time pins everybody anyway."

Fucking Birdy! It's the knife all over again.

"All right, hotshot flying ace! Let's hear your ending. Are we all going to just fly over the walls or something and pretend it didn't happen?"

"OK. This is the way it goes, Al. Before we leave here, after the ball game, we gather up the baseballs and put them in the box. Then we climb up onto the roof of the hospital."

"I knew it, Birdy, I knew it!"

"Listen, Al! Up there, we start throwing the balls out over the walls. It's a beautiful day, blue sky, sunshine with big, soft, fat clouds. We're just whipping those balls underhand and overhand up against that blue sky and watching them sail over the wall.

"Then we look behind us and there's Weiss. He's smiling at us gently, he isn't wearing his glasses. You offer him a ball to throw but he just keeps smiling, a big, soft, loving smile. It's the kind of smile that helps you know inside that you're valuable.

"We watch Weiss as he reaches over his head to the back of his neck. He starts pulling and it's like a giant zipper. He unzips over his head, across his face, his neck, over his stomach and down to his crotch. Then, he steps out of his fat-major-psychiatrist suit. He stands there in the sunlight and he's beautiful."

"Aw, come off it, Birdy!"

"Let me finish, Al. Weiss is thin with long, strong sinuous muscles. His movements are quick and lithe, and he's covered with a golden-colored down like a baby duck. Without the glasses we can see that his eyes are round. He springs to the edge, motioning us to follow him, smiles, then glides, with his back arched, his arms out flapping strongly, quickly but without hurry and his feet flipping gently. He glides across the grounds to the wall surrounding the hospital and lands there. He turns back and motions again for us to follow."

"Not me, Birdy. I'm not even going near the edge. I'm not going to jump off a building and get myself killed."

"I'm not either, Al."

"So what do we do then, Birdy?"

"Well, we take the suit that Weiss molted and we put it in the box with what're left of the moldy baseballs. We go back downstairs and check the box at the entrance. Then we walk right on out of here, out the gates."

"Just like that?"

"Just like that."

"And, so what happens then?"

"Nothing, Al; just the rest of our lives."

"Is that all?"

"That's all?"

"And that's the way it ends?"

"Not really, Al. It's never that easy. Nobody gets off that way."

But it's worth trying.

HB4J